# Short Stories by Alex Frishberg

*The Killer's Life*

*Life on the Outpost*

*Eulogy for a Friend*

*A Midsummer Night's Entertainment*

*Spare Parts*

*Ghosts*

*A Good Friend*

*Just Before the Harvest Season*

*Marriage Made in Ukraine*

*How To Succeed in Ukraine's Business Environment (Without Really Trying)*

*The Neighbor*

*The Party Line*

*Your Standard Kiev Door*

# ACKNOWLEDGMENTS

I hereby dedicate this book to my lovely wife, Lena, who almost convinced me that this story was not worth telling, and to my wonderful son, Daniel, who will not be allowed to read my little novel until he turns 21 (if ever).

I also want to thank my parents, Anatoly and Tamara Frishberg, for the love, encouragement and support they have given me throughout my life. Their sacrifices gave me the freedom to choose my future, something I am truly grateful for.

And last, but not least, a very special "thank you" to my dear grandmother, Cherna Feldman, who insisted on changing all the names in this novel so that I could remain alive a little longer. So far, her advice worked.

# AUTHOR'S NOTE

This novel is about corruption, a business practice that predates Jesus Christ himself. Having moved to Kiev, Ukraine in 1991, I was fortunate to live through a time of unique business opportunities, when Ukraine's economic revolution made overnight billionaires out of well-connected individuals. The saying in those days was, "so long as there is bribery, you can count on justice." Unfortunately, things have not changed much.

To get to the root of corruption, we have to understand its full extent. *The Steel Barons* describes the lives of ordinary people and systematic corruption they face on nearly every level. Those who are unable to "wheel-and-deal" in the semi-criminal world simply end up collecting empty beer bottles in Shevchenko park.

If you wish to join a discussion about the issues raised in *The Steel Barons*, please visit "your say" at www.thesteelbarons.com. I look forward to hearing from you.

Alex Frishberg

# The Steel Barons

Kiev 2008

# Table of Contents

# Chapter 1

The moment white metal doors slammed shut behind Jack, he realized that he had two major problems. First, there had to be some way of explaining to his wife Julie why he was locked away in a filthy Ukrainian venereal disease clinic. Second, Jack did not want to lose his job at Windsor Porter & Gump. All he needed was to create a credible alibi, as Jack had been taught in law school, one that would raise just enough reasonable doubt about his true condition to get him off the hook.

Jack turned to the door and knocked as hard as he could. "There's been a mistake! I don't belong here! Call the American Embassy at once!" There was no reply.

"You are American?" Jack looked over his shoulder to see a clean-cut man in his mid-thirties with a potbelly. An amiable fellow, he seemed grateful for an unexpected opportunity to sharpen his English skills. "And you don't belong here?"

"It's all a misunderstanding," Jack cried out.

"You don't have syphilis?"

"God, no!"

"And you have a wife?" The young man nodded at the golden band on Jack's finger.

"Julie. Her name is Julie. Jesus, how could I have been so stupid?"

"Not fair, is it? Thirty days just for getting laid?"

"What are you talking about? What thirty days?"

"The doctor did not tell you the rule?"

"She didn't even speak English! What rule?"

"Anyone with syphilis must be quarantined for thirty days," he explained, "to prevent the spread of disease. It's infectious, you know."

"But I don't have syphilis," Jack protested vehemently.

"It all depends on the doctor who sees you. If they suspect you have syphilis, you're stuck here for thirty days, no questions asked. That's the rule. Besides, now that you have been exposed to this, there is no way they'll let you out." The fellow shrugged his shoulders and shuffled off back to his cot. Careful not to make any eye contact with the other inmates, Jack walked over to an empty cot next to his.

"By the way, I am Sergei. What is your name?"

"Jack. Jack Parker."

"Welcome to Ukraine, Jack Parker."

"I don't believe this is happening to me," he muttered. Scared and confused, Jack could barely contain himself from crying. What about Julie, who expected her usual wake-up phone call in the morning, New York time? Or his boss, who called him nightly to monitor the progress of his pet project? What would the Ministry lawyer say about Jack's skipping a meeting tomorrow? Jack rubbed his temples.

He looked around for a way to escape. The large, rectangular room was filled with two rows of army cots and night tables, five on each side. Thick metal rods, welded across the windows, confirmed there was no easy way to escape. A lonely light bulb hung from a single electrical wire in the middle of the ceiling. Deep cracks in the ceiling spread out like a gigantic spider web around it.

Altogether Jack counted eight men, representing all ages and demographics. He could easily spot three obvious alcoholics by their weathered features, complete with the classic baggy eyes, red bulbous noses and deep wrinkles, resembling their counterparts in the New York alleyways. Two other patients, sitting on their cots in the corner, were surprisingly young, tough street kids with shaved heads and those small, hard, adult faces. The rest were ordinary, middle aged men, dignified by slightly graying hair.

These inmates must have been here for quite a while, Jack deduced based on their attire: the old, worn-out sweat suits, wrinkled bathroom robes, soft bedroom slippers, anything that a man would ordinarily wear in the comforts of his own home. In sharp contrast, he was still decked out in his white shirt, medium starched, a blue pin-striped Zegna suit, complete with a silky red tie and polished Church's wing-tip shoes. There is no way I can survive this, Jack thought, casting weary glances at the other patients.

# Chapter 2

The next morning Jack's emotional state was stable, but deeply miserable. Yesterday's nightmare continued from the moment he opened his eyes. The dusty light bulb, dangling from a solitary wire in the middle of the ceiling, reminded Jack that he was still in prison. Using his elbows Jack propped himself up on the pillow just when two large male nurses, in white scrubs and masks, started to inject an elderly alcoholic near the door with his daily dose of medicine.

"Don't bother resisting," Sergei quietly suggested. "Otherwise they'll impale you on that needle, the sadists."

"Antibiotics, right?" Jack confirmed.

"Greatly diluted, knowing these apes, but hopefully yes."

Half an hour after the injections a young nurse in a white mask opened the doors and a steel cart with layers of trays rolled in, seemingly all by itself. The girl did not dare to enter the contaminated ward. She quickly locked the door and left the patients to serve themselves. Sergei walked over and picked up two aluminum trays. He handed one to Jack. "This is what you get," he said.

Jack stared at the yellowish mass for a while, trying to figure out what it was. "It looks like mush," he said.

"It's supposed to be porridge." Sergei poked at the mush with his spoon.

"I have never seen anything like this before. Do we get this every morning?"

"Same crap, but with different consistency. It depends on the cook. Sometimes he steals more, and then we get diluted crap. Other times he steals less, like today, and we get more solid crap."

"Right." Jack cautiously tried it. The lumpy texture stuck to the inside of his mouth like glue.

Experiencing the same problem, Sergei pointed to the luke-warm liquid of light sandy color. "Drink tea," he said, "otherwise the crap will glue your intestines together."

"Thanks." Sergei was right: the tea broke up the paste, allowing Jack to swallow the breakfast in tiny portions. "So tell me, how do you know English so well?"

"Not just English, but Polish, German, even a little Hungarian. Name any East European country with a black market, and I can speak their language."

"How do you say, let me out of here?" Jack evaluated the thick steel bars on the windows.

"It's no use," Sergei yawned. "I tried everything with them. Can't even use a phone."

"Shit." Jack was angry with himself, petrified that his dirty little secret would somehow reach Julie. At the same time, he felt utterly helpless as his world spun out of control.

At precisely three o'clock in the afternoon the same young nurse appeared at the door, wearing her little white mask. She cautiously pulled the morning's cart out of the ward and replaced it with another one. This time Jack got up, brought over two trays and handed one to Sergei.

"They are spoiling us." Sergei's sarcasm was well-deserved: on his plate was a thin strip of graying meat, the thickness of a bacon slice, several spoonfuls of dark grain that resembled buckwheat, and a slice of stale brown bread.

The over-boiled gray meat looked like rubber, impossible to chew despite its transparency, and it tasted unbearably bland. The dry buckwheat granules scratched the back of Jack's throat like industrial-grade sandpaper. Instinctively Jack reached out for a glass half-filled with strange, almost sweet-smelling pink-colored liquid with mysterious sediment at the bottom. Hesitating, he looked to Sergei for explanation.

"Must be compote," Sergei guessed. He held his glass to the light. "Either that, or rust. The cook sometimes forgets to filter the water. Rust comes from the pipes, you know."

"I don't care," Jack said, washing down the food. The rusty compote turned out to be peach-flavored water with just a hint of metallic aftertaste, confirming Sergei's suspicion. Looking out of the window through the metal rods, Jack could see people on the street, waiting for the trolleys to take them home. Twenty nine more days of this hell, he thought, and then what?

The annoying overhead light bulb went out at precisely nine o'clock, signaling the end of Jack's first full day in captivity. Soon the alcoholics started snoring in short bursts, loud and violent at times. The next layer of sound was a far more gentle wheezing of the middle-aged men. It was followed by the steady, heavy breathing of the street kids. Jack was the last person to fall asleep in the middle of the syphilitics' symphony.

# Chapter 3

Just one week earlier Jack Parker sat in a sunny, midtown Manhattan corner office. From the sixty-fourth floor, Jack looked past the smiling face of his boss, Mr. Gerald Windsor III, at the city skyline. The morning was especially beautiful because Jack expected to hear that he had been promoted from a senior associate to a junior partner. Windsor Porter & Gump partners had just returned from their annual August retreat in the Hamptons, where they compared evaluations of all associates. The timing was perfect.

Jack's seven-year track record at Windsor Porter & Gump practically screamed that he was partnership material: he joined the firm straight out of Seton Hall and had worked like a madman for Gerald, eventually becoming his right hand man. With an average of sixty five billable hours per week, and only two short vacations, Jack felt that his partnership was well overdue. Jack's anticipation of the good news felt as if he'd had several cups of espresso. Many times Julie complained bitterly that his career was more important than their marriage, that he took her for granted. At last, his efforts were about to pay off.

"I got a call from our client, GPK Telecommunications, yesterday," Gerald said.

Jack's confidence rose. They were the firm's major clients, and they liked his work in the past. This was an excellent start. "Great people," Jack smiled modestly.

"Apparently, there's some kind of a government tender for installation of fiber optic cables, and GPK wants to get in on it. They need a good corporate lawyer to negotiate the terms and get the deal signed. They specifically asked for you."

"I'm flattered."

"You should be. Take a few days to review their files and get ready to travel on Saturday. That will get you there on Sunday, local time."

Jack's thoughts were on his upcoming promotion, which Gerald has not yet mentioned, and it took him a few seconds to realize that Gerald was sending him on one long trip. "Where exactly are you sending me, Gerald?"

"To the Ukraine," Gerald replied without smiling.

"You're joking." The apprehension in Jack's voice was genuine, because he knew that Julie would cause another scandal over this. "I'll have to check with my wife first. Otherwise, there could be trouble."

"Look, Jack, this is a very significant transaction for our client." Gerald paused and then added, "now, this is confidential, so it will stay in this room, agreed?"

"Sure, Gerald."

"I happen to own a little stock in GPK, and this sale could be very, very lucrative. Now, if you seal this deal, I'll make sure the Steering Committee will make you a partner."

So there it was. One final hoop to jump through. "Can we put this in writing?" Jack half-joked.

"You lawyers are all the same." Gerald reached for his cigar, a real Cuban Cohiba. "Just get the deal signed, and I'll take care of my end."

"Thanks, Gerald. That's good enough for me."

"Now look over these files and have a nice flight." Gerald pushed toward Jack two thick accordion files that occupied the corner of his desk. "And give my regards to your wife."

\* \* \*

Jack was the last person out of the customs zone at Borispol airport in Kiev. He saw people holding up signs written in a strange, foreign alphabet. One of the men in the waiting area held a piece of cardboard with JACK PARKER written on it. He was around forty, with a thick black mustache, dressed in a plain brown suit. Jack pointed to his sign and said, "that's me."

"Nice to meet you, Mr. Jack," replied the man in passable English. "I am Igor, your driver. Shall I drive you to the hotel or directly to the Ministry?"

"Hotel," Jack replied without hesitation. He was stuck in a sitting position for more than nine hours. "It's been a long flight."

Igor nodded sympathetically. "I understand, Mr. Jack. Please let me take your luggage and follow me."

They walked out of the airport on a superb early autumn afternoon. The bright sun contrasted against the deep blue sky, trees swayed their yellowing leaves under a balmy breeze. To finally inhale fresh air was pure joy.

The drive took approximately forty minutes according to Jack's watch, though he dozed through most of it. He woke up just as Igor pulled up to a tall, glass-and-concrete building with gold letters "Hotel Intourist" above the entryway. A truly great driver, Igor helped Jack out of his Ministry-issued black Volga and deposited him on the worn-out leather couch in the hotel's lobby while Igor filled out the check-in paperwork. "You will require anything else?" the driver inquired considerately.

"No, thank you, Igor. What time do we meet tomorrow?"

"Nine o'clock ok?"

"Nine is perfect."

In the hotel elevator, Jack could not wait to stretch out on a king-size bed, maybe watch a little CNN before falling asleep. Reality proved to be quite different: his humble room contained a narrow bed, positioned against the wall, and a 19-inch television set from the 1970's. The bed was barely large enough to fit one healthy adult and the television did not work.

The lack of amenities did not matter, though. Exhausted, Jack fell on top of the bed and shut his eyes. For some strange reason, however, he could not relax. His heart pounded with excitement of being in a foreign, former communist country, about to earn the long-awaited partnership wings. At the end of the hallway he heard somebody flushing the toilet. With such fine acoustics, Jack needed a couple of drinks to help him fall asleep.

The Intourist hotel bar turned out to be in the basement. Candles flickered romantically on the tables in private booths that lined the walls. To assure maximum privacy the booths were separated by tall, leather-studded walls. The only source of electrical light were the halogen lamps that brightly illuminated four rows of bottles lined up on the glass shelves behind the bar. Jack approached the bartender, a pudgy man in his early forties, who was sitting on a stool and reading a newspaper.

"A gin and tonic please," Jack said.

"No tonic," the barman replied in heavily accented English. "Only Seven Up."

"Sure. That's fine."

The barman poured far more gin into Jack's glass than any bartender in Manhattan ever would. "Where you from?" he asked.

"New York." Jack was glad to have somebody to speak with, but the bartender picked up his newspaper and continued reading.

Sipping the unusually strong cocktail, Jack started to blank out. With his eyes closed, he could see his office, then the hallway that led out to the elevator, then the airport terminal at JFK. Then a melodic voice asked him softly, "*mozhno s vami pogovorit?*" Immediately Jack opened his eyes to discover a very attractive blond, blue-eyed girl, standing right next to him. She was slightly shorter than Jack, with a petite, triangular face and shoulder-length hair.

Her small, perky breasts stood out firmly just in the corner of his eye. Jack stiffened with embarrassment because she caught him looking at them, but then she smiled back, forgiving this minor breach in social etiquette. Those liberated women in New York City would never let you off without some retaliatory put-down, Jack thought.

The girl's head was playfully cocked to one side. "May I speak with you?" she repeated, this time in English.

Sitting there, unshaven and exhausted by the long flight, Jack realized he must have reeked of gin. Even in his single days, before he was married to Julie, girls never found him "hot" because Jack was an ordinary lawyer, that is five foot eight inches, with brown hair and Lennon glasses; certainly not the Adonis-type with six-pack abs that all the young attractive women want. Considering his appearance, Jack felt especially flattered that this Ukrainian girl, as pretty as she was, wanted to pass her time with him.

"Feel free to join me," Jack said. She accidentally brushed against his leg, then sat down on the barstool next to him. Jack managed to look away from the low-cut blouse, which accurately pinpointed her nipples, before she could catch him again. Their very sight made his pulse race with excitement, even though he knew that nothing sexual could occur between them. It simply was not possible that he would get so lucky on the very first date; Jack never did before in his entire life. Besides, he was married to Julie, who would never forgive him.

The lovely blond angel pointed to the corner booth, occupied by two other young ladies, and said, "my friends want to invite you to us. Want to come?" Both girls playfully looked in their direction and one of them waved, but Jack had an important business meeting in the morning. A brief casual conversation with the blond girl was all Jack really wanted before calling it a night.

"No, thanks. I just flew in from New York, and I'm tired." For some reason, being in a foreign bar with a pretty girl, with each gulp of his drink Jack felt increasingly suave and international.

"How interesting. Buy for me drink? And for my friends?"

Jack smiled back. "Only for you."

"Cognac, Misha," the girl said to the bartender in a familiar way. "*Dva stakana po sto.*" He reached for the most expensive, sleek-looking bottle on the top shelf, but Jack did not care. This was a business trip and the client was picking up all of his expenses. The bartender poured two jumbo doses of tea-colored liquid into the cognac snifters and placed them on the bar.

"Why two?" Jack asked.

"For you." She offered one of the snifters to him.

"But I'm drinking gin," he protested, "it's too much for me, really."

"Not too much," the blond girl smiled. "Not for a real man. Even for a woman, not too much. *Na zdorovye!*"

Then she gulped her entire glass of cognac in several large chugs and exhaled loudly. Naturally, Jack did the same, because otherwise in her eyes he would not be a real man. Amazingly, he did not throw up.

Several minutes later the alcohol in Jack spoke out, loud and clear: this girl is absolutely gorgeous. Meanwhile, her eyes poured more fuel on the fire. I could devour you, they said in volumes without her having to utter a single word. The way this girl openly evaluated Jack, with her mouth slightly puckering out, sent shivers up his spine. There was undeniable, delicious, lustful electricity about her.

Hey, maybe it's not empty flirtation after all, Jack thought. Maybe I have a real chance with her tonight. One last poorly disguised peek at her tightly shaped body and those slender dancer's legs pushed him overboard. She does not even know how beautiful she is, he thought. Her firm, shapely breasts looked like two tennis balls; the waist was tiny in perfect proportion to the rest of her lovely body. This is my one and only time, Jack swore to himself. Besides, Julie would never even know, so what's the harm?

The sexy Ukrainian kitten somehow sensed his temporary weakness. Seizing on that moment, she smiled and seductively arched one of her eyebrows, as if to ask, so are we doing anything or not? That is when Jack breathed in deeply and took her delicate hand in his, just like actors do in those silly romantic movies. They walked out of the Intourist bar without saying another word, though Jack had problems keeping his balance. It was both tawdry and beautiful at the same time.

# Chapter 4

The first consequence of Jack's interlude with the gorgeous blond became apparent the next morning when he got dressed. The wallet, which he precariously left in the inside jacket pocket, was missing. This discovery left an unpleasant taste in Jack's mouth because it confirmed what he had suspected all along: the beautiful girl was only after his money, not good looks. His memories of wild, erotic sex vanished into thin air.

This unfortunate turn of events meant that Jack had no more cash or credit cards for the remainder of the negotiations. Yet he remained calm, safe in the knowledge that neither Gerald nor Julie would guess the circumstances under which his wallet disappeared. Wallets get stolen all the time, Jack would easily explain. He'd have Julie cancel all his cards and wire emergency cash in a matter of hours. By the time Jack arrived to the Ministry of Telecommunications, he was confident that his little indiscretion would remain a secret.

The second surprise emerged several days later, when Jack felt a nasty, burning sensation just after another round of negotiations. On the way back to the hotel, as he twitched in the back seat of Igor's black Volga, a scary thought entered Jack's mind: what if the attractive blond snake infected him with an unkind disease? Then he broke out in cold sweat.

The damned negotiations could end any day, Jack thought nervously, but antibiotics require time and patience. It soon became all too clear: what he needed was a dose of heavy duty, all-purpose antibiotics, and the sooner the better. Even if Jack had several venereal maladies, surely modern medicine would kick in before he could infect Julie.

"Hey, Igor," Jack asked innocently, "can you help me with something confidential?"

"Yes, Mr. Jack," the driver replied readily. "Anything for money."

"Do you know of a hospital in Kiev?"

"For what?"

"For men's problems. You understand? Men's problems." By the pained expression on Jack's face and the desperate urgency in his voice, Igor clearly understood his predicament. Igor abruptly turned the wheel hard to the left, deviating from their daily route.

"Do not worry, I know a reliable doctor." Igor looked in the rear-view mirror and added, "he treats all of my friends, and some of them are still married."

This turn of events was a great relief. "Thanks, Igor. The most important thing is that nobody finds out about this."

"Trust me," Igor said reassuringly, "I know just how you feel."

Each bump on the cobalt-paved road touched off a disturbing alarm deep within Jack's bowels, confirming that his one and only romantic Kiev night had turned into a pathetic mess. By now, Jack definitely felt the stings and arrows of the silent enemy that was creeping up his urethra.

At last, Igor parked his car in front of a gray, dingy building in *Podol*, lower part of Kiev. "We're home," he joked. "This is polyclinic number seven." When Jack entered the dark hallway, he noticed that this hospital was unlike any other he had ever seen before. The paint on the walls of the long corridor was cracked and peeling in random patches. The narrow wooden bench, stretching along the wall, was occupied by three men and one woman. She sported a black shiner under her left eye.

"Wait here." Igor nodded at the wood bench and disappeared in the depths of the hallway. The people sitting on the bench stared at Jack, and with good reason. In contrast to their layered, grimy street clothes, he was still dressed in Western business attire. At first Jack became self-conscious, but then he thought, who cares about what they think? Soon enough Igor will bring me some antibiotics and I'll never see them again in my life. Several minutes later Igor emerged, shaking his head in frustration.

"What's wrong?" Jack expected to hear the worst news possible: that no antibiotics were given out to foreigners with clap.

"The doctor will see you in a few minutes. I've made a special arrangement, so you don't have to wait in line," he said somberly.

"Oh, thank God! And I thought..."

"The problem is that I don't know this doctor personally. She's new around here."

"That's fine with me," Jack beamed with relief, "as long as she'll see me."

"I could make a few phone calls and see if I can get you another doctor, but it would take some time..."

"No, this is fine," Jack insisted, scratching his crotch. "Let's just get it over with."

"As you want." Igor shrugged his shoulders. "Follow me, please."

The doctor was a tired woman, well past her prime. Her greasy yellow hair was pulled up into a tight coil and the large brown mole on her chin sprouted three distinctive black hairs. The doctor faced Jack in her white overcoat and said, frowning, "*snimite vashi shtany.*" Then she pointed at his zipper. By the disgusted look on the doctor's face Jack could tell that she did not want to see anymore genitals, ever.

"She said to take off your..." Igor began to translate, but Jack interrupted him before he could finish the sentence.

"Can you wait for me outside, please?"

"Are you sure you don't want me here? To translate?"

"I think that the doctor can figure out all by herself what's wrong," Jack answered sternly, embarrassed to reveal his private parts in front of another man.

"As you want," said Igor. After making sure that the door was closed, Jack slowly unzipped his pants and allowed them to drop around the ankles.

"*Trusy!*" The doctor barked out a direct order, impatiently pointing to his underwear, so Jack lowered his briefs until they rested just above the knees, fully exposing his fragile and shrunken stump. Naked from the waist down, and still wearing a medium starched white shirt, jacket and a tie, he thought, this is highly undignified, which serves me right for cheating on Julie.

"*Vashi dokumenti, pozhalusta.*" The doctor looked at Jack's wedding band and sneered. As a woman, she sympathized with all the wives, whose husbands carry on torrid extra-marital affairs. As a venereal doctor, she always punished wayward husbands and unfaithful boyfriends, regardless whether the patient actually was ill or not. A mere suspicion of a venereal disease was enough for the doctor to presume the worst case scenario, syphilis, and to take preventative measures.

"What?"

"Passport, *pozhalusta,*" she repeated.

"Oh, I understand." Jack reached for his passport. To break the tension, he tried an old, tired joke, "so what do you think, doc? Am I going to live?" The doctor did not crack a smile. Instead, she carefully studied the photograph in Jack's passport, compared it with his distraught mug, and then reached for the telephone.

Due to the language barrier, Jack presumed the doctor was calling for a translator.

"*Ein moment.*" The doctor spoke to Jack in German, but at least she tried to communicate. He smiled back and pulled up his pants, encouraged by the positive change in her attitude. Several minutes later two men in white overcoats entered the office. They ungraciously grabbed Jack's arms and pulled him outside.

"Let me go!" Jack yelled, "I am an American citizen!" The two goons did not care one bit. They easily dragged Jack past the people on the wood bench, towards double white doors at the end of the semi-lit corridor. Miraculously, Jack caught a glimpse of Igor, who was strolling in from his cigarette break. In a last ditch effort to escape from this lunatic asylum, Jack screamed at the top of his lungs, "Igor, help me, God damn it!"

Jack's terrified voice echoed down the hall. In response, Igor helplessly raised his hands in the air, as if to say, what can I do now?

"This is a mistake!" were Jack's last words to Igor before the massive white doors locked behind him.

## Chapter 5

By the time Jack's thirty day incarceration period had ended, he knew that something probably had gone wrong in his personal and professional lives, but he had no solid facts. Before he was allowed to leave, however, the doctor insisted on calling the U.S. Ambassador Wesley James Pilfer, who chastised Jack over the phone for all the problems he had caused. That is when Jack learned of the domino-like sequence of events that transpired during his thirty-day absence from civilization.

As could be predicted, after two days of unexplained silence, Julie became seriously alarmed at Jack's certain kidnapping or premature death. Presuming the worst case scenario, she called Gerald at the Manhattan office to share her grave concerns about her husband's life. However, since Gerald did not know anything himself,

Julie contacted the State Department. She demanded to place all U.S. citizens travelling in Eastern Europe on highest travel alert because her husband, also a U.S. citizen, has gone missing and is presumed dead somewhere in Ukraine. Then Julie picked up a copy of The New York Times and called them, too.

By mid-afternoon, she dispatched registered letters to both of New York's senators and an identical fax to several congressmen about a mysterious disappearance of an American lawyer in a communist-infested rogue nation. Then she penned a note to the U.S. Ambassador in Kiev. "With all due respect, Ambassador Pilfer, what good is your Embassy if you can not protect U.S. citizens in such obviously underdeveloped nations as Ukraine?" screamed the opening line in her hostile fax. Numerous cc's at the bottom evidenced the breadth of its circulation.

After years of advancing his career via Washington, D.C. party circuit, Ambassador Wesley James Pilfer's sense of political smell was well-honed: this was precisely the type of scandal that could spiral out of control and develop into an international public relations disaster. Surely, it was not good for anyone's career. Reading Julie's fax once again, Ambassador Pilfer could see thunderclouds gathering over his upcoming promotion within the State Department ranks.

At the Ambassador's direct orders, the embassy security attache promptly contacted the Ukrainian Ministry of Internal Affairs (the police) and the SBU (formerly known as KGB). In combination, these two agencies immediately detained and questioned Igor, Jack's trusted driver. It did not take long for Igor to save his own skin by disclosing Jack's location. The police detectives took some photos through the plated glass windows because none of them dared to enter the syphilitic ward. This evidence sufficed as "proof of body" for U.S. Ambassador's purposes.

The grainy black-and-white photographs of Jack's puzzled look accompanied the Ambassador's cover letter, graciously responding to Julie's hysterical fax. It was typed on the official Embassy stationary with an embossed gold eagle, and was accompanied by doctor's analysis of Jack's medical condition, translated into English for ease of reference. To assure his promotion, Ambassador Pilfer sent carbon copies of this correspondence to everyone Julie had previously contacted, including both senators, all of the congressmen, the U.S. State Department and The New York Times.

As it happened, the Ministry of Telecommunications did not purchase anything from Jack's client, GPK. The Ministry's lawyer complained that Jack simply failed to show up for negotiations. Soon after, GPK Telecommunications went bankrupt. Their new lawyers filed a multi-million dollar malpractice lawsuit against Windsor Porter & Gump. In a futile effort to prevent the lawsuit, Gerald dismissed Jack while he was still recuperating in the clinic.

After Julie learned the true nature of the difficulties Jack faced in Ukraine, she promptly filed for divorce. This allowed her to keep the condominium and most of the money they accumulated in the years Jack tried so hard to become a junior partner. About the same time The New York Times carried a small, yet insensitive article about international lawyers and lack of ethics. Jack's case highlighted the point.

Just as Jack was getting used to his daily routine, one rainy October morning he was rudely expelled into the real world to face a completely new life in a foreign country, one without a family or any possibility of re-starting his career in New York City.

Rain drizzled lightly as Jack walked out of the hospital. He did not mind fresh drops on his unshaven face; it was his first sensation of freedom. Although Jack did not notice it, he had aged considerably in just one month. He stood on the sidewalk in a strange city and looked around, without any clue of where to go. For the first time since he was a small boy, Jack felt completely and utterly lost. With nothing left for him in America, he had no choice but to remain in Kiev. That much was clear. The only question of immediate concern was where to spend the night, considering that Jack had no money whatsoever.

Fortunately, Sergei wrote down his address and telephone number before he was released, but Jack did not even have the spare change for a public phone. The rain picked up and continued to pour steadily. Cold, wet and hungry, Jack pounded the pavement for more than two hours, asking strangers in broken Russian for directions.

\* \* \*

The chilly October rain was coming down hard, but Sasha was in a great mood: he was a free man, once again unburdened by life's problems. Proudly wearing his brand new leather jacket, Sasha hurried to Sergei's party straight from the *Bessarabsky* farmers' market. Everyone knew that Sergei, a confirmed bachelor, did not keep much food in his apartment, relying on guests to pitch in.

As Sasha strolled down *Krasnoarmeyskaya* Street, he was in an especially good humor because a brand-new nine-millimeter *Makarov* semi-automatic pistol was comfortably fastened in a holster under his armpit. A bullet in the chamber was ready to penetrate the scull of any bandit who dared to confront him on this wonderful, rainy morning. In fact, the reason for Sergei's party was to celebrate Sasha's newfound freedom from a notorious gang of racketeers called the "Ushaki."

A battle-hardened, sturdy soldier, Sasha returned from Afghanistan as one of the few uninjured men. Because of his unique hand-to-hand combat skills, he became                                           highly sought-after material just when Dmitry Ushak, a notorious thief-in-law, started to recruit experienced fighters for his gang. While walking home one afternoon, Sasha was approached by a muscular man, who spoke to him as if they knew each other for years. It was a very brief conversation.

"Not interested," was Sasha's firm reply. He picked up pace, but the man followed along.

"Ushak will pay you better than anyone," the man insisted. "Why don't you think about it?"

"I just thought about it, and my final answer is no. Get lost."

"If that is how you want it, soldier-boy," the man spread out his arms and backed away, adding from a safe distance, "welcome back to a war zone."

"Next time you see me walking down the street, you'd better cross over to the other side," Sasha called after him, just to show that he was not afraid.

That night Sasha's windows were pelted with rocks, shattering the glass. The next morning he replaced them. A few evenings later the racketeers soaked Sasha's door in kerosene and torched it. By pure fortune he was at home to extinguish the fire, but the psychological damage was done. Like many other young people in Kiev, Sasha lived at home with his parents. They were old and frail people, easy to scare. After the kerosine incident, Sasha's parents refused to leave the safety of their place for any reason, even to purchase groceries or to take a walk in the park. The apartment became their prison.

That is when Sasha decided to put a stop to this juvenile harassment. After replacing the charred door, Sasha went hunting after his enemies. He visited countless bars and restaurants to spot any familiar faces. One afternoon he stumbled upon three of Ushak's soldiers sitting in a cafe on Kreschatik. In view of the other customers Sasha unleashed the full power of his experience unto these unlucky souls. Two of them emerged from the hospital as life-long invalids, walking only with assistance of a cane.

To avoid certain retribution from Ushak's gang, Sasha promptly re-applied to Alfa, his old unit. He was approved on the spot and assigned to serve as one of the bodyguards for the Minister of Trade and Economic

Relations, with a license to carry and use a standard issue *Makarov 9 mm*. This position legally allowed Sasha to kill anyone who crossed his path, including Ushak, with no consequences. That fact, in itself, was worthy of celebration, Sasha thought as he knocked on Sergei's door.

"Who?" To Sasha, Sergei's voice did not sound particularly sober.

"Let me in, or I will shoot something." Sasha was only partially joking, eager to pump a few bullets into a light bulb.

"Don't do it." Sergei quickly opened the door. "Where have you been? Everyone is waiting for the guest of honor!"

"Last-minute grocery shopping," Sasha smiled. He walked straight to the kitchen, where his closest friends were already seated around the table.

"Beat up anyone useful along the way?" Roman greeted his old buddy. They were friends since the first grade.

Sasha looked over the table and shook his head. It was a pityful sight. One bottle of vodka was already finished. The second one looked half-empty. There was one pathetic dollop of sauerkraut and two marinated pickles on a chipped plate. To bring the festivities back to their full vigor, Sasha reached into his grocery bag and pulled out several pork sausages connected by their umbilical cord, a small bag of potatoes, a jar of pickled herring, a stick of smoked sausage and another bottle of vodka. Sergei promptly dumped the sausages and potatoes into a skillet and ignited the gas flame below.

"Well, gentlemen, let's celebrate!" Sergei poured vodka into everyone's glasses. "To Sasha's first week of freedom!"

"Way to go, soldier!" Roman slapped Sasha on the shoulder.

"Thanks, guys." Sasha drank to the bottom of his glass, then bit into a slice of smoked sausage.

"So are you going to show us the gun or not?" Roman said. Just as Sasha was about to hand over his shiny new weapon, Sergei's doorbell rang.

"Funny, but I did not invite anyone else," Sergei said. Sasha lowered his *Makarov* under the table and checked the bullet in the chamber. "Relax, Sasha, it's probably just the neighborhood kids playing a prank. Give me a second," Sergei said before leaving.

"If anyone came by looking for me, just send them to the kitchen," Sasha joked uneasily after him. Meanwhile, he took the safety off the gun in his lap. The other guests also became nervous because everyone knew what Ushak's men were capable of doing.

\* \* \*

Sergei's building turned out to be a run-down old apartment building, hidden discreetly in the back of a courtyard. From the rainy street, the lights that warmly glowed inside several apartments looked very cozy. Jack walked up to the third floor in near complete darkness, carefully following the hand-rail, until he found a wooden door with number nine, just like the instructions read. Jack knocked on the door, praying that he was at the right place. The nearing footsteps sounded encouraging. Then a transparent peephole turned black and Jack smiled straight into it.

"Hey, what a pleasant surprise," a familiar voice said. The door opened, revealing Sergei's grinning face.

"Hello," Jack said, dripping from the rain. He looked like a wet puppy, eager to be invited inside a warm home. "I just got out, and I didn't know where else to go..."

"Well, you came to the right place," Sergei cheerfully replied, "I'm hosting a small party for one of my friends. Come on in and I'll introduce you." When Jack stepped indoors, he was overwhelmed by the fragrance of pepper, garlic and succulent pork. Combined with the smell of fried potatoes, Sergei's apartment made him salivate like a Pavlovian dog. "This way." Sergei motioned to the source of that mouth-watering, almost overpowering aroma that floated freely around his place.

When Jack walked into the kitchen, his hungry eyes became glued to the curled garlicky sausages, frying in the skillet. They were surrounded by golden slices of potatoes. That rich smell of freshly ground pork cooking in its own juicy flavor, seasoned with salt, pepper and sage, drove him crazy.

"You can smell it, eh?" Sergei inhaled the aroma. "The great Ukrainian sausage. Every civilized nation has its own version, but there is nothing else like a Ukrainian kolbasa." Both Sergei and Jack admired the thick links, sizzling in the pan. With great effort Jack tore himself away from that delicious sight to see rather three somber men. They were sitting around a table littered with half-empty bottles of vodka, an assortment of jars containing herring, pickles and sauerkraut, and a plate with sliced salami.

"This is my American friend, Jack," Sergei announced in Russian. The guests visibly relaxed and even started to smile. "He was just released from the Podol clinic. Now, that calls for a drink!"

With his knowledge of basic street Russian, Jack understood the toast and flashed a stupid grin of embarrassment. Meanwhile, one of the guests, an athletic young man in his early thirties, poured a generous portion of vodka into a teacup and offered it to him. "For your freedom, mine friend," he said in decent English but with a strong Russian accent. Then he pointed to the jar with herring and said, "very good. *Na zdorovye.*"

"*Na zdorovye,*" the other guests chanted like zombies, just before everyone at the table, including Jack, emptied their glasses. Jack groaned like a novice, while Sergei easily gulped his bottoms-up in a tumbler-size glass. Then everyone picked at their favorite morsels of food from the communal plates to chase away vodka's medicinal aftertaste, and nodded to each other.

"My name is Sasha," the athletic young man said in heavily accented English. "I am friend with Sergei since school. First class."

"First grade, you mean?"

"Yes. First grade. Good friend, Sergei."

"Very good friend," Jack agreed, hoping that Sergei overheard them. Maybe then he would be more inclined to let Jack stay for a few days. Soon all the glasses were refilled and emptied. Again, Jack almost choked as the burning sensation of pure alcohol attacked his throat. Sasha quickly fished out a pickle from a glass jar and gave it to Jack. It proved to be an excellent chaser.

Out of the kitchen window daylight slowly changed from medium grey shade to a more sinister dark-blue color. The guys kept rattling off their tongues in Russian, offering toasts and gulping vodka every few minutes. Jack did not follow most of the conversation, which switched from one topic to another with seemingly little connection.

"We're talking about business, Jack," Sergei helpfully explained. "The black market days are over. We should be opening our own shops and making real money, instead of getting drunk on a train and selling cheap caviar and vodka in Warsaw or Budapest! You're a lawyer, so you could open a law firm."

"I suppose," Jack agreed. "And what would you do?"

"I haven't decided yet. Sometimes I dream about having a corner booth in the back of my own little restaurant, always open for my friends and me. Other times, I'm thinking really big, like maybe a disco or even a casino. And why not? All doors around here are opened with an envelope."

"An envelope?"

"Yes, an envelope," Sergei answered seriously. "Of course, everything depends on how much is inside, but as a rule, you can buy whoever you want. The envelope is the universal way of finding a common language with any government official whose services you need."

"That's called bribery in America."

"It's called bribery in Kiev, too," Sergei readily agreed, "but as a businessman, I know that sharing money is the only guaranteed method of getting anything done. And the higher the government official, the larger is the bribe, but so is the return on your investment. That's how it always has been, and always shall be."

As a corporate lawyer from Manhattan, unaccustomed to the seedy side of life, Jack was amazed at how easily criminal words like "bribes" and "buying government officials" rolled off Sergei's tongue. Obviously, ethics were not high on his list. "Isn't there some supervision system here? What about the guardians of this country?"

"All of our government employees are dirt poor. Who can live on the miserly official salaries they earn? That is why from the President, all the way down to the customs officers and traffic cops, all bureaucrats put themselves up for sale. Everyone knows their official power is convertible into personal cash. That's the reason police chiefs, judges and politicians are in their positions. Everyone is for sale."

"For sale to whom?"

"To people who have money, who else? To ordinary businessmen, like me."

"For sale to ordinary businessmen like you," Jack quietly repeated. "And how does that work?"

"I prefer to make a one-time flat fee pay-off, but sometimes they insist on having a percentage of the deal. In any case, no government bureaucrat has ever refused an envelope. That's the beauty of the system: everything is possible for money."

"I can't believe it's that bad," Jack shook his head in denial.

"That bad? There's an ancient rule, my American friend, one that existed long before Christ. And in Kiev this rule works the same: so long as there is bribery, you can always count on justice."

Jack cautiously listened as Sergei described a very strange government system with an equally strange set of business practices. Large, heavy raindrops pounded against the concrete windowpane, making the gathering inside Sergei's little kitchen seem all the cozier. Through the entire party, Sergei was fully immersed in his role as the toastmaster; holding vodka shots in both fists allowed him to toast with either hand, like a conductor of a very tipsy orchestra.

The evening progressed well past midnight, and the last of Sergei's guests decided to go home, shaking Sasha's hand respectfully before departing. Eventually Sasha disappeared, too. This left Jack in an unenviable position of being the last guest with nowhere to go.

"Since everyone is gone, I wanted to ask you for a favor," Jack turned to Sergei. Ashamed to find himself in such a situation, Jack struggled to find the right words. "You see, I don't have any place to stay. And I'm kind of short on money."

"I figured that," Sergei interrupted him. "You can stay here as long as you need. No problem."

"Really? It's just for a few days, until I sort myself out."

"Take it easy, Jack. I have an extra cot, so why not lend it to a friend?" Being a gracious host to the end,

Sergei splashed the remaining vestiges of vodka into their glasses and raised his tumbler.

"To a real friend," Jack said gratefully. The two men sealed their friendship with the last shot for the night.

# Chapter 6

The exotic experience of getting drunk all day long with Sergei's childhood buddies became routine after only one week. Occasionally Sasha would bring his seven-string guitar and passionately scream off-color words from Odessa's songs of crime until there was nothing left to drink. When Jack woke up, a cold beer would soothe his splitting headache. The party at Sergei's place was always in progress. None of Jack's colleagues in New York had ever tasted such freedom.

During this lost week Jack found an advertisement in the local daily, offering to rent out a small two-room apartment on *Gorky Street*, near the *Shevchenko Park*. The place was a bit expensive at three hundred dollars per month, but it had a king-size bed and was available immediately. Tired of the round-the-clock partying, Jack wanted to fall asleep in his own bed, under his own roof. Fortunately, Sergei came to Jack's rescue by letting him borrow five hundred bucks. This loan resulted in Jack's immediate relocation to a new apartment; he even had two hundred dollars left over for food.

"Watch your neighbors carefully and don't get involved in their squabbles," was Sergei's parting advice before Jack moved out. "Oh yeah, and don't open the door without looking into the peephole first. That's how most people get robbed."

\* \* \*

Lydia Ivanovna, a pensioner and self-proclaimed veteran of World War II, walked into her kitchen, opened the window and tossed a handful of bread crumbs onto the ledge for the pigeons, as she did every morning since 1953. Although it was mid-October, the weather had turned sunny and warm for a precious last few days. Soon the frigid November winds would arrive. Lydia stood still, so as not to scare off the birds, as she waited for water in the kettle to boil.

Instead of the usual timid pigeons, however, this morning a brazen black raven gracefully landed on her windowsill. The bird looked Lydia directly in the eye, tilting its head, as if evaluating the risks of imminent threat. Its powerful wings reflected the morning sun and Lydia froze, admiring the beautiful black creature from afar.

The emboldened bird majestically shifted its weight from side to side and ambled toward a tea cup that

Lydia kept on the kitchen table next to the ledge. The curious raven dipped its long beak inside to retrieve a shiny object that rested at the bottom of the cup.

"Don't you dare!" screamed Lydia, dropping the kettle on the floor. The boiling water spilled all around her feet, but she did not pay attention. Instead, her eyes followed the large black bird as it pushed off the ledge, flapping its wings, and flew away with Lydia's false teeth clenched tightly in its powerful beak. She remained standing in her kitchen with an empty mouth gaping wide open, amazed at the treachery. For once, Lydia was cleverly duped, and there was nothing she could do about it.

"I have never seen anything like this in my entire life," Lydia shook her head in disbelief, trying to comprehend the situation, "I offered it perfectly good bread crumbs. And this is how I get repaid for my kindness?" To help calm her nerves, Lydia reached to pour herself a cup of home-brewed moonshine, but there were only a few drops left at the bottom of the jug.

As she paced back and forth, Lydia's thoughts revolved around how to get alcohol without spending any money. Suddenly, her eyes lit up with a brilliant idea: she remembered seeing a new neighbor moving into an apartment two floors below her. Surely he would have a bottle or two stashed away somewhere in his apartment. All men do.

Having perfected the various techniques employed in pilfering vodka from her gullible neighbors, Lydia grabbed a screwdriver and took the elevator downstairs to the first floor, to break into a mailbox.

* * *

The doorbell of Jack's Soviet-era apartment buzzed monotonously. It was barely eleven o'clock in the morning and already someone was at his doorstep. Reluctantly Jack got out of the warm bed, threw on his Polish-made bathrobe and went to see who it was. Through the grimy peephole in his door Jack saw an elderly woman, smiling and waving newspapers and envelopes in the air, happy as she could be. Sensing no harm, he opened the door. Across from him stood a short grandmother without a hint of ever having had teeth.

"How can I help you?" Jack inquired politely in Russian.

"My name is Lydia Ivanovna and I'm your neighbor from above." She joyfully pointed to the sky. "Look, I found your mail." Lydia again waived the papers in front of Jack's nose.

"My mail?" Jack wondered who could have possibly sent him anything, given the fact that he moved in quite recently.

"See? Your address." She smiled and handed the entire bundle to Jack. Sure enough, the envelopes contained the right address, though the wrong name. They were ordinary bills, addressed to the previous tenant, so Jack took them.

"Thank you, I really appreciate it." Jack was ready to close the door and return to bed.

"It was nothing, really," the grandmother continued chatting. "I found it behind the trash container."

"Oh?"

"It was just laying there, for everyone to see. I saw your address, and I didn't want my neighbors to get into any trouble. You know how things are these days. Heaven forbid your mail ends up in the wrong hands. So I collected whatever I could find and saved it for you."

"Thank you, that's really considerate."

Just as Jack was about to close the door, Lydia casually added, "I know it's not appropriate to ask, but can I borrow half a bottle of vodka? My husband's upstairs with some of his friends, and I just happened to run out. Silly me..."

Naturally Jack wanted to show his appreciation, so he went to the refrigerator and gave her the full, unopened bottle of vodka that Sergei gifted as a housewarming present. Clearly delighted, Lydia Ivanovna snatched the icy bottle from Jack's hand and skipped into the elevator, giggling like a schoolgirl. Though it cost him a perfectly good bottle of vodka, Jack was glad to know that there were old-fashioned kind of neighbors who still watched out for one another.

\* \* \*

Emboldened by a refreshing shot of ice-cold vodka, Lydia's plans of revenge for the thieving raven had crystallized. In the bathroom she found a handful of sleeping pills and some laxatives. Her magic mixture consisted of finely crushed pills, one egg, a handful of flour and some water. Smiling happily, Lydia pinched off bite-size pieces of homemade time bombs and left them sitting on the window ledge for the raven.

"This will teach you a lesson, you stupid bird," she said. "I may not get my teeth back, but I will wring your bony neck if I find you on the ground!"

From the kitchen window Lydia could see the usual grandmothers, huddling on the benches by the playground, spilling the latest gossip. Two young mothers were happily chatting while keeping a watchful eye on their children, who were playing in the sandbox. A brand new day in the neighborhood was beginning. Lydia carefully locked the door behind her and waited for the elevator to take her downstairs in search of adventure.

\* \* \*

In the afternoon Jack heard gut-wrenching screams coming through the wall of his neighbor's apartment. The sounds made him pause. A resounding echo of a slamming door followed. He listened carefully for any other signs of danger.

Suddenly, a woman's voice just outside Jack's door wailed, "let me in, you animal! You pig!" Walking on tiptoes towards the door, Jack heard her crying out in the hallway, "I live here too! Let me in, you bastard!" Loud sobbing was punctuated by occasional thumping on the door.

Jack silently watched the domestic drama unfold through the peephole. He saw a plump, middle-aged woman standing just three feet away from him, screaming at someone who was hiding behind the closed door. "Get her out here," she roared, "let me take a better look at her!" Then Jack heard a man's voice offering a mumbled response, but could not make it out. The woman shook her head in disbelief and then disappeared inside the elevator cabin.

\* \* \*

On the way down, Tamara Victorovna's brain replayed the raw, pornographic scene she witnessed just minutes ago. Once downstairs, she slowly walked over to the benches in front of the apartment building, still dazed. The usual group of grandmothers already gathered, complaining about the ever-rising price of bread. Everyone became quiet when they saw Tamara's tear-stained face.

"Tamara Victorovna, what happened? Did Anton lay his hands on you?" Lydia asked first. She could see no bruises or any other obvious signs of physical abuse. "Go on, you can tell us," she added encouragingly.

"I can not believe it," Tamara said. The image of her fat, naked husband Anton on top of his skinny, young student nauseated her. Neither her cheating spouse nor his pupil seemed the least bit concerned about being discovered. Especially the young lady, whose legs remained spread open while Tamara screamed at Anton from the top of her lungs. Sobbing, she continued, "there he was, my dear husband, one of the leading professors at the Shevchenko University, parading around our apartment stark naked, completely drunk out of his skull!

And in our bed I found a young girl, almost a child. She was completely nude and equally drunk..."

"That animal," Lydia gasped. "This just goes to show you: all men are dogs. Hump, hump, hump. That's all they ever think about."

"I was standing in our bedroom, and you know what he does?"

"What?"

"He gets on top of her, right in front of me. Like I didn't exist! Is that normal?"

"For a man, anything is normal," Lydia replied sympathetically. This was the juiciest piece of gossip she had heard all week. "So what did you do?"

"I did not want to cause a scandal, so I asked Anton politely, who should leave: her or me? And you know what he said? That bastard did not even hesitate. You, he said. Twenty two years of marriage, and he has the nerve to point his finger at me, while trying to mount her, and say, you! Well, that was the last straw: I threw my keys at them and ran out of the apartment. After I calmed down, I wanted to really let them have it, but we have this automatic lock, and my keys were inside..."

"So he locked you out of your own apartment, eh?" Lydia could not stand by and allow a helpless, decent woman, to be insulted like this. She broke away from the circle of neighbors and went home.

Once inside, she picked up her telephone and dialed 002 to alert the police about the incident. "We have a drunken terrorist," Lydia calmly reported over the line. "He has locked himself inside an apartment and refuses to come out."

"Are there any hostages?" asked a concerned voice on the other end.

"Yes," Lydia said after some thought. "His loving wife, who has a kind heart. Now, please get someone over here, to Gorky number four, before it's too late. We will be waiting for you in the courtyard."

Soon enough a green army truck arrived, containing six men in black uniforms, armed with sub-machine guns. In the courtyard they found a group of Tamara's supporters, which has grown to nine women, including Lydia and three grandchildren. After learning the true facts, however, the police sergeant flatly refused to implement Lydia's recommendation to shoot out the door locks.

"What kind of men are you, if you cannot defend poor women," Lydia delivered her often-used line. She found it to be especially effective with young men in uniform. "I am a widow, a pensioner, who has to pick up bottles for a living. Son, I am old enough to be your grandmother. And now I am pleading for your help. This poor woman's drunkard husband will not let her back inside her own apartment. Think of me as your own grandmother..."

These words were pronounced with just the right blend of humbleness, sincerity and moral conviction. The young police sergeant hesitated. His grandmother was also a pensioner and a widow. He would gladly rip apart any man who dared to offend her. Having found this in common, the sergeant offered Lydia a compromise: instead of shooting at the locks, the police would employ a clever psychological trick to get Anton to voluntarily open the door.

"That's all we ever wanted," said Lydia. Turning to Tamara, she added, "I will be happy to show the nice young policeman where Anton is hiding. Are you coming, ladies?"

* * *

Anton's heart was pounding like a sledgehammer. Large beads of sweat rolled down his back. He was almost on the verge of reaching that glorious release; just another few seconds and all of his efforts would be rewarded in one gigantic explosion.

*Ring!* Anton tried to ignore the stupid doorbell that began to ring during this very inopportune moment, but it would not quit. *Ring! Ring! Ring! Ring! Ring!*

"Don't think about her," Anton said, cursing his wife's poor timing. "It's just you and me, honey." The doorbell stopped ringing and Anton breathed a sigh of relief. "See, I told you she would go away. Now, let's try it again." Suddenly there was heavy pounding on the door, delivered with brute power that Tamara Victorovna did not possess.

"Is it her again?" Tanya asked, lazily stretching under Anton. "Can't you just tell her to get lost once and for all?"

"Open up," they heard a man with a deep voice order authoritatively. "Now!"

"Who the hell is that?" Tanya whispered. She pulled away from Anton and sat upright, wrapping herself up in a blanket.

"Damned if I know. But I'll settle this right now."

"Don't you want to put something on?" Tanya suggested, nodding at the towel on the floor.

"No need. I'll be back in a second. Don't you go anywhere," Anton smiled and winked at Tanya. He walked barefoot on the shiny parquet floor and looked through the peephole. He saw a group of men in dark fatigues with helmets, positioned just outside his doorstep, holding machine-guns.

"Anton Vladimirovich, we know you are in there. Please open the door," said the sergeant. He pointed the barrel of his gun at the peephole for maximum effect.

Anton was profoundly shocked; they even knew his name. "This must be a mistake," he tried to reason through the door. "There are no criminals in here. Only peaceful people."

"Open the door immediately."

"But..."

"I am warning you. Do not try to stall us. *Now!* Open the door *now!*"

More pounding came, suggesting that the door would soon come off the hinges. Anton had no time to think, succumbing to the sergeant's delicate psychological trick. Frightened out of his wits, Anton unlocked the door completely nude to face the police squad, his wife and the elderly neighbors.

"Thank you, officer," Lydia dismissed the sergeant with an unhealthy sparkle in her eyes. "We'll manage from now on. Ladies, let's get that little whore!" Along with several other women she stormed inside the bedroom. They pounced on Tanya, stripping off whatever clothes she managed to put on during Anton's brief standoff with the police. Meanwhile, Lydia walked out on the balcony in search of anything that could be useful in this situation. She emerged victorious, carrying a tin bucket.

"Ladies, Tamara Viktorovna should settle her own scores in private," Lydia said. "Let's take this little slut outside and teach her a lesson in family values that she will remember forever." The angry mob of grandmothers followed their self-appointed leader, shoving the frightened victim out into the stairwell.

* * *

Glued to his door, Jack saw a naked girl. She was surrounded by a group of elderly women, which included the toothless fairy herself, Lydia Ivanovna. He wanted to interrupt whatever was about to happen, but decided to heed Sergei's warning not to get involved, especially after witnessing how Lydia Ivanovna bossed around the head of the local firing squad.

"You little home wrecker," Lydia hissed, "this is so that you will remember what you did today for the rest of your life."

Seemingly out of nowhere, like a magic trick, Lydia produced a tin bucket. She opened the lid and dumped its contents on top of the girl's brown hair. Through the peephole Jack saw slimy green fluid running down her chest, onto the stomach, until it finally dripped from the triangle of her green pubic hair onto the stairwell. The smell was so strong that even Jack could tell it was oil paint. He wanted to go outside and help her get away from the pack of grandmothers. Only Sergei's warning prevented him from flinging open the door. Don't get involved with your neighbors, he said. And don't open the door.

Exasperated, howling like a captured animal, Tanya broke out of the vicious circle. She slipped in a puddle of greasy paint that formed at her feet, tripping and almost crashing against the concrete steps. Tanya flew down the stairs as the grandmothers screamed after her, clapping their hands and laughing. Lydia urged them to follow her outside, and then everyone disappeared from Jack's view.

# Chapter 7

For the first few days, Jack could not believe that he owned a law firm, despite the evidence such as a desk with the black 1950's style telephone, several chairs and even two glass cabinets. Everything was in its place, thanks to another loan from Sergei. Jack's window looked out over the traffic on Lenin Street. Like his former boss, the great Gerald Windsor III, he had an extra-large writing desk, which attested to Jack's position in the law firm.

On the third morning, a thin, balding man knocked on the door. "Can I come in?" he asked and barged in without waiting for Jack's permission. "It will only take a minute, and it's for your own benefit, truly." Well in his late forties, the man had deep, dark circles under his eyes.

Jack pointed to a chair. "What can I do for you?"

The man leaned across the desk and replied, "you are new in this building, so I gave you time to settle in before visiting you. Purely as a friend." Then he paused, to see if Jack understood him. The stranger's breath reeked of sour stench. "I came to deliver a message that could save your life. Lives of your employees, too." He gave Jack a somber look.

Now the man made Jack nervous. Maybe this was a real, live racketeer, trying to shake him down. "What is it? What do you want?"

"The rats have chewed through the elevator cable. Do you understand me?" In other words, Jack's elevator privileges were suspended. What an odd threat.

"Tell me the truth," Jack said, "who are you?"

"Nikolai Novotchek," the man modestly bowed his head. "I am the chief engineer. I am responsible for fixing everything that breaks down in this building. Like elevators crashing, balconies falling off, water and electricity shut-offs, things like that."

"I see." Jack sighed with relief and leaned back in his chair.

"I am like a guardian angel, making sure that everybody is happy in these difficult times, and since your office is new in my building, I figured you could probably use my help every now and then. Practical services at reasonable prices. That's me."

"For example, when rats eat through the elevator cables," Jack surmised.

"Precisely. But don't worry, you don't owe me anything. That was a freebie, because you're new here."

"So can you get us additional electrical sockets, in case we have more equipment?"

"That is exactly what I do," the guardian angel answered. "Three dollars per socket."

"Thank you, Mr. Novotchek," Jack said, understanding his utility. "Three phone lines and ten sockets will be a great start."

"But do me a favor: about the elevator, please tell only your office staff, but no one else in the building. We don't want to start a mass panic, right? Besides, I prefer to notify everyone myself, as you understand."

"I promise, nobody will know about the elevators."

"Thank you for a pleasant meeting, and I will be in touch."

After the guardian angel left, Jack pulled out the divorce papers Julie had sent to him and stared at them. It was a shame the way their marriage had ended, but in a strange way he felt relieved. Being single again was exciting, full of possibilities. Jack signed the last page of the document, wondering if Julie was already dating someone, when his telephone rang. He eagerly picked up the receiver and said pleasantly, "law offices, Jack Parker speaking."

"Hello, counselor," answered a man's voice with a thick Brooklyn accent. "I need a good American lawyer. You interested?"

"Well, I do have some free time today." Jack tried to sound calm and dignified. "How about 3 p.m.?"

"How about right now?"

"Sure," Jack replied, because a prospective client is always right. "Now is perfect."

"See you soon, counselor," said the man with a hint of laughter in his voice.

* * *

Jack liked Antonio from the very beginning. Tall and lean, Antonio was impeccably dressed in a fashionable, dark Armani suit. He sported a heavy gold chain on his thick wrist and a large gold pinky ring with an oversize round diamond in the center. Antonio was a magnificent sight to behold, especially when his long, graying hair was released from its pony tail and allowed to spread on his shoulders like a lion's mane. He was style, charisma and presence, all wrapped in expensive Italian fabric.

But it was Antonio's five thousand-dollar advance retainer that won over Jack's heart. Antonio counted out fifty hundred-dollar bills without any arguments, negotiations or silly jokes about slimy lawyers. After such an introduction, Jack was ready to deliver the world to him on a silver platter.

By nature, his first client was a true "schmoozer," Jack noticed. As smooth as silk, the New York-born Antonio claimed to speak four languages, including Italian, French and some Hungarian. "I manage East European lottery operations for MundoLotto," he explained while lighting a cigarette. "We already have diversified business interests in Moscow and Budapest. Kiev is next on our list to establish similar enterprises."

"And what might those be?" Jack inquired helpfully, eager to earn his fee. Clearly, this discussion was billable time.

"They vary from place to place," Antonio explained. "In Budapest, we own several casinos. Same in Moscow, plus an import-export and distribution company. For moving goods in and out of the country, if you know what I mean. That's what we came here to duplicate. Like in Hungary and Russia, in Ukraine we have our local partners. They want our help in establishing a nation-wide lottery, but I'm more interested in a local distribution company. It's called Podium, Ltd. Ever heard of it?"

"No."

"Good. Your job is simply to document the transaction. General corporate stuff should be a piece of cake for a hotshot young lawyer like you, right?"

"That's exactly what I do for clients."

"The first round of negotiations with our partners takes place tomorrow morning, at ten thirty. Meet me downstairs at ten o'clock sharp."

"You got it, Antonio."

"Stay cool, buddy." Antonio got up and walked out before Jack could thank him for the advance retainer.

At the end of the third business day, Jack had five thousand dollars bulging in his pocket as a wonderful confirmation of success. At last, he could afford to repay all of Sergei's loans, plus have a nice cushion for several months' rent on the apartment and the office, too. It was good to be a single, young and wealthy business owner, indeed.

\* \* \*

The exotic name "Texas Bar-B-Q" erroneously implied that the bar served American quality food and service. Still, it always managed to attract a diverse clientele.

On Saturday nights, heads of prominent Kiev racketeer groups entertained their mistresses and girlfriends in the main dining area; on Sunday mornings, the same tables were reserved strictly for their families, including children.

A separate room had four large billiard tables, which provided additional recreation to a captive audience. Bored expatriates would waste their late nights playing pool there. For Jack, the popularity of Texas Bar-B-Q was rooted in Mexican tequila with a Corona beer, plus the four billiard tables.

While waiting to order a drink at the bar Jack looked across the room and spotted his tip-loving acquaintance, Slava, the man in charge of allocating pool tables. For a couple of bucks, Slava bumped customers ahead of the queue. He was standing inconspicuously in the corner, then smiled and waived, hoping for a discreet reward for prompt service. In reply, Jack nodded, confirming that he was interested in a table.

"One Tequila, one Corona, one lime," Jack turned to the bartender.

"Coming right up."

Jack glanced over his shoulder. The customers were a mix of locals and foreigners, all engrossed in their conversations. He sighed, feeling rich, yet lonely. Jack wanted to speak with somebody, to share this evening with a friend, but there was no one around. When his drinks arrived, he heard Slava's quiet voice. "Your table is ready. But hurry up because somebody else is waiting for it."

"Slava, you're the man." Jack reached over to shake Slava's hand. Usually he slipped two bucks, but tonight

Jack felt like leaving a five-dollar bill in Slava's warm palm. Paying a token fee in advance was important, Jack learned, because one gets far superior service later.

Just as Jack was about to strike the white ball, a young lady in her early twenties rushed over to his table. She was something special to behold. From the moment Jack saw her, he was captivated by her sultry dark looks. Like a wild Gypsy girl, she looked through him with her enormous, beautiful brown eyes.

Those who have never loved before can not understand how Jack felt at that moment. The smooth olive skin, her long, silky black hair, those delicately sculptured high cheekbones. Full red lips. Confident chin. Years of dancing toned her perfect figure and gave her grace more commonly associated with ballerinas.

It was too much to absorb all at once. Stunned by the girl's natural beauty, Jack watched her sweep by, trailed by a sweet smell of perfume. She abruptly stopped and grabbed the white ball from his billiard table, weighing it as if she was getting ready to throw the ball at Jack.

"Listen you, I was here first. I patiently waited for my turn, and that idiot," she nodded toward Slava, "gave away this table, which is rightfully mine, to you. It's the second table stolen from me this evening and you're not taking it! It's my turn to play!"

Her sweet, melodic voice resonated with steel. The girl slammed the white ball hard against the table and stood her ground firmly, with both hands placed on her slim waist. While she waited for Jack's response, Slava wormed his way over to the battlefront. He sensed a distinct possibility of being fired from a lucrative job for small-time bribery and was eager to prevent any screaming or fighting.

Standing next to her, Jack was in awe of the magnificent sight: this was not only an angry young woman, but a very beautiful angry young woman. He could see her flaring nostrils, those smoldering black eyes with long eyelashes that curled up at the ends, the faint dimple on her perfectly sculpted chin. She was within his arm's reach, completely naked under all those clothes, but as much as Jack wanted to, he could not touch her.

Jack's brief opportunity to make a good impression was running out quickly. He had to make a move right away, before Slava ruined everything by saying something stupid. "If this young lady is right, then you are in a lot of trouble, young man!" Jack gave Slava an angry look, to let him know that he wanted to be left alone. Relieved, Slava quickly shuffled off.

"I'm sorry, I did not know this was your table. But I don't have anyone else to play with, as you can see. Perhaps we could play a game or two? If not, I'll understand."

The girl was not prepared for such a reply. Most men stubbornly stand their ground, no matter what. This foreigner seemed humble and sincere. "Alright," she said cautiously. "Maybe just one game."

"So, do you want to break?" Jack politely asked the black-haired beauty.

"What do you mean?" She had such a cheerful, bright smile, that he became disoriented. Looking down at the green canvas, Jack tried to concentrate on the game but his peripheral vision kept focusing on her contours. Of course Jack intentionally lost, and then promptly demanded a re-match. This allowed him to play several games with her, flirting between the shots, sipping white wine. She was beautiful, sexy, charming, and funny. Caught up in the middle of a growing infatuation, Jack forgot about the passing time. At last, she caught a glimpse of her watch. It was nearly midnight.

"I didn't realize how late it is," she said. "I'm sorry, but I have to get up for work tomorrow."

Jack looked into her almond-shaped eyes, silently refusing to let her go, pleading for her to stay. At that moment nothing and nobody mattered. He did not pay attention to the noise, nor the heavy cigarette smoke that surrounded them. The other patrons ceased to exist. They stood by the pool table for several seconds, though it seemed much longer. No words were exchanged because none were needed.

Looking into her eyes, uninterrupted, Jack wanted to say the truth: that she was the most beautiful woman he had ever seen, that a few minutes longer would not matter, that a double shot of cognac would change her mind. Putting all these thoughts together, he blurted out, "so how about coffee and cognac over at my place?"

There was a long, uncomfortable pause. Jack immediately knew that he blew it. Like any nice girl she was offended at such a blunt, indecent proposal. Feeling like a complete idiot, Jack could not think of anything more to add that would dilute this awkward moment, so he continued to look into her enormous eyes.

"I really must be going now," she broke the silence first. "Otherwise my driver will be worried."

"Of course, I understand," Jack said, ready to kick himself. "May I call you sometime? For a dinner maybe?"

"I don't give out my telephone number to strangers." Without saying goodbye, she turned and walked away. That confident demeanor, her cat-like fluid motion, captivated Jack all the more. This gorgeous young lady was unlike anyone he had met before, so he called after the mysterious girl, "at least tell me your name!"

"Lena," she shouted back and disappeared into the night.

Jack's celebration was over as soon as Lena walked out of the pool hall. He left Texas Bar-B-Q and returned home alone, disappointed with himself despite having Antonio's cash in his pocket.

# Chapter 8

At exactly 10:00 a.m. Jack went downstairs, as promised. He saw a navy Volvo, parked just in front of the building. The driver honked twice and a heavily tinted window in the rear lowered to reveal Antonio's grinning face. "Good morning, counselor," he cheerfully greeted Jack. "Why don't you have a seat in the front?"

A well-groomed gentleman sat next to Antonio in the back seat. The man was in his mid-sixties, with a weathered, tan skin. Like Antonio, he had a weakness for gold. Chunky rings with diamonds adorned his leathery fingers. A heavy gold clip, with a thin chain, shined across his silk tie. Large gold-framed glasses with dark brown lenses covered the top half of his face, making it impossible to figure out where he was looking.

Jack climbed in the car and the driver locked the doors. "This is Francesco Napolitano himself," Antonio proudly made the introduction. "He flew in from New York for this meeting."

"Pleasure to meet you, Mr. Napolitano."

"You look kinda young for this business," Mr. Napolitano said with a thick Italian accent. He was cleanly shaven and without a trace of grey hair. Sweet smell of expensive cologne lingered about him.

"Everyone has to start sometime," Jack replied.

"Smart words. Welcome to the team."

"Thank you." Jack fastened his seat belt and pretended to look out the window. Yet Francesco Napolitano's heavy features remained photographically imprinted in Jack's mind, like a police most wanted mug shot. Did the American crime syndicate arrive to Kiev to expand its global network, Jack wondered, and if so, was Mr. Napolitano acting as the mob's international negotiating representative, flying in all the way from New York City to conquer Eastern Europe? Suddenly Jack did not want to be Antonio's local attorney anymore. Getting into a venereal hospital was bad enough, but joining the Cosa Nostra would be disastrous.

"Why are we sitting here, Yuri?" Antonio demanded, losing the playful side Jack initially saw in him.

"We are not going anywhere until back-up arrives," Yuri answered in accented English, looking in his rear-view mirror. "Remember Moscow? It's the same in Kiev."

"I want them over here, now!" Antonio sounded angry. Yuri pulled out a small radio from his pocket and said tensely, "*vi gde, rebyata?*" Something crackled on the other end, forcing him to start the engine. Another identical blue Volvo approached from behind, slowed down, coming to a complete halt. It flashed the brights twice.

"I hate it when people are late," Antonio muttered under his breath.

Twenty minutes later they pulled up in front of a sports complex on the outskirts of Kiev and waited in the car. Several men spilled out of the back-up Volvo and strolled into the building. After a short radio burst of words, Yuri unlocked the doors and escorted everyone inside. Jack felt like he was in some movie.

Musty odor of sweat indicated that heavy athletics, not business negotiations, dominated daily agenda in this gym. There were no elevators, so everyone climbed two flights of stairs and walked down a gloomy corridor. Yuri stopped at one of the doors. He inserted a key and, to Jack's astonishment, they entered a Western office, complete with the mahogany desk, halogen lights and a computer screen.

Mr. Napolitano shuffled over to the leather armchair, sat down impassively and looked at his gold watch. Antonio and Jack sank into the nearby black leather couch. They did not have to wait long. Several minutes later two gentlemen walked in, one more frightening in appearance than the other.

The first one was extraordinarily tall, easily six foot seven inches, surely a former basketball player. His cleanly shaved head, broken nose and protruding square jaw could easily have landed him recurring roles in horror films. The black suit was several sizes too small, leaving his extra-long arms and legs uncovered.

As if mocking the giant's stature, his colleague was quite short, about five and a half feet, but equally broad and stocky. Jack assumed that he was a wrestler, and a darn good one. Like the basketball player, the wrestler wore a wide black jacket, which was tailored to emphasize his well-developed upper body mass.

"Oleg, Ivan, nice of you to drop by," Antonio said venomously.

"Sorry, boss, but we got lost," the basketball player answered while the wrestler translated his words into passable English. "It's our first time in Kiev."

"I hate it when people are late, and you know that."

"You're looking very fit, Mr. Napolitano," the basketball player quickly turned to address the guest of honor.

"Hello," Mr. Napolitano replied coldly.

"Sorry, Antonio." The wrestler hustled over in a crab-like fashion to shake Antonio's hand. Turning to Mr. Napolitano, he bowed his head and said, respectfully, "good afternoon, sir."

"Maybe," the old man answered impassively. His eyes remained hidden behind the thick, dark lenses.

The wrestler extended his powerful, meaty hand to Jack. For a moment, Jack froze because he suddenly noticed a large pink scar etched on the man's round face. It was shaped in an inverse letter L, stretching horizontally under the right eye, then turning 90 decrees at the nose and following through to the mouth. The scar was still fresh, indicating that he was cut fairly recently. Jack could not help but imagine the unpleasant experience Ivan underwent earlier. He must have struggled while someone held him down and carved up his face, causing those jagged edges instead of a clean slash.

"My name is Ivan," the wrestler said. "What's yours?"

"Jack Parker. I'm a lawyer," Jack quickly explained. "I'm also with Antonio and Mr. Napolitano."

"Good people," Ivan smiled. "We've been working for them for the last few years. Really good people," he nodded toward Mr. Napolitano with reverence.

"So you're here..."

"Just to make sure everything is going right," Antonio finished the sentence. "Eventually they will be working with these Ukrainian fellas on a day-to-day basis." Suddenly the office door flew open. A husky young man entered the room, towering over the rest of the group. He acknowledged Oleg's and Ivan's presence with a slight nod. Like a professional boxer in the ring, he moved to the opposite corner of the room. Then an older man appeared, somewhere in his late forties.

Unlike Jack's clients, he was unshaved and wore a simple blue sport suit with white sneakers. The man's composure and his attire showed that he was not about to change his clothes, or his lifestyle, for anyone. From a safe distance Jack observed the deep wrinkles in his hollow cheeks, the front gold teeth. His entire disposition made it clear: this man was used to being in charge, to ruling by force.

"Mr. Dmitry Ushak, I would like to introduce you to Mr. Francesco Napolitano," Antonio said, getting up from the leather couch, as Ivan translated. "He traveled from New York to meet you."

"Tell him that I am glad to meet him, too," Mr. Ushak replied indifferently. "So that we don't waste anyone's time, tell him that we are interested in their help to set up the national lottery and casinos, but the distribution business is already taken."

"Mr. Napolitano says that last week his organization had reached the owner of Podium," Ivan translated the old man's reply, "and they are willing to sit down with our representatives and listen to our offer."

"What do you mean?"

"We are going to buy him out," Antonio explained simply. "Our lawyer over here, Jack, will draft the necessary documents and John Hatchet will sign them. Tomorrow is their first meeting."

"Why would a person like John Hatchet give up such an interesting business as Podium so easily?" Ushak's face remained a mask, without any signs of emotion. "It does not make sense."

Antonio turned to Jack and said, "by your estimates, counselor, how long does company re-registration take?"

"Two to three weeks," Jack replied, "if all the background documents are executed and delivered to me on time."

"That's fine," Antonio said. He looked at his future Ukrainian partner, Mr. Ushak, and added quietly, "by the time Podium's re-registration is done, we'll take over Hatchet's operations. Don't you worry about that, Mr. Ushak. The important thing is that you have no objections or claims over this matter."

"Whatever a thief manages to steal is his to keep," Mr. Ushak replied cryptically, "if he is able."

"Then I'm glad that we understand each other."

"And what about that first thing we talked about?" Mr. Ushak asked. "The lottery and gaming licenses?"

"Those projects will be very profitable, as they always are," Antonio smiled.

"Gentlemen, I am encouraged to hear that everything has been agreed to in principle. It means that we have a basis for further discussions," Mr. Napolitano spoke out, "but unfortunately, I am a little tired from the flight. Can we continue this meeting tomorrow?"

"With great pleasure," Mr. Ushak replied.

"In that case, Antonio, you wanna take me back to the hotel?"

"You got it, boss," Antonio said.

As they walked outside towards the car, Antonio leaned over to Jack and asked, "you got all that, counselor?"

"What part?" Jack said. That he witnessed Antonio and Francesco forming a joint venture with the local scum? Or that a company called Podium, owned by some poor guy, would soon have different, and not very savory, owners?

Antonio fixed his eye on Jack and said, "what do mean, what part? You will prepare legal documents for a man named John Hatchet to sign. Then you will re-register the company to reflect new ownership. Tomorrow morning is your first meeting with Mr. Hatchet. You have a lot of work to do tonight. After that is done, you will be setting up casinos and lotteries. Now, which part didn't you get?"

"Hey, there's no need to be rude, Antonio," Jack said, feeling pressured. "We're all professionals here."

"I'll call you tomorrow morning with the address and the time of the meeting," Antonio growled in response. "And you better start drafting these documents as soon as I drop you off."

"Sure, Antonio," Jack sighed and hopped in the front seat of the Volvo.

"That's better," Antonio mumbled, sitting comfortably in the back with Mr. Napolitano. "And don't argue with me next time."

At this point Jack wisely decided to keep his mouth shut, though he had a bad feeling about his client's true intentions. As the two Volvo's made their way back into the Kiev city center, Jack contemplated the risk of severe bodily injury due to his unilateral withdrawal from Antonio's case.

## Chapter 9

John Paul Hatchet was born in the port town of Liverpool in December, 1938. By the age of twenty three he became a living legend in the discreet, shadowy world of parallel trading, and persona non-grata in most Western countries, including his native England. In 1993, John moved to Kiev in order to organize a Ukrainian import-export distribution company that became known as Podium Ltd. One year later, he was in charge of a cigarette smuggling empire.

His meteoric rise to success was due to a long-term relationship with JRJ Tobacco. For decades, top executives of JRJ Tobacco employed John in countries notorious for harsh business environments, like Colombia, where the only credible wholesale buyers had emerald and cocaine-derived cash. Later, with John's assistance, JRJ Tobacco dominated its competition all over Asia, from Hong Kong to Bangkok, by offering to the drug lords cigarettes as a legitimate money laundering vehicle for their heroin and prostitution proceeds.

Over the years, this aggressive, yet highly effective market entry strategy proved to be a mutually profitable relationship for all parties involved. By using innocent cigarettes, the world's leading organized gangs could launder profits from white slavery, narcotic sales, weapons trafficking, prostitution and extortion. In exchange, JRJ Tobacco gained world market domination with a lovely side benefit of tax avoidance.

Following the 1991 break-up of the Soviet Union, JRJ Tobacco executives correctly predicted that East European organized crime chiefs will soon face similar money laundering needs. To negotiate lucrative deals with a yet another group of slippery outlaws, the company executives once again turned to the most experienced contrabandist in the cigarette business, Mr. John Hatchet, and for good cause.

Just before coming to Kiev, John successfully moved JRJ's cigarettes through the Balkans by making illicit payments to several top-level corrupt government officials, including the President of Montenegro, Milo Djukanovic and the former head of the Montenegro's Foreign Investment Agency, Miluin Lalik. That is why John was granted the exclusive rights to move his cigarettes through a quiet, tiny port in Montenegro without paying any customs duty, value added tax, excise tax or other levies.

With one of the world's leading tobacco companies standing firmly behind Podium's business development efforts, JRJ's contraband cigarettes soon became the currency of choice for Ukrainian, Byelorussian and Moldovan money launderers. Even the organized crime families in New York, which already had considerable interests in other East European nations, took notice of Podium's unique monopoly position in Ukraine.

* * *

In the morning, Jack's taxi driver searched the entire left bank of *Dnieper River* for Podium's offices until he miraculously stumbled upon an isolated, square warehouse, resembling a mini-fort. The hard dirt path was littered with deep potholes, which slowed the taxi down to a snail's pace. Three large, 18-wheeler trucks were parked nearby.

While the driver waited in the car, Jack walked up the ice-covered stairs and pushed a black button. A semi-human voice barked over the intercom, "who is there?"

"Jack Parker." It was the correct password, causing the numerous locks to click open. The thick, vault-like, multi-layered metal door was so bulletproof that Jack experienced significant problems opening it due to its sheer weight. When it partially opened to allow Jack inside, he was greeted by two rows of beefy men, sitting in the hallway on long wooden benches.

On one side were four ex-athletes-turned-racketeers, decked out in their traditional sport suits and sneakers. Broken noses and cauliflower ears were clumsily attached, like play dough, to their abnormally small, shaved heads. Facing their traditional enemies were four pudgy policemen, all dressed up in official blue uniforms, complete with standard issue Makarov semiautomatics in the holsters.

Everyone froze for a fraction of a second, bracing for a band of well-armed men to rush in and kill them. They all visibly relaxed only when the massive green door was firmly in place and locked down. This is not good, Jack thought. "Wait in there," one of the athletes pointed Jack toward a room to the right.

Complying with his instructions, Jack opened the door and stepped into another world, one of technical advancement and Western business hardware. Twelve bright computer screens glowed along the walls, contrasting sharply against numerous laser printers and one enormous multi-function copier.

"Hey, what are you doing here?" It was a familiar voice. Jack turned around, and was dumbfounded to see Lena. This stronghold was the last place on earth he expected to find her. By the look on Lena's face Jack could tell that she was equally dismayed to see him.

"How did you get in here?" she demanded to know.

"I was in the neighborhood and thought I'd drop by to see if you changed you mind about having dinner with me."

"No, really." She was deadly serious and equally beautiful. "How did you find me? Who let you in here?"

"If you must know, I have business to discuss with Mr. Hatchet."

"You have a meeting with Mr. Hatchet? Who scheduled it?"

"My client did. So when are we going out for dinner?"

Before Lena could answer, however, another ex-athlete came in. He said, "Mr. Hatchet will see you now." Jack grinned stupidly at Lena and headed out without getting an answer.

The ex-athlete pointed to the stairs and Jack obediently climbed to the second floor to see another metal door. A large man in green camouflage fatigues, holding on tightly to an AK-47 machine gun, opened it from the inside. The green giant nodded for Jack to enter. Once inside, he saw another soldier, who was standing in a far left corner with his AK-47 trained squarely at Jack, just in case.

Mr. John Hatchet sat at his desk, which was positioned behind the steel door in such a way that a professional assault team would have to eliminate both bodyguards before having an opportunity to kill him. The open door behind his desk revealed a fully functional escape route.

"Oh, hello," John greeted Jack warmly. He was a true English gentleman. "Do have a seat." John wore an expensive Lavan tie, which matched perfectly with his hand-tailored suit. Yet, there was an insane sparkle in his eyes, confirming local pub tales about his state of mind. "So what can I do for the emissary of the great Francesco Napolitano?"

"Just sign right there, sir." Jack produced a two-page binding letter of intent, transferring Podium's equity to Mr. Napolitano's Hong Kong-based shell company, Amalfi Ltd. All other documents would follow. "Unless you have some revisions."

"Here are my revisions." John picked up a thin gold Cartier pen and crossed out both pages.

"What do you want me to put in the contract instead?" Jack's meek protest sounded more like a plea for help instead of principled legal negotiations. He tensed at a muffled noise coming from the room behind John's desk. It was the sound of a money machine, counting bills in short but regular bursts. Along with several large trucks parked outside John's impregnable castle, the rattling noise explained to Jack the necessity of keeping a personal army of jolly green giants with machine guns, plus an assortment of large men with firearms downstairs.

John smiled at Jack paternally and put down his gold pen. "My dear lad," he said, "let me explain something to you. Did you see those trucks, parked outside?"

"Yes, sir, I did."

"The contents inside each and every one of them are worth millions of dollars. Now, if one or two trucks are stolen, I don't mind, because that's the price of doing business over here. But any theft above three truckloads, and suddenly the entire venture becomes unprofitable. In the beginning I had my share of problems, like everyone does. But now, nobody touches my trucks. Neither the government nor the bandits. Sometimes I don't even bother to declare anything at the border. Podium has an excellent distribution network in the primary cities, like Kiev, Lvov, Odessa. I am currently developing similar infrastructure in the secondary cities, like Chernovtsi and Lugansk. We sell cigarettes wholesale and at the kiosk levels. I'm sure you know what that entails."

"Yes, Mr. Hatchet," Jack lied.

"Some of my business partners are very highly placed in the government," John continued pleasantly, "and they will suffocate anyone who disrupts Podium's operations. My customers are equally well positioned outside the government. And the reason I agreed to meet with you is to avoid the kind of war that could easily erupt. Now, please go back to Mr. Napolitano and relay to him the following message. Tell him to leave Ukraine tomorrow on the first available flight because he simply cannot compete with me. Not this time. He will understand."

"I will, Mr. Hatchet," Jack replied, getting up from his chair. "It was a pleasure to meet you." As he was leaving John's office, Jack hoped to run into Lena downstairs. To his disappointment, however, she was nowhere to be seen.

By the time Jack walked out of Podium, he knew that he had to extract himself and Lena from the upcoming battle. That is why Jack placed a call to Antonio's hotel room as soon as he walked into the office. "Antonio, buddy," he started the conversation, "it's me, Jack. How are you doing?"

"Does that mean you have some good news for me, counselor?"

"Well, not exactly. Actually, Mr. Hatchet refused to sign the documents."

"That's what I expected. Did he say anything else?"

"He said that you should leave Ukraine tomorrow on the first flight out because you could not compete with him. He also said that you would understand."

"Is that what the bastard said?" Antonio screamed into the telephone receiver. "Well, you go back and tell him that he doesn't know what he's up against! No more friendly discussions! A couple of my guys will go with you. We'll meet in your office tomorrow. Ten o'clock sharp!"

Jack took a deep breath. "I'm sorry, Antonio, but I am not going."

"And why the hell not?"

"Do you know who your local partners are?"

"Yes. As a matter of fact, I do."

"And I presume you also know who John Hatchet is?"

"For many years," Antonio answered briskly. "So what's your point, counselor?"

"Antonio," Jack continued gently, "my point is that you can leave Kiev tomorrow on any flight and never return, but I have to live here. Do you understand my position?"

"Yup. Sure do."

"Then, Antonio, can you appreciate why I don't want to work for you anymore?" A long, uncomfortable pause followed, causing Jack to break a sweat.

"Yeah, sure, kid, I can understand where you're coming from," Antonio slowly replied, choosing his words carefully. "I've been there myself. But you made a commitment to me, your client, to represent my interests. And I paid you good money, in cash, real U.S. dollars. Now you have to deliver on your end of the bargain."

"Antonio, I don't want to be rude, but you can take your money back, all of it, in cash, real U.S. dollars. I resign. There, I said it."

"That's not gonna work, counselor, sorry. We need somebody to do this job, and you volunteered. Besides, John Hatchet is not going to open up his doors to anyone but you. This much I know. So here's the plan: I will schedule another meeting for you somehow. That's my job. My guys will accompany you as your personal bodyguards. That's their job. And your job is to attend that meeting. Got it?"

"You can't make me do this." Sweating bullets in his suit, Jack felt like he was negotiating for his life.

"Oh yeah? Why not?"

"Because making me represent you under duress would be unethical." It was a weak excuse, but at the moment nothing better came to Jack's panicked mind.

"As your client, I don't mind. See you tomorrow morning, counselor."

After they hung up, Jack recalled the first innocent image of Antonio's smiling face. At the time, Antonio explained his case with such ease and sincerity that Jack practically Salivated at the chance to represent him. Now Jack wanted out of this disaster, at any cost. No immediate solution presented itself, so he reached for the telephone in search of practical advice.

"Hello, Sergei?"

"Hey, Jack, what's up?"

"I really need to talk to you. Can you find some time for me tonight?"

"Actually, I'm a little busy right now," Sergei purred. His voice suggested that he was occupied with some girl, probably in his bed. "How about coming over tomorrow to my place? I'm throwing a party for my first client. Say, ten o'clock?"

"Isn't that kind of late to start a party?"

"I meant in the morning."

"Oh. Great," Jack said, hiding his anxiety. Under the circumstances, skipping out on Antonio was not the best move, but Jack had little choice. "See you then."

# Chapter 10

Jack left his apartment at 9:28 a.m. The sky had a sinister, heavy look, threatening a severe downpour at any moment. Sergei could not have picked a more gloomy, windy November morning to throw a party. Still, Jack arrived well before ten o'clock to the all-too-familiar apartment on *Krasnoarmeyskaya* Street. As always, Sergei quickly ushered him into the kitchen.

"What kind of vodka do you prefer with your coffee? Because I've got two sorts, limonnaya and pertsovka. Or maybe just the classical, unflavored kind?"

"Actually, I wanted to speak with you about this problem I have," Jack started to explain.

"Sure." Sergei reached into the freezer and produced a bottle with a red pepper at the bottom. It grew cloudy after being exposed to air. He poured two icy doses and said, "*poehali,*" which literally means "let's go."

"*Poehali,*" Jack replied and drank his first shot of the day. More guests were due to arrive any moment, so Jack wasted no time. "Here's my problem," he said, "let's say that somebody wants me to help them take over a company, and I don't want to do it."

"So don't do it. Who can squeeze legal work out of you?"

"Antonio, that's who. He's an American, from New York, and I believe that he's connected to Italian Mafia." It sounded crazy to Jack, but Sergei did not seem fazed.

"Then you may need a roof," he replied, "as a temporary precaution. Just to make sure nothing bad happens."

"A roof?"

"Yeah. It's like an insurance policy, an umbrella that shields you from any harm. The question is, which roof is reliable?"

"Right. What are my choices?"

"That depends on your problem," Sergei explained. "There are two basic roofs: private or government. In the private sector you have all kinds of former professional athletes: wrestlers, boxers, weight lifters, gymnasts, even swimmers. After the collapse of the state-funded sports they all became unemployed and formed armed groups. Or you could try any of the government branches, like *Omon* or *Berkut.* They also provide protection."

"And what do you recommend?" Jack perspired even though Sergei's kitchen was fairly chilly.

"My advice? Stay away from criminals in general, and racketeers in particular. That includes the police. There is no sense in hiring bandits to confront their own kind. Even if they protect you today, they'll turn against you tomorrow. And then you will have a real problem on your hands, because no other security organization will touch your case, especially the government. Who needs a certain war, if you know what I mean?"

"So what, exactly, do you suggest?"

"How do I know? You should be talking to Sasha, not me. It's his area of expertise."

"Sasha? What does he know about American mob?"

"He's with Alfa. It's an anti-terrorist group."

Jack's face registered surprise. Sergei went on to explain, "every country in the world has one. As it stands, in Ukraine they are not paid enough, so Sasha supplements his income on the side, like everybody else. That's normal. Just think of him as your personal security consultant."

"You're sure he can handle this?"

"Before re-joining Alfa, Sasha was a member of an elite unit in Afghanistan. He jumped out of helicopters into the mujahedeen-controlled territory to rescue kidnapped Russian soldiers. He also crawled into caves to assassinate Russian traitors. Trust me, Sasha is your man."

"Holy shit! I had no clue who I was drinking with."

"Welcome to Ukraine," Sergei smiled. "He should be here anytime. I'm sure he will be glad to help you out. Plus Sasha won't shake you down afterwards, unlike the athletes. Just talk to me before you agree to pay him anything, ok?"

"Thanks for the advice, Sergei, I really appreciate this," Jack said.

The doorbell buzzed, over and over, announcing Sasha's arrival. As always, he brought along traditional peasant food: moist blood-and-buckwheat sausage, a dark-brown loaf of bread studded with coriander seeds and a hunk of local delicacy called *salo*, which is simply salty pork fat, something that Jack had never put in his mouth before. As Sergei was pouring the obligatory welcome shot, Sasha gave Jack a thin slice of *salo* on black bread, its crust rubbed with garlic. That is when Jack discovered how perfectly *salo* goes with vodka on an empty stomach, especially in the morning.

Just as Jack was about to share his troubles with Sasha, the doorbell sounded again. This time two men in their early thirties walked in. They respectfully placed three grocery bags on the floor as they entered the kitchen and sat down at the table. Before Sergei could properly introduce everyone, however, the doorbell rang yet again.

A few seconds later Sergei ushered into his kitchen the guest of honor, Dr. Kevin Zimmer, who was dripping wet. Wiping off his thick eyeglasses, Dr. Zimmer explained, "sorry to be late, but no taxi would pick me up for the longest time, and it's terrible weather outside."

"Here, Dr. Zimmer, you must drink this." Sergei filled a large coffee mug with pepper vodka. "It will cure absolutely everything."

"Well, thank you very much, Sergei." Dr. Zimmer took off his soaking overcoat and sat down at the table across from Jack. He smiled pleasantly and nodded, like a doctor reassuring a patient on his first visit.

"*Na zdorovye* is what they say around here before drinking," Sergei offered a useful lesson in Russian to Dr. Zimmer. Then, to set an example, he gulped the entire shot.

"*Na zdorovye*, then," Dr. Zimmer said and readily followed Sergei.

The guests, sitting around the table, soon broke up into two camps: those who spoke English and those who could communicate freely only in Russian. Naturally, Jack struck up a conversation with Dr. Zimmer. Skipping the usual where-are-you-from-bit, Jack asked him plainly, "so tell me, what exactly are you trying to accomplish around here? I'm a lawyer, you know. Maybe I can help you somehow."

"Well, Sergei's consulting firm has already set up meetings for me with the Ministry of Health. In fact, the Deputy Minister himself became quite interested in my project. That's why we are having this party." Dr. Zimmer thought for a split second and said, "but you never know when you will need a good local lawyer."

"That's right." If there was any legal work here to be parceled out, Jack thought, it was all his. "So what's your project all about, anyway?"

"It's about giving life. For example, did you know that according to United Network for Organ Sharing, more than eighty thousand Americans are waiting for organs?"

"No," Jack honestly replied. "Never even thought about it."

"Of them, about fifty thousand are in need of a kidney. One of them was Ann Lee, from San Francisco. Her name was put on a waiting list, along with many others. Ann patiently waited for more than three years for a match. Then she decided that she didn't want to wait anymore."

"I'm sorry to hear that." This was a morbid topic and Jack wanted to end it. Only the possibility of landing Dr. Zimmer as a client made him pretend to be fascinated by this. "Poor woman," Jack added.

"Don't be sorry," Dr. Zimmer smiled. "After returning from a brief trip to China, Ann scheduled an appointment with her doctor. To his surprise, while on vacation in Shanghai she had a kidney transplant. Ann only needed after-transplant care, which the doctor provided, of course. To decline would be unethical. Now, she lives a normal life."

"Wow, that's great."

"The point is, if Ann had waited her turn for a donation, she would have been dead and buried by now. To help people like Ann, I came up with a revolutionary concept: creation of a donor database for the first global organ transplant referral service."

"Organ referral service?" Sergei joined in the conversation. "And how does that work, exactly?"

"Let's say a healthy donor walks into our office for a free analysis," Dr. Zimmer explained. "If we find a matching recipient, that donor will receive a fee in exchange for his or her kidney or any other organ. Look, hospitals in India, China and even Thailand gladly accept wealthy patients from South Africa, Kuwait, Saudi Arabia. So why not Ukraine?"

"Sounds like an interesting solution to a complicated problem," Sergei said sarcastically. "But you never said how you found the perfect match for Ann Lee so quickly? I mean, kidneys are not exactly like shoes, readily available in all fits and sizes. Who were the donors in that Chinese database of yours?"

"I don't ask and the authorities don't tell. The important thing is that properly screened organs can finally reach the patients in a methodical and timely fashion. *Na zdorovye*, is that how you say it?" Dr. Zimmer raised his glass of vodka and downed it at once.

Now that Jack understood Sergei's question, he was not sure he wanted to help Dr. Zimmer, even if he paid well. Feeling uneasy, Jack reached to open a crack in the window. Cold air entered the kitchen.

Sasha tapped Jack on the shoulder. "Sergei mentioned that you wanted to see me about something? Should we step outside?" Jack nodded, slowly got up from the table and followed Sasha into the corridor. Leaning against the wall, Sasha asked, "so what's up?"

"You won't believe this, but one of my clients is trying to intimidate a nice English gentleman into giving up control of his company. Now, I don't feel comfortable about that, and I don't want to be associated with this client anymore. Especially since my girlfriend works for the company. That's about it. What should I do?"

"What's her name?" Sasha asked in a businesslike fashion.

"Lena."

"Last name?"

"I don't know."

"Where does she live?"

"I don't know that either."

"Exactly how much do you know about your girlfriend?" Sasha smirked. "What about her work address? Do you know where she works?"

"The company is called Podium."

"What?"

"Podium. They're a distribution company across the river. Near *Levoberezhnaya*." Sasha's relentless questioning made Jack feel as if he was being interrogated.

"I know exactly what Podium is. Alfa has been providing them with security ever since they came here. And I tell you, that is one mother of all companies. You've got to run a background search on that girl."

"You're joking! What the hell for?"

"What do you know about Podium? Nothing. And what do you know about our girls? Even less. Then listen while I explain to you the different ways bandit girls set up people like you. During one of your dates you will accidentally run into her so-called boyfriend with a couple of buddies. He will be deeply offended to catch his girl cheating on him. Then he and his buddies will accompany you home, tie you up and clean out whatever they can carry away. It's all fair game to them. That's why they're called bandits."

First Antonio and now Lena, Jack thought. How could it be that I was surrounded by so many enemies and not even know it?

"Or, better yet," Sasha continued, "what if a few months later your new girlfriend claims to be pregnant? She slips a doctor few dollars, buys the necessary confirmation. And then, regardless whether she's pregnant or not, or if it's your child or not, you will be married to her. Before you know it, your legal obligations will follow, like alimony, child support. I've seen it before, so do me a favor: don't give me any advice and let me do my job. Besides, since you're Sergei's friend, I'll do the research free of charge."

"Fine," Jack answered quietly. "But what should I do tomorrow when Antonio calls?"

"Do whatever you would have done if we didn't meet. Just pick up the phone and say that you agree to everything. What, exactly, did he want from you?"

"To draft a sale-purchase agreement, amend Podium's foundation documents, the whole set of documents to change the company ownership."

"A take-over, huh? Well, let me tell you, nobody can take Podium without a fight. And even then, it's like committing suicide. So when's the meeting?"

"I don't know. Antonio will tell me tomorrow where and when I'll have to meet with John Hatchet."

"Really? You're going to meet with John Hatchet personally?"

"Yes," Jack said, stumped. "You know him?"

"Uh huh," Sasha nodded. "Everyone around here knows about Mr. Hatchet. Are you going by yourself or with somebody?"

"Antonio said I would need his bodyguards, but personally I found Mr. Hatchet to be quite friendly."

"Is that everything?"

"Yup."

"Well, that's it then. You can rest easy after tonight. Let's join the party, shall we?" Sasha slapped Jack on the shoulder and stepped into the kitchen. From Jack's viewpoint, however, the problem was far from being solved, and he was still quite concerned. Jack followed after Sasha, intent on finding out exactly what he should be doing when Antonio appears on his doorstep.

Just as Jack walked back into the kitchen, Sergei announced, "I know this great place; it has the best Hungarian food in town." A hearty round of applause confirmed that his guests were sober enough for a feast. Encouraged, Sergei dialed Miskolc, a restaurant named after a Hungarian town. According to Sergei, it was owned and operated by Hungarian mafia. This trivia and cuisine made it a perfect place to celebrate Dr. Zimmer's future success in giving life to the dying. Half an hour later Sergei's group was at *Miskolc*, ready to be seated. "Please, follow me," said a statuesque blond, flashing a gold tooth. She escorted the guests to a beautifully set table, where fine china plates were already brimming with mouth-watering appetizers: pickled herring with onions in olive oil, liver pate, tiny bowls of black and red caviar, smoked sturgeon. The waiter filled everyone's glasses with chilled vodka from a pear-shaped crystal decanter.

"That lady is striking," Dr. Zimmer said to Sergei. "Are all Ukrainian women that beautiful?"

"Yes," Sergei whispered, "but I would stay away from her. She's the wife of the owner. You don't want to quarrel with this man."

"Point well taken." Dr. Zimmer turned his eyes to another table, occupied by two girls in low-cut blouses. "How about those two lovely ladies? Do you think they..."

"If they are in this restaurant, they are not worth your time. Still, it's a worthwhile toast. To our wonderful Ukrainian women!" On cue, everyone nodded in agreement and gulped their shots.

"But they are so beautiful," Dr. Zimmer continued to whine, breathing vodka in Jack's direction. "If only I had a wife that looked like one of them. Do you know what its like to sit all alone by your swimming pool when the neighbors' kids come over for dinner or a bar-b-q? I'm fifty eight years old, for Christ sake!"

"I think Dr. Zimmer needs a wife," Jack said jokingly to Sergei.

"Damned right I do," Dr. Zimmer cried out. "All of my life I wanted a proper wife. But none of them wanted me..."

"And what do you want to see in your wife?" Sergei asked seriously.

"I don't know..."

"She has to be young," Sasha added helpfully, "because the man is only as old as the woman he feels. Get it?"

"Not that young," Dr. Zimmer frowned. "Late twenties or early thirties would be acceptable."

"Blond or brunette? Short or tall? Are large breasts an absolute requirement or are they negotiable?" Sergei was in his business mode.

"Look, I don't care about her appearance, she just has to be a nice person," Dr. Zimmer said wishfully. "And it would not hurt if she could cook."

"Absolutely," Sergei nodded. "Cooking skills are vital for any proper wife. Dr. Zimmer, you are going to thank me sooner than you think."

"For what?"

"For a life-changing experience. Tomorrow evening be prepared to meet your future wife."

"My future wife?"

"The love of your life."

"But what if I don't like my future wife? Can I send her back?"

"I am sure we can arrange that. And the next evening you will have another willing candidate, eager to become your wife. She will be beautiful and she will treat you like a king. And if you don't like her, either, we'll try again until we find the right wife for you."

"You're crazy, Sergei, but I like your sense of humor!" Dr. Zimmer reached for the vodka decanter to re-fill his own glass, a sign of bad table manners. "Here's drinking to you!"

The waiters were excellent, as was the food, wine and music. Unfortunately, Dr. Zimmer got drunk all too quickly. "The more I drink, the better I sing," he announced. To prove his point, Dr. Zimmer turned to the two single girls he first noticed and screamed, "I love you baby and if it's quite alright I need you baby through all the lonely nights I want you baby..." but then Sergei's hand clasped around his mouth. Dr. Zimmer tried to escape Sergei's firm grip, but in the process he accidentally knocked his dinner plate, filled with food, onto the floor.

Ignoring the broken china, Sergei and Jack placed Dr. Zimmer back into his chair, but he could not keep his balance. "Get me out of here or I'm gonna puke," Dr. Zimmer muttered just loud enough for Sergei to heed the warning. Without wasting any time Sergei and Jack picked up Dr. Zimmer and guided him through the restaurant to the men's bathroom. They left Dr. Zimmer in the toilet cubicle, where he remained for the duration of the evening, periodically vomiting, cursing and moaning.

By the time Sergei and Jack returned to the table, the waiter already served goulash and chicken paprika. The sweet yet spicy aroma of Hungarian dishes was perfectly complemented by a full-flavored, deep ruby-red cabernet sauvignon.

"Listen, guys, Marianna just called, and she's free tonight," Sasha said, smiling in anticipation of a fun evening ahead. "Sorry, but I have to skip out on you. Hope your client's going to be alright, Sergei."

"Don't forget to wear protection," Sergei said with a knowing grin. In reply, Sasha patted his faithful *Makarov*, strapped under the armpit, and smiled back.

With Sasha's departure Jack felt that dark cloud over his head again. Nothing was resolved, and he was legitimately worried. Oblivious to Jack's suffering, everyone else continued to drink, joke and laugh well into the night, through the desert and coffee with cognac, until the other customers went home and the restaurant closed. Sergei's group were the last clients to reluctantly leave.

After the management turned out the lights in the dining room, a large man in a dark suit strolled over. "Hey, guys," he said, "you really should take that American out of the bathroom. He's messing up the whole place."

At first Sergei and Jack tried to talk Dr. Zimmer out of the stall, but he flatly refused to let go of the metal pipes. "I have lost all bodily functions in the lower extremities, including legs," Dr. Zimmer declared, "and I wish to remain here until I regain the full use of my limbs." Still, Sergei could not leave Dr. Zimmer in the bathroom of a restaurant controlled by Hungarian mafia so with Jack's help he grabbed Dr. Zimmer and they dragged him out without engaging in pointless discussions. The party was over.

Standing on the sidewalk, Sergei raised his hand to flag down a taxi. A passing car slowed down and the driver motioned for everyone to get in. Once they settled in the back seat, Jack quietly asked Sergei, "hey, what was all that about finding a wife?"

"You know how it is, anything to keep a client happy," Sergei answered. "Besides, it's no big deal to call an escort service. Just look in the back of any newspaper."

"I'm not drunk," Dr. Zimmer muttered to himself in the front seat, strapped in tightly with a seat belt. "I want a proper wife!"

# Chapter 11

Jack rolled under the blanket most of the night, unable to force himself to sleep. He started to drift into forgetfulness only at the crack of dawn. Just as hard-working people were getting up, he was falling asleep. The alarm clock went off at 8:00 a.m. Jack pushed the snooze button and remained under the blanket. In seven minutes it started to buzz again. His naptime was up.

Two hours later Jack sat behind his desk, waiting for an unpleasant meeting with Antonio. After forty nerve-racking minutes Antonio majestically strolled into Jack's office, dressed in an Italian cashmere overcoat, trailed by Oleg and Ivan in basic leather jackets. Antonio was livid. His nostrils were flaring and he was breathing heavily, like a bull. "What's the matter with you, kid? You think you can just skip out on me?"

"Sorry, Antonio," Jack said quietly but sternly, "but I have another client meeting in a few minutes. Could you please wait outside?" This was nothing more than a cheap ploy so that Jack could call Sergei to inform him that Antonio was about to hurt his American friend.

"Get him out of here," Antonio said with disgust in his voice. Per his instructions, Frankenstein-like Oleg came around the desk, grabbed Jack's arms and easily lifted him out of the chair. Ivan and Oleg escorted Jack to the waiting Volvo.

Ivan-the-wrestler sat beside Jack in the back while Oleg crouched next to the driver in the front, his bald head rubbing against the ceiling. The Volvo gently pulled onto *Lenin* Street, then turned right on *Kreschatik*, careful not to violate any minor traffic rules. Jack did not think Antonio would kill him just because he skipped one day of work, but he could not be sure.

They drove in silence for several minutes. Then Oleg reached to the floor and produced two packages, wrapped in oily newspaper. He handed one to Ivan, who carefully unwrapped the bundle. It contained a small Uzi-like sub-machine gun with two bullet clips and three hand grenades. Jack presumed that Oleg received the same assault kit. "Can I have one, too?" Jack asked Ivan, trying to break the ice with a joke. "Since we're on the same side, and all..."

"The next time, definitely." Ivan had a good sense of humor, but it did not put Jack at ease. Ten minutes later the Volvo smoothly rolled up to *Eldorado*, the most expensive restaurant in the heart of Kiev. Fear-inspired adrenaline pumped through Jack's body when the car came to a halt. Ivan said, "the guy from Podium agreed to meet you here for lunch. Go have a nice lunch."

"There is no way in hell I am going in there," Jack protested vehemently. "Absolutely not!" It was an honest response, having seen his abductors' arsenal and knowing Antonio's violent intentions. Then Oleg turned around, annoyed by Jack's lack of cooperation.

"Nobody is negotiating with you," Oleg spoke through his teeth. "You will go in there or I will kill you right now. One. Two." To prove his point, Oleg raised the barrel of his sub-machine gun to Jack's forehead. Jack froze like a deer, staring into a hunter's shotgun. With the safety off and a bullet loaded in the chamber, Oleg's finger slowly squeezed the trigger.

To save Jack from a certain death, Ivan reached over and opened the car door. He shoved Jack outside so hard that he hit the ground. Then both Ivan and Oleg got out of the Volvo, their leather jackets bulked up, and waited. Jack got to his feet and walked toward the entrance of *Eldorado*, his heart pounding inside the rib cage.

Running away as quickly as possible is my best chance, Jack thought. A glimpse over his shoulder confirmed that their guns were still hidden away. Jack saw Ivan just as a crack of a shot came from a distance. A single bullet entered the side of his round, jovial head. Ivan fell on the pavement, his body sprawling towards Jack in slow motion. Jack could see the lights going out in Ivan's laughing eyes, then dark oily blood running from a gaping wound, forming a red pool under his head.

The second shot came immediately after the first. It knocked Oleg clean off his feet. At the same time, something entered Jack's left knee, which sent a diabolical jolt up and down his leg. Jack shouted in agonizing pain and collapsed to the ground. The last thing he heard were Oleg's screams, then another shot, and then silence.

# Chapter 12

Jack woke up with two plastic tubes coming out of his knee, connected to a nearby drainage machine. Throbbing pain pulsed through his leg. The next thing he saw was Lena's smiling face, slowly coming into focus.

"You're going to live," she joked. "Here, this is for you." Lena handed him a red rose. Still groggy from the sedatives, Jack smiled stupidly at her.

"Thanks." Jack's voice sounded hoarse, not at all like himself. "What's this for?"

"To show you my gratitude. And Mr. Hatchet told me that he would stop by later today. But this flower is from me."

"A red rose?"

"It may not cost much, but it's a symbol that's worth a lot more than money."

"A symbol of what?"

"Are you fishing for compliments? Because that's what it sounds like."

"Never. But since I was nearly killed, a tiny, little compliment would be nice. Even if you don't really mean it."

"You can't force a real compliment; it should come from the heart. Otherwise it's called flattery."

"I'm not that picky."

A doctor entered Jack's room without knocking. "Hello, Mr. Parker," he said. The doctor was in his fifties, with an egg-shaped, balding head.

"Morning. What's wrong with my leg?"

"A bullet ricochet tore your anterior crucial ligament. Can I take a look?" The doctor unbandaged Jack's swollen knee. It resembled a peeled red grapefruit with two straws stuck inside. "Looks good. By the end of the week you can go back to your business. If you still want to, that is. See you tomorrow."

After the doctor left, Jack asked Lena, "what did he mean, if you still want to?"

"He probably knows about what happened yesterday, and he thinks that you're brave to return to work, that's all. I think so, too. Now, that was a sincere compliment. You're quite a hero, you know. There's even a story about you in the paper."

"You're joking." Jack has been in Kiev almost three months and his bad streak of luck was getting to him. He groaned in pain, "why am I in the paper?"

"Here is today's front-page story: Podium Under Assault, Gangsters Killed. A well-known distribution company Podium was defended by the Alfa branch of the SBU special forces, which successfully repelled an attack by well-armed bandits. Due to the efforts of an American citizen, Jack Parker, two criminals were killed. The brave American was wounded. He is currently recovering in an undisclosed location under twenty-four hour police protection. Prognosis for recovery: excellent."

"What do they mean, undisclosed hospital under twenty-four hour police protection? Why is my location undisclosed?"

"You're in a government hospital number one, which is usually reserved for highly placed government officials. Ministers, Parliament deputies, people like that," Lena explained. "In other words, it's not for general public. That's probably why this hospital's location is not disclosed."

"And what about my police protection?" Jack asked a little too anxiously for a genuine hero.

"Well, I had to sign in, but they ask all visitors to do that."

The drawback to being a hero was the risk of retaliation, Jack suddenly realized. As if to confirm his worries, two large men walked into his room unannounced. They wore black leather jackets, just like Antonio's henchmen.

"Who are you?" Jack inquired, but they did not respond. After making sure nobody was hiding in the corners, the thugs froze on either side of the door.

Moments later, John Hatchet entered. He was dressed in a dark pinstriped suit with a gold-and-red tie that contrasted against a dark blue shirt. John approached Jack's bed and said, with a nasal British accent, "my dear chap, I am deeply grateful for your timely warning. Frankly, I had my suspicions about Antonio's presence here all along. He is known to be a bit of a renegade, but I trusted that Francesco would not allow him to do anything silly. Apparently, I was wrong."

"Everyone makes mistakes," Jack replied.

"If not for your assistance, my investors may have lost their Ukrainian operation. And I, my life."

"If I may ask, Mr. Hatchet, what did I do, exactly?"

"There is no need to be so modest, Mr. Parker. Everyone knows it was you who notified Alfa about the attack. And going against the Gambino family was a very brave thing to do." Jack's eyes opened wide upon hearing what he had suspected all along about his first client. "But don't worry about Antonio or Francesco," John continued, "because they will not say anything to anyone anymore. And for that, I thank you once again."

"Not at all, Mr. Hatchet," Jack sighed with relief. "Always glad to help. Let me know if you need any legal work."

"And now, for the goodies." John rubbed his bony hands together and gave a crooked grin. Then he turned to one of the bodyguards, who immediately produced a large box of chocolate candy. "My investors instructed me to deliver this to you with best wishes for a speedy recovery."

"Tell them thank you for me."

"And this," John added, "this is from me personally." He unsnapped a heavy 18-carat gold bracelet on his diamond-encrusted Rolex and placed the watch on top of the candy box. With a quick, respectful bow he handed both gifts to Jack and backed away. Based on John's performance Jack gathered that he was expected to marvel at the watch. The Rolex was the size of a small alarm clock, with hundreds of tiny diamonds sparkling from every possible viewing angle, screaming to draw attention to its owners' new-found wealth. Jack held it before his eyes and squinted.

"I can't accept this from you, Mr. Hatchet. It's way too expensive."

"Nonsense. This is only a small token of my appreciation, Mr. Parker." John's face twisted into a plausible smile. "Oh, and one last thing before I go. If you encounter any problems in the future, problems of any sort, just give me a call." He pulled out a gold-embossed business card and delicately handed it to Jack.

"We're coming out," one of the bodyguards said into a small, hand-held radio transmitter and they followed John outside.

Jack looked at the dazzling watch and wondered aloud, "what am I going to do with this thing?"

"You can always use it as a paperweight," Lena suggested. "Personally, I am more interested in a piece of chocolate, if you're offering, that is."

"Help yourself."

When she opened the box, Lena's hand froze in mid-air. "Jack, you should look at his," she said and tilted the candy box towards him. Instead of chocolates Jack saw ten neatly bundled stacks of one hundred-dollar notes. Never before had he seen so much cash in one place, especially stashed inside a candy box. With a hundred grand, he could take a trip somewhere, buy a car, and maybe even pay off his law school debt.

"This must be your reward money from the investors," Lena guessed.

"If you want to know the truth, I don't care about Podium or John Hatchet. I asked an acquaintance of mine, who happens to work for Alfa, to get you out of a dangerous situation, that's all."

"So you did it for me?" Lena sounded like she could not believe it. "Not for Mr. Hatchet or for his bosses?"

"You mean his investors?"

"That's what he calls them, but it's not who they really are. You know, Jack, I'm really touched that you asked Alfa to protect me," she said softly, almost whispering.

"It was nothing," Jack smiled at her. "Any man would do the same."

"When Mr. Hatchet called me at home and told me not to show up for work yesterday, I thought that he was firing me. I started to cry, right there on the spot," Lena laughed at herself. "So what are you going to do with your reward?"

"Lena, all their rewards are nothing in comparison to the one favor I will ask of you."

"What's that?"

"A kiss." Jack waited out the pause, since there was nothing more he could do. As he hoped, Lena walked over to his bed and said, "this goes together with the rose I gave you." Then Jack felt the warmth of her lips on his mouth. It was the most delicious and sensual kiss Jack had ever known. It tasted like wet flower petals, soft and gentle.

Much to Jack's frustration, the narrow hospital bed could not fit another human body, so they kissed like two high-school kids on their first date. Eventually Lena borrowed an armchair, a few blankets and pillows from some empty room and made herself a plausible bed. She curled up next to him and they fell asleep, holding hands across the bottomless divide that separated them.

In the early morning light Jack woke up and looked at Lena's pretty face, resting on the pillow. The sun was just beginning to rise and it touched her neck with a warm glow. She smiled in her sleep. His first impression was how truly lovely Lena looked at that moment. At first Jack was afraid to move so as not to awaken this beautiful, black-haired girl, but he could not resist the temptation. Ever so softly Jack brushed his lips against Lena's hand, feeling the texture of her smooth, dark skin. Although she was awake, Lena did not stir, so Jack moved closer and ran his fingers through her long, silky hair.

They were interrupted at precisely 6:07 a.m. by a fat, elderly nurse with heavy bags under her eyes. She burst into the room unannounced to inject something in Jack's stomach "to prevent blood coagulation," as she explained. It was the end of a beautiful, romantic morning. After the nurse shuffled off, Lena said, "as much as I hate to, I have to get going, too."

Selfishly Jack pleaded for more time, "can't you stay a little longer?"

"Some people have to be at work by nine," she said, "and before that, I have to get home, take a shower, change into my office attire, and even brush my teeth."

"So you have no more time for your hero? Not even a few minutes?"

"I'll drop by to see you after work, I promise. In the meantime, behave yourself and try not to upset anymore gangsters. And if you want me to bring you anything special, just call me. You know where to reach me."

"Fine," Jack sighed in resignation. It would be another twelve hours before he would see her again. Before leaving, Lena leaned over and kissed him. Then she quickly skipped out the door.

After Lena had gone, Jack noticed how sterile and cold everything in this hospital was. The medicinal odor seemed to come from everywhere, including the marble floors and the metallic green paint on the walls. Lying in a special clinic for the upper-notch government bureaucrats, with its private rooms, frosty tiles and wood-paneled hallways, Jack wondered what to do with the candy box, stashed under his mattress.

# Chapter 13

After a four-day absence Jack was grateful to be back home again, though annoyed at the tiny new tenants who invaded his kitchen. There were two kinds of ants: large black ones and their smaller, reddish brothers. Upon closer inspection of the sink he discovered different types of cockroaches hiding between stacks of unwashed dishes; the regular ones, with brown coloration, and the enormous black bugs commonly known as "American cockroaches" because everything in the U.S. is larger. The American roaches were much more disgusting.

To Jack's distress, one morning he discovered that he had been eating dead food moths for breakfast. They were in the cereal box, barely distinguishable from corn flakes, and he did not notice them until it was too late. Right away Jack spat them out and angrily vowed to eliminate all of his unwanted guests, starting with the largest offenders of them all, the little gray mice that lived in his kitchen. The best way to kill rodents, according to Sergei, was to poison them. The recipe was simple enough: dough and arsenic. Jack mixed up the deadly ingredients, placed poisoned dough pills throughout his apartment and waited.

Several days slowly dragged by as Jack adjusted to his new life with a full-leg cast. To get around, he hired Volodya, a professional taxi driver, who doubled as his personal assistant. As a first step, Jack decided to do something special for Lena, something that she would remember for a long time: he would have a fantastic dinner, with exotic ingredients, ready and waiting for her after work. This entailed making two phone calls.

"Hello, Lena? It's me," Jack said. "Are you busy?"

"Not for you," she replied, although she sounded busy. "So what do you want to tell me?"

"I wanted to invite you for dinner at my place tonight. The menu is a secret and wine selection remains a mystery, even to me, primarily because I don't know what I'm cooking yet. It all depends on whether you accept my generous offer. So, are you interested?"

"Sounds intriguing. Should I come over right after work?"

"Absolutely. And don't forget to bring one of your red roses for me."

"It's just a flower, you know," she said and hung up. Then Jack dialed Volodya's cell telephone number.

Volodya answered, "who wants me?"

"It's me," Jack said. "I need you to do some grocery shopping. Can you take down this list?"

"Go."

"Two lobsters, one kilogram of black caviar, sack of rice, a case of French Chablis and two dozen candles. Make that three dozen."

"No lobster," Volodya immediately replied, "and foreign wine is damned expensive. Who's the lucky girl?"

"None of your business."

"Try Kamchatka crab. It's usually available at the Bessarabsky market. And their black caviar is fresh, too, because they work with Caspian Sea mafia."

"Fine. Pick up a kilo of crab and a kilo of black caviar from the Caspian mafia."

"If this girl is really special, then I would get beluga. And a bottle of French Champagne, not that sweet Crimean stuff."

"Then let's get beluga with French Champagne. And a case of Chablis anyway."

"Vodka would be cheaper. Works quicker, too."

"A case of Chablis and that's final," Jack said. "Just bring the groceries by five o'clock. Use the office cash, from the safe."

Jack considered two distinct scenarios taking place: either Lena will spend the night at his place, or she would not. To increase his chances of success, white wine and candlelights would complement the exotic dinner.

By 5 p.m. the only bottle of Moet Chandon left on the display in the foreign currency store was chilling in Jack's refrigerator, next to the six bottles of real Chablis. Dozens of candles occupied strategic positions throughout the apartment, from the kitchen to the living room, with a special emphasis on the bedroom.

The living room table was lined with a clean, white table cloth; Jack even washed out a glass sugar bowl and re-filled it to the rim with beluga caviar, leaving two silver spoons to stick out from the black mass. It was his first real dinner date with Lena, one that could open wondrous doors in their relationship. He simply could not afford to blow it. Looking over the room, Jack thought, how could anyone with a heart not be romantically swayed by this set-up? By the time his doorbell rang, the white rice was cooking and the Kamchatka crab legs were steaming.

"Come in please," Jack opened the door.

"Smells like something died in here," Lena declared as soon as she walked inside the apartment. Jack sniffed around, and sure enough, she was right: concealed by the delicate aroma of crab legs was a peculiar, skunk-like odor, beginning to settle in the hallway. A mouse must have swallowed one of the magic poison pills and promptly died at this most inopportune time, Jack realized.

"Is that what you're planning on feeding me? Is that your surprise dinner?"

"No. It's probably coming from another apartment. But don't worry, just have a seat in the kitchen and I will fix it, whatever it is." Following the smell of decay was easy. Wearing his cast, Jack limped to the pantry where he stored canned and dried goods, praying the rodent did not die in there. As luck would have it, however, the overwhelming stench inside confirmed Jack's well-founded fear: the mouse passed away, probably in agony, while munching on his food.

Ten long minutes passed while Jack searched for the deceased rodent's corpse without the benefits of a gas mask. He stumbled upon the little fellow's remains behind the last can of beans in the back of the closet. The intestines in its decomposed stomach leaked onto the laminated floor and stuck there, like glue. They produced a most foul odor, totally incompatible with any edible items left in the food closet.

Nauseous, almost vomiting, Jack scraped most of the digestive organs onto a newspaper, gently carried them into the bathroom and quietly flushed them down the toilet. Lena remained blissfully ignorant of Jack's activities as she patiently waited for him in the kitchen. "Is the dinner going to be ready soon?" she sang out when Jack was scrubbing his fingernails.

That awful skunk-like smell seeped into his hands, and Jack could not get it out. "Almost there, honey." Jack rubbed slippery soap between his fingers for the last time.

When he entered the kitchen, Lena said, "so do you want to hear some juicy gossip?"

"Sure."

"While you were stuck at home, someone from the Alfa group came around, asking personal questions about me." Lena dropped that sentence casually, but its implications sent shivers up Jack's spine. By now, he thought that Sasha had forgotten all about his background research on Lena; Jack certainly did. He proceeded, evidently, and rather indiscreetly.

"Questions about you?" Jack dumped the over-cooked rice into a strainer over the sink. It released hot, appetizing steam into the air.

"Yes. They wanted to know about my past lovers, any bad habits, things like that."

"So when do you want me to serve the dinner?" Jack asked, placing the piping hot crab legs into a deep dish.

However, Lena was not easily distracted. "In a few minutes," she said. "So tell me, you don't have anything to do with this, do you?"

"What do you mean?" Jack was getting a sinking feeling about Lena's continuing line of questioning.

"You know exactly what I mean, Jack Parker. Your friend, Sasha, came around a few days ago to speak with our security guys. And you thought they wouldn't tell me?"

"But Lena..." Jack tried to explain.

"If you have doubts about my company, I can understand that. But if you have any questions about me, then you should ask me directly instead of going behind my back."

"You're totally right," Jack said apologetically, "but Sasha insisted on doing this background research. He said it was free." By the angry look on Lena's face Jack understood that he offered a poor excuse. He had to dig himself out of that hole immediately. "He said that Kiev is full of bandit girls. That's why he volunteered to make sure you were not one of them."

"Really? That's all it was?"

"Yes, that's all. Now, can I offer you some Champagne? Please?"

"Before you do, let me tell you this: Podium may have a monopoly on cigarettes, which casts a negative light on the company. But nobody can say anything bad about me personally. When Sasha reports back you, my name will be clean, you'll see. That's all I have to say."

"I am absolutely positive about that, too." Jack was delighted that Lena understood Sasha's concerns and took everything the right way. For a while he thought that she may storm out of the apartment, once and for all. Not quite believing his stoke of luck, Jack asked her, "so are you still angry with me?"

"Not as much anymore," Lena admitted, "but if we are going to start seeing each other, you have to promise me that you will stop doing things like this. It's not healthy for any relationship."

"I apologize, Lena. I swear it will never happen again." Having miraculously averted the second unexpected disaster of the evening, and before anything else could go wrong, Jack said, "and now, can we be friends? Just look at what I cooked for you." He pointed to the crab legs. "And what goes well with this? Champagne, of course." The expression on Lena's face was priceless when Jack produced a chilled bottle of Moet Chandon from the refrigerator. "Please follow me," he invited her into the living room.

The formal dining table was perfectly set. When Jack lit all the candles and turned off the main lights, the living room took on a different glow. At last, they shared a quiet dinner, just like he had imagined they would. The wonderful evening continued for several hours over delicious white wine, playful conversation and flickering candlelights. In the end, Jack's candle-lit, romantic bedroom became their private sanctuary.

Full, rich light of the morning woke Jack up. Their bodies were still intertwined. Lena's burning cheek warmed his neck and he could hear her steady breathing. How beautiful she looks, sleeping next to me, he thought. Lena's skin felt like satin and smelled like fresh morning dew. Sweet baby scent rose up from the nape of her neck. Her breasts innocently pushed against Jack's side. They felt soft and hard at the same time. He remained very still in bed, enjoying each passing second. Soon enough Lena would fly off to work again, leaving him only this lovely moment.

# Chapter 14

"I am sorry to disturb you, but I understand this an American law firm?" Jack looked up to see a man standing at his door. He was older than Jack, in his mid-thirties, with intelligent brown eyes. In his cheap, ill-fitting black suit and a narrow tie he resembled Charlie Chaplin.

"Yes, it is. How can I help you?"

"My name is Alexei Glushko." The man smiled and reached to offer Jack a handshake. "I work with the State Property Fund. I am the senior analyst at the Foreign Investment Section."

Jack wondered what the State Property Fund could possibly want from him. "May I offer you tea or coffee?"

"Perhaps a few minutes of your time instead? And please, call me Alexei."

"So how can I help you, Alexei?"

In response, Alexei snapped open the gold locks on his slim leather attache case, pulled out a piece of paper and placed it on the table in front of Jack. It contained the following information:

| | | |
|---|---|---|
| I. | *Azov Pipe Plant* | *100%* |
| | *Kryvorizh Metal Plant* | *100%* |
| | *UkrSteel Pipe Plant* | *100%* |
| II. | *Donetsk Metal Rolling Plant* | *76%* |
| | *Dnipropetrovskiy Steelworks* | *76%* |
| | *Makiyivka Steelworks* | *76%* |
| III. | *Khartsyzsk Piping* | *51%* |
| | *Nicopol Metal Rolling Plant* | *51%* |
| | *Nizhnodniprovsk Piping* | *51%* |
| IV. | *Lugansk Pipe Plant* | *26%* |
| | *Novomskovsk Pipe Plant* | *26%* |
| | *Yenakiyivskiy Metal Works* | *26%* |
| V. | *Alchevsk Metal Works* | *11%* |
| | *Kerch Metallurgical Plant* | *11%* |
| | *Mariupol Metallurgical Plant* | *11%* |

"Steel and metal pipes, huh?" Jack looked over the list, just to show Alexei that he was paying attention. "Looks like a very impressive list of factories. I bet this covers the entire Ukrainian metal sector."

"These are some of the top-class steel producers, among eighty of the world's largest factories according to the International Iron and Steel Institute," Alexei respectfully said. "Note the percentage of stock across each name. That's what will be auctioned off next week. All bids must be submitted in writing by 10 a.m., next Tuesday."

"I guess privatization is picking up speed, huh?"

"And I am the senior State Property Fund analyst, responsible for reviewing applications and identifying the auction winners. That is why I wanted to meet with you."

"I'm sorry, but what's the reason again?"

"You are an American lawyer, right? It means you probably have clients that may be interested in this auction. You see, I can arrange very cheap deals for any of those steel plants."

"Let me get this straight. You can sell huge steel mills at a discount, and you want me to find a buyer by Tuesday morning?" This was an impossible task. No serious investor would participate in any tender without first performing legal and financial due diligence, which can take several months.

"I can get all other competitor's bids to disappear, plus guarantee your client the absolute lowest price the State Property Fund is prepared to accept."

Jack's mind began to put things together. First, he was eager to get rid of the money under his bed and this seemed like the perfect opportunity. Second, this kind of passive investment into an ongoing, big-scale operation would surely bring a healthy return in the near future. Last, there were no laws or ethical guidelines prohibiting insider trading in Ukraine. Now Jack became very interested in Alexei's one-page privatization shopping list. "So which one do you like?" Jack asked Alexei's professional opinion.

"Donetsk Steel Plant is anyone's first logical choice because of its monopoly in thick stainless steel plates, special steels and steel wire. Unfortunately, it's located in Donetsk, the worst mafioso town in Ukraine. Also, the State Property Fund retains twenty six percent ownership, which means they will exercise financial accountability that nobody wants. The second runner-up, therefore, is UkrSteel."

"Why?"

"Just look at these numbers!" Alexei pulled out a stack of papers from his attache case. "Last month they produced three hundred twenty tons of finished steel and two hundred sixty eight tons of cast iron, primarily for export, though they have domestic content obligations, too. UkrSteel is the largest supplier of metal to China, which annually imports thirty five million dollars' worth of metal. Most of the money is stashed away in offshore accounts for your personal use, tax free. Very lucrative. That's the winner, right there."

"And who is going to run this factory?"

"The factory comes with a director, and his deputy, too. Both are experienced men. They get ten percent cut of the profits. Plus another six thousand employees, who are not in the loop and therefore get nothing."

"And how much does this factory cost?"

"The State Property Fund can go as low as ten million grivna, maybe even lower. There's also a condition about making additional investment in the next five years, but it's not obligatory. Nobody's going to hold you to it. Certainly not me."

If exchanged at the black market rate, instead of the inconveniently low official rate, the purchase price was about three hundred thousand dollars, Jack quickly calculated. This meant he needed another partner, someone Jack could trust. Someone with money. Someone like Sergei. Now his questions became more focused. "Can you tell me exactly how these factories make money?" Jack inquired cautiously.

"They don't. That way there is nothing to tax," Alexei explained. "All metallurgical plants have their own trading houses to evade taxes. Debts remain with the factory while the money ends up in the trading house. Another trick is to leave export sales off the books, pocketing dollars in offshore accounts scattered around the globe. A yet another way..."

"I get the picture." Jack was glad to see that Alexei was in firm control of his pet project. He could always use a good specialist on his team. "So how exactly do the investors become the owners of this steel mill?"

"Each one has to pre-pay fifty thousand dollars and submit the tender documents to me by Tuesday, 10 a.m. I will eliminate the competitors and buy out my share for privatization certificates."

"Buy out your share?"

"With *my own* privatization certificates. Plus the factory workers have a right to purchase stock at subsidized prices. Somebody could buy them for a bottle of vodka each, right? Why not me?"

"So what is your share?"

"Thirty percent. That's my non-negotiable price for arranging this deal, plus using my privatization certificates and arranging the buy-out of workers' shares."

"Alexei, I just may have an investor you are looking for. But I have to talk with him about this first."

"Just let me know tomorrow, ok?"

"You got it."

As soon as Alexei left Jack's office, he dialed Sergei's number. "It's me. How would you like to buy a steel mill, dirt cheap?" Jack deliberately did not mention Alexei's name, just in case someone was listening.

"I could see myself owning a factory or two," was Sergei's initial response.

"Want to go out for a dinner tonight? It will give us time to go over the details."

"How about *Pervak*? Say, six thirty?"

"See you then," Jack said and hung up the phone.

\* \* \*

*Pervak* is a Ukrainian restaurant on *Krasnoarmeyskaya* Street, near Sergei's place. Its name is synonymous with first-rate quality homemade moonshine. Sampling different vodkas throughout the meal is the only logical choice of drink at *Pervak*. That, and proximity to Sergei's apartment, is why it has become one of his favorite restaurants.

To complement its extensive vodka collection, *Pervak* also serves rustic cuisine at its finest, from classic red borsch with sour cream to sweet *vareniki* with cherries. And in between, plenty of dishes to tempt the customers: delicious *blini* with beluga caviar, roast goose stuffed with caramelized apples, rabbit baked in clay with wild mushrooms, and crispy chicken Kiev, just to name a few.

"Would you like an *aperitif*?" the waiter asked Jack and Sergei.

"I'm going to have *varyonukha*," Sergei said. "Not every restaurant offers it."

"What's that?" Jack asked. "*Varyonukha?*"

"It's a hot spiced Ukrainian vodka. If you haven't tried it, you should."

"Actually, *varyonukha* is the drink of the Cossacks," the waiter added. "It's based on honey, dry pears, apples, then our chef adds cinnamon and peppercorns as he heats it all up. Would you like to try it?"

"Sure."

"With that description, make it a double," Sergei said. "For him, too."

After the waiter left them, Jack looked around, making sure that nobody was listening, and said, "apparently there is a large steel plant called UkrSteel."

"A giant," Sergei added.

"It will be auctioned off next Tuesday for the price of a large apartment, in a very special sale, rigged by a guy named Alexei Glushko. He's a senior analyst at the State Property Fund. A deal of a lifetime, as you say. Interested?"

"How much for how much?"

"About one hundred grand. Plus we have to promise to invest something in the next five years. But Alexei said we're not really going to have to do that. It's just a formality."

"One hundred grand for the whole factory?"

"Not exactly. For about one third."

"Who else is in?"

"You, me and Alexei are equal shareholders with thirty percent each and the upper management gets ten percent."

"When do we have to hand over our cash?"

"Fifty grand advance tomorrow, the rest after we win the auction."

"Count me in."

It was that easy. Over dinner and various vodkas Jack and Sergei reached a unanimous agreement on the basic rules of their partnership. First, they would stick together on all fundamental decisions. Second, Sasha would break Alexei's arms and legs if he so much as tried to steal their cash. By the time they left *Pervak*, Jack and Sergei were totally bombed, but in consensus about their investment in UkrSteel.

\* \* \*

Jack looked inside the candy box. It was a lot of money. John Hatchet's diamond watch made it look like a pirate's treasure. The sight of so many green bundles made Jack feel like he was in control of his fate once again. He hated to give them up, but knew that it would be a good investment in the long run.

"So are you going to just stare at it, or can I go?" Sasha said, growing impatient with Jack. He carelessly tossed half of Jack's cash into a small briefcase, together with Sergei's money. Whistling a cheerful tune, Sasha went off to bring Alexei the down payment for their factory. Per Alexei's instructions, Jack and Sergei nervously monitored the developments from the sidelines.

A total of nine investors submitted their applications to the State Property Fund by 10 a.m. the following Tuesday, but only three candidates were admitted to participate in the tender for UkrSteel. One of them was Alexei's offshore company, *Pegasus, Ltd.*, registered in the British Virgin Islands.

The starting price was set at eight million grivna, and numerous conditions were listed, including an obligation to additionally invest eighty three million dollars within five years. None of these formalities mattered, however, because Alexei promptly shredded two of the three envelopes without bothering to open them first. Three days later, the competitors were informed that regrettably they had lost the auction. The declared winner was *Pegasus, Ltd.*

One of the contenders was a large Russian company called RusSteel, owned by a powerful oil/media oligarch named Pavel Berezkov. Unaccustomed to losing valuable business opportunities, especially in his own back yard, Mr. Berezkov became quite upset and rightfully complained to the press about his company's illegal disqualification. Neither Jack, Sergei nor Alexei paid much attention to his gripes, however, because the State Property Fund's decision was final.

In exchange for Alexei's privatization certificates, which he pulled from some highly questionable trust company, plus Jack's and Sergei's cash that was exchanged at a lucrative black market rate, *Pegasus* became the owner of UkrSteel. To his credit, Alexei himself insisted on giving Jack and Sergei each a thirty percent equity ownership in *Pegasus*. Maybe meeting Sasha influenced his decision to remain honest with his new partners.

That is how, thanks to the miracles of privatization, Jack became a minority shareholder in the one of the largest Ukrainian steel plants.

# Chapter 15

Nursing a scotch and ice in his hand, Dr. Zimmer reclined in an arm-chair in an apartment he rented from Sergei for fifty dollars per day, a mere one third of what hotels would charge. An old Soviet movie was flickering on the television screen, but Dr. Zimmer was not following the events. Instead, his mind was replaying highlights of the day.

He visited two medical facilities, interviewed twelve physicians, and came away satisfied. From a technical viewpoint, Ukrainian medical doctors were every bit as competent as Chinese or Indian physicians. With proper advance testing skills, these people could transplant virtually any organ, Dr. Zimmer thought, just as the Deputy Minister assured him during their negotiations.

It was well past ten o'clock at night. Dr. Zimmer finished his drink, turned off the television and went to the bedroom. He undressed and stretched out on the bed with the lights turned off. Several minutes later he heard a gentle knock on the door, followed by the doorbell.

Dr. Zimmer sighed heavily and climbed out of his comfortable bed. He looked through the glass peephole of his door, but it was too dark in the stairwell to identify the person's features. "Who is it?" Dr. Zimmer asked.

"I am Natalie," a young woman voice replied in English. "Your wife."

Dr. Zimmer experienced a flashback. The last two words brought about a vivid memory of a drunken conversation with Sergei. He unlocked the door for a tall, blond woman in her late twenties. The willowy blond towered over Dr. Zimmer, smiling at him from above. "I am Natalie, your wife for this night," the young woman carefully repeated with a slight British accent. She held a grocery bag in each hand, and looked like she expected Dr. Zimmer to ask her inside. "May I come in?"

Dr. Zimmer did not want to make any mistakes, so he asked, "whose wife are you, again?"

"Yours. You called the agency for a wife who must speak English and cook. I am here."

This must be Sergei's blind date, Dr. Zimmer thought, since there could be no other explanation. He motioned for Natalie to enter. "Can I help you with those?" Dr. Zimmer pointed to the groceries.

"No. It is woman's job. Your kitchen?"

"To the right."

Dr. Zimmer became impressed by Natalie's healthy attitude towards domestic chores when she started to peel the potatoes. At the same time, he needed to get some sleep. While Dr. Zimmer was thinking of an excuse to postpone their first blind date, Natalie chopped up potatoes and unwrapped two pork chops. She dropped everything into a frying pan and placed a lid over it. Soon the dinner started to give off a warm aroma of a real home.

"Oh, what the hell," Dr. Zimmer muttered to himself and went to the living room to retrieve the bottle of scotch. He needed another good, stiff drink to boost his energy. When he returned, Natalie was setting the table, like a proper wife. "Care to join me? Real scotch." Dr. Zimmer offered the bottle for her inspection.

"I do not drink alcohol. But you do what you want. You only live one time."

"Then, *na zdorovye*," Dr. Zimmer remembered a familiar toast.

"To my husband." Natalie symbolically raised a glass of water. "But why scotch? You do not like our vodka?"

"Very much. And last night, a little too much, if you know what I mean. This is just my nightcap."

"And you like our girls, too?"

"Well, I don't know about the girls," he blushed. "What I really want is to find a wife."

"That's what they said."

"Oh? And what else did they say about me?"

"That you were hungry and that I should cook for you. Ready to eat?" Delicate and alpine, Natalie lifted the lid off the skillet with one hand and flipped the pork chops, with grease fizzing and sputtering all over the floor. She placed the hot skillet in the middle of the table and served Dr. Zimmer.

The potato chunks were raw and the chops were burned on one side. Every now and then Natalie apologized, like a real housewife. "Sorry about this piece," she would say, modestly lowering her eyes towards her ample breasts. "A little burned."

"Oh, no, it's just right." Dr. Zimmer was oblivious to the dinner, unable to lift his eyes from her bosom. Still, he knew that he could never marry this statuesque woman. They would become a walking caricature in his hometown of Palo Alto, strolling down University Avenue hand in hand. Natalie will make a wonderful wife for some lucky basketball player, Dr. Zimmer regretfully concluded in the middle of their date.

A true gentleman, however, he played out the evening to its logical conclusion, despite knowing that in the end Natalie would smile and leave, probably right after finishing her coffee. It was just as well, because Dr. Zimmer's aging body was telling him that it could use a prolonged rest.

After finishing the obligatory cup of coffee, Dr. Zimmer yawned, as if to announce that the evening was nearing an end. Natalie did not notice this subtle gesture, so he said bluntly, "well, in any case, I'm sure you would like to get home. After all, it's getting late." Natalie looked at him. She finally got the message and hesitantly got up from the table.

"It was very nice to meet you, Natalie," Dr. Zimmer said while escorting her towards the door. "Really, really nice."

"Me too," Natalie said. Then she did something Dr. Zimmer did not expect from his first date: Natalie grabbed his face and squeezed it between her swollen breasts. The smell of cheap perfume on her soft, smooth skin, was more than any man could take. With his head buried deeply in her cleavage, Dr. Zimmer did not utter a sound for several seconds. He was swept away by a powerful emotion called lust.

Natalie moved in a slow, silent waltz, towards the bedroom with Dr. Zimmer attached to her soft, white bosom. He smothered them with wet kisses all the way down the corridor. Once inside the bedroom, Natalie stripped Dr. Zimmer's clothes off. She pounced on his soft, tubby body like a tigress and pinned him to the bed. Her sharp fingernails left red stripes on Dr. Zimmer's white, fleshy skin.

"You are amazing," Dr. Zimmer squealed with delight.

"I am better than other wives. Look." Sitting on top of him, Natalie took off her sweater slowly, teasingly, revealing two large cantaloupes, each with a firm red cherry on top. Their bodies joined at the pelvis and she started grinding against him. In a few minutes a shot of pleasure bolted through Dr. Zimmer. "Oh my God! Oh, yes!" he screamed out loud, jerking spasmodically.

"Are you finished? Good?"

"Not just good, honey. Great!" Dr. Zimmer was positively glowing. "Absolutely magnificent!"

"I am happy for you." Natalie got out of the bed and stretched. "Now, I can go home."

"But it's late. Why don't you stay here until the morning?"

"I cannot do that. My parents will be worried."

"Oh, you live with your folks," he gathered. "Well, that's understandable, honey. Wait one second and I'll let you out."

The astonished look on the young woman's face puzzled him. "No, you don't understand," she said. "It's one hundred dollars. And then I can go home."

"What do you mean, one hundred dollars?" Dr. Zimmer sat upright on the bed, fully awake and sober. "Nobody told me anything about one hundred dollars!"

"But it's always a hundred dollars for a home visit. That's what being an escort means."

"Well, nobody told me anything of the sort," Dr. Zimmer replied testily.

"So that's it? You are not going to pay me?" Natalie asked sadly. Tears were beginning to fill her eyes.

"Oh, no, don't cry, honey. Here, let me see what I have in my wallet. Forty, sixty. There, sixty dollars, American. That's all I have. Really."

"I'll take it. But it's normally one hundred dollars, for your future information. It's ok, you don't have to get up. I can let myself out."

"Good night, honey." Dr. Zimmer's pudgy body remained covered under the warm, cozy blanket. "And thank you."

"Good night, husband," Natalie voice carried from the corridor. Dr. Zimmer heard the sound of the automatic locks and smiled to himself. His unexpected blind date proved to be a delightful encounter, even though Natalie was not his size.

Dr. Zimmer wanted to continue screening additional marriage candidates, so he went over to his suitcase and took out exactly sixty dollars from a secret inside pocket. That night Dr. Zimmer fell asleep utterly exhausted, yet completely satisfied.

# Chapter 16

A few days after *Pegasus*, Ltd. officially became registered as the shareholder of UkrSteel, the director suddenly came down with a severe case of flu and checked into a hospital. The next day, the deputy director also called in sick, coughing loudly into the phone. Neither man said when they would return to work. According to Alexei, something strange was going on.

For a nominal fee, Sasha agreed to investigate the cause of the sudden epidemic that was afflicting their top management. That is how Jack and Sergei learned that both men were threatened by representatives of RusSteel, those pesky Russian competitors whose application Alexei nullified in the privatization tender. According to Sasha, the director and his deputy firmly refused to set foot on the factory's premises for the fear of being killed. This explanation made perfect sense.

To find out more about the enemy, Sasha ran a background research on RusSteel. The next morning he reported grimly, "the owner is Pavel Berezkov, what they call an oligarch. He already owns four major steel mills in Russia, monopolizing one of the world's largest and most criminal markets. All of them were acquired in hostile take-overs by employing the same strategy, over and over: top management is persuaded to step aside while the shareholders transfer their stock to RusSteel, dead or alive. Then top management steps in under the new shareholder, Mr. Berezkov or his companies. Simple and effective."

"If we're looking at a war with the Russian gangsters, then we either have to get a solid roof or surrender before we're dead," Sergei said. "Unfortunately, I see no other alternatives."

Sasha nodded somberly. "Those are the basic rules of business in Russia," he said. "If you can't defend your property, you have to relinquish it."

"Hey, let's hire our own army of assassins with machine guns and send them to kill Berezkov," Jack tried to break up the tension with a stupid joke. "Then let's take over his Russian factories!"

"For an American lawyer, you're beginning to sound more and more Ukrainian every day," Sergei said with approval. "But seriously, Sasha, until this thing blows over, I think we should provide the director and his deputy with some protection. The factory has to continue working. Got any friends, interested in baby-sitting a couple of nice elderly gentlemen for a few bucks?"

"Who doesn't need the money?" Sasha answered with a question.

"Then offer them a starting salary of five hundred bucks a month. Want to split it with me, Jack?"

"Gladly."

"We'll also need someone who could watch over Jack and me, too," Sergei added. "How soon can you find a few good men?"

"Three shifts per person, four people, that's twelve soldiers," Sasha counted. "There are two of you. It might take a while."

"Why?"

"Because all the reliable guys are already working full-time for someone else. I could deliver two, maybe three men on such a short notice, but to put together a larger group you'll need someone like General Kurkov."

"Who?"

"General Kurkov, my commander. One tough bird. Everyone in the forces knows him."

"Where is he now?" Sergei asked with interest.

"Retired, from what I've heard. Lives in a dacha now, goes fishing every day. If you want to, maybe I could arrange a meeting with him."

"That could be useful. Don't you think so, Jack?"

"Absolutely."

When Jack left Sergei's office, he was disappointed that Sasha could not find just one extra bodyguard for him. At least Berezkov gave the administration a fair warning before killing them, Jack tried to comfort himself. Logically, he should extend the same courtesy to the shareholders. Or not...

* * *

General Kurkov was in superb physical condition for any man, although he was in his late seventies. A widower, the General lived by himself in a dacha on the outskirts of Kiev, in a sleepy village called *Borschagovka*. His tiny three-room house, sitting on a small plot of land, was surrounded on all sides by a high wooden fence.

The first few months of his retirement General Kurkov spent fishing in the polluted *Dnieper* River. The catch was so small and infrequent that he finally gave up. Then he came up with a brilliant invention, designed to improve the quality of his retirement. The General requisitioned new recruits to find for him a large empty metal oil drum. The drum was sawed in half and then welded together, side-by-side.

Under his supervision, the soldiers planted the half-drums in the General's back yard, just outside his kitchen window. When they left, the General tested his invention by filling the drums to the rim with water from the garden hose. He now had two in-ground mini-ponds.

Early next morning, after making sure the drums had not leaked, the General excitedly jumped into his black Volga and hurried to the fisherman's market. He bought two dozen live minnows in a round metal bucket and a bamboo fishing pole with extra small hooks. Then

General Kurkov drove back to his dacha very slowly, careful not to overturn the bucket containing his precious minnows.

With great care he released the slippery fish into the pools and smiled at his creation. The rest of the afternoon the General spent exactly the way he envisioned his retirement to be, catching and releasing fish in his own pond. For the first time in his retirement, he went to bed that night with satisfaction of having accomplished something truly enjoyable.

As life would have it, however, when the General woke up at 6:30 a.m., he found two dozen dead fish with their white bellies floating lifelessly on top of the water. This sight shattered the old man's long-held illusion of living happily in retirement, and he lost all control. The General shook his head and went inside his dacha. Seconds later he emerged, gripping his trusty old AK-47, and sprayed the fishing pool with a steady volley of bullets. The familiar burst of gunfire from the much-loved Kalashnikov raised General Kurkov's spirits, and he squeezed the trigger until there were no more rounds left.

To get more ammunition, the General placed an early morning call to Sergeant Korsakov and ordered him to bring several crates from the storage so that "a man could target practice in the forest without running out of bullets." While General Kurkov waited for the supplies, his panic-stricken neighbors bombarded the police station with reports of an armed maniac on the loose. When the police arrived, and learned the identity of the mischievous culprit, they apologized to the neighbors, but declined to disarm General Kurkov.

Until someone was actually injured, the police explained, there was little anyone could do since General Kurkov was one of the most highly decorated Ukrainian officers with powerful connections. Eventually the neighbors accepted their predicament. Still, being civilians, they never quite got used to the rapid machine gun fire that would erupt at odd hours of the night. Golden years of retirement proved to be a living hell for the General and his neighbors, who lived in permanent fear of being shot by the crazy old man during one of his regular anxiety attacks.

\* \* \*

The first time Jack met General Kurkov was together with Sasha and Sergei at *Aragvi*, a traditional Georgian restaurant near the *Vladimirsky* farmers' market. A vibrant man at 78, General Kurkov was still active and strong as an ox. By the grip of his hand Jack guessed that he crushed walnuts for exercise. Fun loving and jovial, the General was the kind of a person you would trust to baby sit your children; there was nothing dangerous in his demeanor whatsoever.

After making brief introductions, Sasha remained outside, guarding the restaurant's entrance. The General, Jack and Sergei were seated at a private table in the corner. Cheap plastic grapes hung from the ceiling in an effort to re-create a rustic Georgian atmosphere.

"What do you prefer, Mr. Kurkov? Or is it General?" Sergei asked politely.

"My friends call me General. But you can call me whatever you want, since you're picking up the tab!"

"So, General, what would you like to drink?"

"Since we're in a Georgian restaurant, then how about Kindzmarauli?" General Kurkov had a dreamy look on his wrinkled, tanned face. Naturally, they started with a bottle of Kinzmarauli, because the General really wanted it. Extraordinarily dense and dark in color, it had a heavy, sweet taste. After his countryside exile, and a few gulps of fine wine, the General was eager to talk about his former life of action and glory, especially to a grateful audience like Jack and Sergei.

"All my life I was lucky," General Kurkov reminisced, "if you can call pulling difficult assignments luck. By the time we left Germany, I had the rank of a full colonel. Those were fine times, indeed. We had a saying, at war, don't be afraid of the enemy; be afraid of the indifference. Well, the soldiers under my command were not afraid of anything. They blocked the machine gun fire with their bodies so that the rest of us could crawl closer and toss that lucky grenade in the bunker. And I always picked men with disciplinary problems over the proper types. They have real character, I tell you. *Na zdorovye*," the General ended his monologue by finishing off all the wine in his glass at once, bottoms-up.

"So what would you like to order tonight?" a waiter with black mustache appeared with a pencil and paper in his hand. "Something from the oven, something from the grill?"

General Kurkov's face frowned as he skimmed through the pricey menu. His index finger rested on the least expensive dish, chicken tabaka, the spicy chicken with walnut sauce in Georgian herbs, then slowly moved to the most expensive plate of lamb. "That's it. *Kharcho* as a starter, followed by a pistachio-stuffed leg of lamb."

"And I'll try Bukharian chicken with apples," Jack said.

"Give me the lamb shashlik," Sergei said. "Plus another bottle of Kindzmarauli for our guest, and your regular, every-day vodka for me. After all, we are still in Ukraine."

Having tasted Kindzsmarauli, Jack began to appreciate why the General insisted on ordering this particular wine. On the other hand, he knew that the reason Sergei switched to vodka was to get the General drunk quicker, so he played along. When the chilled bottle of vodka arrived, everyone drank as proper men do, raising elaborate toasts to make sure that they understood each other correctly. The rest of Kinzmarauli was saved for the main course.

"So General, what kind of men would you choose if you were to put together your own private little army?" Sergei casually asked.

"Me? I like the guys from the Lavanda group. They were trained to jump out of the planes with parachutes, to climb up and down the mountains. A completely fearless bunch. Now they're either extinguishing forest fires in Yalta or catching petty criminals hiding in caves in Crimea. But I prefer men from Alfa, not because it's the anti-terrorist unit, but because it is the most difficult branch to get into. Out of forty eight candidates per class only three men are selected. These days, they mostly cater as drivers and bodyguards to our ministers. What a waste... My favorites, though, are in the mine-clearing business. Not a very forgiving job, mind you. One mistake and you're blown to pieces. A lot of our guys are in southern Lebanon now, and not one has been blown up yet. How about that for training?"

"Very impressive," Jack said, trying to get on the General's good side.

"You bet." The General was proud, and it showed.

"Can you get people that do surveillance?" Sergei asked the General, getting down to business. "Who can sweep my office for bugs, for example?"

"My guys can hear fleas coughing and roaches farting," the General replied, eyeing the crystal carafe of chilled vodka with obvious interest. Jack was only too happy to refill his glass.

When the food arrived, Sergei rubbed his hands. The finest choice cuts of meat were combined with exotic, aromatic spices and fresh Georgian herbs to create the greatest grilled kebab this side of Tbilisi. The General was equally impressed by his kharcho and lamb, which came with a sauce made from ground walnuts and pomegranates. Jack's chicken was tenderly roasted, sealing in the natural juices.

The General dipped lavash, thin bread, into the sauce and stuffed it into his mouth after each bite of lamb. Every few minutes Sergei would announce another long-winded Georgian-style toast, followed by a shot of vodka and a Kinzmarauli chaser. Judging by the amount of alcohol they had consumed, and the conversation that extended well into the evening, the first meeting was a resounding success.

After General Kurkov left the restaurant, Jack and Sergei unanimously agreed to hire him. As it turned out, buying a General was not as expensive as one might expect. Jack and Sergei pitched in twenty five thousand dollars each from their share of the steel mill's revenues. In addition to the General, with this money they purchased a slightly used black four-door Mercedes 600 series. A solid twelve-cylinder luxury-class sedan, the Mercedes looked just like new after it was washed, waxed and polished.

They also hired a full-time driver. This small touch made General Kurkov feel like a part of the downtown Kiev elite. Thanks to Jack and Sergei, he was once again the big man on campus, in control of his life. The General was making a thousand bucks per month, keeping his own hours, flying around Kiev in a chauffeur-driven Mercedes Benz with shades drawn down for privacy.

In return, Jack and Sergei gave General Kurkov one simple assignment: to handpick one hundred soldiers, the best of the best. Not those imbeciles with huge biceps, but true professionals. Jack suggested getting some communications specialists, experts in close combat and surveillance; Sergei insisted on having snipers and detonation people, who can plant plastic explosives and other radio-controlled toys.

As the two friends had hoped, General Kurkov contacted on their behalf dozens of highly trained men, all war-tested veterans. Demoralized, neglected and underpaid, many of them agreed to a job interview.

# Chapter 17

The interviews were set to take place at Sergei's office promptly at 9:30 a.m. Before inviting a viable candidate into the room, the General would briefly summarize the man's experience for Jack and Sergei's benefit.

"The first one we'll see is Stas Melnichenko," General Kurkov read from his notes. "Veteran of all three wars to preserve single and undivided Yugoslavia. Started out in Alfa, went on to join a Serbian paramilitary unit. Later Stas became one of the bodyguards for Milosevich's family. One of our top-notch men in hand-to-hand combat, plus an experienced sniper, which is rare. He would make a perfect bodyguard for either of you."

"Sounds good," Sergei said. "Let's take a look at him."

"Come on in, Stas," the General said loudly toward the door. "We're ready."

Stas Melnichenko was a tall blond man, about forty years of age, with a hawkish nose and a deep scar on his left cheek. Without turning his head, Stas's eyes darted around the room, then settled on Jack and Sergei, sizing them up. He resembled a cornered predator, expecting some sort of a set-up.

"Good morning, Stas," the General said. "I just gave these gentlemen a brief review of your background in Yugoslavia, but why don't you tell them a little about yourself."

"What's there to tell? My unit was officially responsible for reconnaissance, but in reality we cleared out the enemy from the villages." Stas shrugged his shoulders, as if this explanation covered all of the possible questions.

"And what exactly did you do on a daily basis?" Sergei asked.

"Nightly basis," Stas corrected Sergei. "We started at midnight and worked until three or four in the morning. In the daytime, our unit would rest. Then we would go out again."

"I understand. And somewhere along the line you became a bodyguard. What can you tell me about that?"

Stas looked at the General, seeking permission to respond. The General nodded silently, and Stas replied, "at the end of the last war, President Milosevich had sixty bodyguards protecting his immediate family. I was responsible for the security of his daughter. After defeat of Vojislav Kostunica, all of Milosevich's people were thrown out on the street, including myself. It wasn't safe after they killed Arkan, my former boss, so

I came back to Ukraine. And now, there's no money here, either."

"Couldn't you go back now, and make your money as a sniper?" Jack asked.

"Sure I could. My old buddies are still prospecting over there, and I know what they would say to me. Here, pal, take this rifle, here is the scope, now get to work. Ilya just returned from Africa. He was a military instructor for those hand-chopping niggers in western Sierra Leone in exchange for blood diamonds, and he barely made it out alive. He told me everything about the eight year-old snipers, the twelve year-old commanders of the murdering brigades and the fourteen year-old prostitutes that castrated those British soldiers."

"What about the diamonds?" Sergei asked with genuine interest.

"Ilya managed to smuggle out a handful of raw diamonds, not polished yet. That's how he bought a four-room apartment on *Repina* Street. He's set for life, that's for sure. And me? Last year I tried joining a group in Moscow. I spent six months pounding the pavement, drinking vodka with them, but in the end they wouldn't take me. Too many of their own unemployed soldiers."

"It's tough to get a decent job these days," Sergei said sympathetically.

"That is why I'm here, ready to work."

"Well, I don't have any more questions. How about you, Jack?"

"You mentioned earlier that you cleared out the enemy from the villages," Jack blurted out the first thing that came into his head. "How did you do that, exactly?" Right away Jack could tell by the squinted stare that he asked an inappropriate question.

"Sir, you know what he's asking," Stas said to the General. Then he turned to Jack. "Why do you want to know about the mass graves? Are you a newspaper reporter?"

"Absolutely not!"

"Thank you, Stas, you can go now," the General said calmly. "I'll be in touch early next week."

"Thank you, sir." Stas walked out of the room without making another eye contact with Jack.

"So what do you think?" General Kurkov asked Sergei.

"Sounds normal, for a man who was there."

"He is normal," the General agreed. "But the final decision is up to you."

"I like him, but let's see the others," Sergei said with an air of a natural born commander.

"The next one on our list is Fedor Dzyadok. He fought with Stas in Yugoslavia. Technically, he's every bit as good," the General said with some hesitation.

"But?"

"But he's a bit disbalanced, if you know what I mean. After Yugoslavia he went to fight with the Russians in Chechnya, and that place made a bad impression on him. He's still a bit loony, if you ask me."

"So why would we want him to work for us?" Jack asked, feeling uncomfortable at the prospect of meeting a crazy ex-commando.

"Because Fedor can do things that Stas would not touch," the General answered. "Do you still want to see him?"

"Sure," said Sergei. "Let's not rule out anybody at this point."

"Fedor, you can come in here," the General ordered loudly. His tone was formal, rigid. Looking at Fedor, Sergei said, "so tell me a little about yourself. What did you do in Yugoslavia?"

"Same thing everyone did. Went into the villages and shot the Muslims in the name of preserving the Serbian unity."

"And then you ended up in Chechnya, I understand," Sergei continued.

"And what, exactly, did you do there?" Jack inquired.

"Exactly? We would surround the villages, call out the village elders and give them our ultimatum: if you don't give up your arms, we'll raze your village to the ground. At night, all men, including boys, would go away into the mountains on the request of the village elders. By the time we rolled in, there were no more weapons or rebels. Only the elderly, women and children. And nobody could leave."

"Why not?"

"Because we blocked off the main road, that's why," Fedor said as if he was losing patience with Jack. "On approaching any house, I'd fire inside. If anyone jumped out, woman or child, I mowed them down. The guys behind me would torch the bodies with the flamethrowers to get rid of the evidence. We moved through the village, house by house, firing, throwing grenades into the basements, burning. At one train station we hung ten high school kids, and then six more students that were hiding inside a school. On the outskirts we found about a hundred and thirty people, women, children, old men, anyone who didn't run away. We locked them in a grain elevator, chained the door and then torched it. What we left behind were not ruins, just flat ground."

"Are you saying the Russian soldiers killed everyone in some village and nobody has heard of it?" Jack asked him incredulously. It was inconceivable that such a barbaric event could take place in today's world without CNN or BBC dissecting it under a microscope.

"Not everyone was killed. Some of the villagers, the ones who survived, were transported to a filtration camp."

"What's a filtration camp?"

"You really don't know anything, do you? Or are you pretending?"

"Try me," Jack said.

"There is this filtration camp in *Osinovka*. Each room houses twenty to twenty five prisoners, who sleep on the concrete floor. The guards line them up against the wall and practice karate kicks in the head or in the groin. One of our guys liked to put electricity to the bodies, to see them fry. It takes a long time to get used to that smell. If a prisoner tried to untie their hands, the sergeant would cut them off at the wrists. If a prisoner tried to take off the black blindfold, the sergeant would put out his eyes with his thumbs. He was a piece of work from *Archangelsk*, our sergeant.

During one helicopter ride, he dropped three prisoners because he was bored."

"But how is it possible that the world news did not report any of this?" Jack persisted in knowing.

Fedor raised his eyebrows in a manner that made Jack feel foolish for asking such a question. "Simple. For the next forty-eight hours we didn't allow anyone to enter *Samashki*, not even the Red Cross. That gave us plenty of time. Our armored vehicles flattened their bones so that the relatives could not identify them later. Exactly what news are you talking about? Are you from this world or not?" Fedor's wolf-like stare made Jack very nervous.

"Easy, soldier." The General sensed that Fedor may soon become unreasonable and decided to interfere. "This could be your future employer."

"With all due respect to you, General, my future employer is an imbecile who doesn't know anything about real world," Fedor answered defiantly.

"That may well be," the General readily agreed, much to Jack's annoyance. "But while I'm here, you will be on your best behavior."

"Yes, sir," Fedor said bitterly, turning his eyes toward the floor.

"We'll let you know next week," Sergei said, ending the second interview of the morning.

"I won't be keeping my breath." Fedor smirked at Jack as he left the room.

"This guy is mentally defective," Jack voiced his honest opinion as soon as Fedor closed the door. "What do you think, Sergei?"

"I won't go so far as to say that Fedor is completely insane. I will say, however, that I find his behavior peculiar," Sergei replied. "Why go to the interview if you're going to piss off the employer? Not this one, General, sorry."

"I suspected you may not get along," General replied, "but my job is to bring you the best technical experts I know, and your job is to choose the ones you like."

"You certainly know your field, General," Sergei said smoothly. "Who's next?"

"Dmitry Smorodinov," General read a name off his list. "Stationed in Cuba, then Syria and Iraq, where he's been training those dirty Arabs all these years. Knows everything there is about electronics. Our top surveillance guy."

After the intense interview with Fedor, however, Jack felt emotionally drained. Though he tried, Jack simply could not pay attention to Dmitry nearly as closely as he did to Stas and Fedor. Odd sentences flew around the room, but he was desensitized.

"For a bug, all you need is a couple of high-frequency transistors, a few small coils, several capacitors and resistors and a microphone," Dmitry cheerfully answered another one of Sergei's questions. "Telephone bugs are even easier. They can be fed directly to the telephone line through a simple filter. That eliminates the problem of additional power."

"Can you monitor a conversation from my car parked, say, a couple hundred meters away?" Sergei asked.

"The only question is battery life," Dmitry replied. "In most cases, a stack of four small batteries would give us two to five hours of listening pleasure."

Potential employees came and went, but Jack did not care anymore. The first couple of interviews left him burned out; he had to get a breath of fresh air. "Gentlemen, sorry, but I have a meeting I completely forgot about," Jack excused himself. "I'll join you another time, if you don't mind."

"Not at all." Sergei sounded surprised. "But don't be offended if we choose somebody you may not approve of."

"That's all right, I trust you." Jack rushed out the door, gladly leaving Sergei with the responsibility of selecting creme de la creme of the Ukrainian mercenaries.

Altogether, Sergei and General Kurkov held five more days' worth of interviews, rejecting some candidates, hiring the others on the spot and immediately dispatching them on various assignments. In the end, Jack and Sergei were favorably impressed with their investment into General Kurkov. Thanks to him, in the first week they hired eighty six well-trained men, ready for combat at a moment's notice.

In compliance with Ukrainian legislation, Jack registered a joint venture between himself and Sergei called *ProServe, Ltd.*, designed to protect and serve them. The director, General Kurkov, procured a special license, which allowed their men to carry fully automatic firearms. Sasha agreed to work as Deputy Director, in charge of *ProServe's* day-to-day operations. It was a dream job for any enforcer.

In short order General Kurkov proved that he was a graduate of the Soviet system. The General surrounded himself with dour security advisors who worked in military or intelligence posts during the Soveit era, the so-called *siloviki*, many of them colleagues from his long and distinguished career in the K.G.B. Like his ex-bosses in the Politburo, he ruled *ProServe* with an iron fist.

The degree of fire-power Jack and Sergei's private little army soon possessed was impressive by anyone's standards. Nobody could frighten them anymore, not even the great Russian mobster-oligarch himself, Mr. Pavel Berezkov.

# Chapter 18

Christian Huber, an elderly German businessman, had a serious legal problem. He arrived impeccably dressed in an old-fashioned three-piece suit. In the one hand Christian carried a slim attache case and in the other a long black umbrella with a sharp metal spike. As any small business-owner, Jack was delighted to greet such a dignified prospective client.

"Herr Parker," Christian began rather formally. "I am a trusting man, a foreigner in a strange land. It looks like my Ukrainian partners, a father and son, took advantage of my good nature. One week ago I imported ball bearings worth three hundred thousand Deutsche Marks. After that my partners refused to accept my telephone calls. So yesterday I arrived to find out what happened to my ball bearings."

"Go on."

"From the airport I went straight to their office, which is really an apartment. They were surprised to see me. When I asked about my ball bearings, the son told me to leave. Right away I felt that something was wrong. I said to him, let me see the ball bearings for myself, but he pushed me outside and locked the door. Can you imagine that?"

Either the greedy father-and-son team had a serious roof, and felt truly invincible, or they were bluffing. That much was clear. Surely Sasha could find that out. "So what do you want from your partners?" Jack asked Christian plainly. It could be either money or revenge, or a combination of both.

"Money," Christian did not hesitate. "I want my money. Those ball bearings were worth three hundred thousand dollars!"

"I thought you said it was Deutsche Marks?"

"I misspoke. Sometimes you forget the right words when you get to be my age. No matter."

"And who are your partners, do you know?" Jack said eagerly. He was looking forward to putting *ProServe's* resoures to a test while resolving this debt collection case. "Are they connected with anyone? Like the government or racket?"

"What do you mean?" By Christian's puzzled expression Jack could tell that he genuinely did not understand the question.

"Never mind. Let me do my own background research and I will get back to you. Incidentally, do you know our fees for debt collection services?" Jack asked him, just to avoid any misunderstanding in the future.

"No." Christian sounded surprised there would be a fee at all. "What is it?"

"Fifty percent of the collected amount."

"But that is too much, Herr Parker. Twenty," he counter-offered, "and only because I am an old man, who has been taken for a ride."

"I am sorry, Herr Huber, but this fee is non-negotiable because I have to hire sub-contractors."

"But the normal rate is one third. That is the usual amount anywhere else in the world!"

"Maybe elsewhere in the world it may be the norm, Herr Huber," Jack responded firmly, "but here, in Kiev, things work a little differently. If you agree to this amount, then we will begin to work for you. If not, then I will certainly understand."

"You drive a hard bargain, Herr Parker," Christian said after a short pause. "But I agree. We have a deal."

"Wonderful. Do you have their business cards, then? Anything with a name and address on it."

"Of course." Christian reached into the pocket of his vest, producing two business cards. "Here are they are. Father and son."

"Let me look into it," Jack said, making notes on a yellow legal pad.

"Thank you, Herr Paker. I am glad to see there is still justice in this world." As soon as Christian left his office, Jack called Sasha about Christian Huber's unfortunate Ukrainian partners.

"Sasha, it's me. Want to hear about foreigners being ripped off by local scam artists?" Jack began the conversation half-jokingly. After all, he spoke over an open telephone wire. "I'll split half of my collection fee with you, if you're interested."

"Do they have a roof?" was Sasha's first question.

"Since when do you care?" Jack replied.

"Just curious, that's all. Where do I find them?"

"*Luteranskaya* twenty seven. Apartment four."

"Names?"

"Two: Alexei and Kirill Rudakov," Jack read from the business cards that Christian gave him. "Alexei is the father, Kirill is the son."

"Thanks for the chickens," Sasha said. "I'll see what I can do."

After Jack hung up the telephone, he could not help but smile at Sasha's favorite joke, that "a chicken dinner consists of two things: a chicken and me." Somewhere in Kiev two unsuspecting, greedy chickens were about to be devoured.

* * *

Sasha pushed the red button on his telephone and reflected on the information Jack had just relayed to him. Then he dialed Victor's number. "*Privet*, Victor," he said. "We have a job."

"Where?"

"*Luteranskaya* twenty seven."

"When?"

"In half an hour."

"See you there, boss."

Precisely twenty eight minutes later Victor marched down *Luteranskogo* Street, his refrigerator-like body wrapped in a heavy leather jacket. Victor easily spotted Sasha's Landcruiser parked directly across from building number                                                  twenty seven.. He walked over and tapped on the dark window.

"Let's go and meet some people," Sasha said, getting out of his car.

"Anything I should know about them?"

"Two scam artists, stealing money from some foreigner."

Victor slowed down to admire a gray BMW parked across the doorway. "Now, that's a magnificent automobile. Can you imagine how it handles?"

"Personally, I prefer four-wheel drives, but if you like this, then take it," Sasha joked, "I give it to you"

"Sure, just like that."

They walked inside an entryway and stopped at the elevator. "What floor?" Victor pushed the button for the elevator door to open. He glanced inside of the cabin and said, "we are not going to fit in there. It's too small for both of us."

"That's because you're getting fat." Sasha looked at Victor's growing stomach. "It's on the second floor, anyway. Let's see if you can make it. Go."

"Easy for you to joke." Victor breathed heavily, following Sasha up the stairs. "I can't lose this weight no matter what I do. It's like some damned curse."

Sasha paused by a black metal door with number four painted on it. "This must be it. Stand over here, to the side, and let me do the talking."

Victor quickly moved away so that he could not be seen through the peephole. Sasha pushed the doorbell and waited. A slight patter of feet confirmed that somebody was inside the apartment. "Yes," a man's voice said cautiously. "Who is it?"

"I'm from *Zhek*." Sasha meekly looked away from the door and slurred his words for credibility. "The neighbor below you complained about water leaking from your apartment. Their bathroom is flooded. It looks like it's coming from above."

"But we don't have any water in here."

"...I've gotta isolate the leak," Sasha mumbled. "Either that, or I'm gonna have to turn off the water to the whole building until we locate the problem. I don't care."

"It probably sprung above us," the man replied and opened the door, "but if you want to look, you're more than welcome."

"Thank you." Sasha looked into the naive eyes of his victim. "You are the most trusting person for someone who steals from the others. Isn't that ironic?" The young man realized that Sasha was not from the state-run homeowners association, and he tried to shut the door, but Sasha's boot was firmly placed in the crack.

"Argh!" Sasha roared, throwing his entire body into the apartment. With Victor's help he easily overpowered the young man on the other side of the door. "Close that door, Victor!" Sasha ordered the giant. Trapped in his own apartment, the man trembled in fear. Sasha demanded, "is your name Alexei?"

"No, it's Kirill. What do you guys want, anyway? Maybe I can help you."

Sasha remained with Kirill in the hall while Victor went to search the rest of the apartment. "You are Kirill Alexeevich Rudakov, right?"

"There's nobody in here, boss," Victor reported from the bedroom. "The place is empty."

"Where is your father?" Sasha calmly asked Kirill. "Who?"

Sasha's heavy fist landed squarely in the solar plexus. Kirill doubled over and fell to the floor, gasping for air. "Your father is Alexei. Remember him? Where is he?"

"He's not here," Kirill uttered, coughing. "He's gone out for lunch."

"That's unfortunate." Sasha took handcuffs from his back pocket. "But it's not the end of the world. Let's take him with us, Victor."

Sasha was about to handcuff Kirill's delicate wrists together when he heard an older man's voice calling out, "Kirill, you forgot to close the door." Sasha covered Kirill's mouth and listened for the sound of slow, shuffling feet. As the old man passed through the doorway Victor met him with a bear hug and lifted him up in the air.

"Alexei, I presume?" Sasha stepped from the living room with Kirill, who was already handcuffed. "The brains behind this little scam?"

"What scam? There is no scam," Alexei croaked. "Put me down!"

"Drop him, Victor. Can you hear me better now?"

"Yes." Alexei was clearly in great pain. "I can hear you, alright."

"Do you know why we are here?"

"No."

"You owe your German partner three hundred thousand dollars. He is not available to collect it personally, so he asked Victor and me to do it for him. Are you with me so far?"

"But Christian Huber is not our partner," Kirill interrupted, trying to spare his father. "He is an old liar and a thief. He sent us bad quality, worthless ball bearings."

"Alexei, you seem like a reasonable fellow," Sasha addressed the old man. "Please tell your son not to interrupt me again."

"Kirill, stay out of this," his father said.

"Alexei, you and I are grown men," Sasha continued. "And my understanding is simple: you owe three hundred thousand in cash, U.S. dollars. Plus I want the title to this apartment as my fee for having to come over and help collect this debt."

"But I don't have that kind of money," Alexei cried out. "Even if I could sell the damned ball bearings, which nobody will buy, I could not come up with that amount."

Sasha shrugged his shoulders, indifferent to Alexei's problems. "Then steal it from some other foreigner. Or go sell your body at night. Do whatever it takes. I'll call you later about the debt repayment schedule. In the meantime, we will take Kirill with us, purely as collateral."

"But there is no debt," Alexei moaned, but Sasha was not listening.

"Pay us the money you owe, or we will treat your son like treasure and bury him with great care and affection," Sasha said before he strolled out of the door. Victor followed, keeping a tight grip on Kirill's arm. Outside, Sasha nodded toward the grey BMW and asked Kirill, "so how does this baby handle?"

"How do you think it handles?"

"Well, what do you know. Hey, Victor, check his pockets. If I'm right, our collateral may have your car keys on him. Am I right, Kirill?" Without waiting for a response, Victor's meaty fingers patted down Kirill's heavy wool overcoat. From the right pocket he pulled out a key chain with a BMW insignia. Impressed, Victor whistled and said to Sasha, "hey, you're pretty good."

"Like I said, it's all yours." Sasha nodded toward the elegant, powerful car and added, "why don't you ask your new friend Kirill to show you how this baby handles?"

"What? Right now?" Victor asked incredulously.

"Yup. Just follow me."

Half an hour later, two foreign luxury cars slowly made their way down a frozen, mud-covered road. They were in *Koncha Zaspa*, a forest preserve about twenty kilometers outside Kiev, a world away from civilization. In another hour it would get dark. No incidental strangers would come around, at least not until the morning.

The Landcruiser pulled off the dirt road first and stopped twenty feet into the woods. The silver BMW pulled up with its motor purring smoothly. Victor turned off the engine and said to Kirill with sincere admiration, "you had excellent taste in cars when you were alive." Then he laughed at his black humor. By the time Kirill and Victor walked over to the Landcruiser, Sasha already opened the hatch. He pulled out a dirty shovel and threw it at Kirill's feet.

"I'm going to uncuff you, but if you try to run..." Sasha pulled out his trusty nine millimeter *Makarov* and pointed the gun at Kirill's head. "What the hell are you waiting for? Dig." Kirill started to stab at the rock-hard, frozen earth, trying in vain to penetrate the crust of the soil.

"I'll turn my headlights on for your convenience." Sasha climbed into the driver's seat of his comfortable Landcruiser, started the engine and turned on the high beams. He remained inside, with the heater on, for the rest of the grave-digging ceremony. Two hours later Kirill became exhausted, Victor was cold and hungry, and the grave was still nowhere near being finished.

At last, Sasha emerged from his cozy, warm automobile. He strolled over to Kirill and said, "before Victor shoots you, tell me: how much do you want to live?"

"Please don't do this!" Kirill dropped to his knees in the shallow grave and started to cry. "I have a wife and two small daughters. I won't go to the police, I don't even remember your faces. Just let me go..."

"First, let's call your father. Tell him what you just told me." Sasha dialed Alexei's number on his cellular phone and waited a few seconds. "Hello, Alexei? I promised I'd call you. Kirill is here with me, and he would like to say a few words to you. Here, talk to your father." Sasha handed the phone to Kirill.

"Dad, you've got to get me out of here," Kirill cried into the receiver. "I don't want to die!"

"Son, pull yourself together. I'm trying to contact everyone I know."

"What do you mean, pull myself together? Don't you understand where I am? I'm in the..." Before Kirill could reveal their location, Sasha kicked him squarely in the chest. The telephone flew from Kirill's hand and landed in the corner of the shallow grave. It broke into pieces upon impact.

"I guess that's the end of our negotiations for the night," Sasha said. "Too bad."

"So now what, boss?" Victor looked at Sasha and then at Kirill.

"Unless you have a better idea, let's tie him to a tree for the night. Nobody will find him, don't worry. After we get the money, we'll tell his father where to get him."

"Hey, you can't just leave me here," Kirill pleaded. "I will freeze to death before the morning! Then you will have nothing to bargain with. Think about that!"

"He's right about freezing, boss," Victor said. "It's going to be damned cold tonight. Minus fifteen, for sure."

"Maybe you want to keep him in your apartment for a couple of days, with your wife and children?"

"Nope. I can't do that."

"Me neither. So get the damned rope from the back of my car and tie him up. I'll get the money out of his father one way or another, don't you worry about that."

"You are killing an innocent human being! Don't do this, because you will regret this for the rest of your lives!" Kirill tried one last time to save his skin. "Just think about what you are doing, I beg you, please!"

"What are you complaining about?" Sasha answered. "You get to spend a beautiful night in the middle of nature. Tie him up good, Victor."

"Give me your hands," Victor said. Kirill saw there was no point in arguing with him. He obediently offered both wrists to be bound with coarse rope.

"Not too tight," Kirill quietly asked Victor, "I have poor blood circulation."

"When you speak, you annoy people." Victor stuck a dirty, gasoline-stained rag deep into Kirill's mouth to gag him. Then he tied the rope evenly along the body, from the neck down to the feet, to the tree. There was no chance for Kirill to escape without somebody's help.

A few minutes later Victor was in the driver's seat of his new BMW, following Sasha's Landcruiser out of a dark, mysterious forest. For a few bottles of vodka, Victor's buddy at the department of motor vehicles would register a perfectly fake title to his dream car. Working with Sasha was a much better way of making a living than patrolling the streets, Victor thought.

# Chapter 19

As the applause in the audience died down, Gennady Zhukov, the Deputy Minister of Health, patiently finished his speech, "...and in conclusion, I want to say that the Ministry of Health is at the forefront of modern transplant procedures. With the assistance of our esteemed American colleagues like Dr. Zimmer, we shall work together on projects previously considered to be impossible." Dr. Zimmer, standing to the Minster's immediate right, was beaming with pride.

"For instance," the Deputy Minister droned on, "the recent law On Transplantation of Organs and Other Anatomic Materials of Humans allows any foreigner to receive excellent quality, healthy organs from reliable Ukrainian donors. Livers and kidneys, hearts and corneas, all harvested and transplanted right here in Ukraine." The Deputy Minister looked at his watch. "So again, in conclusion, the Ministry of Health is willing and able to offer help to the international community of patients. Thank you."

Everyone politely applauded as the Deputy Minister stepped down from the podium. Soon enough the reception grew loud with casual party chatter. "Hey, over here," Jack heard Dr. Zimmer's voice, "I want to introduce you to somebody!" Jack turned around to congratulate him and froze: Dr. Zimmer's arm was wrapped around a thin waist of a beautiful blond girl. Her angelic face and perfectly shaped legs were intimately familiar to Jack. They had met at the Intourist bar during his very first night in Kiev.

"This is Yana, my fiancee," Dr. Zimmer proudly introduced Jack to the viper, who had infected him and stole his wallet. "Yana, I want you to meet our lawyer, Jack Parker."

"I believe we have already met once." Bitterness oozed from Jack's lips, but he could not help himself.

"Have we? Where?" She sounded genuinely surprised.

"On second thought, maybe not," Jack conceded, unprepared to proceed down this road. "I probably made a mistake."

"Isn't she lovely," Dr. Zimmer pinched Yana's pink cheek. "Absolutely adorable."

The doctor's first opinion of Yana coincided with Jack's: she was a very attractive young lady, armed with a great ass and long legs. Standing across from Yana and Dr. Zimmer, staring awkwardly into his glass of red wine, Jack had a bad feeling about Dr. Zimmer's choice of wives. All evening long he wanted to take Dr. Zimmer aside and warn him about Yana's profession. Instead, Jack kept that dirty little secret to himself.

# Chapter 20

Marina was beside herself with anger. She had been waiting all week for Pavel to take her to the disco on Saturday night, and now it was over, just like that. While all her friends were having a good time on the dance floor, she had to drive back to the village with her stupid, drunken imbecile boyfriend, Pavel.

"So are you coming with me, or not?" Pavel was slurring his words. "Because I'm leaving with or without..."

"Yeah, wait for me." Marina reluctantly got into the front seat of his father's rusty Moskvich because she did not want to be stranded in the middle of the night at the disco. Why did he have to start a fight, she thought, biting her lower lip. Marina knew better than to reason with Pavel after he had a few drinks. And boy did he drink tonight, she thought. Like a pig!

At last Pavel found the keyhole and turned the key in the ignition. The old Moskvich turned over several times and stalled. Furious, Pavel pounded his fist against the dashboard and screamed, "you piece of garbage!"

"Calm down, Pavel," Marina said gently.

"Don't you tell me to calm down, you slut! This whole thing happened because of you!"

"Yes, Pavel, whatever you say."

"Damn right!" He finally started the engine. They pulled out on the main road, heading back to their village. They drove in silence for about twenty minutes. Suddenly, Pavel slammed the breaks, pulled over and stopped the car.

"What are you doing?" Marina asked. She was not frightened of Pavel because they grew up together and knew each other all their lives.

"I'm going to take a piss. What's it to you?"

"Nothing. Just asking."

"Fuck off, then." Pavel clumsily stepped out of the car and slammed the door as hard as he could. Marina watched him stumble through the snow into the woods, until the darkness swallowed him. Soon enough she would be home, with her mother and sister. Father would be there too, drinking with his buddies. What a predictable, boring way to end a Saturday night, she sighed.

Several luxurious Western automobiles flew by, giving Marina an unexpected idea. This would teach the bastard a lesson, she smiled. Before Pavel returned, she jumped out of the Moskvich and put her hand out to signal the passing drivers that she needed a lift. Marina's short, thick overcoat did not shield her legs, wrapped in nothing but a mini-skirt and a light pair of shoes. Several minutes later she was sitting in the front seat of a black Mercedes Benz 600, a car she had never seen up close before.

Pavel emerged from the woods just in time to watch Marina getting into a sleek Mercedes. He screamed to her, "hey, what are you doing?" but she did not turn around. Pavel clumsily tried to run, zipping up his pants on the way, but it was too late. The Mercedes spun its wheels, showering his Moskvich with gravel, and quickly picked up speed along the highway.

"You fucking bastards!" Pavel screamed after them. Furious, he jumped into the Moskvich and twisted the key. It took several times, but he managed to start the ancient engine. Shifting impatiently into the first gear, Pavel moved along the shoulder at the speed of a turtle, slowly gaining speed. Under his breath, Pavel cursed his father's Moskvich that would barely run and the blond guy in the disco who made a pass at Marina. Most of all, he cursed Marina for leaving him alone by the side of the road.

It took Pavel almost fifteen minutes to gain enough speed to make out the Mercedes taillights in the distance, far ahead. Encouraged, he floored the gas pedal, but the car had reached its limit and refused to go any faster.

\* \* \*

"So what does that thing tell you?" Marina pointed at the gauge on the dashboard.

"It measures the temperature outside," Andrei answered. "And this shows you how many kilometers we can go without refueling. Pretty neat, huh?"

"I'd say," Marina marveled at the multi-colored display in front of the driver. "It looks like we're in a cockpit of an airplane."

"Have you ever been on an airplane?" Andrei looked at her skeptically.

"No. But I've seen the inside of a pilot's cockpit on TV." Marina smiled, happy to bask in the lap of luxury even for a short time. As they were driving, Andrei looked over Marina, pleased with tonight's catch. She was perfect: no more than seventeen, with a thin yet muscular body of a farm girl. This is not your typical highway prostitute, he thought.

"So is this your car?" Marina asked.

"You're kidding. Of course not; I'm just a driver."

"I see."

"You want to know who my boss is?"

"If you want to tell me."

"Philip Kirkorov," Andrei said proudly. "Himself."

"The pop star?"

"Yep."

"Get out of here!"

"No, really." Andrei paused and looked at Marina seriously. "Actually, I'm not supposed to tell anyone this, but his Ukrainian promoter is throwing a party tonight."

"You mean Philip Kirkorov is in Kiev right now?"

"Like I said, I'm not supposed to tell this to anyone, but what the hell. Hey, do you want to come with me? I could introduce you."

"Really? You're not pulling my leg, are you?"

"Not at all."

Marina could not believe her luck. "Sure, I'd love to," she said, "who wouldn't?"

"Alright, then." Andrei pressed his foot against the gas pedal. "Hold on."

Twenty minutes later the Mercedes turned off the main highway and went south, towards *Koncha Zaspa*, where the local millionaires and Ministers enjoy summertime in their palaces along the *Dnieper* River. They slowed down before making a sharp left turn onto a narrow road. Andrei flipped on the high beams and they illuminated the pitch-black forest.

To Marina's surprise, the road was perfectly paved, without any potholes. Only somebody with Philip Kirkorov's wealth could afford to have a road like this, she thought. The car stopped at a gate, a thick sheet of steel planted firmly in the middle of two sturdy cement pillars. Andrei rolled down his window and waived into a small camera. The steel wall moved to the left, allowing the Mercedes to drive one hundred meters through a private forest, straight up to a modern, three-story house.

"This is where Philip stays when he performs in Kiev," Andrei explained. "He likes the nature."

"I've read that people like Kirkorov have places like this," gasped Marina.

"You haven't seen anything yet. Want to take a look inside?"

"Sure." Marina jumped out of the car and followed Andrei. She marveled at the solid oak door, adorned with elaborate wood sculptures. "Wow," said Marina, touching the hand-carved figurines on the door.

"After you," Andrei smiled as he opened the door. At first Marina could not see, but then he turned on the lights, and she gasped. The marbled lobby, where they were standing, rose to the very roof of the sprawling house. A glass mini-elevator was built into the center of a staircase, allowing easy access to each of the three floors. The white columns added to the lobby's palatial, grandiose appearance.

"What's up there?" she asked, pointing above.

"The top floor has two bedrooms, each with it's own Jacuzzi. The other floors are for toys, like the TV room, the billiard room. There's also a huge library and an office. But Philip's favorite part of the house, and mine too, is the basement."

"Why? What's there?"

"An indoor swimming pool, a Finnish sauna, a steam bath, whirlpool, you name it. Even a separate room for a Turkish bath. That's when you lay on a hot stone."

"I knew that," Marina lied.

"Looks like it will be a few minutes before Philip will be here. He's always running late. Do you want anything to drink?"

"No, thanks. I don't drink."

"That's excellent. So, while we wait for Philip, do you want to see the basement?"

"Sure."

Andrei pushed the elevator button and the glass doors opened, inviting them. The slow descent into darkness made Marina somewhat nervous. When the elevator doors released them, Andrei flipped a switch on the wall.

All the lights came on at once and Marina could not believe her eyes: Philip Kirkorov had an enormous swimming pool, sparkling with light blue water in the middle of his gigantic basement. To either side of the pool was a row of cedar doors.

"This is the sauna," Andrei pointed at the first door, "and that is the steam bath. You see that door, in the corner? That leads to the Turkish bath. Impressive, isn't it?"

"Well, yes," was all that Marina managed to say. She looked up, hypnotized by the dozens of bright halogen lamps that were built into the ceiling. They cast reflections in the clear water below like bright little stars. Shiny pink marble tiles lined the walls and the floor, dazzling the eye.

"Andrei, is that you?" Marina heard another man's voice.

"Yes, sir," said Andrei. "I'm waiting for Mr. Kirkorov."

"He'll be a few minutes late." The man approached them. He looked at Marina, evaluating her body from top to bottom. "So who is this lovely lady?"

"Well, sir, allow me to introduce you. This is..."

"Marina," she said.

"Very nice to meet you, Marina. My colleagues in the show business call me Veniamin Gennadiavich, but you can call me Venya. Would you like a glass of wine?"

"No, thank you, I don't drink."

"Perhaps some tea, instead, or Coca Cola maybe?"

"A Coca Cola would be nice, if you have it."

"Andrei, can you get us a Coca Cola and a cup of coffee for me? Black with two sugars."

"Right away, sir."

"In the meantime, why don't we sit down here." Veniamin walked over to the plush chairs, which were grouped around a small table by the side of the pool. He plunked himself down and motioned for Marina to sit across from him. "So tell me about yourself," Veniamin said. "You seem like a very healthy girl."

"I worked in the fields this summer." Marina answered timidly, not used to hearing compliments from strangers.

"Have you ever been seriously ill?"

"What do you mean?"

"I mean, have you had any operations?"

"God forbid, no." Marina crossed herself.

"Do your parents drink?"

"My dad does," she nodded sadly, "but who doesn't these days?"

"A lot, huh?" Veniamin asked sympathetically.

"I guess."

"Here are your drinks," Andrei interrupted Veniamin, setting the tray on a side table.

"You can go," Veniamin dismissed the driver. "I will call you when Philip is ready."

"So you must have met Alla Pugacheva." Marina was curious about Philip Kirkorov's famous wife. "What's she like?"

"A wonderful human being, no matter what everyone else says." Veniamin slowly sipped his coffee, occasionally glancing at his watch. He chatted away about their sham marriage of convenience for publicity and Philip's questionable heterosexuality.

"What did you say?" Marina began having problems following Veniamin's words. She forced herself to concentrate.

"I see you are beginning to feel something. Am I right?"

"What do you mean?" Marina tried to pull herself out of the chair. To her surprise, however, the body refused to obey her command. In slow motion Veniamin got up from his sofa and walked over. Marina tried to speak, but nothing came out. She helplessly watched as Veniamin picked up her limp right hand and counted the pulse. She tried to pull away, but her body felt like it was paralyzed.

Veniamin could see the terrified look in Marina's eyes. He leaned over to comfort her. "Don't worry about anything," he whispered in her ear, "just relax and go to sleep. It's only a test; it will soon be over."

As the heavy sedatives quickly set in, Marina watched bright reflections of the overhead lamps bouncing off the swimming pool surface. Then her eyes closed. She did not see a nurse, dressed in a white operating gown, rolling over a wheelchair. The nurse came from the door in the corner that, according to Andrei, was the Turkish bath. In fact, it was a sterilized, fully functioning operation room.

To Veniamin, a simple medical technician, the assignment was routine: the donor's blood and tissue type must be identified in order to be later matched with those of the recipient. The Deputy Minister himself demanded "the works." This meant running tests on the heart, the liver, the kidneys, bone marrow, even retinas. The results had to be hand-delivered to the Deputy Minister immediately.

\* \* \*

In the distance, Pavel could barely make out the exact spot where he saw the little red lights disappear. It took several minutes for him to arrive to the place where the Mercedes had turned off. He stopped to look around. No, he thought, there could be no mistake. It was the only road they could have taken. Besides, the snow tracks were too fresh for any other vehicle.

Turning the wheel as hard as he could, Pavel shifted into first gear and stepped on the gas. The smooth lane, running through the forest, was nearly invisible under the Moskvich's dim headlights, forcing Pavel to drive at a snail's pace. In twenty minutes he came to a dead end. An enormous metal wall barred any curious visitors from disturbing the owners. Pavel reached under his seat and picked up a knife. Hiding the long blade behind his back, he cautiously approached the gate and pushed a black button.

"Who are you and what do you want?" Pavel heard a man's voice coming from a speaker.

"Well, my name is Pavel. I mean, Pavel Dmitrievich Filipov. And you bastards have my girlfriend in there! I want her back!"

"I don't know what you're talking about," answered the bland voice.

"Marina, you've got my Marina in there! And I'm not leaving here without her! Do you understand me?"

"There is nobody by the name of Marina in here. Go home, Pavel Filipov, and get some sleep."

"You fuckers!" Pavel worked himself up, screaming, "let me in there and I'll find her! I know she's in there!"

There was no more response from the speaker. Pavel pushed the black button again. "I said, give me back my Marina! If you don't, I will go to the police and file a report!" Feeling completely helpless in this situation, Pavel flew into a rage. He smashed his fists against the steel wall and hurled terrible insults at the owners from the top of his lungs. In the deep forest, however, nobody paid attention to his ranting.

It was well past midnight. Pavel reluctantly climbed back into his father's Moskvich and carefully navigated his way to the main road. The slow drive back gave Pavel time to reflect on the situation. He clearly remembered seeing Marina getting into a Mercedes. "It turned right here," Pavel said aloud to himself. The bastard on the intercom had to be lying: his Marina was in there with somebody. Then Pavel broke into a cold sweat. What if something went wrong? What if Marina needed his help, right this very moment?

Pavel parked the Moskvich across the main road, so that they would not see him waiting. The knife on the passenger seat was within easy reach. He patiently waited for nearly an hour, shivering, when he finally saw headlamps emerging from the forest. Pavel jumped out of his car, forgetting his knife. The familiar dark silhouette of the Mercedes paused briefly before entering the main road.

ानत

Pavel ran towards the car as fast as he could, waving his arms wildly about his head and screaming, "you motherfucker! I'm going to find you! I'll get you!" The Mercedes sped away, but Pavel could easily make out the license number, KM-237. The Cabinet of Ministers, he noted for future consideration. With little choice, Pavel drove to the nearest police station to report the kidnapping of his girlfriend.

Much to his frustration, however, the policeman on duty refused to take a statement about a missing person "because 24 hours have not yet expired." When Pavel insisted they treat Marina's disappearance more seriously because a member of Cabinet of Ministers was involved, the policeman told him to go away.

"My girlfriend was stolen by someone in a Mercedes," Pavel insisted. "I personally followed that car to a private house in the *Koncha-Zaspa* area." To substantiate his claim, Pavel even gave the policeman a correct license plate number and a detailed vehicle description. Still, this information was insufficient to file a report.

"It is a matter of life and death," Pavel protested angrily, "and if you refuse to do anything about it, then maybe the newspapers will help me. And I will make sure your names will be splattered all over the front page!"

Only then the policeman reluctantly agreed to take down the report. The following evening Pavel was killed in a hit-and-run accident while crossing a street. The car, which ran over him, was never found. Subsequent medical records revealed that Pavel had more than five times the legal dose of alcohol. Nobody who knew Pavel questioned that conclusion. The police report, filed by Pavel earlier, was promptly destroyed.

* * *

"Sorry to disturb you at home, Minister Zhukov, but I have excellent news: your kidneys have matched with a patient." Dr. Zimmer spoke into his cellular telephone while lounging by the swimming pool in the back of his house. It was a beautiful, sunny afternoon in Palo Alto, and Dr. Zimmer felt like a powerful man in the prime of his life. His young trophy wife, Yana, looked like a sexy Playboy bunny, tanning on a lounge chair under the California sun. "The patient is an older woman, in her sixties, from a wealthy European family. She understands all the risks and wants to proceed further."

"That is very good news," Deputy Minister replied. He sat up in his bed and turned on the lamp. According to the clock, it was past 11 p.m. "Where is the recipient now?"

"Hooked up to a dialysis machine somewhere in Geneva. But she can fly into Kiev on Swissair tomorrow afternoon if you can take proper care of her on your end."

Despite the late hour, the Deputy Minister snapped into action because Dr. Zimmer was bringing to him wealthy clients. "I will call the head of the Institute of Surgery and Transplantology immediately. He will organize a team of surgeons, immunologists and nurses to harvest the organs first thing in the morning. Everything will be ready by the time the patient arrives, Dr. Zimmer, including two back-up dialysis machines."

"In that case, I will fax to you the necessary information later today. Pleasure working with you, sir, and good luck with our first patient," Dr. Zimmer concluded.

The Deputy Minister Zhukov turned off the lights, but he could not fall asleep. He was excited about the financial rewards Dr. Zimmer's partnership offered. At the same time, odd questions ran through his mind: did Dr. Zimmer truly care about how these spare body parts became available? How would Dr. Zimmer or his patients know where the organs come from, anyway? With so many unanswered questions, Deputy Minister Zhukov had to take two Valiums to help him fall asleep.

# Chapter 21

When Jack arrived to his office, a short faxed message arrived from Berlin. Christian Huber wrote: *"Stop all work immediately."* This was a most unusual request in debt collection cases, where aggrieved creditors seldom abandon their chase. Confused, Jack promptly got Christian on the line.

"Good morning, Herr Parker," a familiar dignified voice slowly said. "I am delighted to hear your voice."

"Herr Huber, I received your message to stop all work, so I called to find out what is going on."

"My faith in the human nature has been restored," Christian replied. "Yesterday I received a most wonderful phone call from my Ukrainian partner, Alexei. It was all some kind of misunderstanding. He wants to pay me for the ball bearings. So, fortunately, your services will not be necessary. But I thank you for receiving me in your office, and for listening to an old man's problems."

"But Herr Huber, don't you think that I am somewhat responsible for this?"

"Look, Herr Parker, Alexei himself called me with apologies. He explained about the misunderstanding, so everything is okay now. Alexei also inquired about his son. Apparently, he is still missing. Do you know anything about that?"

"No, I don't. But what about paying for my services?"

"Since nothing needs to be done anymore, I see no need to hire you in the first place."

Technically, Christian was right: Jack did not sign an engagement letter with him. Therefore, from a strictly legal perspective, Herr Huber was not obligated to pay Jack anything. This infuriated him all the more. The slimy bastard knew all along he was not going to pay me, Jack realized. He played me for a sucker, while Sasha and I helped to settle his problem!

Jack tried to correct this misunderstanding before it escalated into a full-blown disaster. "Herr Huber, what you are doing is morally wrong," he said. "I solved your problem. You have to pay me. There's a fundamental rule in life's business ethics: don't mess around with your lawyer. Especially with his fee."

"I am prepared to live with my conscience," Mr. Huber replied. "Is there anything else?"

"I guess not." After hanging up the receiver, Jack sat back in his chair and seethed at how easily he was snookered, like small child, by a smooth old con man.

This ungrateful crook has to be taught a lesson, Jack thought while dialing Sasha's number.

"Recognize me?" Jack asked.

"Sure. What's up?"

"Remember that collection case, the one I referred to you a few days ago? Something went wrong. Terribly wrong."

Sasha did not think that Jack would find out about the son's death in the forest. Not that soon, anyway. He mumbled, "I don't know what you are talking about. You sure this a telephone conversation?"

"Listen to me. The client just called to say that his Ukrainian partners agreed to pay him everything. He said our services are not necessary. It means we're not getting paid. How do you like that one?"

"What? The client is refusing to pay us, is that what you're saying?" For some reason, Sasha did not seem at all upset about Christian's underhanded maneuvers. In fact, he sounded downright happy to hear the terrible news. "See you soon," was all he said.

Half an hour later Sasha walked into Jack's office, holding a yellow plastic bag. He was grinning from ear to ear. "This is for you," he said, putting the bag on the table in front of Jack. It was filled with newspapers.

"You came here to deliver newspapers?"

"What newspapers? Open your eyes!" Sasha lifted the top layer of newspapers, revealing underneath tight bundles of one hundred dollar bills, each wrapped by a rubber band.

"What is this?"

"Your client's money. Half of it, anyway." Sasha proudly stood there, smiling down at Jack.

"You actually managed to recover some of the debt?"

"I recovered all of it. And I was going to give it all back. But now, after your phone call, the question is, what are you going to do with your half?"

"My half of what?"

"You are such a clever joker, comrade Parker," Sasha pretended to yawn. "There is a hundred and fifty thousand dollars in here, all yours. I figure that's fair."

"Are you suggesting that we split my client's money between ourselves?"

"Why not? Look, your client tried to screw us, and for that he ends up being screwed himself. That's only right."

"You think?" Meanwhile, a thought ran through Jack's mind. Sure, this may be somewhat unethical, but no worse than what Christian tried to pull earlier.

"Totally fair," Sasha confidently nodded. "Everything worked out perfectly."

"But what about the son? I heard that somehow he went missing." The uncomfortable expression on Sasha's face, his reluctance to look Jack straight in the eye, made Jack pause. "Sasha, you didn't have anything to do..."

"Who do you take me for?" Sasha growled back defensively. "Maybe he drove down to Odessa for the weekend. Don't worry, I'm sure they will find him eventually."

Inside, Jack still felt that something was wrong with this outcome, but he had to agree with Sasha:

Herr Huber deserved a taste of his own medicine. Surely it is not morally wrong to steal from a thief, Jack concluded. "I guess you're right, Sasha," he said and reached for the plastic bag with cash. "Thanks for the dough."

"No, thank you, comrade Parker, for your timely information," Sasha answered mockingly. "Give me a call anytime if you see any other chickens walking around."

"You got it." Suddenly Jack remembered to ask him, "by the way, what did your research reveal?"

"Huh?"

"You know, background research on Lena. The bandit girl from Podium?"

"Oh, her," Sasha said. "I actually talked to several guys from Podium's security. They said she was clean. I was going to bug her apartment, but from the looks of things, she's not your typical bandit girl."

"I thought so." Jack could not help but smile.

"It's too early to tell. You never know about people. Just call me if she starts giving you any problems, and we'll deal with her then."

"Sure, Sasha." Jack was relieved that he found nothing terrible in Lena's background. At this stage, however, there was nothing Sasha could say that would prevent him from continuing to see her anyway.

"Gotta go, Jack. One word of advice: don't keep this money lying around your office. Not even tonight."

"Thanks for your concern, but I'll manage."

Sasha was right, as always. With a hundred and fifty thousand in cash, Jack knew that he would be wise to find some secure hiding place for his newfound wealth. Then he wondered, is there such a thing in Ukraine?

# Chapter 22

As soon as Jack woke up, he looked under the bed to confirm that Herr Huber's money was still there. The yellow plastic bag collected a surprising amount of dust in just a few days. Like a child, eager to play with a new toy, Jack tossed all the cash on the blanket, fifteen green bundles worth ten thousand each. All he needed was a safe hiding place, but who does one trust with such a package? For the time being, Jack's apartment was the only option. He stuffed everything into Sasha's bag and tossed it under the bed.

Pleased with himself, Jack went to take a shower before Lena came over. This morning, however, no water came out of the tap. The reason was clear: the city authorities decided to shut off water to the building, perhaps the entire street, quite possibly the entire city of Kiev itself.

"Why today, God?" was Jack's first moan of the morning, and for an excellent reason: he had invited Lena to spend the Saturday afternoon together, and she accepted. Given their growing mutual admiration, Jack had every reason to hope that their Saturday afternoon date would evolve into an overnight stay. He even planned to serve her breakfast in bed the next morning.

However, Jack's beautiful dream presumed that Lena would be able to use the lavatory, perhaps even take a proper shower. Not willing to take chances, Jack decided not to use the toilet until the water was turned back on. This saved the one and only remaining flush for Lena. Life would be so much easier, Jack grumbled, if I did not have to deal with these inconveniences.

Then he sat down on the kitchen stool and thought about how ironic the entire situation was: there he was, without so much as a drop of water for the morning necessities, while a hundred and fifty thousand dollars were collecting dust under his mattress. In Kiev, this amount of money made Jack equivalent to a multi-millionaire in New York. Yet, he lived like a pauper, in a malfunctioning, animal-infested Soviet-era apartment. Jack's accommodations could use dramatic improvement if he wanted to court Lena in a civilized setting.

Why not purchase one of those enormous communal apartments that house several families, Jack thought, and refurbish it to Western standards? With his sizable cash, the real estate brokers could buy out virtually any communal apartment of Jack's choice. He and Lena could live together in the most fashionable area of Kiev, the famous *Karl Marx* Street, across from all the colorful cafe's and fountains.

Of course, he would have to arrange for a complete reconstruction because some walls will have to be torn out to accommodate the master bedroom with a fireplace. Jack imagined marble in the entryway and the bathrooms, dark parquet floors in the living room, thick carpet in the master bedroom, just like he and Julie once had back home.

What started out as Jack's silent plea for decent accommodations soon developed into a well-focused scheme to drastically change his lifestyle. And why not? He had the necessary financial resources to create a magnificent, upscale New York-style loft, fit for a king and his queen. Now it was only a matter of choosing the right moment to share his dream with Lena.

The doorbell rang. He looked out and saw Lena, waiving her hand and smiling into the peephole. She was much too early. Jack cringed, since he had no choice but to present himself in a disheveled state. "Come on in." He opened the door and stepped aside, trying to comb an unruly patch of hair into its place.

"I got off work early, so I had my driver bring me straight over." Lena strolled in without noticing his appearance. "I hope you don't mind."

"Not at all. Do you always work on Saturdays?"

"Mr. Hatchet likes to gather the upper management in his office for what he calls strategy meetings. From nine until eleven thirty, sharp, every Saturday morning." She stood at attention and gave Jack a military salute. "Today he skipped out early, so I did, too."

"Great."

"So are you ready to get some fresh morning air, Mr. Parker? Come on, put your coat on, you sleepy head. It's wonderful outside! Just like in fairy tales!"

When they walked into the street, however, Jack felt that the temperature was well below freezing and the perpetually gray, overcast skies promised to dump even more snow on the ground. "So where do you want to go?" Jack asked Lena.

A taxi took them to the upper part of *Pechersk* and dropped them off right by the Parliament building. They walked across the open plaza, leaving footprints in the virgin snow. The stately blue-and-yellow *Mariinsky* palace was a delicate, graceful creature from a bygone era. It modestly sat in the shadow of the monstrous, Soviet-era Parliament building, which was unimaginatively plastered with white marble tiles.

Jack stopped to admire the elegant one-story sprawling chateau. "It's absolutely gorgeous. Can we go inside? What are the visiting hours?"

"No, silly, only the President uses it. For official functions. That's why it's next to the Parliament. Otherwise it wouldn't be in such a great condition. Just take a look at how well it's maintained. Must cost a fortune!"

"Is there any particular reason why we came here?"

"To take a look at the palace, to stroll through the park. Just to spend some time together, that's all. Why? Do you have a better suggestion?"

"No, actually this is great." The gusting winds from *Dniepr* River, flowing below, picked up a flurry of snowflakes and spun them in front of the exquisite palace. That is when Jack felt an uncomfortable chill taking over his body. To impress Lena, though, he said, "I love walking in the snow. Helps to energize my blood."

"Me too," Lena cheerfully replied. "I can be outside all day long!"

True to her word, Jack and Lena ended up walking through the snowy park for the rest of the afternoon. Freezing most of the time, Jack looked for a unique, romantic setting where he could tell Lena all about his new apartment. After completing several loops around that enormous, seemingly never-ending pathway, Jack realized that no romantic spot was coming their way, so he blurted out, "I don't like my apartment. There are way too many different bugs. So I decided to change all that."

"How is that?"

"I'll buy an apartment for us, a nice big place in the center, say on *Karl Marx* Street, across from that little park with the fountains. How about that? Let's move in together, Lena, what do you say?"

There was a long, thoughtful pause. "It seems like a good idea for you," Lena replied, "but I can't do that."

"Why not?"

"There are many different reasons. You wouldn't understand any of them."

"Try me." Jack stopped in the middle of the alley and looked into her brown eyes.

"First, moving into an apartment with a man without getting married is wrong. Second, I don't really know you all that well. Third, I refuse to be a housewife; I prefer to have a career. In other words, I am an independent woman. Maybe my views will change when I get older, but for now, I like my independence."

"But that's precisely why we should live together for a while," Jack insisted, "so that we can get to know each other better. Personally, I'm sure that I will love absolutely everything about you, unconditionally."

"Maybe there are certain things I shouldn't know about you. I become disillusioned easily, you know. So could you."

"But that would be a valuable lesson, too," he countered, "because then I could adjust my behavior accordingly to suit your mood." By the look on her face Jack could tell that she was flattered.

"Some things nobody can change, just like a leopard can't change its spots," Lena smiled. "What if I find out things about you that I simply cannot stand?"

"Like what?"

"Like you are married, for one." She looked Jack straight in the eye to catch his reaction. "Well, are you?"

"Nope," he automatically lied, but then quickly corrected himself, "what I meant was, not anymore. I'm divorced."

"So you have been married before?"

"Yes. And you?"

"Of course not. And I want my first marriage to be the last, just like my parents had, so being divorced counts against you."

"I didn't want to lie to you, though I easily could have. Does that count for me?"

"Now, lying would be an extremely serious flaw in your personality. If I ever found out that you lied to me, I would never speak with you again. But I don't think you would stoop so low. You don't seem like the type. So how long were you married?"

"Seven years."

"Seven years, huh? I guess that's pretty good. It means that you don't jump around, that you are solid in your relationships. Have your parents been divorced?"

"They are still together. That's good too, right?"

"You would be surprised, but little things like that can tell you a lot about a person."

It was barely past four in the afternoon, but the Northern sky was getting darker by the minute. Jack's feet were numb and he could no longer feel his fingers and toes. He longed for the warmth of his infested apartment, a plateful of re-heated leftover food and a couple of drinks. Ultimately, the sub-degree torture took its toll: Jack's jaw muscles began to spasmodically contract, causing the top row of teeth to clink against the lower one. Though Jack tried to control the clattering sound coming from his mouth, Lena noticed it anyway. "Are you cold?" she asked.

"N-n-o," Jack stuttered, determined not to be a wimp. "H-h-ow ab-b-out you?"

"You're a pitiful sight, but you look so cute. The trick is to relax, don't shiver so hard. You're losing energy. I think it's time to go home before you get sick. What you need is a cup of coffee with a cognac."

Without uttering another word, Jack stuck Lena's hand inside his coat pocket and they walked out of the park, holding hands. He hailed down the first car that would take them back to *Gorky* Street. In the warmth of the cab, filled with the driver's cigarette smoke, Jack prayed that his water problem was fixed in their absence.

Fifteen minutes later they were back in his apartment, cold and tired. Even though Jack still had no running water, the evening went better than he had hoped. Instead of piping hot coffee, they shared a couple of cognacs, followed by a candle-lit supper of yesterday's scraps.

At the end of the night, right before they went to bed, Lena slowly undressed before Jack. It was a magnificent scene to behold, as she began by pulling the fuzzy red sweater up over her silky black hair. Unfortunately, one of her gold earrings got caught in the sweater, interrupting Jack's viewing pleasure. The earring fell out and bounced off the hard parquet floor, making a distinct metallic sound.

Jack's internal alarm immediately went off. In her search, Lena could easily discover his stash of cash. There would surely be questions for which Jack could not provide honest answers. "I'll get it, honey," he volunteered.

"Don't worry, it's my fault. I'm so clumsy sometimes. It's here somewhere." Lena got on her knees and looked under the bed. "See, there it is!" There was nothing Jack could do but wait for Lena to reach under the bed and recover her earring. "And look at all this trash. It has to be thrown out." Lena reached further than necessary, and that's when Jack truly panicked.

"Don't throw anything out! Just leave my trash where it is!" By asking Lena to leave his belongings alone, however, Jack accomplished quite the opposite result. With a puzzled look on her face, Lena pulled out a yellow plastic bag and glanced inside. Her face did not betray any emotion.

"Is there something you want to tell me, Mr. Parker?" Lena calmly asked Jack.

"As a matter of fact, there is. I started to talk about this in the park."

"Go on."

"I think I love you and I want to be with you for the rest of my life. And to make sure that we are truly compatible, I want to live with you, say, for a year. Then we would know if we want to get married. That way we won't make any mistakes. And this money will buy us a nice place of our own. So what do you say, Lena? Will you move in with me?"

"That was not my question, and you know it," Lena replied sternly. "Where did this money come from? Who are you, Jack Parker?"

"You really want to know?"

"I have to know." Lena looked especially striking when she was angry. "Otherwise I will become suspicious. So tell me, what kind of a person has money like this under his bed?"

Left with little choice, Jack summarized his business dealings with the German client. The way he presented his case, Lena's face changed from sympathy and understanding to indignation and disgust at Herr Huber's cunning and trickery. After Jack finished his interpretation of the story, Lena said, "but you still didn't explain how you got this money."

"Well, we managed to get his debt collected." Jack was intentionally vague, eager to change topics. "So what are your plans for tomorrow? It's Sunday, so maybe I can take you to a champagne brunch?"

"Who is this *we*? You said *we* managed to get his debt collected. So who are *we*?"

It was obvious that Lena was not going to let it go, so Jack explained patiently, as he would to a child, "medical doctors occasionally refer their clients to specialists, ok? And lawyers sometimes hire sub-contractors, people who are experts in their field. Well, on this case I worked with a sub-contractor."

"And who is your sub-contractor? Wait, don't tell me, I can guess myself. Is it the same one that had me researched?"

"You're pretty smart."

"I thought so. So you two kept that German gentleman's money, like thieves?"

"But that's the whole point: he was no gentleman. He was a con man. This is his punishment."

"And what about his Ukrainian partners? They gave up so much money just like that, without any problems?" Lena sounded skeptical.

"Absolutely." In reality, Jack had no idea what the Ukrainian partners looked like, or what Sasha said that resulted in such a quick and easy debt recovery; all he knew was that Sasha ate two chickens. Still, Jack had to defend his position or risk losing Lena's respect and affection. Without knowing the facts, Jack made things up as he went along, "the Ukrainians owed money for the ball bearings, and they knew it. That's why they gave up so easily."

"And how do you know what? Did Sasha tell you this? Or your German crook? To me, what you did sounds very much like banditism. I know people like you. Don't you remember where I work? All of our security, from the guys on the loading docks to the snipers on the roof, are very nice to me, just like Sasha is to you. But to others, they are a nightmare. I hear their stupid adventure stories every day at work, and I despise them for what they do to ordinary, hard-working people just to make a few extra dollars on the side!"

"But why are you lumping me in together with them? If you are such an expert on racketeers, why can't you see that I am just a simple American lawyer from New York?"

"I may be only twenty one, but I know enough to see what you are doing. Nobody gives up this much money voluntarily, so I hate to imagine what Sasha must have said or done to these poor people. But remember, Jack, that what goes around comes around. Someday these things will come back to haunt you. Have you ever thought of that?"

"Sure, honey." By now, Jack was ready to say anything, just to drop this unpleasant topic once and for all.

"So will you give it back?"

"Of course I will," Jack said automatically. Then he quickly clarified, "give what back?"

"The money you and Sasha stole, of course, what else? You can't keep it, Jack. It's not yours."

For some reason Lena was determined to give away his dough, and Jack did not appreciate it. "But I explained it to you already," he said, exasperated, "I'm not giving that German bastard a penny, on pure principle. No way! And from what I heard, the Ukrainian partners are even worse."

"Fine. Then give it to some charity. But you should not be profiting from this scam. Jack, I'm warning you. If I find out that you're involved in something seedy, not to mention downright criminal, I will never see you again. My mother always told me: Lena, never marry a criminal. It proved to be excellent advice so far."

The little spat significantly cooled off the romantic atmosphere in the bedroom. As any man would do in the same situation, Jack caved in and told Lena exactly what she wanted to hear. "Honey, I will gladly give away all the money," he said smoothly, "but refusing to move in together, that's an issue where I can't compromise. Can we work something out?"

Jack did not know where this last-ditch effort could possibly take him, since Lena had already told him no earlier in the park. Still, in this context, he felt it was a fair exchange. By Lena's eyes Jack could tell that she understood the trade-off, and was in the process of making up her mind about what to do with him. Jack smiled brightly, hoping to tip the scale in his favor. It worked.

"So be it, then," she accepted. "If you promise not to stray from the straight and legal path, which you can prove by returning the money, then I will consider moving in with you. But as part of this deal, you will have to abstain from any shady dealings in the future. Is this clear?"

Jack could not believe his ears. It was a hundred and eighty-degree shift in Lena's attitude. "Crystal clear. But what made you change your mind? Back in the park, you said... What happened?"

"You scared me back there, that's what. I didn't want to say no to you, but I wasn't ready to say yes, so I tried to avoid the entire topic, but you kept pushing me, and it came out stupidly. I'm sorry about that.

Since then I had time to think about it, and I decided to re-consider. It's a woman's prerogative to change her mind, you know."

"I am very glad you did."

"And just before I was about to tell you this, it turned out that you were hiding a bag full of money under your bed because you teamed up with some KGB racketeer to shake down poor businessmen. And for what? To earn the money for our first apartment!"

"I assure you, honey, I am not a racketeer," Jack said, spreading his arms out for inspection. "Just look at me. Too skinny."

"You have to do what you promised."

"Baby, we already agreed. Of course I will give away the money," Jack said without blinking an eye, "to a registered charity."

"What kind of a charity? Not a casino, I hope?"

"No. A proper charity that truly needs it. An orphanage, or something like that."

"That's what I hoped you would say." Lena slipped under the blanket next to Jack and whispered, "that means a lot to me," and then she kissed him. This simple kiss turned into another, sparking off a chain reaction of fiery emotions.

Before falling asleep that night, with his shoulder serving as Lena's pillow, Jack thought of how strangely the day turned out. Getting Sasha's money out of his apartment should be easy; Sergei always has an investment scheme or two. And to top it all off, Lena never even noticed that his apartment still had no running water! What a strange, wonderful day, Jack smiled, holding Lena closely.

## Chapter 23

One of the things Jack grew to admire about Sergei was his ability to create new businesses out of thin air. Re-investing some of the profits from the steel mill, and relying on *ProServe* to eliminate legitimate enemies and pesky competitors alike, Sergei plowed his way into the glamorous world of casinos, nightclubs and fancy restaurants. Each time Sergei invited Jack to share in the spotlight by kindly offering a passive minority ownership interest to his quiet American partner, but Jack always declined, mindful of Lena's dislike of all things flashy.

Perhaps that was for the best, because ever since Sergei opened his first casino, he became surrounded by a wall of heavy security. From the interchangeable tall guys in the front seat of his own 600 Mercedes to the ones who silently monitored hidden cameras and searched the clients upon entry in his casinos, an entourage of burly men became an everyday part of Sergei's life.

The General's men could look as tough and surly as they liked, but Sergei insisted that they treat his clients with respect, because one never knows whom one searches or throws out of the premises. Just in one week, for instance, Sergei opened two more casinos, each with its own distinct flavor. Per owner's invitation, Jack attended both openings, and was amazed to see how different each gaming place was.

The first casino was called "Lux." It had a large bar on the second floor with a few gaming tables, but everyone was busy dancing in the disco on the third floor. Sergei explained that it catered primarily to the yuppies, foreigners and the local bohemian crowd, artists and movie stars. The General's men liked working here because the clients did not carry weapons and were not as prone to drunken violent rages as at Sergei's other casino, the "Dnieper Palace."

Situated directly on the *Dnieper* River in a refurbished old cruise boat, the Dnieper Palace catered to a whole different category of people altogether and, accordingly, had extreme security needs. Each individual in the long queue of Sergei's customers was carefully searched in the pseudo-marbled lobby. The General's men would gently take away a wide assortment of guns and hand-grenades, and issue a receipt for each checked item to assure that it would not to be confused with another client's ammunition.

The security would always return the checked items upon the client's departure, very politely. Failure to do so would result in their immediate use. Unlike the Lux customers, the Dnieper Palace crowd was not friendly, nor particularly intellectual. They were simple street thugs, proudly decked out in their finest black suits, who committed various hits at the request of their bosses. A very colorful group of drunken imbeciles, indeed.

To host the first general assembly of the three major shareholders, Sergei offered one of his new places. Jack approached a beautifully polished mahogany door of a two-story light blue building on *Kontraktova square* promptly at 7:30 p.m., as agreed. An elegantly engraved sign "Red and Black" was prominently displayed on a gold plate.

No additional explanation about the nature of this establishment was offered, except for the two large men, stationed outside the front door. Both were wearing identical black bow ties and white shirts, covered by long dark overcoats. "Good evening, sir," one of the men said, holding open the door for Jack.

"Thanks." They were new soldiers in *ProServe*, ones Jack has not met before. Both were exquisitely polite, suggesting this was a first-class establishment. Inside, Jack noticed the walls with etched murals, vast chandeliers of fragmented glass.

"Hey, buddy, sorry to keep you waiting!" Sergei rushed over to greet Jack. Two tall men shadowed him, each wearing an earplug that was wired to an invisible radio transmitter.

"Can I offer you a drink?" Sergei asked, pointing to his own glass.

"Sure, whatever you're having," Jack replied. Sergei raised two fingers and looked at the waitress. She was standing by the bar, wearing a black mini-cocktail dress with a low-cut top.

Unlike Sergei's other joints, brimming with life, this casino was empty, except for the staff. They remained standing rigidly at their stations because the boss of Kiev was in their presence. This place had dark, somber ambiance. Three blackjack tables and one roulette wheel were scattered throughout the enormous playing area. A cute girl was standing behind the blackjack table. Without any customers to challenge her skills, she looked very bored. "So where are the masses of gamblers?" Jack asked, looking around.

"It's not that kind of a casino," Sergei replied. "This is more of an exclusive club for members only."

"Oh? And what are the privileges?"

"Anything you see here is free of charge, twenty four hours a day, seven days per week. Free gambling, free liquor, free girls. There's a swimming pool and sauna in the basement, luxurious suites upstairs, and those are free, too. Anything a member wants, anytime. Those are the privileges."

"So what's the catch?"

"You have to bring something special to the club to become a member, not just money. Something truly valuable."

"And what's that?"

"That's up to you and me to figure out."

"Here you are," said the waitress. She brought Jack's cocktail in a long, clear glass, properly tempered by ice and a lemon wedge. It was double-strength gin and tonic. "Will there be anything else?" she asked, playfully raising her eyebrow.

"Not yet." Sergei patted the waitress on the perfectly sculpted behind when she turned to leave.

"I'll be right over there if you change your mind," she said. It was abundantly clear that Sergei handpicked his waitresses based purely on their sex appeal.

"Nice place," Jack said to Sergei, raising his glass. "Congratulations."

"Glad you like it. Let me show you the office." Sergei invited Jack to follow him to the corner of the casino.

Sergei's office was made of dark oak. It had a serene atmosphere of a place where serious men could relax while smoking Cuban cigars and sipping fine cognac. A large polished humidor proudly sat on an antique French table with bowlegs, which Sergei used as his office desk. A nearby glass cabinet contained three uniquely shaped bottles with tea-colored liquid, presumably cognac.

Across the desk, at the other end of the office, was a large marble fireplace with a pile of logs. A sofa and two armchairs sat around an antique coffee table, near a large, messy brown bear skin. "Let's have a seat over there." Sergei pointed to one of the chairs. He picked up a remote control from his desk and the fireplace instantly came alive. These were real flames, giving off a barely perceptible smell of gas and sweet forest aroma.

"What a great office," Jack said, sinking into a comfortable chair to the right of the remote-controlled fireplace. An antique coffee table was in front of them, with an ordinary Nike cardboard box in the middle.

"While we're waiting for Alexei to show up, let me show you something." Sergei pushed another button on the remote control. This time a steady, powerful beam of a halogen lamp appeared above the shoe box. With a flair of a French waiter Sergei uncovered the box and took out a rectangular piece of cardboard, wrapped in black velvet. When he unfolded the cover, Jack saw stars, shooting off bright rainbows under the halogen. There must have been at least fifty large sparkling drops of white and blue diamonds, all different shapes and sizes, each giving off a rich spectrum of colors. They burned like fire when Sergei's hand moved the tray.

"These are the so-called blood diamonds from Sierra Leone," Sergei explained. "Stas came to me with a bunch of uncut, raw stones, and I had them cut and polished. Stas says that his buddies can get me a lot more of them, so I made him an associate member of the club. That's what started this whole idea." Sergei moved the velvet tray, containing the clear, shimmering stones, closer to Jack. "That is the hardest substance known to man. Did you know that only a diamond will cut another diamond?"

"Nope." Jack was mesmerized by their intense glow.

Sergei placed the stones directly under the light, and they gave off flashes of color, like small bursts of flames before quickly becoming extinguished. "The diamond is valued based on its color and brilliance. Its high brilliance is due to its ability to bend light, and its fire is caused by dividing that light into rainbow colors. See how they're developed to the maximum?

These are the best diamonds in the world, flawless and colorless or, at worst, with a slightly bluish tint, like pieces of ice."

"I have never seen anything quite like this before," Jack had to admit. "They are incredible."

"And every now and then comes along a true natural rarity, a gem that has its own distinct and strong color. Pink, yellow, green or blue, they are extremely rare, like this one," Sergei picked out a chunky diamond in the shape and size of a quail egg. "Thirty seven point three carats. I paid fifty thousand for it, but it's worth at least ten times that amount! Just look at it!"

Jack gingerly took the precious stone from Sergei's fingers and placed it under the halogen beam. It gave off a faint pink coloration, but being a novice, Jack did not think it was more spectacular than any of the others in Sergei's collection; just much bigger.

"So how much do you think this whole tray costs?" Sergei quizzed Jack.

"I don't know."

"The retail price is about four million. The actual cost of bringing it here is less then a million in cash. The rest, minus some bribes, is pure profit. See? That's what club membership is all about: making money without doing too much work yourself." Sergei paused to light himself a fat cigar. "So what do you say, partner? Wanna join me in a little jewelry business on the side?"

"Actually, maybe." Now Jack knew where he would invest Herr Huber's cash: into gems. Unlike the ostentatious casinos and restaurants, with their implied criminal connections, this was a discreet and clean business venture that even Lena would approve of. "Let's say we actually sell these diamonds and make some profit. How do we get the next batch?"

"Easy: Stas will fly out again and get us some more trinkets," Sergei answered without blinking an eye. "African diamonds, Colombian emeralds, Burmese rubies, they're all within easy reach. Why not place some of your play money on the roulette wheel for a few good spins? Strictly on a case-by-case basis?"

"Sounds like a fun opportunity," Jack thought aloud, "and Lena might like it, too. Put me down for a hundred and fifty grand."

"Women can't get enough of these things." Sergei reached for the diamond tray, picked up the large pink, egg-like diamond and handed it to Jack. "Here, give this one to Lena. Believe me, she will love you for it. Don't worry, you can pay me later." Sergei casually dropped the stone in Jack's pocket. "Say, where the hell is Alexei?"

"Busy running the government," Jack quipped. "Last time I saw him, he was talking about becoming a Parliament member. Something about getting immunity."

"That couldn't hurt, having a partner in the Parliament," Sergei thoughfully puffed on his cigar. "If he's not here soon, we'll have another drink without him."

They did not have to wait long. A few minutes later a knock on the door announced Alexei's arrival. "Come on in, Alexei," Sergei called out. "we're in here."

"Good day, gentlemen," said Alexei, strolling into the office. "I hope you're feeling good. If not, then you certainly will by the time I leave." He sat down on the leather chair across from Jack.

"Care for a Cohiba?" Sergei offered. "And a double cognac?"

"Sorry, but I have to run in a few minutes. Meetings, meetings," Alexei replied, all business. "But here's the situation. As of yesterday, three more steel plants are slated to be sold at the auction to the highest bidder. All bids are sealed, as always, which is great for us. I presume we're interested in participating, right?"

"Generally speaking, yes. But it all depends on which plants are offered, percentage of stock, the purchase price," Sergei said. Sitting in the background, Jack nodded in silent agreement.

"Answers: Krivorosh Metal, Dnipropetrovskiy Steelworks, Azov Piping. Buy them, and you'll have a monster: a vertically integrated group of companies. The same percentages as with UkrSteel, thanks to my lobbying efforts with State Property Fund. At the lowest purchase price possible. If we all pitch in and re-invest our profits, we could become billinaires some day! Well worth the investment, in my humble opinion. Think about it, gentlemen. Sorry, but I really must run. The President does not like to be kept waiting."

"The President?" Jack asked incredulously.

"All Presidents need money for re-election. It's called democracy," Alexei winked at Jack, getting up from his chair. "You guys may want to contribute a little, too. Don't you want to keep the same team in the office for one more term? Businessmen like us could always use the President's support every now and then."

"Amen to that," Sergei smiled to his well-connected partner without promising anything. "Go get them, tiger!"

As soon as Alexei was out of the room, Jack asked, "so what do you think about that little offer?"

"Personally, I wouldn't mind investing into those factories. There's no way Alexei could screw us if we pay the same amount of money for proportional percentage of stock. And I can also see the benefits of re-electing our President."

"Especially if Alexei has a personal relationship with the man," Jack added. "I'm in on both counts."

"Then we unanimously agree. The first official gathering of shareholders is hereby adjourned without further delay. And now, how about a friendly game of poker? Or maybe you want to spin the roulette wheel? Did I mention that casinos are truly great money-makers?"

"Many times, but I'm still not interested," Jack replied to Sergei as they walked out of the office into an empty casino. The employees were standing at attention, waiting to serve them.

"You want another drink?" Sergei offered.

"Sure." Jack downed the remains of his gin and tonic as Sergei snapped his fingers at the girl in a black mini-skirt. She nodded, then rushed to the bar to bring over two more cocktails.

"Why not try the blackjack?" Sergei suggested as they passed the rows of green tables.

"Alright, then." Jack took a hundred dollar note from his wallet and placed it in front of the house dealer, a pretty girl in her mid-twenties. She ran a marker across the bill to make sure it was not counterfeit. He joked, "freshly printed and good as new."

"I wouldn't doubt it for a minute," she smiled back while shuffling the cards.

From the very beginning, Jack felt a very congenial atmosphere at the blackjack table. The girl was not an experienced dealer and would regularly overdraw her hand. Every time Jack won, he would share half of his winnings with her, even though he did not have to.

"Another blackjack," the lovely dealer would coo, then Jack would toss half the winnings to her and place the rest in the little green box for the next round.

"Oops, overdraw this time," she said, faking surprise.

"Oh, gosh, I just don't know what to do with all this money," Jack replied. This was not a joke: in several minutes his winnings became uncomfortably large. As Sergei's friend, and business partner, Jack could not just take this money and walk out.

"It's been an interesting evening, Sergei, but I should be getting home," Jack said, leaving all the pretty chips on the table. "Lena is waiting for me."

"Hold on, then, Sasha will take you," Sergei said.

"It's alright, I can grab a taxi," Jack protested, but Sergei would have none of it.

"Sasha, can you drive Jack home?" Sergei said into his sleeve. "We're in the main room, waiting for you."

"Nice toy," Jack said.

"The General thought it was a good idea. He's full of good ideas."

"Are you ready to go?" a familiar voice came from behind. "Sure, Sasha," Jack answered.

"Then let's get you out of here before you lose all your money." Sasha's heavy hand landed on Jack's shoulder. "These people can be ruthless."

"Thanks again for the fun evening," Jack said to Sergei before leaving his new casino. As Jack walked out, flanked by Sasha, he thought of how desperately monotonous and dull the job of security personnel in this casino must be. No steady stream of clients was expected, nor welcome. "See you later, fellows," Jack nodded to the two men, who continued to mind the door in the crisp evening air.

"Good night," one of them yawned indifferently.

Jack and Sasha walked up to a powerful four-wheel drive Toyota Landcruiser, which seemed capable of clawing through the ugliest of terrain. The metal brush-guards with two enormous lamps welded firmly onto the front guard made the vehicle look as aggressive as its owner. Sasha pushed a button, unlocking the doors. Inside, pungent aroma of leather interior filled the car.

Sasha calmly swerved his machine through the narrow Kiev streets at neck-breaking speed, but Jack hardly noticed. His mind replayed the sight of Sergei's diamond tray, sparkling under the light. Out of the blue, Sasha said, "listen, do you want to come to my birthday party?"

"Sure, that sounds great," Jack replied automatically. "How old are you going to be?"

"Thirty three. Just like Jesus when they finally nailed the poor bastard," Sasha joked. "It's going to be a few of my friends, getting together for some shashlik and wine."

"When and where?"

"I'll pick you up at 10 a.m. on Saturday. You'll have a great time, I promise."

"Thanks," Jack said as Sasha turned onto *Gorky* Street. "That's my building."

Sasha pulled up to the doorway and said, as Jack stepped out, "see you on Saturday." Then he honked twice before roaring away into the night.

The author (center) with the real-life steel barons in Sergei's casino "for members only"

The author with Victor and Sasha in Sergei's restaurant, *The Camelot*

The real Jack Parker, enjoying his cigar in Sergei's backyard in San Francisco

"Me, worry?" says Jack, joking around one of *ProServe's* bulletproof Cadillacs

Lena in Kiev, a few days before her departure to
San Francisco

Lena is exploring San Francisco on a moped

**Lena visits Paris on her way to San Francisco**

Lena Ropaeva in San Francisco

**Sergei, entering his office on *Proriznaya* street**

**Sergei, with his own "scales of justice"**

**John Paul Hatchet, persona non-grata in most civilized countries, in a very good mood**

**John Paul Hatchet in a rather foul mood**

**General Kurkov before heading up *ProServe***

**General Kukov one month after joining *ProServe*, with his new Mercedes**

**Antonio Garibaldi, worried about his security**

**Sasha Artamonov, chief of *ProServe's* enforcement branch, smiling for the camera**

Sasha, frowning at the camera

Victor at home

Stas, preparing for another assignment

**Stas Melnichenko, veteran of all three wars in Yugoslavia**

**Lydia Ivanovna in her kitchen**

Oleg Abramov's yacht, The *Aesthasea*, one kilometer from the shore of Cap d'Antibes

Alexei lands on Abramov's yacht in style

Grisha-the-cook, carving up a roasted pig. Note the bullet-proof wall in the background

Grisha-the-cook, offering his finest moonshine

**A rare photograph of Johar Aslanbeck in a relaxed mood**

**Johar Aslanbeck, having his usual "quiet conversation" with a debtor**

**Last known photo of Johar Aslanbeck, captured on KBG cameras**

The boys from *ProServe's* in front of the *Shevchenko* park

Doctor Zimmer at home in Palo Alto after Yana's sudden disappearance

Presentation "Meet The Steel Barons" took place on November 5, 2007, before the Kiev International Womens' Club

Jack Parker, at the November 5 presentation, explaining how becoming partners with Sergei and Alexei helped him to become rich

**Alexei Glushko, describing how he paid $800 million for a steel mill worth over $4.8 billion**

**Alexei, showing his favorite negotiation technique that is commonly employed in steel business**

The author with Viktor after book presentation

The afterparty in Sergei's casino

**Kiev, summer, Sunday, wedding**

Kiev in summertime: taking a stroll through the *Shevchenko* park

Preachers and beggars on *Kreschatik*

**Kiev in the summertime: marriage agencies and wax museums**

**Bogdan sells souvenirs to the tourists on *Andreevskiy Spusk***

**Kiev center is always fun, always with flags**

**Our beautiful and beloved city, Kiev**

# Chapter 24

The next morning Jack dropped off Herr Huber's cash at Sergei's club on his way to work. With the tainted debt collection money out of his apartment, it was Lena's turn to live up to her end of the bargain. From now on, Jack would wake up every morning to see her lovely smile. All he needed was a receipt from a non-profit company in case Lena did not trust him. For a determined lawyer like Jack Parker, this was an easy task.

When his computer screen opened to a new file, Jack typed a letter to himself from Mr. Alastair Bogswell. It sounded like a solid name for a director of an English non-profit organization Jack created and named "Help the Children." His brief letter of self-praise went as follows:

*"Dear Mr. Parker:*

*As a small charity, dedicated to improving lives of unfortunate children in central Africa, we are most grateful for your great humanitarian gesture and the extraordinary gift that accompanied it.*

*Thank you very much, Alastair Bogswell, Director"*

Then Jack created a bogus receipt from Mr. Bogswell's organization for one hundred and fifty thousand dollars, the precise amount he had agreed to donate, and not one penny more. Jack sent both pages to his HP laser printer and smiled. The computer fonts looked good enough to him. After all the loose ends were neatly wrapped up, Jack called Lena at work.

"Podium, may I help you?"

"It's me. Is Lena there?"

"One moment," the receptionist replied and then Jack heard elevator music. The line clicked, causing his heart to skip a beat.

"Hello, you," Lena's voice purred over the line. "How are things in the legal arena? Are you bored again?"

"This time I actually have a good reason for calling you."

"Which is?"

"It's not a telephone conversation. How about if I drop by your office and pick you up around six? Is that alright?"

"Is it anything serious?" Lena sounded worried.

"It's a surprise."

"How about a hint?"

"That was it: be ready at six o'clock. And tell your security not to shoot at my car."

"I'll see what I can do," Lena laughed. "Catch you later."

Sitting in the office, Jack reflected on his new life: he was a shareholder in a huge factory with an inside track to buy a few more steel plants, plus an owner of a boutique corporate law firm, with the most gorgeous girl in Kiev. Things just could not get any better.

The magic hour of 5 p.m. arrived and Jack rushed out the door, trailed by his driver, Volodya. They stopped by the Bessarabsky market to pick up a bouquet of flowers. Seeing the gorgeous roses, elegant tulips and fluffy carnations, Jack wanted to buy them all. Volodya wisely cautioned him that they would not all fit into his car, so Jack settled for three dozen of the finest, ruby-red long-stem roses. The flower sellers seldom get buyers like Jack in the middle of winter, but he had an excellent reason for this excess: he and Lena were moving in together!

By the time Jack reached Podium, it was nearly six o'clock; Volodya's timing was impeccable. As they agreed, at precisely 6 p.m. the heavy metal door opened slightly and Lena slipped outside, wearing a furry fox coat. She skipped down the stairs towards Jack and he greeted her by holding out a thick bouquet of roses.

"You must be crazy buying flowers in the winter," she laughed, smelling the delicate aroma, "they must be so expensive!"

"It's nothing in comparison to seeing you happy, just like this." At that moment, all Jack could see was a little girl, beaming at him with gratitude. Then he reached into the car and pulled out the second bouquet. The sight on her face was worth far more than any flowers. Grinning, he brought her closer and they stood there, kissing in the frosty air, video taped by Podium's security cameras. "Let's get out of here," Jack finally said.

"And where are you taking me?"

"That's part of the surprise."

When Lena climbed into the back seat, she saw the last batch of roses. "Did you buy out the whole market?" she asked incredulously. "These are awfully expensive!"

"But perfectly appropriate for the occasion."

"What are you talking about?"

"I guess you don't remember our little deal. A certain exchange you agreed to?"

"Exchange?"

"So where are we going, boss?" Volodya looked at Jack through the rear-view mirror.

"I'm sorry, Lena, but what's your address?"

"Twenty five *Kominterna* Street," she answered without hesitation.

"We're going to *Kominterna* twenty five, Volodya," Jack said.

"Why?" Lena asked.

"Two reasons. First, I've never seen where you live."

"Alright. And the second reason?"

"Read this." Jack handed to Lena a glowing "thank you" letter from an obscure British non-profit organization called Help the Children. "Does this ring a bell about our little deal?"

"So you actually did it. I didn't think you would, but you did. You are a really decent guy, not one of them."

"Finally, you believe me."

"But why did you have to give the money to England? They are so rich and we have so many orphanages here in Ukraine," she lamented.

"Sorry, I didn't think it mattered. The next time you'll tell me precisely what charity you want me to donate to, and I'll gladly do it."

"Thank you, Jack. You don't know how much this means to me."

"But now that I held up my end of the deal, what do you say? Ready to pack your bags?"

"So that's your surprise! Well, I always keep my word. Let's go pack!"

Jack and Lena were still kissing in the back seat when Volodya parked his car in front of her building. He coughed politely to let his passengers know they had arrived.

Jack followed Lena into the building entrance, where a strong stench of urine hung heavy in the air. "How nice," Jack mumbled, trying to get his eyes adjusted to the darkness.

"Kids steal the light bulbs," Lena explained.

"While urinating?"

"No, that's the homeless. They sleep here at night."

"Lovely."

The elevator did not work, so they walked up six flights of stairs. By the time Jack made it to Lena's apartment, he was out of breath. "Sorry if you're not used to this, but here it is, my place," Lena said while turning the key. Her apartment was small, consisting of two tiny rooms, a toilet with a stand-up shower and a narrow kitchen. In comparison, Jack's apartment was a luxury suite at the Four Seasons.

With Jack's active participation, Lena was fully packed in less than twenty minutes because all of her belongings easily fit into two large suitcases, with room to spare. In another hour Lena's wardrobe occupied the right side of Jack's closet. It all happened too quickly, without any fanfare or fireworks, but at last Jack and Lena moved in together.

## Chapter 25

Jack was on his way home from work when he stumbled upon a homeless man. The bum was so drunk that he was crawling on his knees towards the courtyard. Jack stopped in front of his apartment building, allowing the drunkard to pass. How can people degrade themselves like this, Jack thought, following the man with his eyes. And there are so many of them.

\* \* \*

By now, the pain was eating away at his entire left side, but Boris Vladimirovich continued towards the safety of the alleyway. He wanted to get away from the main street, far from the public view, to take off his jacket and see how badly they got him, but he just could not muster up the strength. The metallic bloody taste in the mouth was making him sick. Drained, Boris sat down on the curb of the sidewalk.

The heavy winter overcoat covered a small, deep hole in the right side, where the kids stuck him with a screwdriver. Damned fool, he thought, I should have given them the money. What's some change, anyway? Boris hoped to slow down the steady stream of blood, dripping from under his filthy jacket onto the pavement. His sticky hand applied pressure to the wound, but it did not help much.

No one paid attention to the pale, elderly, unshaved man, who was sitting alone on a snow-covered sidewalk. In turn, Boris did not bother to look up at the busy people, running somewhere under the falling snowflakes to keep their precious appointments. He never understood their world anyway.

The passing cars spewed out carbon monoxide fumes, throwing muddy slush on his legs, but Boris did not flinch. Instead, his tired eyes focused on a thin, naked tree across the street. It looked very frail, like those trees in East Siberian tundra. With each difficult breath age-old memories began to emerge, one after another, too vivid for any movie.

\* \* \*

Borya heard the sound of their boots before anyone else did. Sure enough, soon after came a knock on the door. His father, Vladimir, heard it also. The last member of the Central Committee to be arrested, he immediately recognized this visit for what it was. All of his colleagues were taken away earlier the very same way, in the middle of the night. Branded as "enemies of the people," they were never heard from again. Their families disappeared afterwards.

Vladimir turned in bed and hugged his wife, Tamara, for the last time. "Be brave, my love," he said to her before getting up. Always a heavy sleeper, Tamara had not woken up yet. She did not realize what was happening as she cuddled her husband in the middle of sweet dreams. They knocked much harder the second time. That is when Tamara's eyes flew wide open in knowing panic. It was half past two in the morning, and this visit could only mean one thing: it was their turn. She looked at Vladimir, as if to ask, is this really happening to us?

"Comrade Pavlov, open the door immediately!" someone quietly ordered from the stairwell. There was no use in resisting, so Vladimir obediently went to unlock the door. He smiled weakly as he passed Boris' bed, and said gently, "it's alright, Borya. Everything will be fine. Go back to sleep."

But Boris could not. Through the wall he could hear his mother's voice. Then three strange men, all wearing long leather overcoats, entered his bedroom. They rudely ransacked everything in sight, searching for something they could not find. Boris kept crying, but his mother did not try to stop them. When the men left, she followed them into the stairwell, screaming from the top of her lungs, "where are you taking him?"

Last memory Boris had of his father were those final words, "everything will be fine, go back to sleep." The next day his mother was arrested, and a week after that Boris was sent away on a long train journey. That is where he saw these trees. Thin and frail, they cast long shadows against the white snow of incomprehensibly enormous Siberian tundra.

\* \* \*

"Wake up, old man, I know you can hear me. Time to move along." Boris opened his eyes with difficulty. He could barely make out the shadows of three men towering above him. Boris tried to explain that he has been stabbed, that he needs medical help, but the man prodded him with a nightstick and said, "get going."

"Hey, the sergeant is talking to you."

Boris looked at a young policeman with unfocused eyes and tried to get up, but it was no use. Another wave of nausea came around and he coughed, spitting blood. "I am the enemy of the people since 1937," he uttered. "*Norilsk* zone number four. You bastards already took my life. What more can you do to me?"

Gathering himself, Boris called upon the willpower that helped him survive incarceration in Soviet Union's harshest facilities. Just like when you escaped from those sadists, Boris kept repeating, you must get up and keep going. This time, however, his body refused to obey.

\* \* \*

By 1954 Boris had spent seventeen years in the colonies, including the notorious *Norilsk* camps. He knew that each breakout carries severe consequences in case of failure: facing the wrath of the *hozyain*, the camp's warden. Still, Boris decided to run in late summer, when the swamps dried up. It had to be in the morning so the guards would only discover his absence during the evening count, after they had returned to the camp.

When the convoy of prisoners crossed a narrow wood bridge, stretching over a creek, on their way to cut down the gigantic tree trunks, Boris slipped in the mud and disappeared into the deep ravine. Ten minutes later he emerged fifty meters downstream, scraped up and dripping wet, and headed towards the railroad tracks. They would lead him to the train station.

Gray afternoon drizzled wet his greasy stubble as Boris stubbornly made his way through the marshes. He tasted the rain, mixed with his own sweat, and smiled. Soon he would be resting in an empty cattle car, free as a butterfly, going wherever the train took him. By mid-afternoon the swamps gave way to a thick, wild forest. Hungry and exhausted, Boris pushed himself, step-by-step. When he reached the tracks, Boris cautiously walked along in the shadow of the forest until the train station came into view.

Positioning himself behind the thick bushes, Boris spied an overnight, long-distance train, preparing to depart from the first track. He remained hidden, waiting to see if any NKVD agents would make themselves known. There were none. Boris took a deep breath and walked out of the woods.

As he casually approached the station, sweeping the area for any signs of danger, Boris noticed a man who was staring right at him. "Damn," Boris muttered under his breath and sprinted forward, running over tracks. The search party started earlier than he hoped. His mind replayed the image of the surprise, written on the man's face at having unexpectedly spotted his prey.

The NKVD agent, assigned to watch the train station for signs of an escaped convict, quickly recovered from his initial shock. He started to chase after Boris, unsuccessfully trying to pull out his handgun along the way. Being younger and more desperate, Boris reached the parallel track first, and rolled under the train wagon, emerging on the other side. The man followed, climbing awkwardly under the first train.

Pumping with adrenaline, Boris dove under the second train, all the while looking for any possible escape routes. With the agent approaching fast, Boris climbed into the nearest empty wagon and held his breath. Through the cracks in the walls he watched the enemy wandering nearby, searching for him under the cars. The agent looked for more than ten minutes before giving up. He went back to the train station empty-handed. Meanwhile, the overnight train that Boris hoped to catch was long gone.

As the evening set in, Boris nervously waited in his empty cattle car, praying for the train to start moving. It never did. Instead, a military truck with several soldiers and their German shepherds arrived. The ferocious animals quickly sniffed out precisely where Boris was hiding. The soldiers delivered him to the zone, straight into warden's paws. The beatings that followed at the hands of the guards left Boris with a punctured eardrum and a broken arm that never properly healed.

* * *

"Fellas, looks like we have another candidate for the school of hard knocks. I'm going to need a courtesy wagon at the corner of *Gorky* and *Saksaganskogo*." The sergeant spoke with authority into the hand-held radio, looking at the homeless drunk sitting at his feet.

"We have one just around the corner," Boris could hear the robotic voice over the radio, answering the policeman. "It's on the way."

"Hold on, chief," the younger officer said to his sergeant. "This guy went through the camps. It's not right. Not after what he's been through."

"Get him out of my sight," the sergeant pronounced his final ruling. Then he added aside, into the radio, "cancel the wagon."

Boris knew the Soviet system all too well and could not believe this unexpected turn of fortune. If they decided to take him to a detoxification cell in his condition, Boris surely would not survive this time. Through the years he had spent his share of nights in that piss-smelling cell full of drunk and violent bums. Each time he swore that he would not wind up in there again.

Gathering his remaining strength, Boris pulled himself towards the nearby apartment building. The police patrol slowly moved down the street. The pedestrians strolled by, some openly disgusted at seeing another hopeless alcoholic, crawling on the pavement. They walked around Boris as he stubbornly headed for the safety of the alleyway behind the apartment building.

The short journey took a long time. At last Boris reclined against the icy brick wall, trying to catch his breath. To his left was a large trash dumpster, heaving with garbage. Boris always hated strong odors, but he could not pull himself away.

He reached out for a cigarette butt that lay nearby and placed it between his lips. "Kids don't have any respect these days, taking money from a homeless man," Boris mumbled to himself. "Probably for cigarettes, too. What a terrible habit." He kept the unlit butt hanging from the corner of the mouth. It was getting cold. So bone numbing, brutally cold that he could no longer feel his legs.

"Excuse me, but this is a decent building," a woman's voice came to Boris, forcing him to open his eyes.

"And I am a decent person, lady," he responded weakly. "The problem is, this is not a decent country. Look at what school children did to me. Is this decent?"

Seeing the trail of blood from a fresh, open wound, Lydia Ivanovna gasped, "you're not drunk, you need medical help!"

"Too late, I'm afraid. Besides, who will pay the medics? You?"

"Don't you worry about that. I just need to get to a telephone. I live in this building, and... But I can't leave you alone like this. Just lean on me, and we'll get into the elevator together." Lydia barely managed to lift Boris. Using her tiny body as a crutch, she guided him toward the doorway. "Let's just hope the elevator works."

## Chapter 26

"Hello, Sergei?" Dr. Zimmer's voice came over long distance line.

"Yes?"

"I need your advice, and I am willing to pay for it."

"What's this about, Dr. Zimmer?"

"It's about Yana, my wife. She's gone out of control. Spending left and right, like there's no tomorrow. Then I found out she has a Russian boyfriend, so I told her we're getting a divorce, but she went to see a lawyer and it's going to be very costly."

"How costly?"

"She knows all about my business. She could have my license pulled, and she knows it. She wants a million dollars plus my house. Can you do something about it?"

"What are you suggesting?"

"I want a divorce. Permanent. Without paying that bitch any alimony or handing over my property. You know what I mean? Can you do that?"

Sergei rubbed his hands in anticipation. By his estimate, Dr. Zimmer would gladly pay a nice chunk of change to get rid of her, a service that required comparatively little of Sergei's personal time. The only issue was the price. "My divorce fees are expensive. Three hundred thousand," Sergei opened the negotiations.

"What?"

"In return, you get to keep your money, property, plus the license. Nobody would ever question why this unfaithful wife decided to leave you."

"How about one hundred?"

"Three hundred thousand, Dr. Zimmer, paid in advance," Sergei closed the negotiations without giving up a penny. "If you agree, I will fax to you my account numbers, and after the money is wired, you will send me your wife's photo, ok?"

"But how do I know you will deliver on your end after I wire the funds?"

"I guess you will just have to trust me. Or go to one of your lawyers. Have a nice day, Dr. Zimmer."

"Alright, I'll be in touch," Dr. Zimmer said and the line went dead.

Sergei pushed an intercom button on his phone and said, "can you ask General Kurkov to come in?" There was a slim chance the General would have the right connections in America, but it was worth a quick consultation.

"Sir?" General Kurkov opened the door and walked in, "you wanted to see me?"

"Yes, General. Can I offer you a cup of coffee?"

"No, thank you, sir."

"Have a seat, please. Let me ask you a question, and please think about it before you answer. Do you have any colleagues working in Moscow?"

"In Moscow?"

"Yes, Moscow." Sergei eagerly waited for the General's reply. In comparison to cash-strapped Ukraine, Moscow was a much wealthier place due to its natural abundance of oil and gas, plus gold, platinum, diamonds and other earthly minerals. Plugging into a global enforcement infrastructure would be easier in Moscow, Sergei reasoned, if only the General knew a reliable, serious person.

"Actually, the only man who I trust with my life happens to live in Moscow. We went through hell together in the Second World War. Maybe that's why we remained so close through the years. Last I heard from him was a few months ago."

Sergei shook his head. "No, I am not talking about old war time buddies. I mean somebody like you, a former military *shishka*, an ex-head honcho. Somebody who is still involved in the business, though. You know what I mean?"

"That's what I am trying to tell you, sir. Gavril is not only a dear, thoughtful old friend, but he's also the chief of worldwide security for senior staff of TuymenNeft. It's an oil company. He's done very nicely for himself, invites me to visit his dacha all the time."

Sure enough, due to the nature of his profession, Gavril Alexandrovich Dvornikov had criminal connections, but Sergei could not imagine how extensive they really were. Even his old Kiev war buddy, General Kurkov, was impressed to learn that Gavril had an excellent working relationship with various Eurasian underworld groups. His great allies were the Budapest-based Mogilevich organization and the *Solntsevskaya* group, Moscow's largest criminal enterprise with more than five thousand members worldwide. It was that easy for Sergei to find the right connection.

"Just send me the address and a photograph or two," Gavril said over a secure phone to his old friend, "and I'll get somebody on this matter immediately. But only on the condition that you visit me this summer!"

"Thanks, Gavril, I will," General Kurkov smiled. "And say hello to Katya."

In less than two hours, Sergei managed to borrow a *Solntsevsky tenevik* to help out Dr. Zimmer, without ever agreeing to pay anything to anybody.

\* \* \*

During the late 1980's and early 1990's, the U.S. opened its borders to people from the Soviet republics. In 1992 alone, one hundred twenty nine thousand visitor visas were issued to persons from Ukraine, Belarus and Russia. Many of these visitors never left, settling in easy-to-hide large cities like New York, Chicago, Philadelphia and Los Angeles.

Of them, some were legitimate individuals, reluctant to return to their homes. Others, in Russian language, were so-called *teneviki*, or "the shadow people," living outside the law. They are the undocumented residents of the former Soviet republics who, for whatever reason, ended up with no permanent place of residence anywhere.

A rather somber group of professionals by any standard, the "shadow people" work either as freelancers or as part of a larger organized group with roots in Russia or another East-block country. Specializing in murder, kidnapping and extortion the *teneviki* travel freely throughout the United States and Europe on various assignments and then quickly escape to the anonymity of their little quiet neighborhoods.

* * *

Exhilarated by her Wednesday marathon shopping spree, Yana proudly walked out of Nieman Marcus store carrying six large shopping bags, three in each hand. She simply adored her daily spending binges in the fashionable Stanford shopping center, in sunny Palo Alto, California, on Dr. Zimmer's account. Strolling slowly in her high heels, wearing a white tennis mini-skirt, Yana looked every bit the part of a trashy young trophy wife of a fat, millionaire that she was.

Yana stopped under a short palm tree that was planted along the walkway. For a brief moment she considered getting a cup of rich cappuccino at the French-inspired outdoor cafe. She glanced at her gold Cartier watch and decided against it. Yana wanted to get home before her hubby arrived from work.

In the parking lot, on the way to her new white Lexus, Yana did not pay much attention to the maroon Chevy van that was parked next to her car, nor to its owner, a large man who was busy inspecting the front passenger tire. Yana pushed the remote control button on her key chain and the Lexus trunk popped open, allowing her to deposit the new dresses.

She got in the driver's seat, inserted the key into the ignition and started the engine. Unexpectedly, the van's burly owner opened Yana's door. His mad eyes glared at her hypnotically, distracting Yana from looking down at the syringe in his right hand.

"What do you want from me?" Yana asked her assailant in English, frightened for her life. "Take my wallet, my purse, take everything, just let me go!" Then she felt a long needle stinging her arm. Feeling dizzy almost at once, Yana never made the connection between Dr. Zimmer and this seemingly random act of violence. "What do you want?" she repeated, fading into oblivion. Then her forehead bumped lightly against the steering wheel.

The *tenevik* looked around to make sure there were no witnesses, then he easily lifted Yana out of the Lexus and stretched her out in the back of his van. She was unconscious, light and passive. Quite a beautiful young girl, he noticed, it's almost a shame to hand her over to the fat Polish pimp in Queens.

The *tenevik* took the car keys out of the ignition and carefully placed them under the drivers' floor mat. Then he swiped the sleeve to obliterate any fingerprints and locked the door. In another hour her American husband will open the car with a separate set of keys and drive away, like nothing ever happened. It was a perfect crime since nobody would report Yana as missing.

\* \* \*

"Our client, Dr. Zimmer, called to thank you, General," Sergei said to the elderly man sitting in front of him. "And please thank Gavril for me. Tell him I am truly grateful."

"But how should I thank him?" General Kurkov asked, and then regretted being so direct. "I mean, what should I say to him?"

Sergei reached under his desk and placed a thin leather attache case on his desk. "This contains one hundred thousand dollars for Gavril. And I included a box of cigars, just in case we'll need to call on him again. Please pass them along when you see Gavril, with my best wishes. The important thing is that he knows how much I appreciate the favor."

"Of course. I will relay this."

As the General turned to leave the office, Sergei added, "there is another package of fifty grand in there. It's for you. Please don't forget to keep it."

"Thank you, sir," the General said modestly and closed the door after himself.

Though Sergei made only a hundred fifty thousand dollars, which was peanuts by his standards, he had no regrets about helping Dr. Zimmer. The newfound business relationship with the Moscow power structures was far more valuable.

# Chapter 27

The first few blissful weeks of living together had passed, allowing Lena to settle in. Having been married before, Jack diligently kept the lid on his toothpaste and the toilet seat in a horizontal position at all times. One thing Jack neglected to consider was their diet.

On a Sunday morning, after finishing breakfast, Lena announced: "today I want to teach you how to shop properly. No more frozen chickens from Germany or tinned fish from Hungary. You are in Ukraine, a country famous for its pork and potatoes, and all your food comes from freezers and tin cans! The only decent meals you bring home are from restaurants, and I don't like eating your clients' leftovers. Do all foreigners live like this?"

"They're my leftovers," Jack mumbled in his defense. "Besides, everybody knows that local produce is poisoned with Chernobyl radiation. Milk, cheese, mushrooms, it's all pure cancer in small doses. No, thank you."

"This radiation is all in your head," she shot back. "Every person in Kiev eats locally grown food, and do you see any two-headed mutants walking around? You have to stop behaving like a foreigner and start living a normal life. That's why I'm taking you grocery shopping today."

"If you feel that strongly, fine, but if anything starts glowing in my refrigerator, I quit."

"Agreed. First, let's try the *Bessarabsky* market. Have you ever been there?"

"Once. To get you flowers."

"Then you haven't really been there. And it's a wonderful, wonderful morning," Lena sang out loud, reaching for her winter coat, "so we are going shopping, shopping, shopping."

"Like an old married couple," Jack added, grabbing his heavy overcoat on the way out.

"That's perfect," Lena said as they walked out the door. "We're going to be just like my parents: a married old couple that still holds hands in the street. Now, give me your hand, and don't you dare to let go until we get to the market."

"You got it." Jack grabbed her by the waist when they got into the elevator. "But you have to kiss me first, and don't stop until we reach the first floor." Without hesitation Lena puckered up her lips and they embraced, kissing softly at first, then more passionately, until the elevator doors opened.

Standing in front of Jack and Lena was a short woman, no taller than five feet, blocking their exit. In her right hand was an empty garbage bucket. The woman wore an old-fashioned wool coat with a heavy scarf wrapped all around her head, but Jack recognized her eyes: it was Lydia Ivanovna.

"What a wonderful time, to be young and in love..." Lydia peeled off her scarf and looked at them, but did not move an inch out of the way.

"That's such a nice thing to say," Lena replied. "You are very kind."

"Can we get out of here before the doors close?" Jack interrupted them.

"I was like you once, you know," Lydia continued, "but that was so long ago. It was a different time, too."

"Food?" Jack reminded Lena, pushing past Lydia into the hallway.

"No, not today," Lydia said. "Boris Vladimirovich is still recovering. He needs food more than I do. For me, a cup of tea and a slice of bread is enough these days. But thank you for asking."

"Oh. Then we will bring you something back from the market," Lena said without missing a beat. "We're going there anyway. What apartment do you live in?"

"Just two floors above this nice foreign man," Lydia nodded to Jack. She added quietly to Lena, as if Jack could not hear her, "he can be generous sometimes." Then she stepped into the elevator and pushed a black button. "Good bye, grandchildren," Lydia waved just before the elevator doors slammed together, taking her up and away.

Without saying anything Jack and Lena walked out of the apartment building into a bright, sunny winter morning. Fresh snow had fallen overnight, covering yesterday's street grime, giving the city a white, pure appearance. It was a beautiful beginning to a marvelous day. When Jack reached out for Lena's hand, however, she pulled away from him. "What's wrong?" Jack asked. "Are you alright?"

"No," she answered. They crossed *Gorky* Street, watching out for icy patches. "Didn't you see anything? This grandmother went to throw away garbage, which is very dangerous for her. One careless slip on the ice can easily result in a broken hip or leg. And what doctor will help her without money? Who will bring her food when she lies in bed for weeks? That's why you never see old people walking on the streets in the winter. Did you know that, or don't you care?"

"How about her relatives?"

"My grandmother broke a hip, and the doctor in her village couldn't fix it. She had all the friends and relatives around her day and night, but she died soon afterwards anyway. Your neighbor just told you that she has had nothing to eat, and you ask about her relatives? What does that say about you? That you have no feelings, that's what!"

"Hold it right there," Jack countered Lena's accusation before she got the wrong impression. "I have plenty of feelings for any fellow human being, but I also know this woman. Do you want to know how we met? She broke into my mailbox, stole my mail, and then had the nerve to return it in exchange for a bottle of vodka. This old lady is a con artist and an alcoholic, too. Sorry, but that's the truth." It came off sounding a little cold, so Jack quickly added, "but I completely agree with you that what happens to the old people around here is just terrible. A real crime."

"You are a foreigner, Jack, so you probably won't understand me, but I'll try explaining it to you. This woman had survived World War II. She is the last of the generation, which liberated this land from the Nazis. My grandparents were a part of that generation, too, before they passed away. Everyone in Ukraine had someone in their families killed in that war. And having lived through it all, your neighbor is probably surviving by collecting empty bottles on the streets for refunds, or maybe begging on the corners. What if she went outside not to throw out her garbage, but to look for leftover food? Ah, nobody cares, not our own government, and certainly not foreigners like you." Then, almost to herself, Lena continued, "still, showing just a little kindness to that old lady wouldn't have hurt you one bit."

"You are wrong, I do care about people," Jack protested vigorously, "but this particular grandmother is different. She is a dangerous psycho. She once called a riot squad with submachine guns on my next door neighbor!"

Yet, Lena defended Lydia Ivanovna to the end. "Everyone of us has their own quirks and peculiarities. Especially the older generation."

After that exchange, Jack and Lena walked in silence down *Lev Tolstoy* Street, towards the *Bessarabsky* market, and he thought about her angry words. Finally Jack said, "do you know what I really like about you?

Under that beautiful face and gorgeous body, you are a very kind, generous person. A warm human being."

"I bet you say that to all your live-in girlfriends. But thanks for the flattery anyway."

"It wasn't flattery, or even a compliment. This was my honest opinion. Thank you for the lesson in humanity. It did not go wasted."

"You're welcome." Lena took hold of Jack's hand once again, which meant that he was forgiven.

Passing through the thick black iron gates of the *Bessarabsky* market, Jack noticed the glass counters, full of exotic seafood: piles of smoked eel, rows of jars with black and red caviar, whole sturgeon, bags of frozen shrimp, anything your wallet can afford. "I didn't see this part of the market last time," Jack said, eyeing the thick sturgeon steaks. "And I bet you this fish is not irradiated, either."

"The sturgeon is from the Caspian Sea," said the plump saleswoman with rosy cheeks. "Fresh or smoked. Delicious. Want to try a piece?"

"Not yet." Jack made a mental note of this counter in case he had to prepare another exotic dinner.

"Over there are your flowers." Lena pointed towards the end of the market. "The fruits are in that section, and the meats are on the other side. The fowl is way over there. Shall we go?"

Holding hands, they walked through the isles among tanned Georgians and Azerbaijani men, screaming to sell their cantaloupes and figs. Across the way, sturdy Ukrainian grandmothers from the villages peddled salty pickles, marinated tomatoes and buckets of sauerkraut. Further along, the butchers displayed skinny, semi-plucked chickens, fat ducks, huge slabs of beef and pork and, of course, that unique Ukrainian delicacy, salted *salo*. Every sales person Jack and Lena passed along the way called out to them, trying to capture their attention.

"How much are your pickles?" Jack asked a little grandmother, who was standing behind one of the counters.

"Two currencies," she replied promptly, eyeballing him with interest.

"What currencies are you talking about, grandmother?" Lena asked her.

"My daughter told me that foreigners should always pay with hard currency, and I want two." She raised two dirty fingers in the air.

"From now on, leave the bargaining to me," Lena said, leading Jack away from the greedy grandmother. "It'll be a lot cheaper."

Lena's approach was simple: each time she would haggle and then turn away. At the risk of losing a paying customer, the sellers quickly knocked off several grivna without any arguments. It was an adventure to walk through that colorful farmers' market with Lena as Jack's guide. In all, they bought two chickens, one for themselves and the other for Lydia, as well as potatoes, tomatoes, cucumbers, tangerines and apples. By the time Lena finished teaching Jack the basics of grocery shopping, he was loaded with four heavy plastic bags, brimming with fresh produce.

When they returned home, Lena insisted on delivering Lydia Ivanovna's package to her immediately. Standing at Lydia's doorstep, Lena pushed the doorbell button and they heard footsteps approaching the door. A round peephole turned dark, indicating that someone was looking at them. "Who is there?" Lydia asked, just in case.

"It's your neighbors from below," Lena said. The lock turned, then another, and the door opened, revealing Lydia in an old, worn-out bathrobe. "We brought you the food as we promised. A little bit of everything: chicken, potatoes, some fruits," Lena said.

"For me? You brought this for me?" Lydia asked suspiciously. "But why?"

"Because you are our neighbor," Jack answered brightly, hoping that Lena would appreciate his participation.

"Well, Boris Vladimirovich is a little tired, but I'm sure he would want to meet you. Come in, please." Lydia stepped aside to let Jack and Lena inside. They followed Lydia into her living room, which looked exactly the same as Jack's, only tidier. An old man was sitting comfortably in an armchair by a lampshade, reading a newspaper. Jack was not sure, but he felt that he had seen him somewhere before.

"Boris Vladimirovich, these are our neighbors, the foreigner and his nice wife," Lydia introduced Jack and Lena. "They brought us fresh produce from the *Bessarabka*, so tomorrow I will make you a real chicken soup. How about that?"

"Thank you." Boris took off his reading glasses and leveled his stern gaze at the surprise guests. "It is very kind of you."

"Don't mention it," Lena replied. "It's nothing in comparison to what you did for our country."

"Me? What exactly did I do?" The old man sounded surprised.

"Why, your whole generation protected our nation during the war, at a terrible cost," Lena passionately replied. "You know, fighting the Nazis, then rebuilding the motherland. I mean, your generation was made of real heroes. You sacrificed everything for us, and now nobody even thanks you. So Jack and I just wanted to say thank you this way."

"I am sorry, young lady, but you are talking to the wrong person," Boris replied. "You see, I have been the son of the enemy of the people since 1937. This country killed my parents and sent me to the labor camps. You seem like a nice young couple, not your regular scam artists. But let me repeat, just in case you did not hear me the first time: if you came here looking for a war veteran with a collection of expensive medals to steal, then you are talking to the wrong man. I am not your hero; quite the opposite."

Both Jack and Lena were stunned to hear such ingratitude and accusations, but Lena recovered quicker than Jack did. "Our being here has nothing to do with your medals," she said. "My grandfather fought for this country during the war. He lost both of his legs and yet somehow he survived. He didn't have that many medals, but he was a real hero."

"You should give your food to him, then," Boris replied and picked up his newspaper. "I'm sure he deserves it more than I do."

"He died two years ago, otherwise I would!" Lena exclaimed, almost crying. "It was a pleasure to meet you, Lydia Ivanovna, but we must be going now."

"Good evening," Jack said and followed Lena.

"Don't forget your groceries," the old man called behind them.

"No, leave everything here," Lena said to Jack. "For her. Our bags, too."

By the expression on Lena's face, Jack could tell that something just occurred that caused her great emotional pain. When he reached out to touch Lena's shoulder, she ran down two flights of stairs and stood in front of his door, sobbing. It was a depressing way to end an otherwise beautiful afternoon.

"Since you gave away everything we bought, we don't have anything for dinner," Jack said, hoping to change her mood. "How about a nice, quiet restaurant that serves a bowl of hot borsch? With black bread and garlic?"

"That sounds nice," Lena said. "But I prefer sushi."

"Done," Jack readily replied. They walked outside, holding hands, and headed towards Nobu, a new restaurant on Saksagansky Street that specialized in freshly flown-in sushi and delicious, hot sake. Unlike Lydia and Boris, they could easily afford it.

\* \* \*

After locking the door behind her young neighbors, Lydia slowly shuffled back to the living room. She sat down on the sofa near Boris and said, "you didn't tell me anything about the labor camps."

"You didn't ask. And does it really matter, after so many years?"

"Just tell me if you were political or criminal."

"Political. Arrested in thirty seven, amnestied in fifty six, released in fifty seven, like everyone else. Should I leave now or can I stay here until tomorrow morning?"

"I was also arrested," Lydia quietly revealed to a stranger her shameful secret, one she never told to anyone else. "In 1942, just three weeks after my Misha went off to the front. One morning I showed up late for work, and that was enough to get me ten years. I was only seventeen years old, but there I went..."

She looked at Boris and knew that she did not have to continue. Of all the people, he knew how easy it was for the People's Tribunal to sentence young girls like Lydia for "breach of labor discipline" and lock her up in a train headed to Vladivostok and its ultimate destination, the *Kolyma* camps or one of the *Norilsk* zones. Lydia's memories returned in patches, the ones she fought so hard to suppress all these years.

It was on that train to *Kolyma* that she first learned of her pregnancy. This predicament saved Lydia from being sent to the labor camps. Instead, she went to the *ElgenDetKombinat*, a prison for mothers with newborn children and pregnant women. There, under strict guard supervision, all young mothers were escorted in formation five times per day to breast feed their babies in a general feeding area. Like the others, Lida learned to grab her baby first and give her up last, just to hold her a little bit longer than others do.

The amnesty for the young mothers arrived two years later, in 1944. When Lydia learned of it, she begged the prison officials to keep her employed on a volunteer basis, just for a few weeks longer, until things settle down. Like the other prisoners, she heard persistent rumors about forced marriages, and Lydia did not want to be married off to anyone but Misha, the father of her child. Yet in the tiny village of *Elgen*, on river *Toskan*, rumors of amnesty for women spread like wild fire.

This remote part of the world was home to gold prospectors and former convicts. Isolated in the Siberian tundra, these rugged men suffered for many years without any female company. Their lonely, tortured existence rendered them utterly indifferent to a woman's appearance, or whether she was already pregnant and would give birth to another man's baby. Nor did these cavemen care about the legal freedom of their newly liberated wives or the existence of their husbands and lovers, who were impatiently waiting for them elsewhere. News of the impending release date was enough to bring prospective husbands by the truckloads, each eager to claim his wife.

On the day of her release, Lydia patiently waited in a group of other women to be reunited with their children. A prison guard walked over and said, "girls, get ready to meet your husbands. They can't wait to see you!" Then the camp gates opened and three trucks rolled in, filled with ape-like brutes. Each of them wanted to be the first to pick out his wife.

Half an hour after the prison gates opened, the women were dragged, some kicking and screaming, by their prospective spouses to appear before a marriage bureau, known as ZAGs. After a brief ceremony Lydia officially became the wife of a former pocket thief.

Unlike the others, he was a good-hearted man who allowed her to leave. Her baby girl, however, did not survive the return journey.

"Hush, it's all over," Boris whispered to Lydia, "even I hold no grudge against life. What use would it be?"

His softly spoken words brought her back to reality. Regaining composure, Lydia swiped remaining tears from her eyes. To her surprise, it felt good to share her secret with someone who has been there, too.

## Chapter 28

Regardless of how Lena felt about Boris Vladimirovich, as a foreigner, Jack thought that it would be exotic to meet a person who had survived the infamous Siberian labor camps. So exotic, in fact, that Jack decided to take an afternoon break just to have a chat with the old man about life in prison under Stalin's bloody regime.

On the way over he picked up a bottle of vodka and a loaf of black bread, as any uninvited guest should. The elevator released Jack on the seventh floor, where he turned to the left and pushed a familiar button, setting off Lydia's obnoxious buzzer. There was no response, but Jack knew that Boris had to be inside, unable to leave the confines of her apartment in the winter. Finally he heard a gruff voice. "What do you want?"

"It's Jack, your neighbor. Remember me?"

"Maybe. What do you want?" Boris repeated.

"To talk to you, if you have some time," Jack answered honestly, smiling into the peephole. "That's all, really."

The door slowly opened, revealing a fragile old man, who was leaning on a wooden cane for support. "As you know, young man, this is not my apartment," Boris answered, standing his ground firmly, "but Lydia Ivanovna spoke very highly of you, so I presume she would not mind you being here. This way, please."

The kitchen was long and narrow, with just enough room at the table for two persons to sit comfortably. The window looked out into the courtyard, letting in plenty of daylight even on this hazy winter afternoon. Jack placed a loaf of bread and the vodka bottle on the table, and asked Boris casually, "how about a hundred grams between you and me?"

Without saying anything superfluous, the old man reached into a cupboard and pulled out two teacups. Jack poured vodka generously, to the very rim. There were no objections, he noted, which was encouraging.

"To meeting you," Jack raised his teacup in a traditional introductory toast.

"*Na zdorovye,*" Boris gave an equally neutral reply. After drinking, he wiped his mouth with the back of the hand and said, sounding surprised, "this is real stuff, not moonshine." Then he tore the loaf of bread into two halves and smelled it, deeply inhaling the earthy aroma. This must be something they did in his generation, Jack thought.

"We did not mean to offend you," Jack began to mend the bridges. "I hope you understand that."

"That's what Lydia Ivanovna said. These days, you have to question why young people would give you anything for free. Some want your apartment, others want your silverware. People are being killed for their World War II medals, or coin collections. These are the times we live in..."

"Well, I wanted you to know that Lena, the girl who was with me, did not mean to insult you. She does not know anything about the labor camps, or why the people were sent over there. Nobody knows about that."

"Nobody cares," Boris corrected Jack. "Because we are not people. Quite the opposite: we are the enemy of the people. And the people, in turn, became our enemies. This entire nation is infested with enemies, starting with children. Have you noticed those twelve year-old kids? They wouldn't think twice about stabbing you, and they are our future."

Even though Boris spoke in monotone, the somber words could not suppress his anger; Jack could hear the rumbling of an emotional volcano inside him, ready to overflow. All it would take was one more well aimed toast, Jack thought, refilling their teacups with vodka. "To those who remained behind," Jack said, drinking out of his cup. Jack and Boris reached for the same piece of bread, but Boris quickly backed away, so Jack tore off a large chunk of freshly baked dough and respectfully handed it to him.

"You seem to be a good man." Boris squinted at Jack. "But tell me, why did you come here, really?"

"I've never met anyone who was in a labor camp before," Jack answered honestly, "and I want to know the truth about how it really was."

Boris closed his eyes and said, "we were freezing most of the year. I was so desperate to get out of *Norilsk* before the winter that I volunteered to fight on the front, along with forty eight other men. That was in the fall of 1943. The Soviet army was losing many soldiers, so Stalin gave us, the prisoners, a choice: either go and protect your motherland, or freeze to death in the camps. As part of the deal, anyone who volunteered would be set free, if they survived the war. Even some of the thieves had volunteered."

"The thieves?"

"And for them, it was going against the code."

"The code?"

"And in the end, they paid dearly for that mistake."

Without making a big deal out of it, Jack generously splashed more vodka into their cups. The next sip stirred up the old man's memory, and he began to explain that like the Communists, the Russian czars also imprisoned criminals and forced them to do hard labor in similar Siberian penal colonies. There, reliance on each other meant the difference between life and death. That is why in 1682-1725, during the reign of Peter the Great, the hardened criminals, known as "thieves-in-law," first banded together in Russia's remote prisons.

These thieves, much like their Sicilian colleagues, formed a fraternal order that no one since could eradicate. Tight networks of prisoners spread throughout the region. The members were sworn to abide by a rigid code of behavior that included never working in a legitimate job, never paying taxes, and most importantly never, under any circumstances, cooperating with the authorities, unless it was to trick them.

To announce their status as professional criminals, the thieves carved in their skin elaborate tattoos. Images of predators, like eagles and wolves, were proudly splattered across their burly chests and backs. They had developed a secret language that was virtually indecipherable to authorities. The thieves even set up a communal criminal fund, called the obschak, which was used to bribe officials, finance business ventures and help inmates and their families.

Through the centuries, the brotherhood of thieves grew in strength to the point that in the early 1900's they helped Lenin's gangs to rob banks to fund the communist revolution. Later, the communists relied on thieves to spread fear and chaos amongst the population. Through the years one thing became clear: no one could tame the thieves. Nobody, period.

During World War II, Joseph Stalin devised a clever plot to annihilate the thriving subculture by recruiting them to defend the motherland. Those who fought alongside with the Red Army, hoping to gain freedom in return, knowingly defied the age-old prohibition of helping the government. They were grouped into penalty battalions or *shtrafniye batalliony*, and sent off to face certain death.

"We ended up fighting in a house-to-house street-by-street battle in Stalingrad. You probably don't even know where it is. After the Luftwaffe finished their bombing campaign, Stalingrad looked like a moonscape of debris. All around us there was nothing but collapsed rubble. We were hugely outnumbered, but what did we have to lose? So we kept firing even as they pushed us back within a few hundred meters of the *Volga* River cliffs. At the time, I didn't think I would survive. Most of my comrades were dying all around me."

After the war ended in 1945, however, all surviving prisoners were promptly arrested and thrown back into the same prison camps. The thieves who crossed over to work for the government were branded *suki*, or bitches, by the thieves who had refused to join the war. At nights, when the weather grew especially frigid, the two sides unsheathed their sharpened knives and hacked each other to pieces.

When the Bitches' War was finally over in 1953, only the thieves who adhered to the code, and refused to battle the Nazis, had survived. By then, they wielded ultimate authority in prisons, over guards and wardens, openly importing liquor, narcotics and women. "They slept near open windows, away from the communal toilet, where only the homosexuals and other weaklings were fit to reside," Boris remembered. "Of course, this included us, the political prisoners."

"Did anyone try to escape?"

"Once a year, in the summer, someone would make a run for it, but they always got caught and punished. One time I tried to escape, too. Even made it onto a train, but they brought in the dogs, and they sniffed me out. That's how I ended up in the *Norilsk* zone during the summer of 1953."

While the rest of the Soviet Union passionately mourned the passing of its great leader, Joseph Stalin, on March 4, 1953, hundreds of thousands of prisoners, criminal and political alike, celebrated the bloodthirsty dictator's unexpected demise. "Stalin croaked!" inmates everywhere screamed and jumped for joy. They hoped that an amnesty, or at least a reduction in their sentences, would soon follow.

By mid-May, however, it became apparent that Soviet Union's new leader, Lavrenty Beria, continued with Stalin's repressive tactics. That is when the prisoners started to stage organized mass protests and strikes. By 1953, the *GorLag's* six groups, called "zones," housed thirty five thousand prisoners; men and women, criminal and political. They started to fold like dominoes. First, *Vorkuta's* prisons went on strike, then Khazakstan labor camps joined, until the uprisings reached *Kolyma*, where the inmates in one camp disarmed their guards and made a desperate run for Alaska. All but two were tracked down and shot.

The real explosion took place in the *Norilsk* group of camps within the GorLag penitentiary system, when the prison guards shot six leaders from the first and fourth of *Norilsk* zones. On May 25, the protesting prisoners in the third and fifth zones went on strike, refusing to build the *Norilsk* copper plant. Others joined soon after, including the second and sixth women's zones.

The prisoners' demands seemed quite reasonable: decrease the work day from twelve to eight hours, introduce a two-day rest period, grant mail privileges with relatives, improve the quality of food. The official response was brutal: on July 1, 1953, armored vehicles entered the fifth zone, killing everyone in sight. The other zones were destroyed the next day.

Another chug of vodka, and Boris' eyes glazed over. His rough, leathery hands moved left and right, pointing to invisible objects that seemed very real to him. Through rich, detailed narrative, Jack could also see the events unfolding before him.

"In our zone, the cells were opened by the idiots, the criminally insane from the other labor camps. We had this small psychiatric ward that housed them. Somehow one of those blessed idiots pushed the magic button and the metal bars opened, releasing us all at once. I immediately understood that something horrendous was about to occur. Sure enough, the thieves started to throw stones at the soldiers in the watchtower, who mowed them down with short bursts from machine guns until they ran out of ammunition. Then in a matter of minutes, the soldiers were thrown from their bunkers in the sky and torn to pieces by the angry mob.

"The rest of the prisoners took this as a signal to pursue their own objectives. The sexual deviants broke into the women's barracks and raped as many girls as they could hold down. The drug addicts raided the medical ward and drank any medicine containing alcohol. In the process of looting, they found the prison doctor and two nurses, and dragged them out into the courtyard. They wanted to cut off the nurse's heads to show the authorities how serious they were.

"Meanwhile, I climbed up on the roof to escape this madness. From there, I could see a long formation of armored vehicles with mounted machine guns approaching the camp, so I spread out flat to avoid being noticed. While the soldiers were taking their positions, the prisoners already torched everything that would burn. Mattresses inside the barracks gave off this black, putrid smoke and fire, and I heard screams and curses.

"A group of idiots charged through the courtyard, covered in blood. After slaughtering much of the livestock on the camp's territory, they were chasing three remaining pigs that somehow managed to escape, trying to cut the meat off live animals on the run. Then a voice came over the loudspeaker: "we are opening the gates and ordering you to come out. If you are not out in fifteen minutes, we will use force. Is that clear?" We all heard it, all right, but nobody made a move.

"True to their word, exactly fifteen minutes later an armored vehicle broke through the prison gates, followed by seven trucks filled with soldiers wearing helmets. They jumped out and began spraying machine gun fire at everyone in plain view. The prisoners in the yard were quickly mowed down. Some of the wounded couldn't move, writhing on the ground in pools of blood. Others crawled, as fast as they could, to the safety of barracks. The soldiers ran after them to finish the job, but they were afraid to enter the buildings. Instead, the cowards tossed hand grenades through the windows and ran away. In the courtyard, the other soldiers finished off the wounded prisoners.

"It took the authorities almost four hours to bring things under control. In the end, hundreds of prisoners were killed, and even more were hospitalized with heavy trauma wounds. That was how they subdued everyone. And only three years later, in 1956, we were forgiven in connection with sudden discovery of Stalin's cult of personality. To amnesty, young man."

"To amnesty," Jack repeated, drinking with him.

As life would have it, Boris celebrated most of his birthdays in zone four of *Norilsk* camps in a traditional, low-key fashion: with a cup of prison-brewed coffee or tea, strong enough to the point of inducing euphoria, perhaps half a jar of oily moonshine that tasted more like kerosene. His twenty eighth birthday Boris spent in Kiev, released under the amnesty for political prisoners.

"And all these years I tried to find my parents' graves," Boris continued, "but that information remains a state secret, along with millions of similar secrets that were buried by our dear leader, Comrade Stalin."

Suddenly, alcohol-inspired creativity took a hold of Jack. Maybe Sasha would know someone with access to those ancient documents for a minor fee, Jack thought, if they were still kept somewhere in the KGB archives.

"I can't promise you anything, but maybe I can help you," Jack said. "What can you tell me about your parents?"

"Everyone knew my father, Vladimir Pavlov. He was the leading member of the Central Committee. We lived on the second floor of this magnificent building on *Grushevsky* street, where the Chinese embassy is now located. The first floor was reserved for Moscow-appointed hierarchy. That's where Lazar Moiseevich Kaganovich lived. I even became good friends with his daughter, Maya, before they moved to Moscow. Everyone else who lived in that building was either shot or sent off to prisons. My father was the last one to be arrested."

"When was that, exactly?"

"On November 3, 1937, at 2:35 a.m.," Boris replied automatically. "My mother, Tamara Pavlova, was a doctor in an orthopedic institute. After father's arrest she called in to say that she would not be going to work that day, or ever again. So they came to her instead. My mother was sentenced to fifteen years without a subsequent right to reside in a major city. First, she was held in the *Lukianovka* prison, but later everyone was transferred to Siberia. After that, I lost track of her, too."

"Like I said, I can't promise any results," Jack said, feeling genuinely sorry for the old man, "but I promise that I will look into this matter for you."

"I will pay you whatever it costs." Boris' bony fingers were shaking as he scribbled his parent's names on a side margin of yesterday's newspaper. "If you could tell me what happened to my mother and father, I would be very grateful."

"Stranger things have happened." Jack finished off the remainder of vodka that was floating at the bottom of his cup, and got up from the kitchen table. "It was a pleasure to meet you, Boris Vladimirovich, but I'm afraid I must get back to work."

"What did you say your name was, again?"

"Jack Parker."

"Be careful of those children, Jack Parker," Boris warned him before closing the door.

Sure enough, Jack saw the kids Boris hated, standing in the alleyway, but they did not appear very menacing. Just five children, standing in a circle, drinking beer and puffing on dirty cigarette stubs they picked up from the pavement. The ringleader was constantly spitting globs of saliva and tried to look cool. They watched Jack pass by and then someone muttered a joke that caused a massive hysterical laughter.

# Chapter 29

Russia has thirty six billionaires. Collectively they own nearly twenty five percent of Russian GDP. They are estimated to be worth more then one hundred and twenty billion dollars. This does not include approximately ninety thousand common, run-of-the-mill multi-millionaires.

One of the multi-billionaires is the 37 year-old Governor of Chukotka, an oil tycoon by trade, Mr. Oleg Abramov. In fact, according to Forbes Magazine, Abramov was the youngest and wealthiest Russians of them all. He was also listed as the twenty first richest person in the world, with an estimated fortune of $13.3 billion.

And for excellent reasons: Oleg was the governor of Chukotka, an oil-rich territory, using his territory as a tax haven for his business deals. Moreover, President Yeltsin provided Oleg with protection from any attempts of prosecution for criminal activities, making him virtually untouchable. Unless Oleg angered the President, of course, in which case he would be bankrupt and in prison the next day.

Geographically, Chukotka is the first bit of Russia you would come to if you crossed the Bering Strait from Alaska. Bisected by the Arctic Circle, Chukotka has little except the native Chukchis and their reindeer, some impossible-to-extract gold and an aged nuclear power station. It is a desperately cold and bleak place, rife with disease and alcoholism. People would do anything to be able to leave. But where would they go? To Miami, Barbados or London town? Actually, to any of these places, if they were Oleg Abramov.

It was a sunny May afternoon, and Oleg was enjoying his spring break off the coast of Southern France. Per his instructions, the captain dropped off an anchor one kilometer from the shore of Cap d'Antibes. Oleg was relaxing on an Art Deco-style cream sofa on the upper deck of his 115-meter super-yacht, *The Aesthesia*, waiting for his lunch to arrive.

And boy, was it a beautiful ship! The newest and largest of Oleg's flotilla of four super-yachts stationed around the globe, *The Aesthesia* was custom-built per his personal specifications. The naval architects were given an unlimited budget, with just one instruction: make it fun. For a mere three hundred and fourty two million dollars they created the world's finest yacht.

It had all the James Bond toys that any highly security-conscious baby billionaire could dream of. In addition to the elevating helicopter deck, the ship contained a missile-detection system and a hovercraft launch. There was a mini-submarine dock inside the hull, with the sub that detected limpet mines. The underwater cameras would broadcast to large LCD monitors throughout the yacht. All electronics were linked to a sophisticated computer. There were also jet skis, diving equipment, a floating golf range and shotguns for clay pigeon shooting. It was a blend of a modern warship and an incredible floating palace.

The yacht's interior was the height of luxury. Naturally, all of the glass was bullet-proof. Aside from a cinema, there was an in-door swimming pool, state-of-the-art fitness center, a steam room and a massage area. Each of the bedrooms had floor-to-ceiling windows, contemporary furniture in cool, muted tones, plus a giant plasma screen. The bathrooms had marble walls and mosaic floors. In fact, this masterpiece created such an excitement among the French Riviera's super-rich that it was even short-listed by the pompous Superyacht Society for a prize in their annual design awards.

The sound of whirling helicopter blades captured Oleg's attention. The captain activated the deck, allowing the on-board helicopter to land. According to Oleg's Patek Philippe Perpetual Calendar watch, it was 1:12 p.m. Lunch had arrived at last! It was quite important, because as everything else in life, Oleg loved fresh food. He would always fly it in from his favorite restaurants in Nice, Paris or London, rather then eat the stuff that has been sitting around for a few days. Whenever Oleg was at sea, his gourmet dinners would be delivered by a helicopter. This time, along with his take away lunch, the pilot was bringing a rising star in the neighboring government of Ukraine. Oleg just could not wait for his chopper to land.

To Alexei, the ship's dimensions were breathtaking. The collosal, four deck-high liner towered over the calm sea like a giant spaceship. It's impossible, he thought, that one person could own something of this size. Someday, if Alexei played his cards right, he would also possess one of these toys. He just knew it.

Three little Gurkha soldiers ran across the platform. One of them opened the helicopter's door. He pointed at Alexei's feet and said, "good afternoon, sir. I am terribly sorry, but no one is allowed on board in shoes. Mr. Abramov likes his yachts spotless. Over there is a container with flip-flops for the guests." The soldier politely gestured aside.

The views of the picturesque Mediterranean coast from the open helicopter deck were spectacular. There was something magical, even medicinal, about the salty sea air and green scenery in the distance. Alexei inhaled deeply and went over to pick up his pair of flip flops. He wondered, would I make my guests take off their shoes?

Alexei was escorted by his Gurkha guide to the upper deck. Cream leather armchairs were grouped together for private chats over cocktails. A tanned young man of about 35, with unshaved cheeks, was waiting for him. "What football teams do you like?" the man asked out of the blue, as if he knew Alexei for many years.

"Being from Kiev, I'm kind of partial to *Dynamo*."

"That's already one thing we have in common. My first choice is Milan because they've got Andrei

Shevchenko. But they don't want to sell. Guess I'll have to settle for Chelsea."

It took a few seconds for Alexei to comprehend the subject of the conversation. Was the Governor talking about investing into a soccer club? Surely this could not be the reason for his long distance flight to the French Riviera. Still, if Abramov wanted to talk about athletic events, Alexei was willing to oblige his host. "But why bother with sports teams? Seems like a waste of money to me."

"It's not about making money," Abramov replied, stretching lazily on the sofa, barefoot. "And it's not about prestige, either. It's about access. The beauty of a football club is that sooner or later you get to meet everybody important in life. That's why you buy a football club. Whenever Milan plays, you may get Berlusconi in your box. You'll probably have a couple of drinks afterwards, and then the Prime Minister will invite you to his humble Villa Borghese. Or if you purchase Chelsea, then Tony Blair will be your invited guest. It's like buying membership to a nice posh club in Rome or London. You know what I mean?"

"I guess," Alexei said, absorbing the theoretical possibilities. "In that case, maybe I should make an offer to buy Formula One."

"Maybe not. I'm in negotiations with Bernie right now," Abramov said somberly. "It's one of the world's most glamorous sporting events. Hollywood types flock here like bees to a honey pot. Monaco in May, during Grand Prix time, means Brad Pitt, George Clooney, Hugh Grant."

"I was only kidding about buying Formula One."

"Ask me later. Maybe I'll sell it to you one day."

"I am looking forward to that day."

"Let's go inside," Oleg offered. "You never know who could be listening out here."

With a gesture befitting any head of state, Oleg motioned for Alexei to proceed to the main deck VIP stateroom. Alexei left the art deco terrace with great reluctance and entered an enormous room. It spanned the entire width of the yacht. He whistled, clearly impressed. Indeed, it was the preserve of a very wealthy few. Alexei immediately noticed one of Oleg's many indulgences: the gigantic room was full of art. Judging by the quality of the pieces, it was obvious that Abramov knew a thing or two about serious indulgence.

It was quite an imposing gallery with a superb collection of museum-quality world-famous paintings, including Van Gough's *Prison Courtyard*, Cezanne's *Pierrot* and *Harlequin*. Much to his embarrassment, Alexei could not recognize the names of many Soviet artists, whose familiar paintings depicted socialist realism: eager workers, well-fed peasants, Stalin and his generals. There were also the finest original works by Mikhail Larionov, Piet Mondrian, Wassily Kandinsky, Lyubov Popova.

"Are all of these are..." Alexei pointed around the walls.

"On a permanent loan to me from the *Tretyakov* Gallery and the *Pushkin* Museum," Oleg finished his sentence. "And this beauty came from the *Lenin* Museum, in Moscow." He pointed to a beautiful oil portrait of Lenin. Nearby in a glass frame were Lenin's original Communist party cards, dated 1920 and 1927.

Alexei looked at the cards, numbers 224332 and 0000001, nodding in appreciation of their historical value. Abramov added proudly, "you'd be amazed at what artifacts are available these days. A friend of mine is the director for the State Center for Museums. He had the museum curator deliver them to my door. "

"I bet that helps."

"Doesn't hurt," Abramov shrugged his shoulders modestly. "The problem is, where do you find decent forgeries to return to the museums?"

The amount of wealth surrounding Alexei was mind boggling. And yet to him, it all made perfect sense: when you have all the cars, mansions, private helicopters and football teams, buying a brand new super-yacht with a world-class private art collection seemed perfectly reasonable.

In sharp contrast with the expansive, grand VIP stateroom with its exquisite art, Abramov's office was sparsely furnished. The floors and walls were made of Norwegian wood. The couches and chairs were upholstered in understated beige colors. His titanium-and-glass desk was fastidiously neat, offering astounding views through sloping bullet-proof glass windows.

On top of the desk was a photograph, a color portrait that showed Abramov and President Yeltsin in swimming trunks, holding chunks of skewered lamb cubes. It was snapped during one of the barbecues at Abramov's datcha in Barbados. If a visitor did not get the message, another black-and-white photograph on the wall showed Yelstin and Abramov, enjoying a shot of vodka against the orange sunset on the deck of *The Aesthesia.*

"I know what you must be thinking," Oleg said. "And you're almost right. Politics are close to me. But there are different ways of participating in that game. I can't afford to be indifferent to politics. At the same time, I don't have personal grand ambitions. I have only one task connected with politics: to help the President. Now, I'm not a close buddy of his. I treat him with great respect. People like us must not get in the way of people like him. Don't you agree?"

"One hundred percent," Alexei honestly replied. He knew that the government could always reach back into the history and pull out criminal, civil or tax charges. Obviously, Oleg had a great roof.

"You know, I heard good things about you."

"Like what?"

"Like you have a business mind. Plus, you've got both feet firmly planted in the system: you're an unofficial advisor to the President and a member of the Parliament. And most importantly, you have the same go-for-broke instinct, just like me. I can see it in your eyes."

"You may be right. Who knows?" Alexei modestly replied, "only time will tell."

Oleg peered at Alexei as though he was making a quick assessment. Then he said, "the reason I invited you is to make you an interesting offer."

"One I can't refuse?"

"This is not a joking matter," Oleg said sternly. "I have a couple of ideas I wanted to run by you. For example, how about putting together a new, vertically integrated company, from some of the choicest parts of the old system? I bet you could arrange this with the Ukrainian State Property Fund. They'll sell us a few cherries in a cozy auction for a reasonable amount. Say, up to a billion dollars. I'll finance my half in cash. In a few years, the company's real worth, probably several billions, will become apparent. Then we'll float it on London Stock Exchange. Now, that's a great deal! Trust me."

Alexei was concerned that Abramov's great idea was exactly the same as his, but he did not show it. "That's an interesting concept. Certainly worth exploring." Alexei intentionally did not mention his plans to implement this concept without Abramov's participation.

Encouraged by Alexei's positive attitude, Oleg continued, "in President's Yelstin's election, for example, it was a fair trade of state property for financial support to the President during a difficult re-election battle. A few of us threw our financial muscle behind the President. In exchange, we got some of Russia's most valuable companies below their market value." Oleg fell quiet and then marvelled aloud, "as a result, to some degree, I am the real government of Russia. For example, I can dismiss ministers and nominate people who are loyal to the President in their ministerial positions. So could you."

According to Oleg, so far Alexei was on the right track to becoming a baby billionaire too. "I'm open to all of your ideas, Mr. Abramov," Alexei smiled pleasantly.

"You can call me Oleg," his mentor-in-waiting replied. "Another idea is for your National Bank to set up a stabilization fund. It's like a national piggy bank during times of financial uncertainty. Plus an anti-corruption fund, to pay officials a decent salary so they don't have to hustle for bribes. I'll get my Harvard advisors working on it. Believe me, after their reports, the IMF, the World Bank, the IFC, the USAID, everyone will gladly wire us billions upon billions of loans and grants. It's a big enough pie for everyone to profit, including your President."

"Sounds perfectly feasible to me."

"Good. In that case, there's a banker I want you to meet. He's helped me in the past. Does this sort of thing all the time. I have a meeting with him next. Afterwards may be a good opportunity for you two to have a chat."

"I'd love to," Alexei smiled. With his earning potential, an international banker would be a great connection, even if Oleg's attempt to muscle in on Alexei's plans was doomed to failure.

"I have a few other ideas, but let's start with these projects first. What do you say?"

"Sounds tempting, but I have to think about it."

"What's there to think about?"

"For one thing, I have to consult with my other partners."

"Do you really need to? I was hoping we could keep this between ourselves."

"I can understand that. Still, I'd like to have a few days, if you don't mind."

Immediately Oleg knew that something was wrong. Nobody refuses an offer of obscene wealth without an excellent reason. Still, there was nothing he could do but wait. "Just don't take too long, ok? I want to start working in Ukraine with someone, and soon."

"Of course," Alexei smiled pleasantly.

Something drew Oleg's attention beyond the bullet-proof glass windows. One of his hovercrafts was quickly approaching the yacht. "It's my next appointment," Oleg said. "Excuse me."

"No problem," Alexei replied. "Should I just wait out there, on the deck?"

"Yeah, why don't you do that," Oleg replied, his spirit dampened by Alexei's ambiguous, non-committal attitude. "I won't be long."

Standing on the huge upper deck, absorbing the serene atmosphere of the sea, gave Alexei a strange feeling of exhilaration. He had been insulated in his Kiev business world for so long that he forgot all about the fresh air. At last, he was all alone. There were no big fat men, accompanied by people wearing ear-pieces and strange irregular-shaped bulges under their jackets, no young women with mink coats and tight leotards with leopard patterns.

"Hello," a woman's voice called out in perfect Russian. "Do you get here often? South of France, I mean." Alexei turned to see a stunning tall blonde with a gorgeous figure, approaching him. She was fashionably dressed in an all-white business suit with a low cut blouse that revealed her cleavage.

"Every now and then," he lied, trying hard to disguise his provincial roots. "But I'll be spending more time here, believe me."

"In that case, you may need me," she smiled seductively and moved closer to him.

"You're absolutely right," Alexei flirted back with the attractive, sophisticated lady.

"I mean, what do you do after you've already remodeled your apartment, built a country home and bought your Bentley?" She was so sensual that he wanted her, right there on the spot. "The next step is buying a place in the South of France, of course. That's where I come in. Enter DeLux Solutions, a one-stop, all inclusive shopping consultant agency."

"You don't say." Alexei was disappointed to learn that the beautiful blond was just a real estate agent, and not a high-class escort that Oleg thoughtfully provided to his guest.

"For Mr. Abramov, for instance, I provide what we call the Oligarch Package. We advise him on the best-selling yachts, and who's buying them. We also offer the most elite property on the market and things like security."

"Got it," Alexei replied, hoping to end her sales pitch. "Thanks."

But as any great sales person, she refused to take no for an answer, continuing with her canned speech, "DeLux has a don't-call-us-we'll-call-you philosophy. We don't need to advertise in golfing or yachting magazines. Our customers are usually well-known people, who socialize in the same circles. They're at least multimillionaires. Most of them are Russian, and the number of those wanting to be invited keeps growing."

"Like club for members only?"

"Precisely. We publish what we call a Catalogue of Very Expensive Things. In fact, Mr. Abramov wanted his copy right off the presses, so here I am, his delivery girl. It's purely for the ultra-rich. Our slogan is, if you've only got ten million, you can't afford it. Jets, collection cars. Just place your order and our consultants guarantee the rest. So when your time comes to invest into planes and vacation villas in the South of France, just call me."

"Maybe later. Excuse me." Alexei turned his back and walked off to the opposite side of the deck. He did not feel comfortable with the pushy saleslady, especially since he was not prepared to spend as lavishly as she wanted him to. Had she known the truth, in her eyes Alexei would be merely a millionaire, practically a nobody. Unfortunately, Alexei had no choice but to agree. After seeing Oleg's display of wealth, he knew that they were in different leagues, and he did not like it.

A few minutes passed. Curious, Alexei turned to see if the blond was still there, but she disappeared. Instead, a plump, elderly gentleman stepped out from Oleg's private museum. He approached Alexei and introduced himself. "Hello, I am Eduard Safran," he said. "And I hear you are from Ukraine?"

"Well, yes," Alexei admitted reluctantly. "And you are..."

Safran smiled modestly. Apparently the young Ukrainian fellow did not know that he was on Forbes Magazine's list of the top 200 wealthiest individuals in the world. In fact, Safran's total worth of $2.5 billion was in large part due to Mr. Abramov. "I am in private banking," Safran explained, "and my business is to know all the secrets of the financial planet. These days, I work with Mr. Abramov. For the Yelstin family."

"Really?"

"Yes. As a matter of fact, Mr. Abramov suggested that I introduce myself to you. Perhaps we could do business together, he said. After all, many governments use my banking services. Russians and Americans, Panamanians and Colombians, you name them."

Impressed, Alexei said with interest, "and what services does your bank usually offer to governments?"

"In your case, we could clear any amount of foreign aid without a trace. For instance, Russia received more then twenty seven billion dollars worth of aid from the World Bank and IMF, some in grants, but mostly in loans. Seventeen billion went through my New York Bank alone."

"Nice haul," Alexei whistled, impressed.

"Plus, each of my clients has independent projects. In Russia, part of the money flows from over-abundance of natural resources: aluminum, steel, oil and gas, precious metals and minerals. And everything is extracted on industrial scale, if you can imagine that. Ukraine is a different animal altogether, one without the natural resources, not that I have to tell you that. But if you manage to become someone like Mr. Abramov, and end up coordinating the various advisors to the President, then you should definitely call me."

"Very interesting," Alexei replied. "May I have your business card?"

"Naturally," Safran gently wrapped up his presentation. "Incidentally, I spend most of my time in Monaco these days. If you're ever in the neighborhood, please drop by for a glass of wine."

"Thank you, Mr. Safran," Alexei smiled and shook the old man's hand. "I will be in touch." Alexei remained on the sunny deck long after Safran shuffled off and retreated into Oleg's office. Having consulted a vacation guide before arriving, Alexei expected the host to take him on a short cruise down the coast, or maybe even a day trip to St. Tropez. The island of Ibiza was a long-shot possibility. Anticipating the upcoming trip, Alexei patiently waited outside while Oleg conducted business with the private family banker to the governments.

At last, the meeting was over. Oleg appeared from the main stateroom, looking somber, and said, "listen, Alexei, I wanted to spend some more time with you, but there's a situation developing that requires my presence in Moscow."

"Nothing terrible, I hope."

"Potentially, worse then terrible. But that's not your problem. If you want to, feel free to hang out on this boat as long as you wish. Or if you have urgent business back in Kiev, my Bandit will fly you out there today."

"What bandit?"

"It's one of my airplanes," Oleg explained. "It will get you back to Kiev in comfort. By the way, if you want to borrow it anytime, or use any of my yachts, just give me a call. Everything I own is open to my partners."

Alexei was disappointed about the cancelled cruise, but he knew that business takes precedence. Especially when a president is personally involved. "Thanks for everything, Oleg, but frankly, I don't want to stay here all by myself if you're not here," he smiled sadly. "It just wouldn't be the same."

"I can certainly understand that. Let me call you when I'm done with Moscow, and we'll do it again. Maybe even next week?

"Maybe. I'll check my calendar."

Escorting Alexei to the helicopter pad, Oleg offered, "and when the time comes, I'll show you everything you need to know about structuring a web of ownership. Companies nested within companies within companies."

"Great," Alexei responded without enthusiasm.

As the helicopter blades picked up speed, Oleg gave Alexei one last bit of advice, "try to get into your Parliament's Anti-Corruption Commission. Or the National Security Council. Then, at least the government won't be coming after you. And remember, the most important investment you can make is your contribution to your President. You've got to keep close to him."

"Thanks, Oleg, I'll keep it in mind," Alexei said loudly over the smooth churning of the rotors. "And don't worry, I'll let you know in a couple of days. Thanks for everything. It was really useful."

The look of suspicion was written all over Oleg's face. He backed away from the helicopter, half-scowling, still hoping to do business with the sly Ukrainian politician. Alexei waived goodbye and waited. Finally, the helicopter lifted from the super-yacht. That is when a dreadful thought occurred to Oleg for the first time, that perhaps he made a strategic error by sharing his confidential business secrets with a potential competitor.

Ten minutes later the helicopter landed on the territory of Nice airport. Alexei looked in awe at a commercial passenger wide-body jet with a name *The Bandit* plastered on its side in huge black letters. Oleg even had a scull and bones painted on the tail for maximum effect. It was an adapted one hundred eighty million dollar Boeing 767, an airplane designed to carry up to three hundred and sixty passengers.

The interior was decorated with mahogany and gold-plating. Since he was the sole passenger travelling directly from Nice to Kiev, Alexei had at his full disposal a large master bedroom with a huge bathing area, an office, a cinema room, a fitness room, and lots of spacious cabins for guests, personal assistants and bodyguards. Of course, there was a plasma screen TV in every bedroom, and other amenities for a long flight.

During the brief guided tour, one of the pilots explained to Alexei, "this custom-made bird even has its own anti-missile system. It's the next best thing to the U.S. President's Air Force One in terms of security, and far superior in terms of comfort."

"But who really needs an anti-missile system?"

"You'd be surprised, sir," the pilot replied, a little too seriously for Alexei's comfort.

In the open area inside the plane, the comfortable, sturdy furniture was screwed tightly to the floor boards. The dark wood, the luxurious carpet on the floor, all somehow reminded Alexei of Sergei's club for members. Sipping a glass of Krug Grande Reserve, Alexei looked out of an over-sized window on the world beneath him and thought about Oleg's offers.

On the one hand, Oleg's love of the good life, pride in his political reach, and undying loyalty to the President, were truly inspiring. On the other hand, Alexei did not feel obligated to go into business with a new partner. Especially a dangerous one, who had Gurkha soldiers, helicopters, mega-yachts and Boeing airplanes.

Besides, Alexei did not need Oleg. He was doing quite well on his own. In fact, Alexei was well ahead of his time. When most Ukrainians were too naive to understand what was going on, he purchased UkrSteel for almost nothing, and managed to turn it into a profitable company. Inept managers and alcoholics alike were quickly dismissed. The best young executives were hired, including several Americans. With their help, Alexei capitalized on the huge difference between state-subsidized and Western market prices for raw materials. UkrSteel's output and profitability soared, making its shareholders very rich men.

And after listening to Oleg's words of wisdom, Alexei wanted to take his portfolio to the next level. Not only would he set up a vertical integrated firm, one that extracts, refines and sells steel products -- in another few years, his shares would be traded on the London Stock Exchange. Billions upon billions of dollars would follow. While other Ukrainian billionaires-to-be were not yet dreaming of the riches they would acquire, Alexei was well-positioned to take his chunk of wealth.

Flying high in the clouds above Germany, he remembered a delightful decoration on one of the yacht's walls: an oil painting of Lenin in the Finland Station, his arm waving toward the future. Smiling at the irony, Alexei could not wait for his ultra-capitalistic future to arrive. Meanwhile, Alexei's official monthly salary as a deputy to the Ukrainian Parliament would not have bought a business lunch at a nice restaurant in Manhattan.

In all, the day trip to the South of France was an eye-opening, life-changing experience. In the beginning, Alexei half-expected to see a street bruiser who muscled in on his billions. But Abramov did not steal anything. He was able to take billions of dollars out of Russia in full public view, with the blessing of his president. Oleg's exuberant lifestyle and spending practices left Alexei dizzy with the unlimited possibilities. These billionaires have everything to excess, he thought. God, it's fantastic! The partnership between government and business could be extremely lucrative, he concluded, no doubt about it.

# Chapter 30

Lena's taut back was facing Jack, curving like a guitar at the waist, rising under the sheets around her hips. Such a voluptuous, womanly figure on such a young girl, he thought. Ever so lightly Jack scratched his nails across Lena's shoulder blade and she purred like a kitten, stretching. Finally she turned to face him. As every morning, Lena's long, black eyelashes did their magic: Jack was completely hers for the taking.

"That's certainly one way to wake me up." Lena reached over to give Jack what has become their customary good morning kiss. Her puckered lips felt like a tight young rose bud. From past experience Jack knew that a few more minutes of playful kisses and they would end up rolling around in bed all afternoon. And today was only Saturday, leaving the weekend wide open. Lena smiled and wrapped herself around

Jack. "You know, I really love these moments we spend together, just cuddling in bed."

"Me too," he said, breathing in her natural sweet aroma. Jack and Lena were comfortably snuggling in their bed at 10:04 a.m., until an uninterrupted sound of a loud horn blared under the window, assaulted their privacy. Lena said, "I am always amazed at how many idiots there are in the world."

Just to make sure this massive disturbance had nothing to do with him, Jack walked over to the window. Right away he recognized the roof of a Landcruiser, confirming his worst fear: the public offender was Sasha, which meant that he was not about to stop. Like an alarm, three words suddenly flashed in Jack's mind: Saturday-Sasha-Birthday. To confirm this, the birthday boy himself was inside his shiny black car, disturbing the peace on an otherwise quiet street. And it was a Saturday morning.

Then Jack noticed a long line of shiny, foreign automobiles behind Sasha. Jack's neighbors, including complete strangers in the building across the street, also stuck their heads outside for a better view. Their sleepy, bloated faces reeled in disgust at such inconsiderate, antisocial behavior, exhibited so early in the morning, yet no one dared to throw any rotting produce at the obnoxious Landcruiser or its entourage. At last the horn went silent and the sunroof opened. Sasha's torso popped out and he looked straight up at Jack. "Hey, are you ready, or what?" he yelled. "How long do we have to wait for you?"

"Give me a minute," Jack mouthed silently to Sasha and gave him a hand signal. Then Jack froze as hundreds of prying eyes shifted towards his balcony. Deeply embarrassed, Jack jumped to hide behind the wall, where nobody could see him.

"Take your time!" Sasha screamed in return, cupping his hands around the mouth for greater resonance. "We will be waiting for you down here!"

"Who were you waving to, Jack?" Lena asked.

"Oh, I completely forgot. It's Sasha's birthday today. He invited me to his party."

"But I thought we agreed that you weren't going to associate with criminals."

"Lena, I told you already: Sasha is not a criminal. Quite the opposite. He works for the government."

"You know exactly what I mean, Jack. That was a part of our deal. Remember?" She sounded deadly serious.

"But Lena, honey, how can I possibly tell Sasha that I'm not coming to his party? He drove all the way over here to pick me up. Besides, I've already agreed to attend," Jack pleaded, but it was no use.

"Well, maybe you shouldn't have told him you would be going in the first place."

Jack got dressed as quickly as possible, all the while apologizing to Lena for having to leave so suddenly. By the time he made it to the street, an orchestra of car horns was blaring from around the corner. A traffic policeman was politely informing Sasha that his party was interfering with the flow of city traffic, blocking the buses and taxis. The policeman, with great respect bordering on fear, kept looking over his shoulder at the vehicles behind Sasha's Landcruiser.

Admittedly, it was a mighty sight to behold: the next three cars were long, shiny Mercedes sedans, six hundred series, no less. The rest were clones of Sasha's monstrosity: overly large utility vehicles on enormously wide wheels, complete with tinted windows, front and rear brush-guards, overhead lamps and even one with custom-made chrome exhaust pipes. All of them were polished to perfection by hours of continual buffing; several were filled to capacity by large men, while the others contained one or two passengers with a driver. Some of the men had small black earphones implanted in their ears; the others were civilians.

"I don't care, let them wait," Sasha said to the policeman jovially as Jack negotiated a steep climb into his vehicle. "It's not every day a man turns thirty three."

Minutes later, a row of inappropriately expensive, foreign automobiles slowly passed through Kiev's streets. Sasha was leading the way, proudly ignoring all the red traffic lights. While entering the freeway, he pulled off a maneuver only an Alfa man can get away with: Sasha stopped the Landcruiser perpendicularly, blocking off all oncoming traffic. This move allowed the other cars in his convoy to gracefully enter in one row, unimpeded.

As expected, the people Sasha had cut off patiently waited. Not one of the drivers, sitting in their rusty Moskvich or dilapidated Zhiguli cars, and even those in prestigious black Volga's, dared to blow their horns in protest. With a procession like this, who would?

Overall, it proved to be a longer ride than Jack expected, but he always enjoyed listening to Sasha's war stories. Sometimes Sasha came up with hilarious anecdotes, other times they were not as funny. Even though Jack never knew whether Sasha was telling the truth, Jack always enjoyed hanging around with him.

"Today you'll meet an interesting fellow, David. Last week we shared a ride in a bullet-proof Mercedes, just like the one behind us." Sasha glanced in the rear-view mirror. "The only problem was that it had no license plates."

"Why is that?"

"Because David took it as partial payment from one of his debtors, but that's not the point. So here we are, driving the car out of Odessa city limits; the police checkpoints are posted every ten kilometers, but none of them try to stop us. This is unheard of in Kiev, so I pulled up to one of them and showed them my identification. The cop saluted me. Out of curiosity I asked him, we have no license plates; why don't you guys stop us? Do you know what he said?"

"What?"

"He says, it's not worth it. Every time we try to stop one of you guys, you just start shooting without giving us any warning, and we're sick and tired of it. What do you think about that one?"

"Funny."

"Yeah, David thought so, too. Now he wants the same identification card I have," Sasha laughed. "By the way, I brought something for you."

"For me?"

"Look behind you, in the back seat."

It was an antique, Soviet-style cardboard file with two ribbons, tied together so the contents can not spill out. The cover page was filled out in faded black ink.

It clearly stated "Vladimir Semyonovich Pavlov," and only then Jack understood the importance of the documents in his hands.

"This is the original file. Sorry, but there was nothing about Tamara Pavlova," Sasha said, staring at the road. "I have to return it in a few days, so please don't lose anything. By the way, this guy was rehabilitated. His whole family, too."

"What does that mean?"

"Just that his name is now officially cleared, that's all. He is no longer the enemy of the people. Under the law on Rehabilitation for Victims of Political Repression, people fall into two categories: enemies of the state or socially dangerous elements. It's a long story, just read the file yourself; I did. This guy was something else. No wonder they killed him."

"Thanks, Sasha." Jack could not believe his eyes. That rascal somehow managed to snatch from the KGB archives the file Boris Vladimirovich wanted to see so badly. "You've done a good thing, my friend."

"Glad that I could help out with a favor."

Sasha drove in silence for several minutes, and then he said matter-of-factly, "so you're from New York, huh? I've only seen it in movies. Is it as great as they say?"

"It sure is. The city that never sleeps. You can get anything you want anytime of day or night."

"I always wanted to see it," Sasha continued wistfully. "To breathe that air. So I wanted to ask you, can you help me out with a little favor?"

Under the circumstances, still holding the file in his hands, Jack had no choice but to reply, "you know me, Sasha. Of course I'll try. What's the favor?"

"I need a visa. You're from New York. You can invite me to visit New York. And I'll even pay for everything myself, don't worry."

"Sure, Sasha, I'll be happy to try, but I can't guarantee the outcome."

"What do you mean?"

"As a U.S. citizen, I'll be happy to give you my invitation. I can even write for you a recommendation letter to the consular officer, but you'll have to go through the interview yourself."

"An interview, eh?" Sasha shook his head doubtfully. "That's the whole thing: I was hoping that you could by-pass that for me. The problem is that technically I'm still working for Alfa. Even if I lie on the application, they'll weed me out at the interview. Just look at me: is this the face of a pencil pusher?"

Jack had to acknowledge that Sasha's military appearance would probably raise questions about his professional qualifications. "No really."

"That's why I wanted you to talk to some of your friends at the Embassy informally. Surely for a few bucks they could stamp a visa without my having to go through an interview. Avoiding the interview would be the best option for me. Just tell me how much they want."

"To tell you the truth, Sasha, I don't have such a good relationship with the Embassy," Jack said, knowing that Sasha would not accept any excuses, justified or not. "Ambassador Pilfer himself does not like me. A lot."

"You know the Ambassador? What a great connection! Why didn't you tell me this before?"

"Because I've never met him, but the Ambassador knows all about my stay in the clinic with Sergei. And none of it helps my reputation with the Embassy. Actually, my direct lobbying on your behalf could be a detriment."

"So you will try?" Sasha asked Jack coldly. "Or not?"

Under the circumstances, Jack felt obligated to help Sasha with his favor. Not only was Sasha a useful friend; equally important, he could become a vicious, potent enemy, one to be avoided at all costs. "Of course I'll try," Jack replied. "But like I said, I can't promise you anything."

"Thanks, buddy," Sasha smiled with appreciation. "I knew I could count on you." So that's why the tricky bugger invited me to his party, Jack thought. Staying in bed with Lena would have been the right decision at the time.

For the next twenty minutes Jack and Sasha drove in silence. At last they came to rest in a clearing, surrounded by an ancient, majestic forest, complete with wild mushrooms and pungent cow manure. Five long tables were waiting under the tall pine trees. They were brimming with appetizers and numerous bottles of liquor.

An occasional ray of sunshine pierced through the thick, green canopy of pine trees to highlight one dish or another. Deep inside the meadow was a man, standing over a makeshift grill, turning two animal carcasses on a spit. Beside him was a huge oval cast-iron pot, which he occasionally would stir with a long thick stick, releasing exquisite aroma into the air.

Several of the bodyguards pressed fingers against their ears, stiffening up. Then a boxy, silver all-terrain Mercedes utility vehicle came out of the forest at a high speed. It rolled over boulders and stumps without bothering to slow down. "It's David, the friend I told you about," Sasha said, smiling. "He's something else." At the last second the driver slammed on the breaks, bringing the car under control. Before the Mercedes came to a complete halt, a short man with bulging arms jumped out from the front passenger seat.

The muscle man eagerly opened the back door for his employer, like a well-trained valet, and a bald man, about fifty years of age, slowly emerged. He was wearing a black sport suit with red stripes, and blindingly white, brand new Adidas sneakers. Although first impressions can be deceiving, Jack thought that David looked like a vicious villain. The sinister gleam in his eyes attested to a great capacity for raging bull violence. Swarthy complexion and permanently scowling, pockmarked face did not help.

David's girlfriend followed behind. She was probably seventeen years old, but looked no more than fifteen, with her blond hair pulled back in a ponytail. Nearly all of the men at Sasha's party instantaneously stopped what they were doing to look at her. And for an excellent reason: this virginal blond was blessed with a hard body and a hot, flat stomach, unburdened by any fatty deposits that come naturally with age. Everyone, including Sasha, silently marveled from a distance.

Witnessing such a reaction, the bald-headed bandit leaned over to his girlfriend and whispered something in her perfectly sculpted ear. By those pouting lips Jack could tell she was disappointed. Still, the girl obediently retreated into his Mercedes, the driver made a sharp U-turn and took off at the same neck-breaking speed as when he arrived.

"David, let me introduce you to my friend, Jack," Sasha cheerfully greeted the bald man. "David controls Odessa ports," Sasha quietly explained as David modestly smiled, flashing his gold tooth. From his physical appearance, and the arrogant demeanor, Jack could see that he was the perfect man for the job.

"It's nice to meet you, David," Jack said gently, as he would to any Neanderthal.

"You too," David said and inhaled the smoke that lingered in the air.

"And my buddy Jack owns a steel plant in Krivoy Rog," Sasha finished the introduction, and David's face stretched in a menacing smile.

"Oh, really?" David raised his eyebrow and said, "then you could probably use a bullet-proof Mercedes. It's fully loaded and I'm asking only fifty grand. You interested?"

"Nope," Jack replied. "But if that car is bullet-proof, it must be worth twice as much. Why is it so cheap?"

"A friend of mine at customs is in charge of confiscated goods," David explained, but Jack did not believe him. Sasha's version, that David has confiscated the car himself and wanted to get rid of it, seemed more plausible. David looked at Jack hawkishly, like he was hypnotizing his victim, and asked, "so what do you say?"

"I don't think so, David, but thanks for the offer."

"A rich young factory owner never knows when he might need a bullet-proof vehicle," David said in a changed tone, like he was warning Jack about a specific problem that only he knew about.

"Oh, yeah? What for?" Jack asked innocently.

"Because wicked people could steal you." David's face continued to wear a lizard-like rubber smile, but his eyes became deadly serious. That got Jack's attention, loud and clear; threats always do. David stood across from Jack with his bow-shaped legs, like a ferocious pit-bull, waiting for a response.

Just a few months ago, before Jack had his own private little army, he would have played everything off as a joke and then quietly walked away from this thug. But David's vanity, the smugness with which he tried to dominate Jack, had the opposite reaction. That is why Jack said, "an old dog should not show his teeth if he can't bite."

Jack delivered that sure-fire insult straight to David's face, knowing that Sasha was standing right beside him. If it came down to it, Sasha would eliminate the disturbance right there, on the spot. The General's men would settle any lingering problems at a more convenient date with just one well-positioned sniper, no matter who David thought he was. It was one of the benefits of owning *ProServe*.

At once David's hairy eyebrows lifted in disbelief, sending waves of wrinkles across his forehead. His thick, hairy, pumped-up arms reached out for Jack's throat. Fortunately for Jack, Sasha jumped in between them, preventing David from tearing his victims' limbs off with his bare hands.

"Hey, hey, David, relax! This is my friend," Sasha said. "We're having a party here."

As Jack expected, Sasha's presence had an immediate calming effect on David. He slowed down considerably, and even allowed himself to slap Jack on the shoulder. "Anybody who speaks to me like that has real balls," David scowled in Jack's direction, extending his hand in peace. "You're welcome in Odessa anytime."

"I'll be sure to give you a call," Jack replied sarcastically, making a mental note to avoid this man for the duration of the party.

"To friendship, then," Sasha said, handing to David a bottle of cold vodka his valet quickly brought over. They passed it around, drinking straight from the bottle, since there were no cups in the immediate vicinity. Then Sasha said, "if you don't mind, David, I am going to introduce Jack to some of my friends."

"Sure thing," David replied. Slowly, with dignity, Jack and Sasha went off in opposite direction from David.

"Don't take him so seriously," Sasha said. "He just got out of prison and hasn't gone through the socialization period yet."

"So is he what you would call a thief-in-law? Like that Ushak and his gang?"

"Not anymore. Real thieves don't work with the government, no matter what. Last month the guy that used to run the Odessa ports was shot. He went for a morning jog with his dog and bodyguards, and two guys jumped out from the bushes. Since then, a friend in the Cabinet of Ministers picked David to run the ports in his place. That's how David got his amnesty. I'm sorry if there was some bad air between the two of you, but David is really a nice guy underneath it all."

"Somewhere very deep underneath," Jack added, "and even then, maybe."

While walking towards the row of tables, brimming with food and alcohol, Jack looked at a rather strange man, who was standing by himself. His face bore a sinister burn across the forehead and he was mumbling to himself. Sasha quietly steered Jack out of his way, saying, "that's an old buddy of mine. Don't talk to him, OK? It's for your own safety. Now, over here is Victor, a man I would trust with my own life." Sasha pointed to a large man who was barely able to sit upright at the table. "Hey, Victor, look over here, I want you to meet our employer."

"Hello," Jack said.

"Wake up, Victor, it's a great day," Sasha shook his friend's shoulder. Victor opened his eyes and then Jack could tell that he was not sleepy at all; Victor's mind was somewhere else. He looked as if Sasha interrupted a soul-to-soul conversation he carried on with himself. "Meet my friend, Jack."

"Have a seat, Jack," Victor smiled weakly. He seemed like a genuinely nice guy, so Jack decided to stay with him for a quick drink while Sasha went off to pal around with David.

"So, what's on your mind, Victor?" Jack asked the gentle giant. "You seem kind of down."

"We were patrolling the streets, like we always do, when I spotted him," Victor quietly started to explain. "This darkie was walking along, all by himself, so we pulled over to take a closer look. Right away I could tell that he was not from Kiev. He could been from Azerbaijan, or Georgia or Chechnya, from the mountains, that is. In any case, he was obviously a foreigner, and our job is to make sure that no criminals roam our streets, so the sergeant asked him for identification papers.

"Yes sir, he answered, but real slow, like he was dumb or something. We were waiting for him to offer us money to let him go, but he didn't say anything. He just stood there, smiling like an imbecile, pretending like he didn't understand the situation. By now, I could tell he wasn't going to pay. The sergeant saw it too, so we shoved him into the back of the wagon. We have the right to detain any suspicious individual for seventy two hours without charges, and we exercised our legal right. To my surprise, the darkie didn't resist, which is unusual with these mountain people. There is no need for violence, I will get in myself, he said, but I wanted to make sure he realized that we were serious, so I punched him a few times. "At the station we took him downstairs to the interrogation room. I chained him to the heating battery, just to soften him up. After a few shots of vodka we returned, and the sergeant showed him a kilo bag with marijuana, the one we confiscated last year from the gypsies. You see this? the sergeant asked him. We found this on you tonight. Do you know how many years you will spend in prison for drug dealing in Ukraine?

"No, he said, this isn't mine, it's a mistake. When I looked at his face, I realized what was wrong with him: this darkie was mentally slow. He was retarded. I didn't know if the sergeant saw that, but it probably would not have made any difference at that point anyway, because the process had already began. The sergeant said, I'm afraid it's you who are making a mistake. He nodded to me, and I knew what he meant.

"The first time I beat him so badly, he could not speak anymore. We left him alone for a few hours, still chained to the battery, until he came around. He just lay there, covered in blood, moaning, so I did it again. And again, for nothing. The third time I just didn't have the heart to do it. Even the sergeant told me to leave him alone."

Victor opened his eyes, begging Jack for sympathy and forgiveness, but none was forthcoming. Looking at Victor, Jack has never seen such emotional pain; guilt was gnawing away at the poor man's insides. The more vodka Victor drank, the more ashamed he felt about what he had done.

"So what happened to the darkie?" Jack asked, speaking in Victor's language.

Victor's tear-stained eyes opened wide as he looked straight ahead, horrified, like he was revisiting the gruesome scene. "We put him in a cell with the others and then went upstairs to drink some more vodka to forget him," Victor said, tears swelling up in his eyes. "But I still can't... And before that, I would deliver homeless bums to the training camp all the time. Strange, but it never bothered me."

"What training camp?"

"You're with Sasha, so you must know... The training camp, just outside Kiev. We supply homeless bums to them. Instead of the drunk tanks, we take them out for karate practice. Our guys literally kick the life out of these drunkards, breaking their bones to reach the vital organs. Personally, I never cared because they're homeless scum, but the look of that dumb kid, the stupid smile on his face, it really got to me. The next day I went to church and then I quit the police department. Thank God Sasha gave me a decent job."

"It was very nice to meet you, Victor," Jack said, getting up from the table, "and congratulations on your new employment." To own a protection firm is one thing, Jack thought, but there is no need to know personal information about his employees. To get away, Jack made a beeline for the cook, a jovial man standing by himself, turning the baby pig on the spit. As an introduction Jack asked, half-joking, "killed anyone lately?"

"Just these two," the chef pointed to the lamb and the piglet. "But it was for a worthy cause."

"I see that you have good wine, too."

"The best Georgian wine available," he nodded to the tables. "Care of the customs police, freshly confiscated just three days ago from a real live Georgian. Help yourself. By the way, I'm Grisha, the cook."

"Very nice to meet you, Grisha."

The confiscated Georgian wine had a silky texture, a little tart, but very satisfying. After sharing with Grisha the rich, full-bodied bottle of wine, Jack's taste buds salivated over the luscious roast suckling pig that was rotating on a spit. Light breeze carried over the aroma of perfectly spiced lamb. Standing near this outdoor kitchen was becoming unbearable.

"So when is the food going to be ready?"

"If you're hungry, try this." Grisha cut off a juicy slice from the lamb, another from the pork, and placed them on the china platter nearby. The concentrated, sweet and smoky flavors and the unique blend of seasonings covering Grisha's roasted meats were out of this world.

"This is fantastic," Jack smacked his lips. "Truly magnificent. How did you get it so tender?"

"The main secret is the marinade. The pork is first marinated in adzhika and then refrigerated for two days. Then you baste and turn until the meat falls off the bone."

The next bottle of confiscated Georgian wine had a different taste. Although it was also thick-textured, this juicy red wine had a slightly herbal note, accented by licorice. And so Jack remained drinking with Grisha-the-cook until the rest of the company ambled over to a nearby long makeshift table, which easily exceeded fifty feet.

As the guests poured deep glasses of vodka in preparation for the first toast, an assortment of dishes from the Central Asia were brought to the table, starting with plov, the lamb-based rice dish. The aromatic plov was prepared in the kazan, a separate huge oval cast-iron pot, which hung low over a charcoal fire. Then came two large bowls with the Georgian lamb stew with cumin and coriander.

The first person to deliver a toast was, naturally, David. By that reptilian smile Jack could tell how much David enjoyed playing the role of a criminal celebrity. David rose from the chair as if he was the only logical opening act at Sasha's party, raised his glass and waited for the restless group to grow quiet.

"Dear friends," David's voice sounded tough, coarse. "The time has arrived when the thieves and the law are no longer mortal enemies, but simple businessmen, working together in the name of prosperity. So let me be the first amongst the thieves to raise this toast to our newfound cooperation that has coincided, and not accidentally, with Sasha's birthday!"

Sasha's merry gang drank up, leaving their glasses empty. By this time, Grisha finished carving up the lamb and the roasted piglet. He proudly presented large chunks of meat to the guests on two huge silver platters. An enthusiastic round of applause followed. Of course, Sasha had the first pick, before Grisha served the others. The scene of a feast in the middle of a forest could have easily taken place in the days of horse-drawn carriages and highway robberies.

The sun shone through the old pine trees as the guests poured out their hearts in beautifully phrased toasts, one by one standing up, all in Sasha's honor. Today Sasha turned thirty three years of age; a man of wealth and respect by anybody's standards, especially in Kiev. That was why only the finest Georgian wine, with the most tender and perfectly spiced meats, would do on this occasion. Like everyone there, Jack was relaxed, enjoying the tranquility and fresh smell of pine air, when Victor raised his glass to offer a birthday toast to Sasha.

"Thank you for taking me in when I was going down. Long life to you, Sasha, and may you die in your own bed," Victor slurred his words and swallowed another shot of vodka. He must be very drunk to deliver such a somber toast at a birthday party, Jack thought, but looking around the table he noticed that many guests were nodding at the wisdom of Victor's words.

While Sasha's guests were sitting in the middle of a grassy meadow, getting drunk, it dawned on Jack that he was the only innocent lamb in the middle of a social function normally open strictly to big bad wolves. Fierce-looking men sitting around the table, surrounded by bodyguards with far more disturbing facial features, supported this conclusion. Then again, Jack thought, how innocent could I be if I hire people like them?

Fortunately, the animals were neither hungry for money nor thirsty for blood. That, and Sasha's watchful presence, made Jack feel relatively safe in this company. The party went on for many hours, though he did not manage to stay awake until the end. Sasha and his buddies got Jack so drunk that he fell asleep in the forest, on a carpet of soft, green grass.

# Chapter 31

Jack's first sensation of the morning, and the reason he woke up at all, was a steady, burning pain. Slowly Jack pulled out his throbbing left hand from under the blanket to discover a bloated, dark-blue quarter-size tattoo, which was crudely etched into the skin prominently between his thumb and the index finger. Jack cringed at the ugly sight of a circle, surrounding a five-point star with a crown, whatever that meant.

This stupid tattoo will kill my legal career faster than any venereal disease ever could, Jack thought. How the hell did I get it? No immediate explanation came to mind, which is understandable, considering the amount of alcohol Jack had consumed the day before. Then he froze, afraid to face Lena's wrath.

Turning to her, Jack wanted to apologize for leaving so abruptly yesterday morning, to ask for forgiveness for being tipsy last night, but Lena was not there. The only thing Jack found, on her pillow, was the official-looking KGB file that Sasha let him borrow. According to Jack's watch it was 2:25 p.m. Lena could be anywhere by now, Jack thought, probably sitting in some cafe with her girlfriends, complaining about my rude behavior.

With his injury-free right hand Jack tugged at the strings that kept the ancient file together, and it unfolded before his eyes, releasing an old, musty smell. Inside, Jack found several official-looking, typed reports along with one hand-written note and two black-and-white photographs. He skimmed over the first page:

*"V. S. Pavlov. Arrested at 2:30 a.m. on May 4, 1937, based on a tip from an informant Konstantin Vasilievich Karasik that starting in 1928 Comrade Pavlov collaborated with the Polish intelligence."*

Apparently, despite five months of brutal interrogations, Vladimir refused to confess to any crimes. The attached sheet of paper, dated October 3, 1937, was hand written in large, bold letters, and read as follows:

*"I am not guilty of any crimes, and I can not understand what is wanted from me and what I should confess to. I wrote many requests for explanations, but the prison warden provides no answers. I consider this to be inhumane treatment and a personal insult to my dignity. The prison guards under the Czars granted prisoners better conditions than the Soviet country does.*

*My conscience prevents me from meekly accepting the current predicament, where someone checked off my name from a list, forcing me to serve twenty five years in prison. And exactly for what, nobody has explained, and still will not tell me. You can try to extract a confession by slowly destroying a person, but in this case, you are wasting your time. You will get my confession only when I go insane."*

According to the next official report, Vladimir was sentenced to twenty five years' hard labor and sent to *Solovetsky* camp, located on the grounds of a former monastery. He became one of the worst prisoners the guards had ever seen, judging by one of their complaints:

*"The prisoner told the guards that unless he is informed about his family, nobody would be allowed to enter his cell and he will behave as disruptively as possible so that "the executioners would strangle him faster." Afterwards, the prisoner continually violated internal rules by singing and whistling loudly, disturbing the rest of the population. The prisoner ignored the guard's repeated demands to stop singing and whistling, and was transferred to the isolation cell for one month."*

While turning these ancient pages, Jack got the impression that Boris' father was an unusually stubborn man; one entry after another supported this conclusion. The next comment, entered four months later, spoke loudly about the strength of this man's character:

*"The prisoner continues to disrupt the internal order by whistling and singing, as well as throwing objects including human waste against the cell walls and bars. When ordered to stop, the prisoner denied any wrongdoing and called the guards "executioners." The prisoner resorted to using fists, injuring one guard, and received two months in the isolation cell."*

Unable to resist the temptation, Jack jumped to the last page of the file. In the end, the Stalinist camp system did not break Boris' father; a bullet did. He was shot near a small Karelian town called *Medvezhyegorsk* on June 3, 1938, along with one thousand three hundred forty seven other prominent individuals. It was a sad, but not entirely unexpected, ending. Jack thought that hopefully this information will allow Boris Vladimirovich to get some closure.

"Lena?" he called out from the bedroom, "honey, are you here?" There was no reply, which confirmed that she must have stormed out for the afternoon. Jack got out of bed with some difficulty and stumbled into the kitchen to make a cup of coffee. On the table he found Lena's short note. It read:

*"I asked you to stay away from bandits, but I see that you can not. Your tattoo says that you are a thief-in-law, and I saw some prisoners' secret file. So are you a thief or a spy? Either way, you are a liar. Goodbye, thief, spy and liar. Do not call me again."*

That brief note hurt Jack more than his new tattoo and pounding headache, combined. It was not fair, Jack wanted to scream, but he was too nauseated. The obvious solution was to find Lena and explain the simple truth. Unfortunately, the only telephone number where he could reach Lena was at her work, effective no earlier than Monday morning. And the simple truth was that Jack did not know how he got the damned tattoo.

In an effort to resolve the tattoo mystery, Jack remembered David's opening toast. That's when he switched from drinking wine to gulping vodka. From that point on, things got fuzzy. Concentrating hard, Jack reconstructed a mental image of David, his bulletproof boxy Mercedes and a shotgun in a hard-shell case. Suddenly, a vivid flashback: Sasha was not supposed to know that the engraved Remington was his birthday gift from David's organization.

The last thing Jack recalled was David inviting him to a sauna, and then Jack did not remember anything at all. Surely I could not have possibly gone with this criminal into a sauna, Jack gasped at the thought. As much as he tried, though, Jack experienced a complete memory failure. The more he stared at his inflamed left hand, the more Jack's moronic tattoo began to look familiar, just like one on David's hand.

David showed Jack some of the other tattoos he earned while running the prison, including a crude eagle that looked like an evil chicken, displayed across his hairy back. So that's why my little masterpiece looks so familiar, Jack realized. David had one just like it etched into his skin, exactly in the same spot. Now Jack remembered how proud David was of the tattoo, going on about the honor of being inside the circle of thieves-in-law, until Jack passed out.

This is why Lena was so upset, Jack thought. Finally he understood: while working at Podium, Lena probably saw similar markings on some of John Hatchet's buyers. Naturally, she presumed that last night he was sworn in as a real thief-in-law, a mini-king of the criminal world, just like David once was. This ludicrous misconception could easily be corrected, Jack was certain, after Lena learns that it was all a bad joke.

The only problem was finding Lena on a Sunday afternoon. Jack had no clue where to start looking except, perhaps by sheer luck, he might run into her at the place they first met, that cheap joint called Texas Bar-B-Q. The odds were minuscule, but worth pursuing. Half an hour later he was seated at the familiar bar.

"Bartender, I'll have a beer and a shot of that tequila," Jack pointed at a square bottle with a worm at the bottom, "and a cheeseburger platter." The tequila shot was surprisingly ineffective in comparison to good old vodka, so Jack had another. Then his burger arrived, the bartender started cracking jokes, and the rest of the afternoon flew by in a flash.

Soon enough it was past 6 p.m., and a steady stream of customers began to arrive for the happy hour. Everything was peaceful until Jack returned from the bathroom to discover that a large, bulky man with a crew cut was sitting on his barstool. He looked like an American farmer, grain-fed and satisfied. An unruly combination of alcohol and built-up frustration took the better of Jack. "You're in my seat," he said in English. "Get out."

"Forget it," the man replied and turned away. His English was tainted with a Southern drawl and the crew cut on his head indicated that he considered himself to be a tough guy. The man continued to occupy Jack's stool, sipping his beer, acting like Jack was invisible. Something had to be done. While looking around the bar Jack bumped against him, delivering a sharp elbow jab into his side.

The large man swallowed the bait. He turned to Jack and said, "hey, what the hell... You'd better watch yourself, son!"

"Listen over here, asshole," Jack looked him directly in the eye and spoke through teeth, just like Clint Eastwood, declaring open war. "Get off my seat and run away from this bar, as far as possible, while you still can walk."

"What did you just say to me?" The man slowly got up, surprising Jack with his height: at six foot four inches, the giant towered several heads above him. This display of muscle did not intimidate Jack, however, not after his standoff with David at Sasha's party. If this bully wanted to prove himself, then Jack was glad to introduce him to an even bigger bully, Sasha, free of charge.

Measuring at the man's chest lever, Jack looked upwards, into his flaring nostrils. "My good friend will drive over here in ten minutes to kill you," Jack said calmly. "If you don't get out off my stool, pal, you won't make it home tonight."

The man sized Jack up and down, emphasizing the enormous height difference between them, but did not respond. By the puzzled expression on his enemy's face Jack saw that he could not believe the audacity of this conversation, especially coming from a person much smaller than himself. Muscles flexed under the man's sweater, suggesting that he was getting ready for a fight.

In response, Jack reached for his cell telephone and dialed Sasha's telephone number. He paused before pushing the green "send" button, giving his opponent one last chance to plead for mercy. It worked. "Listen, partner, I don't know what your problem is, but I have twenty Marines in that room, playing pool," the man said, becoming worried. "Do you really want to mess with all of us?"

Drunk and boisterous, not quite listening to him anymore, Jack said what was on his mind: "it's all the same to me. Bring 'em on! I'll have all of you motherfuckers killed." Then Jack's pickled mind slowly registered something about "twenty Marines," so he clarified, "wait, did you say you were a Marine? With the U.S. Embassy, I presume?"

"Yeah," the large man replied cautiously, "I'm in charge of the Marines. What about it?"

"Actually, I'm an American, too," Jack explained, putting away the telephone. He did not want this incident to reach Ambassador Pilfer, because threatening to wipe out his Marines would surely count as a second strike against Jack. "No sense fighting each other, huh? Can I buy you a beer?"

"Sure," the Marine said with a sigh of relief.

"Two Coronas and two tequilas," Jack called out to the bartender. "Cheers."

After taking a gulp of his Corona, the Marine asked Jack, "so what the hell was that all about?"

"I'm going through a bad time with my girlfriend right now," Jack answered honestly. "Sorry you had to put up with my crap."

"No problem, pal, but take it easy next time, alright?"

"Sure. What's your name, anyway?"

"Sergeant Joseph T. Cane from Crawford, Texas, but my friends call me Joey. Pleased to meet you, partner."

"Jack Parker. No hard feelings, I hope."

"Hey, shit happens," Joey said. "Been there myself."

They sat together at the bar, trading war stories and old jokes, until past 2 a.m. Even though Lena never showed up, Jack still had a good time with his new drinking buddy, Joey. It turned out that Joey was recently transferred to Kiev from South Korea because of unspecified problems with local girls, but he refused to expand on the topic.

"Don't forget to call Lena first thing in the morning," were Joey's last words of brotherly advice before Jack stumbled out of the bar.

# Chapter 32

As Volodya drove Jack to work, they passed the Parliament building on *Grushevsky* Street. Jack looked at the large black Mercedeses, Audi's, BMW's and Landcruisers that were parked along the way. Across from the luxury automobiles were rows of coal miners, sitting on their oil-stained sleeping bags. When Jack saw similar vehicles on parade at Sasha's birthday party, they seemed perfectly appropriate for the occasion. Now, against the background of dirt-poor coal miners, with their dusty, cracked faces, the same cars looked obscene.

The Donetsk and Lugansk coal miners were once again picketing in front of the Parliament, demanding that the government finally pay their miserly salaries. Their mines were privatized late last year, however, just like Jack's steel mill. The real owners also kept their profits in offshore accounts, leaving the miners without salaries. In this case, the government was not to blame for their poverty: it was the real owners, those former directors with large stomachs, that moonlighted as democratically elected deputies to the Parliament.

The bosses privatized the coal mines just like Jack and his partners did with the steel mills, but unlike Jack, the Donetsk and Lugansk chiefs refused to upgrade equipment to provide their workers with basic safety. They also forgot to pay minimal salaries on a regular basis. That is why the coal miners were protesting: to be able to buy food for their families, and only secondarily, for their own safety. Does this make the new owners of the coal mines robber barons? Jack wondered. And, more importantly from an ethical viewpoint, are we in the same category?

The press sometimes critisized the new millionaires for blatantly flaunting their wealth while ignoring their own country, vast and impoverished, cursed with low living standards and high mortality rates. But Jack believed their accusations missed the point entirely. His riches were excusable because they were earned by running a legitimate business. Good old fashioned capitalism, investment in assets for profit. Salary payments of the coal miners was not Jack's obligation. And providing for the general safety and welfare of Ukrainian citizens was their government's function.

By the time Volodya reached the bottom of the Parliament hill, Jack counted a total of thirty-two very expensive cars. All of them were purchased for cash because no bank, Ukrainian or foreign, would extend auto loans to Ukrainian citizens. They always default, leaving nothing to collect. By Jack's rough assessment, the Parliament hill had more than two million dollars' worth of automobiles on that sunny morning. Similar vehicles can be found parked in front of Sergei's casinos and restaurants, Jack compared, and yet none of us are criminals. We are businessmen who make our own money, not politicians who steal from the budget.

As Volodya waited for the traffic light to change, Jack looked into the weathered faces of those grimy, tired coal miners. Unlike their Western colleagues, who would surely have pelted the government leaders and their cars with rotten eggs and tomatoes, the Ukrainian miners did not dare to touch the precious shiny vehicles. Without salaries, they could not afford to repair even a minor scratch.

Jack knew that in contrast to the owners of these vehicles, for most Ukrainians it was a daily struggle to survive. Unemployment and alcoholism were rife. Life expectancy was falling. The inequality between the Parliament members and the rest of the country was stunning. Soon, breaking out of this predicament will become impossible, Jack predicted.

Volodya's car moved slowly past the Stalinist gothic Ministry of Finance on their left. The coal miners continued to peacefully picket outside the Parliament, hoping against all reason that the government bureaucrats would feel guilty and somehow allocate the money from the budget to pay them. By the time Jack arrived to his office, he almost managed to deflect his own accusations. Almost, but not quite.

As soon as Jack got behind his desk, he thought about what to say to Lena. He had to get in touch with her today, come hell or high water. Just as Jack was about to dial Lena's work number, a short pudgy man in his mid-thirties stormed inside his office. His head was heavily bandaged with white gauze. "I need a lawyer to sue the bastards!" he demanded in English.

"Do you mind if I make a quick phone call?" Jack asked politely. All he needed was five minutes to speak with Lena privately, but the unannounced visitor did not want to hear it.

"I'll be brief," the man said, sitting in the chair across from Jack's desk. "By the way, can I get a cup of coffee? I take cream and sugar."

"Tanya," Jack called out to his receptionist, "can you get our guest a cup of coffee? He wants cream and sugar."

"He already told me that," Tanya replied loudly from the next room. "No please, no thank you, no nothing."

As Tanya's employer, and the owner of a corporate boutique, Jack felt that her comments were inappropriate because any potential client, as rude and obnoxious as he may be, is a source of income. "She's new," Jack said apologetically.

The man replied, "don't you require your secretary to speak Ukrainian? After all, we *are* in Ukraine."

"Tanya is from Kiev, so she is used to speaking Russian," Jack explained diplomatically. "Generally, people from the Western Ukraine are more fluent in the Ukrainian language."

"This is Ukraine," the man replied coldly, "and if you can't speak the language, then you should either learn or get out."

"Of course, you are right," Jack said, deliberately avoiding an argument with a die-hard Ukrainian nationalist. "So what can I do for you today?"

It took several minutes for Jack to see that Mark, or Markian as he preferred to be called, rode into Kiev from New Jersey on a high horse of self-righteous indignation. As proud members of the American-Ukrainian diaspora, that is Ukrainians born in America, from an early age Markian's parents instilled in him a moral obligation to help the old country.

Trying to stay true to his heritage, Markian relocated to Kiev in order to remedy all things gone wrong in the Ukrainian society. After living in Kiev for several weeks, like many foreigners, Markian became alarmed by the level of open corruption and social injustice in the country he came to save.

By now Markian wasted almost ten minutes of Jack's precious time. Jack resented being stuck listening to a babbling idiot, whose goal was to change Ukraine for the better, while he could be patching things up with Lena. "So what do you want from me?" Jack finally asked him plainly.

"I want to sue the bastards who did this," Markian demanded angrily, pointing to his bandaged head. "This country needs a wake-up lesson!"

Apparently, while walking down *Pushkin* Street the previous night, Markian noticed three policemen in uniform, and yet completely drunk. In broken Ukrainian, which he learned as a child, Markian chastised them. "What kind of an example are you setting for the citizens?" he remarked, passing them by. He continued walking, but not fast enough, because a nightstick smashed the top of his skull. Markian fell to the ground, bleeding. Each of the policemen took turns kicking him in the groin and kidneys, but soon they lost interest because he no longer responded.

"And they let you go?" Jack asked incredulously.

"Those animals threw me in the trunk of their police car," Markian's eyes had tears of self-pity. "Fortunately, I came around while they were driving. I could feel a trickle of blood running down my neck, and through the cardboard wall I heard them laughing, but this time I kept my mouth shut."

"Good decision."

"I knew something wrong was about to happen, so I was ready to fight them regardless of the outcome."

"That was very brave of you."

"You bet," Markian nodded in agreement. "Then the car stopped and I heard them getting out, so I played dead. They unlocked the trunk, yanked me out and carried me to the river. I knew we were getting closer because I could hear the water splashing. Probably I must have been too heavy for them because one of the cops accidentally dropped my legs. The other two also decided to rest and they let go of my arms. Before they could get a better grip on me, I jumped up and ran for my life as fast as I could."

"And they did not bother to shoot you? Nobody ran after you?"

"I didn't see, I was just trying to make it around the corner and get out of their sight. And I made it, too. So now, what are you going to do about it?"

Glancing at his watch, Jack explained to Markian that nobody was going to fight on his behalf with the police department. Not in Kiev.

"What can they do to me? Nothing! And you know why? Because I am an American citizen, that's why. And the last thing Ukraine needs is an international diplomatic scandal."

"Get over yourself. Nobody is going to start a third world war over you. In the meantime, you could get into real trouble."

"So what are they going to do? Kill me?"

"Worse. Just like police in New York, Chicago or L.A., the Kiev cops are an uncontrollable bunch of armed thugs. If they so much as get a whiff of you attempting to mess around with them, they will stop you on the street and ask to see your identification papers. Regardless of what you'll say about being an American citizen, they will haul you into detention. Do you know much about the conditions in the Ukrainian detention centers?"

"No," Markian answered, puffing angrily.

"They can hold you for up to three days without filing any charges. That gives them seventy two hours to do what they want with your body. The usual routine involves beatings and sodomy. Please do not misunderstand them: they are not all homosexuals. It's a form of torture. They want you to lose your dignity as a human being, to break you. After that, you will be labeled a "rooster," which in prison dialect is a license for everyone to fuck you in the ass. In U.S. prisons, under similar circumstances they would call you a "bitch," even though biologically you are a man, but I digress."

"This is not..." Markian began to protest.

"No, please don't interrupt me." Jack wanted to finish his shock therapy session and get Markian out of his office. "After the initial three-day period is over, you will be released on the street, hopefully still in walking condition. Suddenly, another police patrol will approach you, asking for your documents. You will present them, only to be taken in for another three days on a suspicion of raping some grandmother. This will continue indefinitely, until you are no longer a menace to the police society. Now, tell me, Markian, when should I file your complaint? Later today or tomorrow morning? Or maybe you want to think about it some more, until your head feels better?"

"So you are not competent to file a law suit, is that what you're saying?"

Clearly, experience taught Markian nothing. He still harbored the illusion of attaining justice in a legal arena against the law enforcers. By now Jack's patience had run out. Markian was an easy mark, the kind Jack would gladly charge double the billable hourly rate. This morning, however, calling Lena took priority over parting this fool with his money.

"Drop it, Markian," Jack advised him, "and next time think twice before teaching the locals how to live their lives. Excuse me, but I have to make an important phone call."

"And I thought you were an honest lawyer," Markian hissed before leaving. "I'll complain to the American Embassy about you. Just you wait!"

If this bastard actually complains, that's strike number two, Jack thought while dialing Podium's main line. "Podium, how can I help you?" The familiar voice of the receptionist meant that any second Jack would be connected to Lena, and his hands became moist with nervous sweat.

"May I please speak with Lena?"

"Who is calling?"

"Jack. Jack Parker," he said and immediately regretted his honesty. What if Lena did not want to speak with him?

"I am sorry, Mr. Parker," the receptionist answered, "but she does not wish to speak with you."

"Wait a minute..."

"And she requested that you do not call her, ever again. I am sorry and good bye, Mr. Parker."

Feeling lost and confused, Jack wanted to drop everything and rush over to Podium to see Lena, to talk it out with her face to face, but he knew enough to wait until she left work at 6 p.m. The security at Podium definitely would not let him in.

At precisely 5:25 p.m. Jack turned off his computer, ready to sprint outside to Volodya's car, which would deliver him straight to Lena. At that moment, Tanya announced, "Sergei is on the line for you, Jack. Are you available?"

"Damn," Jack muttered under his breath and reached for the telephone. "What's up, Sergei?"

"Alexei just called. He said there was some bad news." Sergei sounded sober and serious, which was not a good sign. "He wants to hold an emergency meeting of shareholders as soon as possible."

"When and where?" Jack did not ask any other questions, because clearly this was not a telephone conversation.

"In thirty minutes, at *The Camelot*."

This was terrible timing, indeed. Jack tried to weasel out of the meeting, pleading, "can't you handle it yourself? I kind of have a prior commitment this evening."

"This is business. Do you really have more important things to do?"

"No, I guess not," Jack nearly cried into the receiver. "I'll see you soon."

Instead of greeting Lena with flowers that evening, Jack ended up at Sergei's new restaurant, *The Camelot*, on *Klovsky Spusk*. From the outside, the place looked like a fortified castle, from the thick iron bars on the windows to the gargantuan double doors with ancient engravings. As Jack approached the solid doors, two cameras above moved a little. They were mounted across each other in such a way as to monitor the visitors as well as the street. The heavy door swung open just as he reached out to grasp the brass doorknob. A large man, with a metal armor plate on his chest and a long sword at his side, invited Jack inside.

"Welcome to *The Camelot!*" The tin man respectfully held the door ajar. The entry was lit up with several antique torches, giving the customers an impression they had entered the Middle Ages. Broad-blade swords and large knives adorned the walls. Four realistic mini-cannons were positioned in each of the corners. To the left Jack noticed two other knights, decked out in identical shining armor and holding long spears, guarding a massive, iron-studded wooden door.

"This way, please." One of the knights opened the heavy wood-and-metal door. Sergei was waiting behind the bar in an empty, dark chamber, illuminated by three candelabras. He was already nursing a healthy dose of scotch. The bar area was paneled with dark mahogany, giving it aristocratic, serene atmosphere.

"Alexei isn't here yet?" Jack asked.

"Nope. Running late, as always. What are you drinking?" Sergei was playing the role of a bartender, as bosses sometimes like to do.

"Same as you." Jack sat down across from him. "Nice guys at the door. They're new, right?"

"Yup. The General hired thirty two more soldiers, six for this restaurant and the rest for the casinos. This makes *ProServe* the largest privately owned security company in Ukraine. The small businessmen are beginning to hire us for protection from the criminals! How about that? It's us against the racketeers! And I bet we'll win every time."

"That's good news. It means business is picking up and regular folks have more money to spend," Jack said, looking around the well-decorated bar. "You know, I really like the atmosphere in this place. Any plans to open it to the public?"

"As soon as we find the right chef." Sergei poured single malt scotch over ice for Jack. They nodded to each other and sipped without saying anything. Then Sergei suggested, "why don't we wait for Alexei in the dining area?"

Sergei escorted Jack through a yet another thick door into a grand hallway, filled with dark, heavy wooden tables and solid oak chairs. Silk drapery fell in folds down the walls. From the ceiling hung thirteen rich, purple velvet flags, each embossed with gold threads of a knight's coat of armor.

For some reason Jack was not surprised to see more steel-plated men standing on the stone pedestals along the walls, confidently holding double-edged swords. When his eyes adjusted to the darkness Jack realized, to his disappointment, that these ones were fake. After they sat down at one of the tables, Sergei considerately asked Jack, "by the way, are you hungry?"

"Maybe just a little," Jack replied politely, feeling like he could eat a moose. "I didn't have lunch today."

"Great!" Sergei snapped his fingers and a waitress appeared from the shadows. "Order anything you like, as many different dishes as you want. And if you don't like something, I'll kill the chef."

"Sounds like you don't like the guy," Jack said, sipping the strong drink. "Why not just fire him?"

"Premature. The last chef couldn't cook worth a damn, so now I'm testing this Italian guy we stole from *DeMario*. And before I can open this placed to the public, someone has to taste everything on the menu at least twice, just to make sure he can duplicate the same dish."

"I see." Jack glanced at Sergei's expanded waistline.

"Yeah. I can't eat anymore food, just look at my stomach. It's your turn to gain weight."

"Sounds good to me!" Jack envisioned a thick, juicy double-cut veal chop, or maybe even a rack of lamb. "But you're not really planning to kill the chef just because I don't like one or two dishes, are you?" It was a prudent question to ask before ordering.

"It was a joke, Jack. I don't kill chefs. If this one is also no good, we'll keep trying until we find the right man."

"Let's see the menu, then." Jack was relieved that Sergei retained his famous sense of humor despite becoming the boss of Kiev. "And the wine list."

"Remember, this is supposed to be an exclusive restaurant, extremely sophisticated," Sergei said while Jack flipped through the menu. "So, what do you think?"

The first several pages reflected the owners' passion: Jack saw at least thirty different vodkas, all infused with different fruit, including strawberries, raspberries, sour cherries and fresh peaches. Jack noticed that Sergei even offered hot mint and honey vodka, along with an impressive assortment of French wines, brandies and cognacs, as well as Cuban cigars.

"Do you have anything non-alcoholic to eat?"

"Try the next page."

The second-to-last page of Sergei's menu described food that Jack would not ordinarily order, given a choice. He scanned the menu twice, feeling that he had entered a previously uncharted culinary zone. The new chef is either a brilliant artist or a nit-wit, Jack thought. The full-page menu that Sergei was so worried about read as follows:

*Oxtail-Stuffed Baby Squid with Cremini Mushrooms, Mustard Oil and Oxtail Braising Juices*

*Baby Eel with Olive Oil-Poached Tomato Cucumber Sauce and Seaweed Salad*

*Frog Legs with Roasted Eggplant Puree and Saffron*

*Sea Urchin and Osetra Caviar with Vodka Creme*

*Duck Gizzards in Veal Stock Reduction and Olive Oil*

*Skate Wing with Zucchini, Black Trumpet Mushrooms, Brussel Sprouts and Curry*

*Chilean Sea Bass with Pinot-Noir Stewed Shallots and Veal Stock Reduction*

"Does anything strike you as being particularly appetizing?" Sergei asked.

"The combination of Thai lobster tail, pigeon breast with black trumped mushrooms and pigeon jus," Jack finally read the very last dish at the bottom of the page. From the corner of his eye Jack could see the waitress writing down his order and then disappearing into the darkness. Since Alexei was running late, Jack decided to get Sergei's opinion about the coal miners on the Parliament hill.

"Let me ask you something, Sergei. We all have a few million bucks stashed away, right? But do you think that we're doing something corrupt or criminal? I mean, we pay quarterly bribes to the Minister's family, contribute millions to the President's re-election fund. In return, we get the first right to buy huge steel plants in rigged auctions. To me, that's corruption."

"Not in my view," Sergei replied without hesitation. "If one equates corruption with crime, then the entire nation of Ukraine is a work of crime in progress. Especially people who work in the government. Countless employees in the Ministry of Interior, the tax authorities, courts and customs officials alike. From a lowly traffic cop on the street to the President himself."

As a practicing lawyer, Jack had to admit that the cops, judges and customs were by far the worst at blatantly demanding bribes. Still, Sergei's simplistic explanation was not enough to clear his conscience. "But if we give out bribes, and the government officials take them, then aren't we as bad as they are? It's like a chicken-and-egg problem. So who do you think is responsible for the start of this corruption cycle?"

"Just ask yourself: would any businessman willingly part with his hard-earned money, unless some government employee was standing in the way, extorting a kick-back? Of course not! And it's getting worse each year. We are being forced to pay our way through life like never before. You wouldn't believe it, Jack, but the cost of the average bribe has sky-rocketed. Officials now have price-lists for bribes! Now, you know as well as I do, if a businessman doesn't pay, he can't play. We have to share our profits with the government parasites only to be able to carry on working. And they're becoming more greedy because sooner or later they will lose their jobs, so they're trying to grab all they can before retirement. In my opinion, the government is the source of corruption, not business."

Again, Sergei's logic was rock-solid. Everyday, on every level of society, bribes were demanded: by the respected university professors to get into their universities, by the doctors for services that are supposed to be free, by military officials for an exemption from mandatory conscription, by the judges for ruling in your favor, by the traffic cops just for stopping you on the street. The list of offenders went on and on.

"Yeah, but hiding our profits offshore without paying taxes is not exactly clean living, either," Jack tried to play the Devil's advocate. "How is that justified?"

"The way I see it, the government can either take my taxes or my bribes. They can't have it both ways. And frankly, the services they offer in return for taxes are just not worth it. Their hard-working police? Their unbiased judges? No thanks."

"Got it," Jack said, feeling better about his rating on the corruption scale. "Thanks for clearing this up for me. You know us, lawyers. Ethical appoach and all."

"Go forth and continue with your business, my son," Sergei laugingly crossed Jack, playing the Pope. "You hereby are absolved of your sins. Now, relax. Have another drink."

"Sorry for being late," Alexei barged into the dining area unannounced. He was all business, dressed in a tailored dark wool suit and an expensive-looking tie, just like Jack's former boss, Gerald. At last, Alexei's transformation from an awkward government geek to a suave oligarch was complete.

"Please sit down, have a drink, order something from the menu," Sergei said. "It's a free degustation day, so try a little bit of everything."

Alexei flipped to the very last page of the menu, one that Jack did not see, and said, "I'll have the chef's choice: soft-shell crab with hazelnuts, followed by African pompano with macadamia nut crust and white asparagus. Now, can we talk about business?"

"Sure," Sergei said. Like Jack, he was impressed with a marked change in Alexei's sophistication and taste.

"The good news is that the Anti-Monopoly Committee approved our proposal to merge all the plants into one integrated concern. Congratulations, gentlemen, we are now officially the kings of steel."

"Holy shit! You actually pulled it off!" Jack exclaimed. They now held a monopoly on the Ukrainian steel market. Neither Sergei nor Jack dared to expect this result, especially from the strict Anti-Monopoly Committee, despite Alexei's assurances to the contrary.

"My dear Alexei," Sergei beamed, "I love you. With all of my heart, I truly do."

"It was the President's way of telling us, thank you. Our contribution was generous and timely."

"Tell the President to call us if he needs our help again," Sergei chuckled.

"And now, for the bad news."

Jack looked at Sergei, and they both asked in unison, "what bad news?"

"This morning all four of our factories received the same nasty telegram from the Ministry of Industrial Policy. They're concerned that in the last six months their raw materials and energy resources have not justified our poor performance. In other words, they're asking, where did your products go? Remember: our plants may be privately owned, but we still depend on the Ministry for raw materials. We also have to satisfy domestic content requirements before exporting our steel abroad. And we have to start paying taxes. Sorry."

"Damn," Sergei said. As the sole three shareholders had planned, in the first quarter their total output fell thirty four percent to three hundred seventeen thousand tons. The next quarter was even worse. Overall, they officially lost just over one hundred forty four million dollars, which was bad news for the state budget, but in reality the overall production and export sales increased dramatically. Per Alexei's advice the unofficial profits were stashed away in the trading company's offshore account in Cyprus.

Even with a fourteen and a half million dollar pay-off to the factory's top management, and another ten million payment to the son-in-law of the Minister of Natural Resources, Jack's tidy share of profits in the joint off-shore account grew by more than forty million bucks in three short months. It was a phenomenal return on his investment.

Naturally, the partners wanted to continue officially losing money, but the telegrams made their point: Alexei's clever business plan of siphoning off cash and depositing it in an offshore account was in plain view of the Ukrainian authorities. Unless all of their steel plants started to show some profit soon, the government supplies of energy, metal and other raw materials would stop.

"I'm sorry to say this, gentlemen, but we have to start keeping less cash off-shore," Alexei said. "We have to show some profit. And pay taxes on it, too."

"No way in hell," Sergei protested vehemently. "Let's send the Minister another bribe, this time bigger and better than ever."

"A beach-front house in Miami," Jack offered helpfully, "or maybe an apartment in central London?"

"It's not up to the Minister anymore," Alexei replied tersely. "There's a new commission appointed by the Parliament. I'll make sure to be on the panel, of course, but in any case it's going to be tight for a while."

"Well, I guess showing a little profit never killed anyone," Sergei mumbled. "Just a little, though."

"Little, little profit." Jack held his thumb and index finger slightly apart. They all resented having to share their money with the government, but there was no choice: they were busted.

"Then the question for you Alexei, our trusted analyst and partner, is how to achieve as little profit as possible without attracting anymore attention," Sergei said. "Any ideas?"

"Absolutely." Alexei came fully prepared, as always. "If we upgrade domestic deliveries of pig iron from sixteen percent to eighteen percent of monthly sales and increase rolled metal slated for internal market to twenty four percent of sales compared to twenty two percent recorded the month before, we can keep exporting scrap metal. That way, everyone will be happy for a while."

"So how much can we expect to receive, in the end?" Jack asked for the bottom-line.

"I estimate that if we stick with official quarterly profit of one million three hundred forty six thousand dollars, which is a small yet visible improvement over the disastrous last quarter, we can expect to lose about seventy one million dollars per quarter. If we leave all expenses for raw materials and energy with UkrSteel, our little trading company should net a quarterly profit of about one hundred and twenty one million, minus twelve million for our top guys and ten more for the Minister, which leaves roughly thirty three million per person."

"That's not as bad as I thought," Sergei said. "I can live with that."

"Me too," Jack nodded. His mind quickly calculated that if Alexei was right, in three months he would have nearly seventy five million dollars. More then half of this uncomfortably large amount of money was already sitting in a communal bank account, to which Jack had no access. Trying not to appear suspicious, Jack casually asked, "now that we have some money, Alexei, what's the procedure for me to transfer a few dollars to another account?"

"An excellent question, as always," Alexei said. "Each of us should open several off-shore companies, with numerous bank accounts. Setting up a company runs a couple grand and should take no more than two weeks. I suggest that you spread your deposits evenly in your accounts to avoid attracting attention of the Interpol."

"Makes sense to me," Sergei said. "I will get on this tomorrow morning."

"Same here," Jack said, just as the pretty waitress emerged from the darkness of the kitchen with an enormous tray, containing different plates. Jack's grilled Thai lobster was delicious; the pigeon was boned and plated at the table, served with lemon and herb-infused olive oil. Alexei was similarly awed by the preparation of his dish.

The first emergency meeting of shareholders at The Camelot continued well past midnight. By that time, Jack and Alexei were stuffed to the gills and happily drunk, all the while sincerely praising the amazing culinary skills of Sergei's new chef.

The next morning Jack arranged to have a company called "Magnexo Ltd." to be registered in the British Virgin Islands, with four accounts: in New York, Geneva,

Tel Aviv and Turks & Caicos. In a couple of weeks, the trading company's offshore bank was due to wire the first tranche of ten million dollars to Geneva, followed by similar transfers to the other accounts.

If Alexei's estimate was right, a few months later another thirty three million tax free U.S. dollars should follow, Jack calculated, which was enough to set him up for life. Having this wealth, however, did not mean that Jack was about to retire. Under the circumstances, what reasonable businessman would?

# Chapter 33

Francois wanted Galina to accompany him on a business trip to San Francisco, as any loving husband would. With great reluctance, and much prodding from Francois, Galina agreed to visit the consular section of the U.S. Embassy to apply for a tourist visa. She heard all about the Embassy, and did not want to be humiliated and then rejected.

After nearly two hours of waiting in a long line outside the gates, her turn finally arrived. The security guard waved her through the metal gate. Galina cleared the X-ray machine, where an American soldier swept her, making sure she carried no weapons. The third, and final, queue placed Galina before a plastic bulletproof window.

"*Dokumenti,*" said a middle-aged American woman on the other side of the window, trying her best Ukrainian accent. She was bored and did not hide it.

"They should be all in order," Galina answered in her high-school English, smiling sheepishly.

"Oh, you speak English," the woman wondered aloud, weighing the probabilities of Galina remaining in the U.S. forever.

"I am accompanying my husband. He is going there on business."

"On business," the woman repeated skeptically. Still, she accepted the documents and said, "come back next week, after three o'clock."

"I have been to France several times, and the Netherlands, too. All of my European visas are stamped in that passport."

"I said, come back on Thursday after three," the woman replied to her indifferently. "Can I help the next person in line, please?"

"Thank you," Galina said quietly and left the building. While walking towards *Artema* Street to hail a taxi, she decided not to worry. She accepted that unlike Francois, who did not need a visa because he was a French citizen, the American Embassy had the right to deny her a visa without offering any explanations.

And yet, even with her low expectations, Galina was unprepared for the phone call that came later that evening. "Hello," said a deep voice on the other end, his Russian tainted by a heavy American accent. "I am calling from the U.S. Embassy. Is this Galina Martinova?"

"Yes. But we can speak English, if it's easier for you."

"Oh. Yes. I'm actually calling from the consular section." The man sounded nervous, excited.

"Is something wrong?" Galina looked at her watch; it was well past eight o'clock. Surely the consular section is closed by now, she thought, and this American would not be calling this late in the evening unless it was something urgent. "Is there some problem with my documents?"

"No. Not really. Nothing that can't be taken care of, if you know what I mean."

"Actually, I don't understand." Galina was getting a strange feeling about the phone call. "What do you mean?"

"I suggest that we meet tomorrow, about this time. We can discuss it then."

"But please, explain to me, exactly what do you want to discuss?"

"You are interested in getting a visa, aren't you?"

"Yes, of course," Galina hesitated.

"Well, if we get together tomorrow evening, and get along, then you can get your passport back with a visa. And if you don't want to come, well... That's your loss. So how about it?"

Galina sat down, feverishly searching for an alternative explanation to his blunt proposal, but there was none. This man, this American from the consular section, was asking to have sex with her. No, not asking; he was demanding sex as a fee for entering America.

"So what do you say, honey?" the man repeated.

Galina barely kept her anger from spilling out. "What do the other women say?"

"They say, yes sir, may I have another," the man on the other end chuckled. "So how about it, sweetheart? This time, tomorrow, we meet by the Golden Gates?"

What did he expect her to say? That she, a married woman, would agree to prostitute herself in order to visit America? Galina's heart pounded heavily, but she never lost control. "Call me tomorrow evening, this time. I will have an answer." After hanging up, Galina broke down and cried.

Fifteen minutes later she managed to regain her composure. Galina reviewed the entire disgusting conversation in her mind several times, revisiting the things she should have said. More than anything Galina wanted to find out who he was, to somehow punish him. But what could she do against the power of an anonymous, invisible bureaucrat? And it was all due to her dear husband, Francois, Galina thought, who insisted that she apply for the stupid American visa in the first place! She sat quietly in the living room, staring at the wall, waiting until Francois came home to unleash her anger at those Americans upon him.

"Damn you, Francois!" Galina screamed at her husband as soon as he opened the door. "And damn them, too!"

"What's wrong, Galya?" Francois froze at the doorway, frightened by his wife's disheveled appearance. In their short marriage Francois had never seen her quite like this before. Lines of black mascara ran down her cheeks, but Galina did not bother to wipe off the ugly stains. She sat in the living room, clinching her fists, cursing in Russian. Francois came over and tried to put his arms around her, but she pushed him away.

"What happened, my love? Did somebody hurt you?"

"I knew it was useless, but you wouldn't listen, would you?" Galina looked at her husband with hatred.

"You knew what?"

"That these Americans are parasites, that they abuse people. To hell with them, and their country. I never want to see or hear about America again!"

"Galya, please, calm down, you are not making sense, my love," Francois said, deeply concerned. "Tell me what happened."

And then, sobbing, she told him everything.

\* \* \*

Francois Mounier was a client, whose company Jack registered several months earlier. He called the next day to invite Jack for a cup of coffee at Slavuta, a tiny restaurant near Jack's office. Over coffee and a glass of cognac he described to Jack an ugly incident that took place the previous evening. According to Francois, these kinds of things go on all the time, unreported and therefore unnoticed.

"The reason we never hear about them is because it happens only to Ukrainian citizens! Well, this time they made a big mistake," Francois hissed, shaking his finger in the air after downing the second cognac, "and I am not just a jealous husband, either; I am a French man, who knows that no civilized country treats its visitors like this! This is unacceptable behavior!"

And yet, being a French citizen, Francois also knew that he had no influence over the U.S. consular section. Feeling helpless, he could do nothing about the insult to his wife, so he did the next best thing: he consulted an American lawyer. "To these arrogant Americans,"

Francois wailed after his fourth cognac, "the Ukrainians are third world citizens. The Russians, they get visas, even people from Kazakhstan. But for Ukrainians, it's totally impossible."

Defending a married woman's honor against indecent proposals of a slimy government bureaucrat was the right thing to do, Jack's moral voice said, regardless which government that bureaucrat happened to work for. At the same time, his Kiev-honed legal mind calculated that if Francois was telling the truth, it was an excellent opportunity to help Sasha with his favor, the coveted U.S. visa. "Francois, I am deeply sorry this happened, especially since it involves my country," Jack said sympathetically. "If I were in your position, I would do the same thing: try to find and punish this piece of human garbage."

"So you will help me?"

"Not only will I help you to nail this pig, but your wife will have a multiple-entry visa next week."

"Are you serious?"

"Deadly. But I will need your assistance."

"Absolutely!" Francois was ready for anything. "What shall I do?"

"If this man actually calls your wife tonight, I want to tape-record the conversation."

"Yes, I understand. But I do not have the correct equipment."

"That's okay. A friend of mine, Sasha, will do it for you. The important thing is that Galina should try to schedule a date in the daylight, sometime in the afternoon."

"She should meet this man?"

"Yes, so that Sasha can record his face on a professional quality video. Can you imagine if CNN got a copy of this tape? Francois, I guarantee that you will get your revenge and a visa, too." In disclosing his strategy, Jack did not reveal his intention to have Sasha piggyback on Galina's upcoming settlement.

"I understand," Francois smiled slyly. "That would be perfect."

"Alright, then. Sasha will call you in an hour to arrange a convenient time to set up tonight's recording."

"He can reach me here." Francois scribbled his home telephone on the back of the business card. "And by the way, how much shall I owe you for this service?"

Jack did not want to rip off Francois, so he threw out the first round number that came into his head. "How about one thousand dollars? Is that too much?"

"Not for something like this!" Francois excitedly got up from the table before the bill had arrived and bowed his head. "I am truly grateful, Mr. Parker. I will tell Galina the good news right away. Thank you again."

"My pleasure."

While waiting for the waiter to come around with the check Jack finished the remainder of his coffee. His approach may not have been entirely ethical, but under the circumstances it was the right thing to do. Someone at the consulat section was abusing their government position, which is a form of corruption. And ordinary people like Galina should not feel molested by this faceless bureaucrat, no matter what his nationality is. I am eradicating corruption in the U.S. Embassy, Jack concluded, which is a good thing. As a nice side-benefit,

Sasha, a member of the KGB's elite security force, could obtain a U.S. visa without having to undergo the dreaded screening interview.

Through the huge glass window Jack could see Francois crossing the street, hurrying to tell his wife the good news. Then he noticed two dark-skinned men in leather jackets, who stepped out of a brown Zhiguli. They carefully watched Francois, and then one of them spoke into a hand-held radio with a small antenna. By the time Jack put on his overcoat, the brown Zhiguli was gone. Maybe Francois has more problems than he knows about, Jack thought.

# Chapter 34

Every morning Jane Murdock poured herself a cup of coffee on the way to her tiny cubicle, regardless of what country she happened to be residing in at the time. Jane's portable office accompanied her all over the world, down to the framed photographs of her parents and their two cats. Nearing fifty years of age, Jane spent the last twenty two years in her mini-office, snugly tucked away behind her desk, documenting various reasons for denials of visas.

Jane looked outside the bullet-proof window at the never-ending line gathered outside the Embassy gates. From Jakarta to Kiev, these people waited for days in all kinds of weather for an interview with one of her junior officers. As head of the consular section, Jane's job was to screen all parasites who could potentially remain in the U.S. after their visas had expired.

Having lived in third world nations for most of the past twenty two years, Jane did not hesitate in issuing business visas to local politicians, wealthy shadow businessmen and other loathsome mini-kings. Though they may be corrupt and even criminal, she reasoned, these people could be relied upon to return to their fiefdoms. Besides, they would get entry visas anyway by engaging the Ambassador's attention or submitting official-looking letters of support from dubious local authorities. Ordinary citizens, however, were likely to remain in the U.S. forever, and therefore had to be screened much more thoroughly.

In screening applicants, Jane employed a two-prong test: an applicant had to present not only a good reason to enter the U.S., but more importantly, solid evidence of intent to leave the country. Since most applicants did not know about the second part of this test, they were summarily denied entry. The denial could only be reversed through a Catch-22-like "appeal process," which required presentation of new evidence that the applicant's situation has changed since the initial rejection. Those were the rules of engagement, and Jane prided herself in applying them evenly across the board.

\* \* \*

When Sasha first showed Jack the color glossy eight-by-ten photographs, he was astounded to recognize his drinking buddy, Joey. How could such a nice guy victimize helpless local girls? It can't be true, Jack thought. Then Sasha played the telephone recording. It explained what Joey was doing after the consular section closed for the day: leafing through the photographs attached to recent applications, picking out the cutest girls, and inviting them out on dates. Jack did not need to see the videotape to know that Sasha had just earned himself, and Galina, a U.S. visa.

Jack's appointment with the chief of the consular section, Ms. Jane Murdock, was scheduled with unexpected difficulty, and only after he threatened unspecified legal action. Apparently, it was Ms. Murdock's policy not to meet with anyone unless it was absolutely necessary. With Sasha's evidence tucked under his arm in a manila envelope, and dozens of cameras watching his every move, Jack entered the heavily guarded consular section compound.

"Keys, chains, metal objects," said the young kid in a green uniform with a shaved head. He was one of the Marines, guarding the X-ray machine in the building. "Leave everything over there."

"Fine, but this envelope has to stay with me," Jack said, offering the package for inspection. He obediently emptied everything from his pockets, including the cellular phone, keys and coins, onto a plastic tray. Meanwhile the Marine pulled out cassette and videotape, along with the photographs.

"Hey, that's Joey!" he exclaimed with a Southern drawl that sounded a lot like Joey's. "Are you a friend of his?"

"Kinda."

"So you want me to pass this envelope to him?"

"Absolutely not. Give it back!"

The Marine looked at Jack suspiciously, but did not try to pull anything funny. Rushing through the X-ray machine, Jack grabbed his precious envelope and walked to the empty waiting area. The visitor's hours were over. An elderly woman struggled to push open the lead-heavy, tank-proof door that separated Embassy employees from the visa seekers.

"This way, please," she said politely with a heavy Ukrainian accent, having trouble holding the lead-filled door open. "Ms. Murdock is expecting you."

"I sure hope Ms. Murdock is in good mood today," Jack tried to engage her, but the woman did not answer; she just sighed heavily. At the end of the corridor she stopped in front of an office, knocked on the semi-open door and announced, "Mr. Parker is here." This was Jack's cue to come inside and negotiate two multiple entry visas.

For a person in such a responsible position, Ms. Murdock's office was quite small and informal, filled with photographs of odd pets and relatives. "Good morning, Ms. Murdock," Jack greeted her professionally and sat down across from the desk.

"What can I do for you, Mr. Parker?" She was all business. It was just as well, given what Jack had to say.

"My client retained me to discuss with you..." Jack started to explain, but Ms. Murdock shook her head.

"Please don't waste your time, and mine, discussing individual client cases. As a lawyer, you should know all about a process called an appeal, where your client can address their grievances within our well-defined system."

"But sometimes the system doesn't address individual concerns," Jack tried again.

"Our procedures are transparent. They are applied evenly, across the board. To everyone. The only thing you can recommend to your client is to file an appeal. Good day."

After such a brief, combative exchange, Jack enjoyed sharing with the consular chief the eight-by-ten color glossy photographs, clearly displaying Joey's masculine face. "If you like transparency," Jack said, smiling, "this is an advance copy of tomorrow's front page news. You can keep it. Everything here will become perfectly transparent in the nearest future."

Ms. Murdock flipped through the photos showing Joey alone, grinning in anticipation, then his surprise at seeing Galina, ending with an angry slap on his face. Slowly Ms. Murdock's eyes narrowed, becoming little slits in the middle of her mug. She knew what Joey had been doing all along, Jack gathered.

"Do you know this man? I believe his name is Joey," Jack said, watching her grimace. "Isn't he one of the Marines responsible for guarding the consular section?"

"What's this about?"

"It seems that my client can't get an entry visa unless she has sex with Joey. That's a problem. Don't you agree?"

"What if I told you I don't know what you're talking about?"

"In addition to the photographs, there are two tapes in this envelope: audio and video. They are self-explanatory. My client is prepared to give you the originals in exchange for a three-year multiple entry visa. Otherwise, they will be released to the Washington

Post, the New York Times, the BBC, the CNN, Reuters, Financial Times of London, among others. They all believe in transparency, just like you do."

"Alright," Ms. Murdock interrupted, "you can just leave these tapes with me, and I will get back to you."

"Sure," Jack smiled back. "And can her friend get a visa, too?"

"What friend?"

"The one who was in charge of photography and video editing. He has the negatives and the original tapes."

"I already told you to wait for my call," Ms. Murdock repeated tersely. "Now, good day!"

"It was a pleasure to meet you," Jack replied pleasantly. He wanted to leave on a good note, though he knew that their relationship had no future. Having burned any remaining bridges with the U.S. Embassy, Jack walked out of their gates, satisfied that his sacrifice helped Francois and Sasha.

Around the corner, on *Artyoma* Street, Jack quickly flagged down a passing car to take him back to the office. Several minutes into their ride the driver looked at Jack in the rear-view mirror, and said, "do you have many enemies?"

"Excuse me?"

"There's a green Moskvich behind us. It's been following us ever since you got in," the driver explained. "That's why I asked about your enemies."

Unable to control himself, Jack spun around and, sure enough, there was a green car right behind them, with two men sitting in the front seat. They looked like Georgian fruit vendors at the *Bessarabsky* market, with dark skin and those wide, black mustaches that indicate virility. The men chatted, completely oblivious to Jack's stare.

Every now and then Jack would turn around abruptly, trying to locate the green Moskvich in the traffic, but it disappeared behind them. By the time he reached the office building, Jack suspected the driver was delusional. Still, just to make sure he was not being followed, Jack ran inside the doorway and positioned himself behind the door.

From that vantage point, through the crack he could see a familiar green Moskvich, rolling slowly down the street. Jack's heart sank when the car parked twenty feet from him and the passenger started speaking into a hand-held radio with an antenna. What if the all-powerful Gambino family somehow learned of his involvement in disappearances of Antonio and Francesco, Jack thought. Everyone has skeletons in their closets these days. Instead of following on Jack's footsteps, however, as serious contract killers would do, they simply drove away.

# Chapter 35

Ever since the day Lena left Jack, he ordered three dozen of the freshest, longest-stemmed roses to be delivered to Podium's doorstep every Monday to await Lena before she arrived for work. And yet, expensive flowers did not melt her heart. Like an obsessed love fool, Jack would dial her office number, but each time Lena was not available, so he toned it down to calling just twice a day. This Monday morning was no exception.

After the third week, the usually stone-cold receptionist began to flirt with Jack, semi-jokingly revealing that she was available if Lena was playing too hard to get. The receptionist became gravely offended when Jack did not reciprocate, but he wanted Lena and only Lena; no other female in her place would do.

From his desk drawer Jack pulled out Sasha's passport and looked at the visa again. Unfortunately, both negative and positive consequences of Jack's visa procurement fiasco materialized, just as he had predicted. The bad news: Jack was blacklisted by the Embassy from any and all social events, including the 4th of July picnic, that was open to everyone. The good news: both Sasha and Galina received their three-year multiple entry visas in exchange for the original tapes and negatives. Plus, Joey was transferred to Okinawa, Japan, far away from the Ukrainian girls.

The watch on Jack's wrist informed him that it was only 9:43 a.m.; Sasha was coming over at ten. With extra time on his hands, once again Jack found himself wondering what Lena was doing that very minute. Did she get his flowers? Even if he accidentally bumped into her on the street, how could Jack explain with a straight face that he was not a branded thief when the tattoo on his hand has not fully healed?

While waiting for Sasha to show up, Jack dialed Lena's number again. Outside his window Jack could see an old chestnut tree across the street. It had fully blossomed, with flowery, white pyramids contrasting brightly against the newly green leaves. It was late May in Kiev, the time of young lovers.

"Podium, may I help you," answered that familiar bored voice.

"It's me. Is she there?"

"Yes."

"Did she see the roses?"

"Yes."

"Did she tell you to throw them away?"

"Yes."

"And did you keep them?"

"None of your business."

"Sorry," Jack quickly apologized. "Any other news?"

"No."

"Talk to you later."

"As if I have a choice," the receptionist said and hung up. Although Jack should have grown used to it by now, he still found Lena's ongoing rejection brutal and unnecessary.

"What's the matter? She doesn't love you?" a familiar voice behind Jack chortled mockingly, nearly giving him a heart attack. Jack spun around to see Sasha, sitting across the desk, arms folded across his chest.

"Jesus! You could really frighten someone like that!"

"That's what they all say," Sasha smiled, pleased with himself. "So I hear you have some good news for me?"

"Sure do." Jack handed over Sasha's passport and sat back in his chair. "Is this what you wanted?"

Sasha read carefully every line in his visa and slapped the passport against his knee. "I don't know if I'll need to use it, but I'm sure glad I got it! Thanks, Jack."

"Let's just say we're even." Jack picked up Vladimir Pavlov's original file from his desk and handed it to Sasha. "Thanks, and you can return this to the archives."

"Oh yeah, I meant to ask you about it. So what was the son's reaction? I mean, did he cry, or what?"

"I photocopied everything, but honestly, I didn't have the time to give it to him yet. I'll do it in the next few days."

"Whatever."

"While you're here, Sasha, can I ask you a silly question? Maybe I'm paranoid, but I think I am being followed by dark-skinned people with hand-held radios. I've seen them twice now. Maybe it's a coincidence?"

"Nothing is a coincidence. You should know that by now. I'm going over see the General anyway, so I'll explain everything myself. He will probably assign a few guys to you. Are you okay with that?"

"Yeah, that would be nice. Just for a few days, you know?"

"Yup. Oh, before I'm out of here, I couldn't help but notice when I first came in that this girlfriend of yours doesn't want to see you. Is that right?"

"Kind of."

"Let me tell you about my first wife, Nadya. She was a model, tall, gorgeous girl. When she let her hair down, Nadya looked like a wild animal. Then we got married, and she refused to prepare dinner for me. It didn't matter to me before, but a wife must cook and clean for her husband, right? So I took out my handcuffs and connected her to the refrigerator. Then I went out for the night."

"So where did she go to the bathroom?"

"On the kitchen floor, where she sat. After that, she had dinner waiting for me every single night. Until we got divorced."

"Makes sense," Jack said, referring to the divorce.

"If you ask me, a little kidnapping could be interpreted as a romantic gesture, a sign that you really care about this girl. Now, the General has a great extraction team, a really charming bunch of guys. They could even bring along a bottle of champagne with a bouquet of roses for her."

"Kidnapping is a crime, Sasha!" Jack laughed at the thought of approving a romantic extraction of Lena. "But thanks for your suggestion, anyway."

"It may be a crime when you kidnap people for ransom, and sometimes not even then. Look at any of Shakespeare's classics, when young lovers would kidnap each other all the time and elope. That's real passion, real romance! They still do this sort of thing in Georgia. Then everybody makes up and celebrates the wedding. It's very nice."

"Thanks, Sasha, but I can manage myself." Jack noticed that Sasha was becoming a little too insistent, which was a bad thing.

"I'm from Kiev, Jack, and I know how the local girls like to be treated: they want to be pursued and then taken. It will be a small favor from me to you, in return for the visa. No need to thank me now." Sasha placed his passport in the pocket, picked up the KGB file and got up to leave. "See you around."

"Stop right there!" Jack jumped between Sasha and the door. "I want you to promise me one thing: you will *not* kidnap Lena. Otherwise, it will interfere with my long-term plans."

"Alright, I can appreciate that. But if you change your mind, you'll let me know, right?"

"Sure." Jack slapped Sasha on the back to make sure he knew they were still friends. At the same time, Jack was relieved to have Sasha out of his office before he could bestow any other favors that would require repayment in the future. By now, Jack knew better then to accept free favors from Sasha. Then he picked up the telephone and dialed Lena's number again, just to make sure she did not change her mind about hating him. According to the receptionist, she did not.

* * *

Sergei arrived to work well past 1 p.m., tired and hung-over from the prior night's festivities. General Kurkov insisted on seeing him right away notwithstanding his unsteady condition.

"I'm afraid I have some disturbing news for you, sir," the General reported somberly. "A well-organized group of people are following you. Something has to be done at once."

As an owner of several metallurgical plants, prominent casinos and restaurants, Sergei was well aware that kidnappers existed, and that they were usually after the money. And ProServe was created specifically to eliminate such dangers. Unfazed, he asked, "so who are they?"

"We don't know that yet."

"Then what, exactly, do we know?"

"Two days ago we noticed that an unidentified group of people had placed your office and home under surveillance. Your daily movements about town were carefully monitored, too."

"Can you be more specific?"

"Yes, I can." General Kurkov pulled out a report he received earlier in the morning. "This was observed yesterday at 9:28 a.m. Brown Zhiguli, license plate number 839 KIB was parked in front of your apartment building. Inside the vehicle were two male individuals, dark skin, in their late twenties."

"Did you say dark skin?"

"Yes, sir. 9:43 a.m., your car picked you up. Brown Zhiguli was replaced with green Moskvich, license plate E9807XT, which followed your car. The driver of Zhiguli meanwhile parked his vehicle at the cafe *Kozak* and had a cup of coffee. 10:07 a.m., your car reached the office; the green Moskvich followed behind. 10:00 a.m, our video recorded a male subject watching the office entrance. He was gone by 10:14 a.m. During this time he had no contacts with anyone else. 12:37 p.m. Your car left the office. This time, a black Volga follows you to *The Camelot*. 3:04 p.m. The Volga returned with you to the office. 7:14 p.m. Brown Zhiguli followed you to your apartment, where the green Moskvich was waiting. Should I continue?"

"No, I can read the report myself. Just leave it here on the table." Sergei was glad that General's men had identified the threat in time to take preventative measures. This meant the situation was still under control. "General, what can you tell me that's *not* on this piece of paper?"

"At least five different vehicles are involved in carrying out the surveillance. These vehicles are equipped with radio telephones, and they change every two to four days. This group consists of numerous members. By their skin color, and general appearance, I'd say they're darkies from the mountains."

"You mean the Chechens?" Sergei asked cautiously. Like every businessman in Eastern Europe, he feared the violent Chechens, a very special group of Muslims from the Northern Caucuses in southwestern Russia. A lawless region resembling Afghanistan, the Transcaucasia includes the notorious Chechnya, Dagestan, Ingushetia, Azerbaijan, and the relatively civilized Armenia and Georgia.

The Chechen's distinction as a bloodthirsty bunch was well deserved even amongst the most notorious Russian gangs. Relentless as the Golden Horde that once thundered across the Russian steppes and sacked its cities in the Middle Ages, in early 1990 the Chechen mafia successfully invaded Russia. Using military-grade weaponry and hardcore determination of professional warriors, they left Moscow's Georgian, Armenian and Slavic mobs in disarray. The degree of carnage in the early 1990's was unprecedented. Even Moscow police and special security forces could not stop the Chechen mob from taking over the city.

"So are they Chechen, or not?" Sergei snapped at the General.

"We don't have such detailed information yet," General Kurkov responded calmly. "At this point, our darkies could belong to any of the Moscow groups. They're all being squeezed out, so they're relocating to greener pastures, like Kiev. In any case, I would like your permission to implement countermeasures."

"Can you be more specific?"

"I want an immediate increase in security both in the office and around your apartment building. I also want to put counter-surveillance on those savages and then round them up for questioning. In a couple of days we'll know who sent them and why. In the meantime, you'll have to stay indoors, sir."

"Thank you, General." Sergei nodded respectfully, dismissing the chief of his security. Obviously, being targeted by the Chechens worried Sergei greatly. But these things were bound to happen at some point, Sergei comforted himself with a glass of cognac. Now, it was up to the General and his army to earn their keep.

\* \* \*

As he did every evening, Alexei waved goodnight to his bodyguards and punched in a four-digit code to open the front door of his apartment building. He waited for the automatic lock to spring. After it clicked, Alexei pulled the door handle and entered the usual world of darkness. He cursed under his breath and steered to the right, trying to avoid the sharp corners of metal mailboxes. One day he would buy the entire building and repair the damned entryway, he thought.

Taking six familiar steps forward, Alexei found the elevator button. His finger fell through the hole in the plastic, melted by young hooligans with their cigarette lighters. The ancient elevator slowly and loudly started its descent until the doors finally opened. To Alexei's surprise, he saw a beautiful young woman standing inside. She hesitated to come out.

"Sorry, but I forgot my purse upstairs," she apologized. Alexei nodded understandingly, walked inside and pushed the button to his floor. They stood next to each other, both staring at the elevator doors, until they came to a halt. Always a gentleman, Alexei allowed the girl to exit first. He was a little surprised when she turned around and pointed her tight little fist at him. The reflection of the cold, gray steel made him squirm, but it was too late.

The young woman squeezed the trigger several times, sending three large caliber bullets into his abdomen, one by one, until Alexei slid down to the ground. The silencer muffled all the shots. This is a professional hit, was Alexei's last thought. He looked into the barrel just before the last chunk of lead smashed into his left cheekbone and exited from the back of the head.

The assassin broke the light bulb in the elevator with her gun and pushed the top floor button, sending Alexei's bleeding body upwards. She listened attentively for several seconds. Hearing nothing unusual, the young woman lightly skipped down five flights of stairs and discreetly exited the building through the back door.

# Chapter 36

When Jack saw the front-page news, he was in shock. The cover story reported that his partner, Alexei Glushko, fell victim to a contract killing, mafia-style. According to the article, one bullet passed a few millimeters under Alexei's left eye, barely missing the brain. The others perforated his bowels and lungs. Reading the words over and over, Jack refused to believe that his clever business partner had died a gruesome death in an elevator last night. Feverishly he dialed Sergei's number.

"Yes," Sergei barked abruptly into the telephone.

"It's me."

"I guess you heard the news."

"Is it true?"

"I'm afraid it is."

"So what do you think?"

"I think we have a problem. I want you to stay at home until we get a firm grip on whoever is behind this."

"Are you saying..."

"We don't know yet," Sergei interrupted him. "The General is here and we're reviewing various options. Don't worry, I'll call you as soon as I have more information. In the meantime, don't leave your apartment until I call you, okay?"

"Great." It was all Jack could say. Knowing that professional assassins were hunting after him, Jack turned off the lights and draped up all of his windows, making a sniper's job more difficult. What am I, a multi-millionaire, doing hiding in the darkness of this crummy, third-rate apartment, Jack thought. Instead, I should be enjoying exotic drinks with tiny umbrellas on some South Pacific beach with my love, Lena. If I get out of this mess alive, he swore, that's exactly what I'll do.

Sneaking a peek through his bedroom window, Jack could see four of the General's men sitting in a car across from his building. They would remain there day and night, patiently waiting for someone to come and kill him. The life of a self-made millionaire proved to be more stressful than Jack had ever imagined. The only source of comfort was knowing that professionals at *ProServe* were working on his liberation.

\* \* \*

"Jack is also concerned," Sergei said to General Kurkov after he hung up the telephone. He reclined in a leather chair, puffed on a fat *Romeo Y Julieta* and asked, "so what's the latest information?"

"We tracked the license plate numbers of the vehicles, and four of them are stolen from identical cars. This explains why they appeared to be Ukrainian from the first glance. The fifth car, however, still had Russian plates, so I called Gavril."

"Sounds promising." Sergei nodded in appreciation of the General's resourcefulness.

"As you know, Gavril works closely with the Moscow police department, and he gave me some background information."

"Like what?"

"So far, Moscow police have identified six major organizations they cannot eradicate. Three of them are controlled by the Chechens: the *Tsentralnaya*, the *Ostankinskaya*, and the *Avtomobilnaya*. Together, the Chechens have about three thousand men spread out among their three different groups. It's quite an impressive structure, actually. Like all organized groups, they share a central *obschak*. The earnings they pool into *obschak* are used to pay lawyers, bribe government officials and provide financial support to imprisoned gang members, the usual thing."

"That means they enjoy protection of the government."

"Exactly. According to Gavril, the Chechens are connected at the highest levels of the Moscow City and national governments. They go out of their way to recruit former KGB and police officials, especially those in charge of investigating organized crime. Anyone who refuses to comply is killed without warning: policemen, governors, mayors, parliament members, newspaper reporters. It makes no difference to them."

"What a pleasant bunch of fellows," Sergei said. "I would have no moral problems whatsoever in having them bumped off."

"That's what everyone in Moscow says, but nobody's managed to accomplish. And that's why in Moscow the Chechens control most hotels, casinos, and restaurants. One American fool, a manager of Hotel *Slavianskiy*, was killed because he refused to give up the hotel. The Chechens now own it."

"Is that all?"

"No. They compete for power with two Russian criminal organizations: *Solntsevskaya* and *Podolskaya*. Both are involved in counterfeiting, arms trafficking, kidnapping, smuggling and extortion. They're in constant conflict with the Chechens. This means we are on the same side, if you decide to strike back at anyone in Moscow."

"The question is, who is responsible for ordering this?"

"Right. So I asked Gavril to check the Russian license plates through the police. It belongs to Johar Aslanbeck, one of the lower-level soldiers in the *Tsentralnaya* group. If it had been anybody else, including the *Solntsevskaya* or *Podolskaya*, Gavril could approach them in Moscow to work things out through negotiations. The problem with the Chechens is that those dark-skinned bastards simply refuse to negotiate with their enemies. It means that nobody can guarantee your safety."

"Shit. So what are you suggesting?"

"Gavril said that based on his experience, we have to get rid of them before they have a chance to put down their roots in Kiev. Otherwise, he said, we will have a repeat of Moscow on our hands, and nobody wants that. Not you, not the KGB, and certainly not the local cops, whose lives will be on the front lines. It's that serious. Gavril even offered to send some of his specialists, but I declined. Instead, I'll call in some favors with Alfa. With this situation on our hands, I'm sure they'll back us up."

There was no point in refusing extra help, Sergei thought, especially if it does not cost anything. "You have my permission to do whatever you think is necessary."

"Hopefully, we'll soon have the darkies in custody. Trust me, I'll find out who sent them."

"I'm counting on you, General Kurkov."

"I won't let you down, sir." The General saluted his superior before walking out of Sergei's office.

# Chapter 37

Jack's phone rang several times, and he rushed over. "Hello?"

"Everything is taken care of, buddy. It's safe to come out and play." Sergei's voice sounded tired, worn out.

"Are you sure?"

"Absolutely. Plus, I have some interesting news that requires your input. How about joining me for a cold beer in the park? It's a beautiful evening outside."

"I'd love to. When and where?"

"Actually, I'm calling you on my cell phone while sitting in *Shevchenko* Park, right in front of the statute."

"I'll be right over." Jack eagerly left the confines of his apartment, looking forward to having a few beers on some wooden bench in the park, where thick chestnut trees towered over azure fountains.

As Jack entered the park, he was not entirely surprised to see Sasha. He was sitting on a bench, reading a newspaper. Sasha nodded in recognition and whispered something into his left sleeve. Then he pretended to continue reading, all the while scanning the public for potential signs of trouble. This meant the General's people had the entire park surrounded.

"This way," Sergei called out, waiving his hand. "Cold beer over here!"

"Enough for me, too?"

"Plenty." Sergei smiled and held out a bottle of *Slavutich*, arguably the finest Ukrainian brew. By the look on his face, and dark rings under his eyes, Jack could tell that he was pretty tired. Sergei raised his bottle and said, "well, congratulations, partner."

"What for?" Jack asked, taking a swig of beer.

"For getting out alive. We found out who killed Alexei."

"Oh?"

"Funny thing, this metal business," Sergei shook his head. "Seems that our old friends at RusSteel never forgot how Alexei cancelled their privatization bid for UkrSteel. This time, when Alexei excluded them from the last auction altogether, Berezkov went ballistic. It was Pavel Berezkov who sent the Chechens to get Alexei. You and I were next on their list. Berezkov must want our concern pretty badly."

"And how do you know all that?"

"Because I spoke with the girl who killed Alexei. She told me everything herself. Last night our guys raided their garages and apartments, all at once. The

Chechens didn't even have time to fire a single shot, and they had quite an arsenal."

"Thank God." At first, Jack was genuinely relieved that the danger was identified and eliminated. Then a dark thought crossed his mind: what about any future unwelcome surprises? The solution was obvious, so Jack blurted out, "we have to send someone on a midnight train to Moscow after Berezkov. Purely in self-defense. We have no choice."

"That was my first thought, too. But earlier today some lawyer from RusSteel called me from Moscow. Somehow the bastard got a hold of my cellular number. He knew exactly what happened to the Chechens and why. One amazingly well-informed guy. He made us an offer."

"Oh, really?" That ugly, nervous energy returned, pumping blood to Jack's head. "What did he say?"

"That Berezkov demands an unconditional release of his Chechens, unharmed. Plus our ownership in the steel mills."

"On a silver platter? After what he did to Alexei? No way in hell!"

"...in exchange for one point eight billion dollars, payable anywhere," Sergei concluded. Then he took a big gulp from his bottle. "So what do you say now?"

"Did I just hear you correctly? You said billion, right?"

"It's well below what our going concern would fetch on the open market," Sergei replied, "and Berezkov knows it. That's why he made the offer."

"One point eight billion dollars," Jack repeated to himself. "Well, that's a totally different approach. And what's your position on this?"

"I would take the money. If we don't, the lawyer mentioned something about RusSteel continuing to pursue its business interests in Ukraine, and we all know what that means. Who needs round-the-clock bodyguards, these life-and-death dramas? Do you really want another war with the Russians or the Chechens?"

"Even if it's less then our factories are worth," Jack thought aloud, "just a year ago I would have sold my soul to the devil for a fraction of this amount."

"Plus, don't forget: we don't have to worry about paying any investment obligations on the factories. That's a savings of another three hundred and eighty three million, right there."

"Does Berezkov know anything about that?"

"Do you really care? I suggest that we just take his money and retire in some warm spot under a palm tree." From many drunken party conversations Jack knew that by "a warm spot under a palm tree" Sergei meant a villa on the beach in southern France or Spain, with an accompanying yacht that has its own helicopter. Now he could add an airplane or two to his shopping list.

"You'll be bored out of your skull in two weeks," Jack teased him.

"On the contrary. There's so much to do: buy a mansion, order a ship, travel the globe. And I don't mean tourist traps like Paris or London. Let's charter a private plane to Borneo or Madagascar, where life stood still for centuries. Want to go?"

"But what about your restaurants and casinos?"

"Even after paying off the Minister and our management, we'll end up with eight hundred million dollars each! And that's in addition to what we've already earned! For all I care, Sasha can take over the restaurants and casinos. He needs the money more than I do."

"How about *ProServe?*"

"The General can keep my half of the company, if you want him as your new partner. You might consider giving him your half, too, if you're going to be leaving Ukraine anyway. I mean, do you really need *ProServe* anymore?"

"I guess not. How about our little jewelry business?"

"Jack, who needs the headache? I'll buy you all the jewels you want."

"But I still have your diamond. The one you let me borrow, remember?"

"Don't worry, I have more of them than I know what to do with. Give it as a present to your girlfriend. That's what I give to all my dates if they show me a good time."

"Thanks, Sergei, that's real generous of you." All of a sudden Jack looked around the park in a different light, knowing that he may not be here for much longer. "You know, it's funny, but I never believed you," Jack said. "I thought it was all a big joke, us becoming rich. And here we are, sitting on a park bench, drinking beer to having become billionaires. Too bad Alexei didn't live to enjoy it."

"To our partner. Without him, we would not be who we are today," Sergei raised his bottle Alexei's memory. Then he confessed, "between you and me, I never thought this would happen, either."

"So when are you leaving to look for your palm tree?"

"As soon as Berezkov's money hits my account," Sergei beamed with anticipation. "And after that, a whole new life begins. No more gorging on rich foods, or spending endless nights on the town, drinking and gambling. It's time to slim down, enjoy life's fruits and berries, yachts and fast automobiles."

"I'll join you once I convince Lena." Jack saw no reason to mention her absolute lack of interest in him, because he still harbored hopes of overcoming that barrier. Then Jack recalled another impediment: Ms. Murdock's burning hatred of him. Without getting into details, Jack added, "there is only one tiny problem: Lena will need a U.S. visa."

"So you decided to take her with you, huh?"

"Sure, if she wants to go." With that statement, the urgency of meeting Lena had reached a whole new level for Jack.

"But you are an American citizen. You should have no problems getting her a visa."

"Unfortunately, both the Ambassador and the head of the consular section hate my guts. They would deny my invitation on sheer principle."

"Then why don't I invite Lena?"

"Because you are a Ukrainian citizen, with no legal right to invite anyone to visit America."

"True, but I also own a company called *InterQuest Acquisitions, Ltd.*, which is registered in Delaware. My company's lawyers can invite Lena to visit them in Washington, D.C., for some bullshit business reason. We submit these kinds of invitations to the consular section all the time. So far, nobody has been refused."

"You must be kidding. Countless people are denied entry to the U.S. every day, and you make it seem so easy."

"Why not? The American authorities are scared that our tourists will stay in U.S. illegally. Businessmen, however, tend to return to their jobs. That's why all of my invitations through *InterQuest* are issued strictly for business reasons."

"Man, if you could pull it off, that would be fantastic!"

"Tomorrow your office will receive a faxed invitation from my lawyers concerning a meeting in D.C. It's that easy. Sorry, Jack, but I gotta run. Glad that you agreed to become super rich."

Sergei left Jack sitting on the park bench, nursing the rest of his beer in solitude. Now Jack started to worry: even if he somehow ran into Lena, and they became friends again, there was no guarantee that she would accept his offer of early retirement in America. Try as he might, there was no easy solution to this dilemma.

A few minutes later Jack noticed Lydia Ivanovna. She carried a plastic bag with several empty glass bottles that chimed as she shuffled by. Feeling a light beer buzz, he called out to her, "how are you, Lydia Ivanovna?"

"Well, this is a surprise," she slowed down. "What a nice evening. May I sit down?"

"Of course." Jack moved over and Lydia carefully settled her fragile bag on the ground. "So how is Boris Vladimirovich?" Jack inquired politely.

"He can't walk outside, but otherwise he's alright."

"What happened? Did he break a leg?" Jack was genuinely concerned about the old man's health. He also felt ashamed of forgetting to pass along to Boris the photocopied documents after all this time. "Does he need medical help?"

"What medical help? Last week I went to the open-air market and bought him a new pair of foreign shoes, imported from Iraq. During the rain, they came unglued. These shoes were made for funerals, for the deceased, I later found out. Now I'm saving for another pair. Until he gets new shoes, Boris Vladimirovich can't go outside. Are you finished with that bottle?"

"Sure." Jack gently placed his empty beer bottle into her sack. Then he made a mental note to buy a pair of shoes for Boris tomorrow. Jack's next thought was, what will happen to Boris and Lydia after he leaves Ukraine? Jack looked at his neighbor, this feisty grandmother, who was as old and poor as he was young and wealthy. How can I help her survive the upcoming winter, Jack wondered, short of giving her a large chunk of cash that some drug addict would kill for? As if she could read his mind, Lydia said mysteriously, "actually, I wanted to make a business proposition to you."

"Oh? What is it?"

"You have been to my apartment. It's exactly like yours, sixty two square meters of total area, including the hallway, the kitchen and the bathroom. It must be worth at least ten thousand dollars, no?"

"More, I should think. Three or four times more, easily."

"See? That could be your profit," Lydia answered quickly, and then measured Jack's reaction. Coming from an old lady who had no money, this talk of profit sounded strange.

"My profit?"

"My memory is not what it used to be, son, and I don't have that long to live. So this is my offer: if you give me one hundred dollars every month until I die, you will inherit my apartment after I'm buried."

"What?"

"You yourself just said that my apartment is worth at least thirty thousand dollars. If only I could get one third of that money before I die, then I wouldn't have to pick up bottles anymore. In return, you'll get a sunny, two-room apartment in the center of Kiev, with a balcony. We would sign the necessary documents up front, of course. I just thought this would be a beneficial arrangement for both of us," Lydia concluded.

Her morbid request made Jack pause; talk of death is always unpleasant. "I will think about it, Lydia Ivanovna," Jack replied politely. Although her offer made good business sense, Jack felt uneasy accepting it, as though he would be profiting from Lydia's demise. Besides, he did not need the extra money.

Lydia noticed his hesitation. "I can see the answer in your eyes, and I understand. You don't have to feel obligated, we'll make due." She took hold of her plastic bag and stood up with some difficulty. "Please give my best to your wonderful wife." Then she slowly walked away in search of more empty beer bottles.

Setting aside his concerns, Jack got up and ran after Lydia as fast as the beer in his swollen belly allowed. He caught up with her, and said, "I agree. I will pay you five hundred dollars each month. That, plus my driver, Volodya, will help you with minor errands. In case there's anything you'll need in the winter months."

The look of surprise on her wrinkled face, followed by an enormous, grateful smile, made Jack feel all the more guilty. Maybe he really was a callous, penny-pinching foreigner that Lena once accused him of being. I should have offered Lydia and Boris my help sooner, Jack cursed himself, even if it was only a few bucks every now and then.

"Can your Volodya drive me to the cemetery, to visit my daughter's grave?" Lydia quickly asked.

"Of course."

"Then I will need him to take me there two times a year: in November, when she died, and in late spring, to clean up around the plot. As a part of our deal." Lydia was squeezing as much out of Jack as she could, but everything she was asking for Jack would have gladly given anyway.

"No problem."

"Oh, that would be very useful, indeed," Lydia started to ramble. "I haven't visited my baby's grave for the last three years in a row, and I feel terrible about it. But to get to the cemetery, you have to take two buses, and then walk a kilometer and a half to reach the grave. One day I became so frightened, thinking that I wouldn't be able to make it home, that I just stopped going altogether."

"Lydia Ivanovna, I am very glad that we ran into each other tonight," Jack interrupted her. "And remember: Volodya is the name of the man who will take care of you from now on. He will knock on your door tomorrow afternoon with the first payment, plus some groceries. He'll also arrange for a new pair of shoes for Boris Vladimirovich."

"But when do we sign the documents? You know, for the apartment."

"There's no need. We trust each other, right?"

For the first time since Jack met her, Lydia Ivanovna was dumbfounded; she did not say anything, not even a thank you. Maybe she doesn't believe me, Jack thought. There was nothing more to discuss, so he went off to buy another cold *Slavutich* from the corner kiosk.

The park was brimming with students, enjoying the warm evening. The outdoor cafes were full of foreigners and locals alike. Sitting all alone on a wooden bench, nursing his beer, Jack could not decide which of his accomplishments was greater: becoming an overnight billionaire or providing life security for Lydia and Boris. "*Na zdorovye* to you on both counts," Jack said to himself, taking a generous congratulatory gulp from the bottle. "If only Lena knew what a nice guy you really are."

## Chapter 38

The fax from Didier Nobel, Jack's personal offshore financial consultant in Geneva, Switzerland, confirmed that Berezkov's payment of eight hundred and fifty million dollars had safely reached his account. Jack read the one and only line in Mr. Nobel's fax over and over again, trying to comprehend its long-term implications.

With this transfer, Jack's combined offshore savings were a little over nine hundred eighty two million dollars. At last, Jack could live like a king for the rest of his life, free to go anywhere on a moment's notice in first class accommodations. Closing his law firm and getting out of Ukraine became Jack's absolute top priority. The only problem was Lena; he had to see her immediately.

To accomplish this feat, Jack devised three steps: first, he would try calling Lena himself one last time.

Based on past experience, however, Jack knew this was futile. As a fallback position, he was prepared to ask an intermediary to set up a meeting on his behalf. It had to be someone Lena knew and respected, such as her boss, the all-powerful John Hatchet himself. Third, and final, option involved enlisting Sasha to organize a romantic kidnapping.

Following through on the first step, Jack dialed the painfully familiar telephone number. "Podium, may I help you," a woman's bored voice said on the other end.

"It's me." Jack knew by heart all of the upcoming lines in this pathetic conversation. "Is she there?"

"Not for you," the receptionist replied. "Don't you ever give up?"

"No. Can I talk with her?"

"You're a good man," the receptionist sighed, "but no."

"Don't hang up: this time it's important."

"You said that before. Many times. Is there anything else I can help you with?"

"Yes." As Jack anticipated, his gentle attempt to reach Lena failed miserably, so without blinking an eye, he moved straight to step number two. "Let me talk to John Hatchet."

"I'm sorry, but Mr. Hatchet is away from the office."

"Then find him, tell him my name and remind him about the favor he owes me."

"Are you sure you want me to do this?"

The hesitation in the receptionist's voice confirmed everything Jack already knew about Podium's business.

Under any other circumstances he would never bother a person like John Hatchet with such a silly request. However, John was the only person who could perform this miracle peacefully, before Jack resorted to using romantic extraction teams.

"Put me through, please," Jack insisted. "It's that important."

"I hope you know what you're doing. Please wait."

An insipidly sweet version of *Moon River* played in Jack's ear until something clicked. "Yes, Mr. Parker, what can I do for you this morning?" John's British accent was breaking up in pieces, as if he was talking on his cellular phone.

"I know that you are a busy man, Mr. Hatchet, so I'll be brief. May I drop by sometime this afternoon to discuss a matter of importance to me?"

"Of course you may, Mr. Parker, but unfortunately I won't be there to greet you since I am currently in Monte Carlo. Can this matter wait ten more days, until I return, or is it something urgent?"

"Actually, it's urgent. You mentioned once that if I needed anything done, I could call you personally, so I'm taking this liberty now. Do you mind?"

"By all means, I am at your disposal," John said blandly.

"My request is simple. I'm asking you to set up a meeting between myself and Lena, one on one. In a neutral setting, like your office, so that she's not worried about my intentions."

"A meeting with Lena?" John asked incredulously, almost talking to himself. "And you can't arrange this yourself?"

"Something like that." Jack did not offer any explanations. "So can you help me?"

"I would be delighted. Name a convenient time for you."

"Twelve o'clock today. Two hours from now. Or any other time she's free."

"You will be expected at noon. Is there anything else I can do for you?"

"No, Mr. Hatchet, but I appreciate you setting up this meeting very much."

"Good morning, then," John replied politely. After they hung up, Jack's stomach turned with nausea: he had one final chance with Lena, and simply could not afford to blow it. Though Jack had plenty of time to think about what to say, the only words that correctly expressed his true feelings were simple and honest: I love you. Such a blunt approach could well frighten her off, Jack thought, but it's the truth.

As arranged, Jack arrived to John's warehouse just before noon, and was pleased to see that he was not just expected, but welcome. The otherwise impregnable green door slowly opened, releasing two large men in sports suits. They rushed outside and one of them carefully opened his car door. "This way, Mr. Parker," the man respectfully said, stepping away for Jack to get out of the car. Like with many former athletes, his broken nose had shifted to the side of his face.

To Jack's disappointment, and at the same time great relief, Lena was not waiting for him in Mr. Hatchet's office. This gave him a few more minutes to come up with something besides the banal three-word opening line. "I wanted to tell you..." Jack practiced,

while looking out of the window, "I am not what you...
That I think you..."

"You?"

Caught completely off guard, Jack turned to face
Lena. She slipped unannounced into John's office and
stood by the door, glaring at him. The look on her face
said it all: Lena's beautiful charcoal eyes first filled with
disbelief and then anger. The only three words Jack
came over to say got stuck in his throat. Standing by the
door, Lena looked as gorgeous as the very first time he
saw her, but now her steely voice cut him deep inside.

"So you are the mysterious foreigner Mr. Hatchet
told me to meet with! Is that how you get your dates
these days? You stooped so low that you had to ask
Mr. Hatchet to arrange this meeting?"

That opening was something Jack did not expect.
"What do you mean?" was all he could utter in shock.
Trying to regroup, Jack focused on his better deeds.
"What about all the flowers? Didn't you get any of my
flowers?"

"Big deal, so you spent some money on flowers. You
thought that if your employees buy out the entire
flower section I would come crawling back to you? Is
that what your little gardening exhibition was all
about? What good are your roses if you couldn't even
find the time to give them yourself? Not even once!
Such a busy man! Well, I'm a busy woman. Get lost!"

So *that's* it, Jack realized. She's mad at me because
I did not give her enough of my personal attention.
Lena's enormous eyes betrayed her sadness, as if she
was saying farewell. It became too quiet and Jack
instinctively felt that unless he said something,

anything at all, Lena would leave this room and he would never see her again.

"I love you, Lena," the opening line spilled out from his lips unwittingly, and then Barry White's genius suddenly took over. Familiar words shamelessly rolled off Jack's tongue, "you are my sun, my moon, my guiding star — some kind of wonderful, that's what you are." The corners of Lena's mouth were no longer frowning and the look on her face confirmed that Jack was on the right track. "You're my first, my last, my everything," he quickly wrapped up. Fortunately, Lena had never heard of Barry White or any of his songs, and Jack's translation into Russian did not rhyme. Otherwise, she would not have believed him as readily as she did.

"What did you just say?" Lena was stunned to hear such romantic words spoken so freely. "Did you just make this up?"

"I really love you, Lena," Jack repeated his original opening line, with extra feeling. "Can we please start over?

"You are like a modern-day Pushkin. If that's how you really feel, then I will have to think about it."

"Thank you," Jack hugged her tightly, inhaling the sweetness of her smell. "I knew you'd understand."

"Not so fast, Jack. I'm still not sure about you. You have a lot of answering to do."

"Then let's take this afternoon off, and I will prove to you that I'm not so bad. Please?"

"It sounds tempting," Lena smiled, "but I really have to get back to work."

"Don't make me call your boss in Monte Carlo. He's on vacation, so let him get some rest. Come on, just take this one day off for Mr. Hatchet's sake, or I'll have to bother him again."

"Are all lawyers so persuasive?" Lena smiled, and suddenly Jack felt like laughing and dancing. It was an silly, giddy sensation that only true lovers would know.

"My car is waiting for us outside." Jack offered his hand to Lena and she accepted. The security guards, sitting on the benches in the hallway, smiled at Jack and Lena knowingly as they walked out of Podium; one of the athletes even gave Jack a thumbs up sign.

When Volodya slowly pulled out of Podium's parking lot, driving carefully between the deep potholes, Jack felt like a real thief because he had just captured Podium's most precious jewel: Lena. His arms were wrapped tightly around her, as if she would disappear if he let her go. "I missed you," Jack whispered, breathing warm air into her ear. She giggled and pulled away.

"So where are you taking me?" Lena asked.

"Wherever you want to go."

"How about the botanical garden? It's one of our last chances to see the autumn colors before the winter gets here."

"Funny you should say that. Volodya, can you take us to the botanical garden?"

"Anywhere you say, chief."

The botanical garden is actually a magnificent mini-forest, preserved in the center of Kiev. Jack and Lena strolled passed massive trunks of ancient oaks that reached towards the sky, blocking the sunlight. Underneath, a layer of bronze-colored leaves littered the ground at their feet.

"I am really glad to see you," Jack said. "You don't know how many days I dreamed about you. And how empty everything was without you."

"And I'm just glad that you made time to see me," she countered sharply. "But why pull out the big guns?"

"What?"

"You didn't have to call in your favor with Mr. Hatchet on account of me. You should have just come over, that's all."

"But how was I to know you would let me in? You wouldn't even accept my flowers," Jack defended himself weakly, knowing that she was right. "Look, the important thing is that we're here, together."

"We are not together yet, Jack. I have plenty of questions for you before we are together, if ever."

"Ask away, then. I have nothing to hide."

"What about that tattoo on your hand? Why were you hanging out with some bald-headed bandit who dropped you off in the middle of the night, dead drunk? And what are you doing with those KGB files about some labor camp prisoner?"

"They're all excellent questions, for which I have perfectly innocent explanations. First, I got the stupid tattoo when I was drunk. Honestly, I don't remember getting it done, and I don't even know what it means, but there it is. Second, the bald bandit is not my friend. He is someone I met at the party, and I will never see him again. Third, the file you saw was about Boris Vladimirovich's father, the enemy of the people. A son wanted to know how his father died, and I helped him, that's all. Even you would approve of that. Any other questions?"

"Yes. Do you really love me?"

"With all of my heart."

"Then take this as my second, and final warning, Jack: stay away from the criminals. No more parties like the last one. No more stacks of cash under your bed. And no more excuses. Of all the people, I know about racketeers, and nothing good ever comes from them."

"Agreed. And I apologize for everything, I really do."

"Accepted."

Jack and Lena strolled by the delicate white birch trees, their branches covered with yellowing leaves, shimmering in the autumn breeze. Feeling a bit more confident, Jack asked her openly, "so does it mean we're together again?"

"Maybe. For now."

"That will do, for now." Without any warning Jack kissed her lips and Lena leaned gently towards him. They remained standing by the birch trees until a small, white poodle started to bark. A frowning elderly woman, walking the obnoxious dog, also did not approve of their behavior. She coughed twice, then cast a dirty look in their direction. Holding hands and laughing, Jack and Lena moved down the garden path towards the willow trees. Jack steered Lena to a bench, conveniently positioned on the edge of a pond.

"What a romantic place, this garden," Lena sighed, sitting next to him. "I can't believe we're in the city, can you?" She was right: the emerald pond was covered with algae and an occasional patch of lilies. The reflection of the clouds passed across the surface. This peaceful, serene environment was an ideal setting for

Jack to raise a rather sensitive topic of Lena's relocation to America with him.

"Being here is like going on vacation," Jack began innocently enough.

"Exactly." Lena breathed in clean air.

"Actually, I was thinking of taking a vacation soon. Somewhere nice. Do you want to join me?"

"That all depends on where you're going."

"How about America?"

"Sure, like the American Embassy is going to let me in. I'm young and single. They'll reject me on the spot. Besides, what's there to do in America?"

"Ha! We could swim in the Atlantic Ocean in Miami, then fly in for a few days to Chicago and listen to some blues, then watch the sunset over the Grand Canyon, or dance the nights away in San Francisco clubs."

"You're crazy," Lena said, laughing at him. "Nobody does that. It's too much!"

"I want you to see the bright lights of Las Vegas. Then you'll understand the meaning of too much. Because I love you too much, I will get us first class tickets, and a visa for you, and then we're out of here. So what do you say?"

"If you can get me a visa, then of course I'll go. What girl in her right mind would refuse?"

"Great!" Jack practically screamed, delighted that his plan of luring Lena to America has worked out so well. "I'll need your passport and you'll probably have to fill out an application, but wow! I can't believe this is happening!"

"It sounds too good to me, too. Imagine, me in America! But when are you planning on going? I have to give Mr. Hatchet notice, you know."

"In a few weeks. That should give you enough time to get your visa and for me to wrap up my cases."

"And when do we return?"

"That depends on you," Jack answered slyly. In his mind, there was no coming back to Ukraine; whether Lena chose to remain with him in America would be her choice entirely.

"I get one month vacation per year," she said.

"Then we'll return one month later." Though Jack may have lied to Lena again, this time he did not feel any remorse. He had enough money to last several lifetimes, and a burning desire to spend as much as he could before he died. Surely Lena would extend her vacation once she gets into her new, glamorous lifestyle.

# Chapter 39

As Volodya drove Jack and Lena to the *Borispol* airport down the freeway, Jack saw the first Bentley in Kiev overtake them on the highway. It looked grotesque and inappropriate against the background of rural poverty, even in comparison to the usual Mercedeses and BMW's. The good times have arrived for Ukraine's super-rich, Jack thought, holding Lena's hand in the back seat.

Two hours later they sat inside the first class travelling section of the Swissair's widebody jet, flying towards America. A chunky gold bracelet with a large Rolex, and its hundreds of tiny diamonds, dangled from Jack's wrist. He was going to leave it for Sasha, but at the last moment decided to keep John Hatchet's gift for sentimental reasons.

The flight back to the America proved to be much more civilized than Jack's was used to. Lena was glued to a romantic comedy on her personal mini-TV set, giggling at the actors' hilarious antics and clever punch lines. The filet mignon tasted just as Jack remembered. The nice stewardess in red uniform allowed him to sample all of the alcoholic beverages, twice. No smoking was permitted anywhere in the cabin, including the lavatories.

According to Jack's gaudy watch, the plane would land in San Francisco in a few hours. The reason for Jack's choice of destinations was simple: right after Lena got her visa, Sergei had invited them to a housewarming party at his new place. The address was in Jack's wallet, next to the large diamond that he carefully wrapped in a piece of cloth and smuggled out of Kiev.

Soaring high above the clouds, Jack looked back on his short and equally strange journey. A colorful kaleidoscope of characters turned in his memory, one by one: Antonio, the smooth yet venomous viper; Dr. Zimmer, the body snatcher; Herr Huber, the old con man; Alexei, his dead partner. Jack wondered where they all were, except for Alexei. His only regret was that he did not get a chance to see Boris Vladimirovich's face as he read the contents of the envelope, which Volodya delivered along with the first monthly payment to Lydia Ivanovna.

Jack reclined in the seat and closed his eyes. Spending a month in a venereal ward completely changed his life, he thought. Only a year ago Jack was a white, fluffy bunny rabbit, ignorant of realities that surrounded him. Since then, he learned that people are nothing but flimsy paper boats, floating on top of life's unpredictable, often cruel and unforgiving, ocean-size waves.

After his shipwreck, Jack faced adversity and survived. More, he learned to thrive in the dark undercurrents, becoming a part of the super-wealthy crowd. But at what price? By now, Jack could easily afford several private airplanes of his own, with an army of servants. He could fly away to any luxury resort in the world, far away from the daily misery of an ordinary coal miner's life. Any yet something inside Jack gnawed at his conscience.

Then it struck him: it was the way Lydia looked at him with disbelief when she realized he would help her. That happy toothless grin was worth far more then his millions could buy, because it was real. But there are so many other pensioneers out there, he thought. Will they survive the upcoming winter without medical care or decent food? Will anyone notice if they don't? The feeling of guilt was ruining his otherwise well-deserved vacation.

Whenever Lena got angry at the unfairness of this world, she would say that people like Jack perpetuated corruption in the society. But Jack strongly disagreed: this nation, as many developing countries, was for sale to the highest bidder to begin with. If not him, then another oligarch, a nasty piece of work like Pavel Berezkov, would have stepped into his shoes, that's all. Several times Lena accused Jack of becoming a bandit, but she was always wrong. For example, unlike Berezkov, Jack had never extorted money or had people killed, even though with *ProServe's* resources he easily could have.

At worst, Jack became one of the millions of participants in the so-called "shadow economy," but in his opinion, no morally repugnant crime was ever committed by moving your own cash into a few secret bank accounts. In fact, everyone did it. Technically, it was called money laundering, but who really got hurt? The nebulous concept of government, which the politicians employ for self-gain? The currency regulations and tax laws were a joke: the government leaders themselves demanded their bribes be wired to anonymous offshore accounts.

Far worse, they depleted the national budget to buy themselves expensive cars, leaving people like Lydia Ivanovna to pick up empty beer bottles merely to survive. And yet not one of them got punished for money-laundering activities and extortion that they regularly perpetrate. Or for the permanent, degrading state of poverty surrounding their shiny, new vehicles. In comparison to the government crooks, nobody could accuse Jack of having done anything wrong, except for Lena, who had no clue about the true state of corruption. The irony was not lost on Jack.

Someone should treat this stricken nation before darker times arrive, he thought. A major housecleaning in high politics and mid-level bureaucracy is long overdue. In more civilized nations, the leaders simply resign when they get caught financing their luxurious lifestyles with public money. But resignations are unheard of in Ukraine. No matter what the media reveals, no matter how strong the evidence is against those alleged of misappropriation, nothing ever happens. The bureaucrats enjoy their immunity too much.

Then Jack wondered, how do you begin building a transparent, effective state in a country where a dishonest, thoroughly corrupt government system exists? How could anyone eradicate corruption when it's the most effective business around? There's just no way to resurrect the ligitimacy of this government, Jack concluded, no matter how many funds George Soros sets up to fight corruption. Poor Lydia Ivanovna...

The landing at San Francisco Airport was surprisingly smooth. The officials at passport control were unexpectedly pleasant. The customs officials seemed abnormally cheerful. Everyone wished the arrivals a nice day with a smile. Neither Jack nor Lena were used to this kind of treatment from the authorities. When they walked outside, a man in a red jacket approached Jack. "Do you have transportation waiting for you, sir?" he asked.

"Not really, but if you could hook us up with a nice stretch limo, I would appreciate it. And so would you."

"Yes, sir, just follow me." The man grabbed theie luggage and practically ran toward the exit. By the time Jack and Lena caught up with him, he found a driver with a six-person brand new Lincoln Continental that just missed a client. It even had a small television set and a fully stocked mini-bar. For a measly two hundred bucks, plus a twenty-dollar tip to the entrepreneurial baggage handler, Jack and Lena were treated like royalty.

"Tiburon, please. 25 Cliffside Drive," Jack gave Sergei's address.

"Yes, sir," the driver said, "right away."

"Is everyone in America so polite?" Lena whispered in Jack's ear as they headed North on Highway 101 towards downtown San Francisco.

"Absolutely, honey. And friendly, too."

"For some reason I'm a little tired," she said after a while. "Do you mind if I close my eyes, just until we get there?"

"Not at all." Jet-lagged himself, Jack offered his shoulder to Lena as a pillow, and she relaxed. Forty five minutes later they woke up in front of an impressive iron gate with an electronic device.

"Do you have the key, sir?" the limousine driver asked Jack.

"No. Just pull up closer to the speaker box." Rolling down his window, Jack pushed the chrome button of the intercom and waited, wondering if he had the right address.

"Who is that, lurking in my bushes?" a familiar voice came over the speaker.

"Your dear guests," Jack answered. The tall gates slowly opened, allowing them to enter. Coasting slowly down the long and winding driveway, which curved upwards for nearly half a mile, Jack thought, this is probably the most secluded estate in the entire Tiburon. Not surprisingly, the driveway was lined with palm trees that Sergei always wanted to live under.

"Look at those birches and pine trees," Lena said, "just like we have in Kiev."

"I guess we're high enough on a mountain," Jack replied as the limousine approached the top of the hill. Sergei's house looked like a real Italian villa on a postcard. This was not just a mansion; it was a

Mediterranean mini-palace. A French 19th century white marble fountain with a scallop basin prominently occupied the center of the circular gravel driveway.

The driver parked by the main entrance and whistled, impressed. Jack did not want to admit it, but the sheer size of Sergei's estate overwhelmed him, not to mention Lena. Considering her lack of experience with outrageous wealth, she was blown away. They stood in awe in front of the door until Jack recovered and rang the doorbell. The melody, which reminded him of a Lawrence Welk tune, pretentiously chimed inside the mansion. A few seconds later Sergei's voice came out of thin air.

"You must be tired from your flight," Sergei greeted his guests over an invisible intercom system. "Why don't you leave your luggage in the hall and join me for a little drink by the pool? The door is unlocked." At once, the locks of the glass-and-iron door disarmed to welcome Jack and Lena inside. They waited by the grand central staircase, which spiraled upwards, for the host to greet them. The perfectly polished marble floor reflected intricate crystal and wrought iron chandelier that hung high above their heads.

"Guys, the fastest way to the pool is through the living room, then make a right and follow the corridor to the end," Sergei's voice said. He must have the latest surveillance cameras and microphones rigged throughout the house, Jack guessed, knowing Sergei's love of modern gadgetry.

"Which way is the living room?" Lena asked Jack.

"Straight," Sergei answered, confirming Jack's suspicion. "Just in front of you."

The living room was framed by a soaring grand window. It looked out on the natural beauty of the gorgeous landscape that unfolded before their eyes. The house was perched high on a sun-drenched hilltop, with an in-ground swimming pool overlooking the San Francisco Bay on the one side, and scenes of the mountains and canyons on the other. From the spacious living room they absorbed the panoramic view of the San Francisco skyline and Golden Gate Bridge. Lena and Jack stared at the vanishing edge of Olympic-size pool below, surrounded by a large deck, and the shimmering ocean beyond the bridge, unable to tear themselves away.

A giant glass fish tank separated the living room from the formal dining area. It was a custom-made salt water fish aquarium with strange looking sea creatures, containing at least five thousand gallons, Jack guessed. It flowed like a giant wave across the living room.

"Why are you still inside the house? I've got fresh air, sunny weather and an open bar out here. What else can I do to drag you out of the house?" Sergei was standing two stories below, by the poolside, holding a small telephone in one hand and waiving to get his guests' attention with the other.

"Sounds perfect," Jack said, reluctantly turning his back on the view of Golden Gate Bridge. "So what do you think, honey? How about a dip in the pool?"

"It's absolutely gorgeous," Lena finally said, recovering from the initial shock.

"That's why California is such a special place," Sergei's voice followed them. "Now, just take a right turn, go straight for a while and make a second left.

There will be stairs that will lead you down. I'll meet you just outside."

"You got that?" Jack asked Lena.

"Yup. Second left."

On the way to the pool, Lena noticed a collection of exquisite blue-and-white Chinese porcelain figures that were displayed in the glass case in the corridor. An identical glass case, standing across, contained various carvings from ivory: long African tusks with rows of elephants, delicate Asian boats and fishermen.

"Just look at that vase, how fragile it is," Lena said. "You can practically see through the porcelain."

"I never thought Sergei was into these things," Jack mumbled as they walked downstairs. To him, they seemed unnecessarily wasteful and extravagant. Jack could not help but wonder if the new life in sunny California had changed Sergei for better or for worse.

"Great to see you!" Sergei exclaimed, opening the door at the end of the hallway. He had lost more than thirty pounds, got some color and looked younger than when Jack first met him at the clinic.

"I was going to ask how you were doing, but now I don't have to bother," Jack said. "This is some house you've got. Wow, Lena, look at this picture!" They stood on a top of a hill, overlooking the Bay, with the city's landmarks in the background. Wide marble steps, lined with classic armless and headless Italian sculptures, led down to the swimming pool.

"Better view than from your balcony in Kiev, eh?" Sergei asked Jack.

"Undeniably." Jack looked around, absorbing it all. Then he saw Lena frowning, and quickly added, "not that Kiev is all that bad."

"Let me show you around," Sergei said proudly, and his guests followed him down the grand marble stairs, toward the swimming pool. The warm, clear water of the mosaic-tiled pool was inviting, especially after a long flight. They passed the length of the pool, which curved around the house, to the edge of the terrace. There, perched on a cliff, high above the ocean waves like a swallow's nest, was a delightful mini-patio. A wind-protected glass-surrounded area consisted of a full bar and an outdoor gourmet grill; Sergei even had a gas firepit with lava rocks.

"Can I impose a Bloody Mary upon you?" Sergei politely asked Jack and Lena.

"Sure," Jack said. "Make mine Kiev-strong."

"I prefer water," Lena said. "With gas, if you have it."

While Sergei was preparing drinks, Jack asked him a question that was relevant to both of them. "So how are you keeping yourself busy these days? Was I right about being bored?"

"Bored? I wish I was bored! When I got here, I was young and stupid. I started buying everything, left and right, for cash. Big ticket items, too, like this house, the yacht, the cars."

"You have a yacht?" Lena asked incredulously. "A real yacht?"

"Yup. Three staterooms, projection TV, full bar and even a small jacuzzi! It's like being in this big, beautiful condominium on the water while you're catching salmon. There's even a private marina just down the hill. All I needed was a captain to teach me how to sail the damn thing. I ordered it before this whole mess began, and now it's like a noose around my neck."

"I don't understand," Jack said. "What, exactly, is the problem?"

"As it turned out, I bought too much, too soon. My mistake was that I paid for everything in cash. This is America, land of capitalism, I thought. Who knew someone was watching me? Now the INS is asking why I'm residing here if I'm on a business visa, the IRS wants to know my source of income and the FBI has questions about my ties to the Ukrainian mafia. What Ukrainian mafia? I'm a small-time businessman, I keep telling them, but it's useless. This global fight against corruption and money laundering is causing me one massive headache. Don't these people have anything better to do than to sit in their vans down the street, bugging my phones, taping everyone who comes and goes? It's perfectly acceptible in Ukraine, but I thought America was different. If things keep up like this, I'm going to buy myself an island somewhere in the Caribbean and move there permanently!"

"I didn't realize the situation was that bad," Jack said, concerned. He was aware of the risks associated with receiving Berezkov's eight hundred million dollar payment into his secret Swiss bank account. Such a large amount, transferred all at once, could easily be noticed and scrutinized by authorities. What was a perfectly acceptable business practice in Ukraine is considered to be downright criminal behavior in America. Sergei's legal problems considerably heightened Jack's well-founded fears.

"It's impossible," Sergei lamented, "they're coming at me from everywhere! Money laundering, wire fraud, conspiracy. All of them are felony charges, and that's just the FBI! Naturally, I hired a bunch of accountants and lawyers to help me out, but they flatly refused to bribe anyone. And as a lawyer, Jack, you know there's no chance in hell of winning anything without an envelope."

"Sorry to hear this news," Jack sighed. "But sooner or later, all things eventually pass. This will blow over, too."

"Sure. Unless they confiscate everything and then deport me. It's like a curse that's hanging over my head. Sometimes I wake up in the middle of the night, sweating bullets, thinking I'm inside a prison cell. But no matter what, I'm keeping my Ferrari. I'll drive that baby off a cliff before I give it to the bloodsuckers!"

"You've got a Ferrari, too?" Lena asked.

"It's up there." Sergei pointed upwards, to a large, wooden structure sitting high on the hill behind his mansion. "Come on, I'll show it to you. Let's take a short-cut, though."

Sergei, Jack and Lena climbed up four levels of narrow, wooden stairs. At the top, Jack saw a horse barn. Unlike the ordinary, animal-oriented shelters, this one had four extra-large garage doors on one side. "Like I said, when I first arrived to America, I was like a kid in a candy store: I wanted to buy everything in sight," Sergei said with a childish grin. "So I did. Look at this." He pushed a rectangular button on the side of the building, and all of the doors opened simultaneously, slowly uncovering four polished vehicles: a sleek black BMW, followed by a shiny candy-red Ferrari, then a sporty sky-blue Mercedes coupe and a cream convertible Bentley with its classic design.

"Each of these babies has twelve cylinders," Sergei nodded to the cars, "and yet they're all different. This BMW has Dinan super-charger and more than three hundred and eighty-horse power, which makes it fun. Handles much tighter than some of the other ones here."

"And what about that?" Jack could not help but stare at the voluptuous red shape of a low-sitting automobile. To him, everything about this car looked just right: the low grill, set below headlight clusters, the hood-mounted air intake, the wide, custom-made twenty-inch alloy wheels.

"That little Ferrari has five hundred and twenty horsepower, four hundred thirty pounds per foot torque," Sergei answered. "It's like driving in a bullet. Want to go for a spin down the hill?"

"Maybe later." Jack knew that one of the reasons Sergei kept a personal chauffeur in Kiev is because he never learned how to drive a car himself. Flying around the corners of Tiburon hills in a sports car with Sergei at the wheel was not safe, especially after a few drinks. The Ferrari itself, however, called out to Jack. He could not resist taking this chance. "Can I sit inside it?"

"You can do anything you want. The keys are in the ignition and it's ready to go. Just back up carefully. Is Lena coming with you, or should I get in?"

Just before Jack reached for the key, he admired the oversize, professional-looking tachometer. The steering wheel was a work of art in itself, fusing leather and aluminum into a powerful tool. "Here we go," Jack said to himself and turned the key. The engine purred softly under the hood, but you could tell that it was a monster.

When he pressed the gas pedal half throttle, Jack heard the sound of an airplane jet, steady and powerful.

"Isn't she amazing? I would buy this car again for the sound alone. Now, this one, in comparison, is pure luxury," Sergei pointed to the next vehicle, the convertible two-seater Mercedes. "It's a 600 series, also V-12, but a completely different breed of a cat, something they call the AMG package. It provides in excess of five hundred horsepower, but it's more conventional, not tuned to be an aggressive sports car. Much more forgiving, not as responsive."

"Not as responsive," Lena repeated under her breath, just loud enough for Jack to hear. "Must be a terrible car."

"And this is a Bentley." Sergei pointed to an elegant convertible coup with a sleek shape. Right away Lena recognized from photographs the long hood that seemed to stretch forever, split by a riveted seam. Its mesh grill was unmistakable. She admired the sexy, rounded aerodynamic curves of this work of art.

"Wow," was all Lena could say. "Now, that is really something."

"It's the first time Bentley offered twelve cylinder twin turbochargers, boosting its power to five hundred plus horses, so I decided to try it. It's sturdy, not nimble like the smaller sports cars. You definitely feel the weight and yet it handles beautifully. The only real detraction: it's a six speed automatic. Unfortunately, it's not available with a manual transmission."

"Absolutely perfect for a woman," Lena chimed in. She looked over the Bentley with some interest, and for a good reason. The open cabin was lined with soft, creamy light brown leather and plush carpeting. The instrumentation panel contained an abundance of gadgets. She playfully asked, "so when are you going to get something like that for me, Jack?"

"Why ask Jack for this car? It's mine to give," Sergei said, "and I hereby give it to you. Consider this to be my present to you upon arrival to America."

"Right," Lena said.

"No, I mean it," Sergei insisted. "I already drove it around, and it's not nearly as much fun as the Ferrari. I insist; in fact, you would be doing me a favor." Hearing that, Jack could not help but wonder whether Sergei's generous gift was somehow related to his legal problems with the U.S. authorities.

Unlike Jack, Lena did not take Sergei seriously at all. "Get out of here," she waived him away. "I don't even know how to drive a car! Besides, what am I going to do with a Bentley in Kiev?"

"I'm still getting used to driving myself, but I'm sure that Jack can teach you. You can drive a car, Jack, can't you?"

"Sure, but..."

"...and this is as good a car as any to learn on," Sergei continued, refusing to take no for an answer. "And when you get a license, Lena, you can send me a bottle of wine. That's it, end of discussion." Sergei's adamant insistence confirmed what Jack had already suspected, that Sergei needed to minimize the appearance of his wealth before the U.S. government. Besides, for a man with Sergei's money, a super-charged convertible Bentley was nothing but a cheap toy.

"Here are your keys," Sergei said, handing a keychain to Lena. "Well, dear guests, please follow me." After they walked out of the horse barn, Sergei pushed the garage button and the doors closed automatically. This time, everyone walked down a perfectly paved asphalt road that led away from the barn, past a red clay tennis court, back to Sergei's house.

"Out of curiosity, how did you find these cars? They must be rare," Lena asked. She knew that it was impolite to ask how Sergei obtained his wealth, a question that has been bothering her all along.

"By accident," Sergei shrugged his shoulders. "I was browsing through the magazines in the airport and found myself glued to the beautiful color pictures of sports cars, luxury boats, small airplanes, old castles. All of them were for sale, so I just circled the ones I wanted. For an extra few thousand dollars these beauties were delivered to my doorstep in less than a week. It's that easy in America! Now it's just a matter of keeping them."

Looking back at the barn that housed Sergei's dream machines, Jack thought that all of them were fine thoroughbreds, but the little red Ferrari was definitely the sprinter among this pack of world-class distance runners. His next thought was, what innocent explanation could I possibly offer to Lena for being able to afford a private island, an obscenely large motor yacht and a personal aircraft, too? Until Jack came up with a believable explanation for his own wealth, he could not afford to buy any toys like the Ferrari.

On the way back, Sergei offered, "why don't you get settled into your room? Then we can hang out by the

The Steel Barons/Frishberg

pool. It's heated, you know, so you can still swim in the evenings. And then a few people might drop over for a little get-together. How does that sound?"

"Great!" Jack and Lena replied together and laughed at each other. They followed Sergei through the maze of his house to the foyer, where they found their humble, beat-up luggage, looking inappropriately poor on the shiny marble floor. Jack picked up his suitcase while Sergei considerately carried Lena's.

"This house used to belong to some Hollywood movie actor, but I don't remember which one," Sergei explained as they walked up the grand staircase. "It has a total of seven bedrooms, including the master bedroom and two guest apartments. Your suite is my favorite because it has new Brazilian walnut floors, plus a few other amenities."

The entertainment room of Jack and Lena's apartment had the same incredible view that first captivated them from the main living room, with their own private floor-to-ceiling window overlooking the pool deck and the Bay. They became hypnotized once again. Ever a thoughtful host, Sergei opened the double doors to their bedroom, which housed a large four-post antique French bed. Lena went inside to explore and disappeared into a yet another adjacent room.

"Oh my God," Lena exclaimed somewhere from within deep bowels of the bedroom. "Jack, you've got to see this!"

Jack went over to find out what all the fuss was about. As he walked into a side-room, where a toilet and shower usually belong, Jack froze along Lena's side at the sight of a built-in oval swimming pool. The water was completely still, like a mirror. Extensive use of glass and marble gave this room a flashy feel. Gold faucets and peach-colored marble floors set the tone. There was even a Travertine marble shower big enough for four people and a matching jacuzzi, shaped like a giant Roman tub, able to accommodate six adults.

"By the way, the swimming pool has a lap stream," Sergei said, "in case you want to exercise. Just push that button in the corner. Well, now that you're all settled in, what's your pleasure? A dip in the pool, a drink at the bar, a nap on the terrace? Maybe a round of tennis against the evil cannon-ball machine?"

"Give us a few minutes to change, Sergei, and we'll meet you out by the pool," Lena said, beaming like a child. Looking at her, Jack had to smile because he knew that she was genuinely happy.

\* \* \*

"A girl from Kiev could get used to this," Lena said, stretching lazily on an inflatable raft while Jack swam beside her. "But it's all just a little too perfect, you know what I mean? A little too much of everything. How can Sergei afford all this?"

"How should I know?" Jack answered, holding to the side of her raft. By now, he knew better than to answer Lena's questions honestly.

While they were floating in the shimmering pool, Sergei went over to the bar, high above the golden Bay. He mixed a few drinks and brought them over on a silver tray. "Two more Bloody Mary's for civilized people like Jack and I, and a glass of fizzy water for the lady."

"Thank you, Sergei," said Lena. "You're the perfect host."

Their calm afternoon was suddenly disturbed by the sound of big band instruments. It seemed as if an entire orchestra was tuning up just around the corner, like the beginning of the *Sergeant Pepper's Lonely Hearts Club Band*, only much louder.

"That sound system is awesome!" Jack said. "The speakers sound just like a symphony, even the drums."

"You don't say," Sergei smiled. "That's because the musicians are setting up on the other side of the house."

"What musicians?"

"I hired a Russian band from L.A. to fly in for the night. They're here to play for us."

"I see. Do you believe this man, Lena?"

Knowing Lena, Jack could tell that she did not approve of such extravagant gestures. "The frightening thing is," she said, "I think Sergei is telling the truth."

"Of course I am," Sergei said, smiling happily. "It will be a wonderful party, I promise. You'll meet some of my new American friends."

The portable poolside phone rang out. Sergei pushed a button, looked at the five-inch black-and-white screen at the base of the station and said into the telephone, "I'm glad you could make it, Jesse! Come on in, we're downstairs by the pool." Then Sergei turned Jack and Lena, and said, "these are the first guests."

"I thought you said it was an evening party," Jack said, taking a towel to dry himself off.

"I said no such thing," Sergei answered. "I only said there would be a party later. Well, now is later in relation to when I said it."

"Jack, I don't think Sergei is joking about this one, either," Lena said, quickly climbing out of the swimming pool. "Let's get dressed before we become the joke of the party. Please?"

"Relax, guys, everyone is easy in California," Sergei said, leisurely sipping his cocktail, but Jack and Lena did not listen. They speed-walked in wet swimsuits across the marble steps, ran into the house, up the stairs, and zoomed through the corridor with porcelain and ivory. They made it to the lobby of Sergei's mansion just as polished Porsches and BMWs, driven by well-dressed guests, piled into the circular driveway. The doorbell rang again. Jack and Lena could hear conversation outside the door, just a few yards away from them.

Bursting with laughter, they scrambled, dripping wet, up Sergei's grandiose staircase and ran down to the end of the hallway. Like naughty children who were about to be caught, Jack and Lena jumped into safety of their plush apartment just as the guests entered through the front door.

Curious, Jack stuck his head into the room with the swimming pool and turned on the lights. "I still can't get over this," he said. The sight of still water in their private pool was inviting. "Want to get in?"

"I completely forgot about that little room," Lena said. "Sounds like a perfect idea. But do we really have time for this? I mean, there are guests downstairs."

"Lena, I hate to shatter your illusion, but this party is not about us," Jack said, testing the water. "Sergei likes to throw parties, that's all. Nobody will miss us for the next hour or two. Besides, we need time to recover from our jet lag. Get in here, it's very nice!"

"He's *your* friend." Lena wriggled out of her bathing suit and submerged in the calm water. "This is fantastic!"

"Not too much?"

"Oh, shut up, you!"

Following her lead, Jack also undressed and stepped into their swimming pool, though not nearly as gracefully.

* * *

By the time Jack and Lena made it downstairs, the guests had gathered around the gigantic swimming pool, enjoying their drinks in the late afternoon sun. From a distance, they resembled an oil-and-water mixture of strong colors and eclectic patterns, holding champagne glasses.

It was windy, but surprisingly warm. The sun would be setting soon, casting the last of its rays across the San Francisco Bay. Several waiters in black-and-white tuxedos carried wide silver trays, brimming with champagne and hors d'oeuvres. One of them approached Jack and Lena.

"Oysters with Beluga caviar, and foe gras with Black Forest mushrooms on toasted French bread," the waiter announced, extending the tray to Lena for a better view. She nodded, eager to try the delicacies. The waiter snapped his fingers with a free hand, and a busboy quickly stepped out from his shadow. He placed two appetizers on a small plate. "Champagne? White wine? Red wine?"

"Champagne, please," Lena smiled.

"White wine for me," Jack said. It was an oaky Chardonnay, with a lovely aroma of fresh green apples.

As they passed among groups of people, searching for Sergei, Lena whispered to Jack, "look at how they're all dressed. It's not normal." She nodded toward one middle-aged woman, who walked by wearing outlandish satin military fatigues with black leather mini-boots. Looking around, Jack had to agree with Lena. Sergei's newfound friends were mainly rich trash, the local high rollers with one thing in common: a flair for fashion.

In contrast to the flashy dressers, Lena looked quite contemporary in her simple black cocktail dress. Making their way through clusters of people, who were deeply involved in their conversations, Jack managed to catch a sentence or two. The same names kept popping up: *Prada, Armani, Dolce & Gabbana, Gucci, Chanel.* All they talked about were clothes and the latest styles. Halfway through the poolside terrace Lena squeezed Jack's hand and nodded towards the ocean. "There he is, by the bar," she said. Jack looked over to see Sergei, pouring himself a glass of white wine, and walked straight towards him.

"Is that some special reserve wine, or the same swill you force upon your guests?" Jack joked.

"It's one and the same. Chateau St. Jean makes the finest Chardonnay in Sonoma Valley." Sergei reached for two more large tulip-shaped glasses. He appeared to be very comfortable, wearing casual leather loafers. "That is why it's here, for all the guests to enjoy. May I offer you a glass?"

"Sure," Lena said, setting aside her Champagne flute.

"So who are all these characters?" Jack asked. "They seem, um, interesting."

"Local socialites. Some own art galleries, others dabble in fashion, and they dress the strangest of them all," Sergei said. "Actually, I am a neophyte in their world. As far as I can tell, it boils down to attending charity events and parties. And each time it turns into a fashion show for the semi-rich and sometimes famous. This is just another opportunity to see and be seen. Maybe I'm missing something..."

"And how did you hook up with this crowd?" Jack asked.

"Easy: I always overbid at their silly auctions, plus I invite them to all of my parties. Actually, Yanni, my decorator, introduced me around. Want to meet him? There he is." Sergei waived to someone.

"Hello, darlings," came a high-pitched voice from the crowd. Yanni was a thin Chinese man in his late twenties. He was wearing a pink chiffon shirt with rhinestone buttons. It was wrapped by a thin gold belt around his white Versace jeans, giving the appearance of a dress.

"This is Yanni Woo," Sergei introduced him. "The best and the most expensive decorator on the West Coast."

"You have done wonders with this place," Lena complemented him. "Truly amazing. Especially the vases."

"Yes, I am like this old-fashioned couturier who dresses up the clients' rough edges." Yanni's face broke into a broad smile, but then he caught himself. "Plus, Sergei has been an exceptional client. He allowed me to be as creative as I wanted, without imposing any limitations, so I picked from various cultures and devoted one room to each style."

"Sounds interesting," Jack said, barely managing to keep the sparkling buttons on Yanni's shirt from distracting him.

"Since the Japanese perfected the art of tranquility and serenity, Sergei's day starts by waking up in Tokyo, then enjoying his breakfast in modern Copenhagen, followed by a leisurely morning swim in sunny Tuscany. Incidentally, the statute in the driveway, and those lovely marble busts along the stairway, were all shipped from Florence, as were many other antique pieces in the house."

"I have these sixteenth century samurai warriors, decked out in full armor gear, in the corners of my bedroom," Sergei shook his head. "They scare the hell out of me at night when I have to use the bathroom!"

"We already went over this, Sergei," Yanni said. "We have to make the most of the available space and light. That's why the master bedroom is in Oriental style, because of its syncopation of form and color. And those samurai warriors belong at the side of the emperor, which is you. Otherwise they become ronin, outcast predators."

"I can see you really enjoy your work," Lena said.

"Oh my, yes, I just love the fabric research, the colors, the details," Yanni moved his delicate hand in circles. "I'm a constant shopper, always on the lookout. And

what about you?" he turned to Jack and smiled
invitingly.

"No, he's not on the lookout," Lena answered,
protectively putting her arm around Jack. "He's with
me."

"Right," Yanni bowed his head. "I must circulate,
darlings. Ta-ta, Sergei, his friends." Then he slithered
back into the crowd without looking back. "It's all
about glamour, sparkle and romance," Yanni's voice
could be heard in the distance. "If it's not fabulous,
it's meaningless!"

"As I was saying before that little hurricane passed
through," Sergei raised his wine glass, "to us, friends
through all kinds of adventures, from Ukraine to
America. *Na zdorovye.*"

Fortunately, Lena remained oblivious to the fact that
Jack and Sergei were toasting to their entry into a new
stage in life, where everything was easy and pleasant.
Delicious, oaky California Chardonnay tickled their
taste buds, its rich taste complemented by the fantastic
view from the pool deck.

"You want to know what I really miss?" Sergei said,
out of the blue. "That fat, juicy Ukrainian *kolbasa* we
used to have. Remember?"

"In your kitchen," Jack smiled fondly at the distant
memory, "with vodka."

Winking at his guests, Sergei pulled out his hand-
held transmitter, pressed a button and said, "we're
over here, by the pool-side bar. Can you send us some
real food over here? Just grill everything on the tray I
set aside, and bring it over as quickly as you can. It's
urgent!"

Ten minutes later a dapper young waiter rushed over, carrying a silver bowl with hot, sizzling garlic sausages. Sergei walked behind the bar, pulled out an icy bottle of vodka from the freezer and poured three shots. "Let's drink to today," Sergei said bitterly, feeling a little tipsy, "because who really knows what tomorrow brings? God damn those American government agencies, every single one of them! They call it capitalism, but it's just like the old Soviet Union. Ah, welcome to the life under a palm tree, Jack!"

"Speak for yourself," Jack reminded him, drinking vodka and sinking his teeth into a homemade, juicy *kolbasa*. Lena looked at Jack for explanation, but he avoided her questioning stare. I can always plead ignorance later, if she accuses me of anything, he thought. From the cozy bar of Sergei's residence Jack watched an endless river of French champagne washing down mounds of cracked Dungeness crab claws and grilled tiger shrimps on skewers.

To him, this opulence proved that Sergei had not changed much: he still lived life to its fullest, but this time on a much grander scale. That's why all these guests keep coming over, Jack thought, like fireflies flocking to a bright light. Partying high above the San Francisco Bay, everyone basked in the last glow of orange fire. The skyline in the East turned from pale blue to deep violet as the sun slowly faded on the horizon, drawing sighs of awe from the crowd.

"Everyone, dance!" Sergei's booming voice came from the forest. He was still sitting at the bar, speaking into a wireless microphone. "Just follow the waiters!"

A procession of waiters, each holding a burning medieval torch, just like the ones Sergei kept on the walls of *The Camelot*, ushered the guests to the paved road that ended at the motor-barn. Behind the barn was a large clearing in a forest, easily able to accommodate a small orchestra and all of the guests. Informal blankets and pillows surrounded the grassy dance floor for those unable or unwilling to dance. Glass-colored lanterns of yellow and green hung low from the surrounding trees, giving off a magical glow.

In a matter of minutes everyone disappeared, including the gracious host. The aquamarine light, emanating from the powerful lamps imbedded in the swimming pool, confirmed that Jack and Lena were completely alone. Standing on the edge of Sergei's deck, they watched the fog creeping in from the ocean and settling under the Golden Gate Bridge. The rhythmic sound of the ocean waves, crashing against the rocky shore, whispered seductively below. There was no other living being in sight, only the misty clouds below and flickering lights of downtown San Francisco in the distance.

Jack and Lena held each other in the fresh, salty breeze, not saying a word. The longer they gazed into the distance, the more Jack wanted to tell her about his feelings, about their future life together. Rugged nature surrounding them made it the perfect moment. Taking a deep breath, Jack got down on one knee, reached out to take Lena's hand and said, "I love you, Lena. Will you marry me?"

"What?" Lena's eyes opened wide in panic.

"I said, will you marry me?" Jack repeated with fading enthusiasm and reached for his old, worn-out alligator wallet. Stashed deep inside the left side was Sergei's pink diamond. Jack carefully unfolded the small piece of plain white cloth and offered the large sparkling stone to Lena on the palm of his hand.

"What are you giving me?" she asked.

"This diamond ring is incomplete without a setting, I realize, but that's only because I don't know your exact ring size. But I do know that I want to spend the rest of my life with you. So what do you say, Lena? Will you marry me?" Jack asked for the third, and final, time.

Lena remained silent. She kept staring at the diamond. "You're crazy," she finally said. "First class plane tickets, friends who give away Bentleys, and now a marriage proposal? All in one day? And you expect an answer, right here, on top of some American cliff?"

"Why not? I love you..."

There was a long pause. "You are a lunatic," she said, "but I love you, too. Yes, I will marry you, Jack Parker!"

The orchestra was playing a soft, familiar melody as Jack kissed Lena, just the two of them in the world.

* * *

"Alfa one. What the hell did he give her?" Leutenant Stern said with authoritative voice into a microphone and wiped the sweat off his forehead. All the electronic equipment inside the van made it unbearably hot, despite the cool evening. "Did anyone see what he gave her? Delta one respond."

"Not me," one of the waiters in the procession whispered discreetly into his sleeve. Like the other servants, he was dressed in a black tuxedo, carrying a hot, burning torch that sstunk of kerosene.

"How about you, Delta two?"

The guitar player pretended to check his strings. "I'm in some forest, sir, I can't see them," he muttered into a microphone implanted inside the bow tie. "They're probably still out there, by the swimming pool."

"Damn," sighed leutenant Stern. Before relocating to San Francisco to head up the FBI's West Coast Task Force on Money Laundering and Racketeering, he was in charge of investigating organized crime in New York City. Any business partner of a suspect was a suspect, too. Guilty until proven innocent, no matter what anybody says. It was just a matter of waiting for the evidence to surface. And whatever Sergei's partner was showing to his Ukrainian girlfriend by the poolside could have been the evidence leutenant Stern was looking for. "I'll get you one of these days, partner," the leutenant promised, taking a gulp from his luke-warm can of Coke. "Just make one wrong move."